SUNBRINGER

Also by Hannah Kaner

The Fallen Gods Trilogy
Godkiller

SUNBRINGER

A FALLEN GODS NOVEL

HANNAH KANER

HARPER Voyager
An Imprint of HarperCollinsPublishers

SUNBRINGER. Copyright © 2024 by Hannah Kaner. All rights reserved. Printed in the United States of America. No part of this book may be used or reproduced in any manner whatsoever without written permission except in the case of brief quotations embodied in critical articles and reviews. For information, address HarperCollins Publishers, 195 Broadway, New York, NY 10007.

HarperCollins books may be purchased for educational, business, or sales promotional use. For information, please email the Special Markets Department at SPsales@harpercollins.com.

Harper Voyager and design are trademarks of HarperCollins Publishers LLC.

Originally published in the United Kingdom in 2024
by Harper Voyager UK, an imprint of HarperCollins UK.

FIRST U.S. EDITION

Map and interior illustrations copyright © 2024 by Tom Roberts

Library of Congress Cataloging-in-Publication Data has been applied for.

ISBN 978-0-06-335010-6

24 25 26 27 28 LBC 5 4 3 2 1

For my mother,
who taught me courage, grit and power.

CHAPTER ONE

Arren

ARREN'S HEART SCREAMED.

He fell back from the fireplace. The god in his chest was howling: *Hseth! Hseth! Hseth!*

'Stop!' Arren cried. He grappled with the tangle of twigs, moss and flame that filled the rift in his ribs. Fire licked the sides of his fingers, burning him.

Hestra, the god of hearths who lived where his heart had once beaten was usually quiescent, but now she shrieked the name of another. *Hseth.* The great Talician god of fire.

'Please,' said Arren. 'Stop!'

She did not stop. Worse. Sparks ran down his stomach and landed on the floor. There, lint, straw, pine roots and tiny bits of bone sprouted, catching light in the fireplace where he had been kneeling. She was crawling out of his chest.

What had happened? They had been waiting for Hseth to return in glory, filling Arren with the power of the strongest fire deity to have ever existed, in exchange for the life of his friend.

Not a friend. Not anymore.

But Hseth had not returned, and neither had her promises. Arren's god, Hestra, spilled out onto the hearthstone, dragging her heat and light from him and leaving a void of darkness. As she built herself outside of him, he fell back against a low table, gasping. First, she was a bud, a cocoon of twigs. Then the cocoon cracked open, splitting into the limbs of dried grass, moss and kindling. A face of branches and eyes of flame.

'Hestra,' he wheezed. With her gone from his chest, he could feel his blood cooling, the strain of his breaths. His death, it came at him like a wave, long held back by flame. 'Please.'

In Blenraden, the morning sun had struck open the sky, but here in Sakre, in the far west of Middren, the windows were still thick with the grey before dawn. The only wakeful ones would be the guards outside his room or the folks in the kitchens. They must not see him like this. He had built himself up as a godslayer, a breaker of shrines. No one could know he needed a god to live.

Hestra did not heed him. He reached for her, but she stepped backwards into the fireplace and disappeared in a hiss of anger.

And he was left with nothing. Less than nothing. She had vowed to keep him alive, had entreated him to speak to Hseth and understand the will of a god, his potential. She had helped him betray every law he had ever made. In a moment, all of it was gone. Without a word, she had left him to die.

The whims of gods. As fickle as a false spring.

Arren had never been so easily turned. But look what it had earned him: in Hestra's absence, the world grew loud. Gone was the crackling of his heart, the warm rushing of his blood. Instead, he could hear the snap of embers in the fire, the sparks that hissed minutely as they died on the stones, the rain that thrashed against the window, thinning as the sky brightened. Most of all he could hear the desperate dredging of his lungs as they tried for air. It did no good, not without Hestra, his secret, his shame. Without her, he would be dead before the sun rose. All his hopes lost.

Help, he thought. Unbidden, his friend's name crept into his mind. *Help me, Elogast.*

Elogast was not coming. He was in the east. Betrayed and wounded. Betrayed by him.

Arren was alone. He had sacrificed his closest friend, his brother, his one remaining love, for the power to change the world, and it had gained him only a pathetic death in a locked room.

A tap at the door to his chambers. Soft, tentative at first. He couldn't answer. Then knocking came harder.

'Your majesty?'

The guards. They had heard.

'There were noises? My king?'

They could not find out this secret. Not yet. They weren't ready.

The door shook on its hinges, the guard shaking the lock. Arren tried to drag himself upright.

'Don't . . . come in,' he tried, but barely managed a croak of air. He fell on his side, knocking the table, and the compasses and writs he had spread across it clattered to the floor. His vision blurred. Hseth had promised him, *promised him*. Talicia and Middren, united as one, coast to coast claim of the Trade Sea. The beginnings of an empire, of indisputable love and power. He should have known their promises would come to nothing.

The door splintered, slamming back on its hinges and smashing into the wall hard enough to shake the dust from the tapestries. In came Knight Commander Peta, shoulder first. She drew her slender sword and cast around for an intruder, finding none. Just a mess of twigs, a crackling fire.

'My king,' she gasped in her alarm, dropping to her knees beside him. He struggled for air, for control, but he could not hide it now: no blood, no covering, just an open, empty wound. Peta's eyes found the chasm in his chest, the darkness where death should be.

It had been years since the axe of the god of war had gone deep into his bones, ripping through his breastplate and cracking his ribs into pieces. The marks remained where the metal of his armour had made a mess of his skin, healing into dark red scarring threaded with Hestra's smoke-script. That, a vivid black. A god's promise.

'Please,' Arren whispered, though he did not know what he was asking for.

Peta's face paled with horror, her hands hovering over his shoulders. Her eyes and mouth were lined by a life of hard living, her grey hair cropped, no-nonsense, close to her skull, and shining in the light that had crept through the dispersing clouds. She was upright and fierce, desperately loyal. One of the few aged generals who had not run in the worst days of the war, nor had she faltered at hanging would-be assassins from the gallows, one of them her own cousin. She had even passed his command to burn the Craier steadings to the ground. And he had lied to her.

'My king, I . . . When?' Her calloused hand hovered over the gaping space in his chest. When did this happen? How long had he lied for? It was too late now. He was dying again, and Elo wasn't here to hold him.

'The war,' Arren managed. His vision swam, darkness crowding in at his eyes. Let them know, let them all know. He had tried to live. They should be grateful.

But the look on her face was not the disgust he expected. It was awe.

Arren had seen that look before. Given to his mother when she was queen. Given to gods. His commander did not hate him. She admired him.

Hestra and Hseth had assured him he would be dragged through the streets as a traitor if the world found he had harboured a god. They would think him weak like his mother, disloyal like Elo. He had believed them.

Arren's brain raced as he neared death. It was what Elo always praised him for, his quick thinking, his decisiveness. What if Hseth had been wrong? What if he did not need her power to be loved? What if there was a story here, capable of winning their faith? That was how gods were made.

'I gave my life for Middren,' he said, resting his fingers on his open chest. 'All I have done . . . for Middren . . .'

Peta nodded. 'I know . . .' she said.

The other knights were beginning to understand. Arren heard a creak as one, then another, then all of the guards fell to their knees.

But it was too late. Too late for this last grasp at hope, at love. His hand dropped to the floor. His breath faded. None of them dared say a word.

A spark from the fire leapt out just as the dawn broke through the clouds. The ember ran across the wooden floor, the carpet, racing up Arren's arm and into the cavity where his heart had been. There, it bloomed.

Hestra. She took root in his heart and once more her power

filled him, warming his blood and sending it rushing. His gasping lungs swelled with air, bringing light and life to his body. He breathed.

He gripped the commander's arm, dizzy with the sudden change. Death to life. Dark to light, as the sun illuminated all of them in gold.

Another chance.

Arren forced strength into his voice. 'It is well,' he said, and sat up. 'I am well.' He had learned this on the battlefield, suffused with fear, breaths from death, to channel strength, power, certainty. He stood on shaking legs without Peta's help, trying not to show how terrified he had been. His commander stepped back, scared to touch him.

He would show no shame; nothing good would be built on shame. He stood tall, softened the planes of his face from pain into something gentler, then held out his shaking hands and showed his bare chest fully. The darkness within was now lit by Hestra's fire, crowded with green moss and twigs.

The guards looked up at him, agape, uncertain. Uncertainty he could use. He saw himself in their eyes: a tale they could whisper, a myth he could build.

Hseth is dead. Hestra did not care for the crisis she had caused. Instead, her thoughts slammed into Arren's mind, agonising. No acknowledgement, no apology. *The great god of fire is dead. Her shrines broken, her power gone.*

Dead. Arren gritted his teeth. One damned crisis at a time.

'We failed you,' Peta whispered. Two of their guards deepened their bow, another gasped, horrified at the thought.

'No,' said Arren quickly. 'No, Knight Commander. I gave my life, willingly, to kill the god of war and save our lands from destruction.' That was not all true – Arren had not killed the god of war – but the truth didn't matter. All that mattered was the story. The myths that made gods, brought them to life in their shrines. Stories bind hope and love to make it faith.

Peta touched her hand to the badge that pinned her cloak at her shoulder, the stag's head before a rising sun, the symbol of Arren's kingship. His defeat of the god of war, the gods he had risen beyond. Before his symbol had been a young lion, but that he had come to share with Elo; the king's lion, so his friend had been called. Arren had to be something else.

'I did what I must,' he said softly. How many times had Hseth said such a thing to him? 'A sacrifice is not a loss. We had to fight the tide of darkness, the chaos of the gods. We still fight it, we still must fight it.' Hestra flared in his chest, and he put a hand there.

Wait, he thought towards her, hoping she understood him.

'To bring sunlight back to us, to Middren,' said Arren, threading his hopes together, 'to bring ourselves back from those nights of terror, we all must be willing to give our lives, even if it hurts us, even if it challenges our very soul.'

Hestra was still. Arren let the light of the sun brighten his curling mess of hair, let the flicker of the god's flame twist impossibly in his heart. He was vulnerable. A single briddite blade would end him here and now.

'If you, too, will make such offerings,' he said, 'then pledge to me.' He splayed out his hand and put it over the rift in his heart. Like sunrays, like his symbol. His story.

Peta dropped to her knees and copied him: hand over heart, fingers spread wide. The others followed, hand after hand. Hestra's flames stirred again, this time with delight, sensing what she also desired, more than anything. Faith. For a moment, in their eyes, they were both more than they had ever been. More than his mother's unloved son. More than a lucky prince who won a war and no longer had the commander who won it with him. More than a little god of littler shrines, chipped away and forgotten. Together, they were greater than his flesh, brighter than his crown. All he had ever wanted to be.

'Sunbringer,' said Peta. Arren almost laughed with half pleasure, half delirium. This was more than an alliance with Hseth, a reliance on her power.

This was him.

The others murmured with her. 'Sunbringer.'

'Sunbringer.'

It was not enough, not yet. He needed more. He needed a nation. He must become a god.

CHAPTER TWO

Skediceth

THE RINGING OF HAMMER ON METAL MARKED THE END OF their journey.

Twenty-three days. Back over mountains forests and rivers.

Skedi wasn't the only outlaw these days. Inara Craier, his heart's companion, knew now that it was the king who had burned her home, and she had not been meant to survive. Her life itself it seemed was kept secret from Middren. Elogast too, the knight on the run, grizzled with pain and anger, and set on stopping Arren's bloody ambitions before they swallowed the Trade Sea whole. For all the journey they had relied entirely on Skedi to hide their presence with his sweet white lies.

For the first time, he was needed, truly needed. And, now he was not so alone, he did not mind hiding. Nor did he regret leaving Blenraden behind, with its spectres of forgotten gods and broken shrines. It had been a fool's errand to think he could find a home there on his own in a dying city, where no one needs lies.

So, when they had seen Lesscia rising on the horizon, as beautiful as a flower open on the wide river, dread filled him from his belly to his ears, and shivered the tips of his wings. On the road, they had been dealing with only 'now'. Surviving. Being safe.

Lesscia was 'next'. Skedi was afraid of 'next' and his place in it.

Still, he helped them shuffle past the makeshift steadings that crowded safer parts of the marshland, and through the afternoon crowds and food trade of the outermarket, whispering the lies he had practised to death: *we are no one special, no one interesting, you have tasks to do, errands to run, places to be.* He was too weary to discern whether it was his small power or the business of the city that protected them.

The evening bells had not yet rung as they passed by the guards at the gates, so the streets were brimful of noise. Runners carrying messages or delivering merchandise sped past, their barrows clattering on the flat cobblestones as they whistled loudly at people to get out of their way. Pilots of canal boats bellowed to each other over full hulls, ferrying to and from the harbour, side to side of the canals, under bridges and crashing against stone jetties. Inside the city, too, were artisans; tilers sitting smoking by their samples outside the factories, brushmakers selling the finest rabbit-fur ends, haggling with newcomers on prices. And researchers, biographers, merchants, travellers, arguing everywhere over hot tea, peach-infused hipgin, or charcoal-laced water, depending on their stomach.

It was a relief to find their way back to the residential lanes near Kissen's home, where the ways were quiet and calm. They walked beneath the drips of hanging washing, or children playing in the street with black and white kittens. Kissen's horse, Legs, swished his tail, impatient, knowing where he was going. He all but dragged Inara towards the smithy where Kissen had first brought them. Where her sisters were waiting for her to come back.

Inara's quick steps faltered as they heard the song of the hammer, the sure clanging of a smith at work, and reached the large gate on its metal runners. It was open, and above it hung a crisply worked sign of gears and a hammer, telling passersby what lay beyond. Yatho didn't work near the other smithies, where the ginnels were too narrow for her wheelchair. And smithing, Skedi had learned, wasn't a common practice in Lesscia, the city of knowledge, so her experimental, intricate work had a home all of its own.

It was there, their destination, that Inara stopped completely. Skedi looked up through the satchel in which he had been hidden. He could see her colours, her emotions, churning in conflicting shades. Hard to read. Inara's colours had once been jewel-like: corals and amethyst, citrine and emerald. Bright, unfettered joys and woes of childhood. No more. Day by day, the shine of her emotions had clouded with forest-murk and glimmers of the orange flame that had burned her home and had fallen with Kissen into the sea. Inara carried her journey with her, and it had changed who she was. It was strange. Gods did not alter so swiftly, not like humans.

But somewhere hidden within those shades of Inara's was the sky-blue of her will. Her power that had broken Skedi's lies, unravelled Elo's curse, held the great god Hseth at bay. Power that did not belong to a human at all.

'You've done so well, Inara,' said Elo, stopping beside her. 'It's all right. I will tell them.' Elo, too, had changed. The upright, clean-shaven man was now bent with fatigue and pain, shoulders dipped protectively towards his chest. His hair and beard had grown out, dry and unkempt around eyes that were shadowed with lack of sleep. The smell of his wound had lightened, at least, though the herbs tucked into the yellowed bandages on his chest still could not fully hide the stink of healing skin.

Skedi poked his head fully out of Inara's satchel. He misliked its muck of mud and foraged food. Unfit for a god.

'Must we tell them?' he said, twitching his whiskers. He was a god of white lies, but this was cold, hard truth. 'I do not like this. We could say we don't know what happened, that she might still be . . .'

'Please, Skedi,' said Inara, her voice tight. 'Please don't.'

Skedi dropped his ears at her tone. They had all seen Kissen plummet into the sea. Even if she had survived the fall in Hseth's arms, she would have drowned. It just felt wrong to Skedi to quench all hope, to tell a truth that would cause such pain.

Inara took a breath. 'I will tell them, Elo,' she said. 'They know me. They should hear it from someone they know.'

Elo grunted with understanding. Legs, however, would abide no more waiting. He snorted, gave his reins a smart tug out of Inara's hand and trotted straight through the gate, going nose-first for the trough. Trust a horse to know where their water was. The second pony, Peony, they had sold many days before for balm and clean bandages, but Legs they couldn't part with.

Inara followed Legs into the courtyard, clutching Skedi's satchel as he hunkered back inside, Elo a close and steady presence behind them. The courtyard was as Skedi remembered it: mud-beaten, criss-crossed with wheel tracks save for a small vegetable patch by the stable, out of reach of the milkgoat and thick with spring greens. The smithy was open to the air and one of its three furnaces was lit. By it, Bea, Yatho's apprentice, was beating a long piece of folded metal. He wore a wool hat over his ears, despite the heat, and was humming gently to himself. The boy struggled when there was too much noise, but his colours seemed calm and focused. Yatho herself was standing with the aid of a metal contraption and a tilted saddle, rolling a wire through a compressing wheel. No one else was around, so Skedi poked his head back out of his hiding space.

Legs began drinking noisily, and Yatho looked up from her work.

'You're back!' she said, her colours brightening to lemon yellow. She saw Inara first and lifted a lever to lower her seat, then unbuckled herself and moved into her wheelchair. 'Thank gods, we were starting to worry . . .' She rubbed her face, smudging dust, burns and freckles together with smoke-stains and sweat from the furnace. She had recently shaved her hair back behind the ears, showing more of her leafy tattoos.

Then she stopped, noting their silence, Elogast in the place of Kissen, and Skedi. Kissen had left to separate Skedi from Inara; she had not succeeded.

The yellow faded, and instead the shine about Yatho became stained with a stormy, doubting grey, the colour of cold metal. 'Where's Kissen?' she asked.

The change was so sudden, so complete, that Skedi knew she had been holding this fear just beneath her skin, like a breath she never fully exhaled.

'Kissen . . .' Inara's voice stopped before she could speak and the darkness around Yatho deepened, thick with dread.

It will be all right, Skedi said directly to Inara's mind. *It's all right.*

Don't lie to me, Skedi, Inara said, with a sharpness that made him shrink. She cleared her throat, and Elo put his hand on her shoulder, his own shades awash with pity.

'I'm so sorry,' said Inara, her voice hoarse. 'Yatho . . . she died.'

Skedi knew she was picturing it, the fall. Or worse, when she had told them to run, and they had obeyed.

Yatho's darkness stretched out, filling the space around her. She stared ahead for a moment, her gaze unfocused, then looked down at her hands. Strong, muscled, empty.

'Your sister gave her life in Blenraden,' said Elo, unable to bear it as Inara shook. 'Protecting Inara, Skedi and myself. She's the bravest woman I've known.'

Yatho put her palms to her eyes. Skedi shrank to the size of a mouse. She was so quiet as her colours consumed her like a choking cloud, and it frightened him. Skedi wanted to save her from this truth, lie it away. But her grief was too much, too great, too deep. Such emotion was not in his power to change. He was not strong enough.

'How?' Yatho said, her voice so tight it was a whisper.

'Hseth, the fire god,' said Inara. 'Yatho, Kissen told us what happened to her as a girl. They fell together, into the sea. She had her vengeance.'

Yatho let out a dry sound – a sob, or a laugh? Both? She looked over at Legs. Her eyes were dry, but Skedi could see the greyness sinking into her skin, curling around it like the vines of her tattoos. Her eyes roved to the house, to the gate, to the workshop. Skedi followed her gaze. There, on the wall, were the fine briddite pieces of a new prosthesis. For Kissen.

'Did it hurt?' she asked.

Inara and Elo hesitated. They both knew that death by flames was not kind. Skedi stepped in, a good lie if he ever told one.

'No,' he said. 'It was quick.'

Yatho narrowed her eyes at him, though despite herself she was soothed. 'Did you have anything to do with this, liar god?'

Skedi rustled his fur, but he found he didn't have the energy to grow in size and pride. Days of making lies, averting curiosity, shielding them all, had taken its toll.

'No,' said Elo. 'It wasn't his fault. It was mine.' Skedi twisted up to look at Elo, whose jaw was set and determined. Bad idea. Bad truth to tell.

'Kissen gave her life for Middren,' said Elo, 'and for me.'

Yatho's shades turned sharp, her anger tipping the darkness with green. 'And why would she do that?'

Elo showed the bandages that wrapped his chest beneath his shirt. Even now, the wound still seeped, and the shape of Hseth's great hand could be seen, darkening the fabric.

'So I could kill the king.'

CHAPTER THREE

Kissen

FOR THE SECOND TIME IN HER LIFE, KISSEN WOKE IN THE arms of the sea god.

Everything hurt. The cut on her shoulder, the burns on her right leg where her half-melted prosthesis had seared her skin. The nicks, scratches, and aches of long weeks of fitful nights and being hunted through the wild lands. Her body was keeping score of its battles.

But now all was quiet save for the rush and breath of waves striking stone, dragging chiming pebbles and shells out, inch by inch, into the deep. It had been so long since she had heard the sound of this particular shore.

She opened her eyes with a snap. Above her, the sea god of her childhood looked out to the east, contemplating the water. Behind him, the sky was dark with evening and potential thunder.

'Fuck,' Kissen hissed, tipping herself out of Osidisen's embrace and landing in an ungainly heap on the rocky ground. This shore was as she remembered it, though she had not seen it in almost fourteen years: filled with black stone rising and crumbling like an empire's ruins. The cliffs surrounding them loomed high and dark, circled by cormorants.

Osidisen looked down. Here he had brought her after the fire god Hseth had destroyed her family, broken, orphaned and burned. His holy cove, known to all the village as the place the sea god would take his rest. Kissen touched her chest where she had carried the wish her father had made for her: his life for her life. The writing had turned from dark to light, the promise fulfilled, her father's life gone.

'Why did you bring me back here, rat-drowner?' she said, her voice cracking. 'I asked you to save me, not drag me back to nowhere.' This was leagues from the Trade Sea where she had fallen from Blenraden's shrines. Inevitably, she found her eyes drawn to the black cliffs north of the bay. There, as a child, she would have seen the struts of her village's houses clinging to the edge, shaken by the wind and spray of the sea. No more. The cliff had fallen, the houses too. The village was gone.

'It might occur to you,' said Osidisen quietly, 'not to insult a god on his own land.'

'It might occur to you that I don't give a shit.'

She struggled to her feet, trying not to look at her warped and twisted prosthesis. She could sense the ache of her missing right limb below the knee. Phantom pain; her calf, shin, and ankle squeezed in a bone-splintering vice of agony. And so it should hurt; if the leg hadn't been metal Hseth would have burned her through to the bone. But she wouldn't look at it. Not yet. She had to convince herself that it was still her leg, and it would still hold her, or she would crash to the ground.

'Tell me why,' Kissen demanded. She didn't want to be here, so close to her childhood pain. What would her still living family think of her disappearance? Her friends? Elo and Inara?

They would think she was dead. Her heart knotted in her chest, tightening her lungs. How could she tell them she was alive? She was weeks away from home on foot, and in a land whose god she had just killed.

'The "why" is a warning,' said Osidisen. His face drifted as he spoke, turning from a rush of water and a beard of foam into something more human. His skin hardened into flesh, the froth turning to grey-and-white strands of hair, though his body remained a cloak of waves, eating the light where it touched. A warning? This was the god who had watched her steps as a child, who helped her find good pools of cockles, who had helped her swim through stormy waters. What warning could he have for her? 'An obligation,' he added.

Kissen shook her head. His love had made her family a target, a sacrifice to Hseth. She wanted nothing from him. 'You have fulfilled my father's wish,' she said through a scowl. 'The promise that tied us is done.'

Osidisen laughed, his beard foaming and curling as he chuckled, disappearing further into the water. His hair ran green, turning into fronds of seaweed, then returned again. The light of the setting sun was golden, dancing over the foam of the waves until it met the purpling cloud of an incoming storm. She had been there for a whole day.

'You waited half your little life to let me fulfil your father's sacrifice,' the god said. 'Then you deliver me another boon.'

Kissen winced.

'The fire god. Hseth,' Osidisen continued. 'She drove me out of these lands and my people's hearts, to live on the secret wishes of fishwives and their folk. You gave her death to me—'

'It was not for you,' said Kissen through gritted teeth. It was for Inara, for Elogast. For her family. And herself.

'This warning is what I will pay for it.'

It did not matter to him, her intention, only what was. She cursed under her breath. 'You give me a warning, then what?' she said. 'Then you leave me here again? Demand another gift to take me home? What will it be this time? My finger? An eye?'

'I swear to take you to those shores you now call home once the warning is done,' said Osidisen dismissively, as if he had not brought her half the world away. 'These are the whispers of the wild, of the water. You have had them before, but you did not understand them.'

When Middren falls to the gods, your kind will be the first to die.

The mutter of a nothing-god rose to her mind. A river spirit too big for its little pond had paid her threats with her last breath.

'And I know,' Osidisen continued, his gaze boring into her, as if searching for her soul, 'you would not believe a god's word, only your own eyes.'

There was movement out on the water; ships drifting under the storm clouds and a low veil of rain, some from the south, some from the north. Osidisen ignored them, his focus on Kissen. If he wished, he could press his voice inside her mind, impress his will on her and fill her thoughts with terror and drowning. Weakened as he was, he was still an old, half-wild god with many shrines. She ran a tongue over her gold tooth, then shifted to sit warily on the ground. Of all her weapons, only her cutlass was left, its briddite blade perhaps enough to sting Osidisen if he decided to crush her. Even the leather gloves she still wore, that she had used to drag Hseth down to the water, had been torn to rags, the briddite plates gone. She was at a disadvantage, and she didn't like it.

'Then what is my warning, sea god?'

'War will come with summer,' said Osidisen, 'and Talicia will bring it.'

Kissen blinked, then scoffed. 'I'm a godkiller, war is nothing to do with me. A game of monarchs and politicians, or greedy raiders. You yourself guided Talician ships to Middren's shores in the years before I was born, and bore them back fat and bloody.'

Then, after a decade of raids and sunken ships, an alliance of Middren, Pinet and Restish had come for the Talician kerls and their raiding families. They had ravaged the coast and its people to ruin, and scattered their leaders' bloodlines to the winds. Kissen had grown up on the edge of a Talicia that was a mess of feuds and corruption, petty battles, blood debts and starvation. Her parents had kept well clear of it, till Hseth came and brought wealth back with her.

'This is no squabble over sails and sheep,' said Osidisen. 'Hseth plans invasion.'

'Hseth is dead.'

'Her will remains, and with it she will live again.'

'Bah. That will take years.' Even with the popular gods, it took time to build up the love of their followers, the sacrifices, the offerings, for them to manifest again at their shrines. Once revived, they still retained no memories of their previous life, so most gods never lived again after death, their followers instead drifting away to other gods still living.

'Not this time,' said Osidisen, his beard washing once more into his breast, his cloak running into the sand. 'Hseth will return before the shortest night, sooner perhaps, and she will be reborn in the shape of the will she left behind her. The shape of power, the shape of war.'

Kissen bared her teeth. Fuck no. The crazy god of fire had had her chance and lost. 'You're spouting lies, old god.'

Osidisen bristled. He grew in size, and his body deepened into angry water. 'I am no trickster god, like your feathered companion,' he growled. 'I am a god of the north seas, of water and storm. I am what I am, and I do not tell lies.'

Kissen's hair rose with the intensity of his anger. How did he know she had been travelling with Skediceth, the god of white lies? She glanced past him at the ships, a foolish part of her hoping for succour. Something was odd about them.

'Not three miles to the south,' said Osidisen, pointing, his waters calming. 'Beyond my reach from the shore. Go. See what I say is true.'

That was it: the ships, three of them, were low in the water, far too low, and dragging rafts that were barely visible above the waves. They bore strange cargo: small nests, it looked like, of metal and chains. Familiar. Like the smell of burning was familiar.

Kissen was wholly distracted now from Osidisen's nonsense. The ships were coming closer. Another rounded the edge of the cove, from the direction he had indicated. It was the largest Talician vessel she had seen, not like the copper-trading vessels she had seen in Blenraden, nor even with the briddite on their bows they used to ward sea gods away. Perhaps that was why Osidisen hadn't noticed them. Perhaps she could draw them in, beg passage further south, make her way home. To her family.

There was movement on the rafts, crews spreading out and using huge poles to tip the cages forward. Anchors? The first one tumbled into the water, quickly followed by the others, their placement marked by red barrel-buoys that splashed on the surface.

Osidisen flinched. Foam frothed from his hair and beard. Pain. He tore around to see what had happened, but then his right shoulder erupted in a spray of water. The god roared, and Kissen saw he had been struck by a briddite-tipped harpoon.

Kissen scrambled to her feet. The cages, the chain. They must be briddite too, forged from bridhid ore and iron. Tipping them into Osidisen's waters would make a wall he could not cross. No, a prison.

She hadn't seen briddite used on such a scale since Blenraden.

Osidisen pulled out the harpoon and threw it back towards the boat, striking through its jib but doing no further damage. A second harpoon slammed into him, this one at the end of a rope that was quickly winched tight. Kissen could see someone on the ship in white, snapping out orders as they dragged the god onto his back and towards his sea.

This wasn't a random attack: this was planned. A godkilling.

The god of her childhood cried out as his body hit the stones of the cove, the sound like the creaking of a ship as a storm took it. Briddite was more deadly to gods than any metal was to human. The salted smell of his inner flesh burned Kissen's nose, the blood of old sacrifices mixed with ancient sea and smoke.

What could she do? What should she do? This was her job. She hated gods. She hated Osidisen. She had for years. She should feel satisfied to see the bubbles of salt pouring from his wound as he was hauled like a sack of haddock into the waves. Even if he had been her father's lover. The protector of her mother and brothers. The god who had just saved her. So what if he was dragged to his death?

His dark-grey eyes bored into hers. Frightened, caught. Vulnerable. Like Skedi, like Inara.

She gritted her teeth, drew her cutlass.

He had remembered her, after all these years. He had honoured his promise. That was more than most humans she had met.

'Shit,' muttered Kissen. She brought the blade's edge down on the rope, which snapped and hissed back into the water.

Freed, Osidisen grasped the harpoon and tore it out of his shoulder. He glared at Kissen, his flesh darkening, his eyes turning from grey to the black of the cold depths. He knew she had been one instinct away from finishing him herself.

With a roar, Osidisen lifted his hand and the sea surged in around them, flying up the cliffs in ragged sheets of water. A shield for her.

'Get to my caves!' cried the god, then threw himself into the salt waves of the briddite-tainted sea. The boats turned their harpoons towards the water, and one was quickly overwhelmed by a wave that tore through its sails.

What had she done?

Too late for regrets. All Kissen had to do now was survive. She moved, relying on her memories to guide her steps to the north of the cove. Each movement shook pain from her bones and reminded her that the prosthesis she relied on was irrevocably warped.

There, where she remembered, out in the water; a half-hidden split in the cliff face with the tide almost up to its brim. She sheathed her cutlass and leapt into the bitter cold, pushing forward with her arms and dragging her legs behind her. Waves surged around her, tossing her sideways, slapping into her nose and mouth. She struggled.

Then, the current came like a hand at her back. It pushed her into the shadow of the cliff, straight through the narrow entrance. She broke the surface, found air, and gasped for breath. The sea fell back with a suck and gasp and left her in the dark.

CHAPTER FOUR

Elogast

PAIN COULD KILL A PERSON. THAT WAS WHAT HIS MOTHERS had told him. Exhaustion, grief, injury, heartbreak, betrayal. One needle to the heart could be healed, but a hundred would stop it beating. With his every breath, Elo felt the Hseth's flaming hand in his chest, the pain of Arren's betrayal and what he had done to him, to Inara, to Kissen. And the fear of what he might do next.

Now he sat in the home Kissen should have come back to, filling the space that she left for him, waiting to explain to her sisters what he had done. He had to make amends.

Not just to Kissen's memory, but to Inara, who sat staring dead-eyed and tired at the empty hearth. Twelve years old, her mother lost, her home, and now her guardian. The girl had spent almost two fortnights digging willow-bark and boiling it to clear his wound, changing and tightening his stinking bandages, foraging for their food and hiding her face from him when she cried.

Arren would pay for making Inara cry.

'They will understand,' said Skedi softly, into the silence of Kissen's kitchen. He was sitting on a large table amid paper and metal wires, fascinating twists and cogs of which Elo had never seen the like. This space was not like his mothers' luxurious manors, or the hive of activity of the Reach or the Forge in Sakre. It reminded him a little of his bakery; sparse, but homely.

'Don't lie,' whispered Inara. She was thumbing the remaining buttons of what had once been a very fine velvet waistcoat, now caked with dirt, its threads run ragged. Skedi's ears flattened. It was not the first time she had dismissed his comfort.

'Some lies are made with good intent, Ina,' said Elo quietly, feeling for the poor little god. He couldn't help but feel affection for Skedi. He was useful, caustic at times, but kindly overall. Elo had met worse gods.

'Like you lying when you tell me it doesn't hurt? Or like my mother lying when she kept me locked at home while leading a rebellion that got her killed?' She turned her bright brown eyes to Elo. 'Or Skedi lying, telling me that this is all going to be all right?'

Skedi shuffled on the table, he flicked his wings. 'Have you lost all your faith in me, Ina?' he said.

Inara softened visibly, and swallowed. 'N-no. I didn't mean . . .' She paused. 'Kissen brought us here,' she said at last. Elo could imagine Kissen in this place, weary and cheerful in that crass, obscurely charming way of hers. 'She didn't know me, but she brought me home. And now she's dead.'

Guilt. It filled them both to bursting. In all the days they had travelled there, when every step had been survival, they had not explored the emotions that choked them. Elo was used to it: the horrors of war had forced him to pack the fear, the grief and death down tight, folding it into dough to bake in the oven of his gut till it burned up in shattered, heart-tearing fragments. Even now, three years since the final battles, a shaft of light on metal, the scent of mud, a spray of water, and he was overwhelmed, his breath quick, his body aching. He had been a good soldier, his body healed well, and he still paid a price.

Worse, he had taught others to do the same; to push it down, close their inner heart, see nothing beyond the flash of their blades, the call of orders, the rush of their blood. To see people and gods as nothing but dust and desperation, their screams just the same as lightning. Passing.

And now, intentionally or not, he had taught it to Inara, to hide what she felt, to fester in unspoken shame. A child. Not a warrior.

'Ina, none of this was your fault,' said Elo, leaning over the bench to put his hand on her curly head. It was so ragged in plaits and knots that he had suggested cutting it short, but she had refused. 'None of this burden is yours to bear.' It was his. He had called the fire-god. He had put his faith in Arren. 'If you need to blame me, if you need to weep, or scream, you can.' He wished someone had told him this, but he no longer knew how. 'You should.'

Skedi sat up on the table, his ears twitching, tense, as Inara looked up at Elogast. Her hand clutched her buttons so tightly her knuckles had gone pale.

'I can't,' she whispered, her eyes dry. 'I don't think I'll stop.'

'You don't need to stop.'

'I can't lose you too.'

Elo didn't know if his heart could break again. He closed his eyes, unsure what to do. So he put his forehead on Inara's the way his mothers did to him when he was a boy, to make him feel calm, safe. 'I owe you my life, Inara,' he said, honestly. 'I will always be in your debt. If I am anyone's knight now, I am yours. Your protector, your brother, uncle, father, villain. Whatever you need me to be, I'll be it.'

The girl sniffed, shifted slightly, then: 'Be my commander,' she said. 'Teach me how to fight.'

Elo drew back.

'I have power,' she said. 'I can use it somehow. To help. I'm sure of it.'

Elo hesitated. Could he use her for her strange power? Her ability to somehow communicate with gods, undo or control their power and will, could be valuable.

No. No matter how angry, no matter how powerful, Inara was owed a childhood.

'I—'

A stir of footsteps in the hall, a creak of wheels on mud. The kitchen door smashed open, and a wild-eyed woman charged in. Her dark hair framed a delicate, scarred face, and her robes were the dusky greys of an archivist.

Inara stood, and Skedi moved too, flapping his wings in fright and leaping straight to Elo's shoulder. The woman didn't speak, but signed at Inara; deft, clean strokes of communication. This must be Yatho's wife, whom she had gone to find. Telle. Inara had described the woman as calm, kind, but her gestures were sharp as blades, her expression beseeching.

Inara signed one of those she had taught him in their journey back. *Sorry, sorry, sorry.*

Elo stood and stepped before her, holding up his hands, palms out in a sign of peace, though they trembled. Telle stared at him, then turned her ire his way. Her hands danced through a language Elo could only grasp by her face, and her face showed fury.

'She says if you don't understand her what's the point of you being here,' Skedi whispered.

Yatho appeared at the door, out of breath, then touched her wife's elbow, stopping her mid-sentence. Telle whirled on her, shaking, and the two stared at each other, the silence thick with feeling. Then, Yatho put on her brakes with one hand, stood up, and put her arms out to her wife. After a moment, Telle fell into them. Yatho held her tightly, kissing her neck, stroking her back as she shook with sobs. Inara grabbed Elo's sleeve and held on.

After what seemed like a long while, Yatho and Telle broke apart. Telle helped Yatho into her chair, then went to the cask of water and scooped some up to cool her face and neck, before putting her hands on the side of the barrel to steady herself. This time, she made the sign. *Sorry,* then added something to Yatho. Her wife nodded to Elo.

'Please. Tell us slowly, and clearly. I will translate anything she needs.'

Elo told the tale as plain as he could, from Arren begging for his help, to his brush with Canovan, meeting Kissen, Inara, Skedi and the demons. Yatho tapped at a small clockwork mechanism as Elo talked and the movement seemed to soothe her between signing. Then he told them about Blenraden, his discussion with Aan, his fight with Kissen, carefully omitting their lovemaking.

'*You* did it,' said Telle out loud, before Elo had even come to the end. 'You summoned the fire-god that killed her. That killed her whole family.'

Yatho put her item down slowly, carefully, as if afraid of crushing it. 'Get out,' she said, then pointed at the door. 'Get out of our home.'

He did not know what would happen, said Skedi, his voice making all except Inara flinch as it bored into their heads. *He did not ask Kissen to stay and fight her.*

'Forgive us,' snapped Yatho, 'if we do not trust a god of white lies.'

'I thought I was saving a man who was family to me,' said Elo calmly. 'I had no intention of Kissen or Inara being involved. I intended to die.'

'Then why didn't you?' said Telle, reading his lips. 'You had demons and a god on your back, but here you are breathing where my sister is not.' She stopped and rubbed her throat. Gods, he was hurting her by making her speak. Kissen would either be laughing at him now or throttling him.

'The curse was broken,' said Elo, not looking at Inara, who had drawn it from his flesh like poison. He felt her eyes on him, but Kissen's family was a veiga's family from Blenraden, whatever Ina was, she had to be cautious. 'Kissen killed Hseth so we could run.'

'Show us then,' said Yatho. 'This broken curse. Should be white, shouldn't it?'

Elo hesitated. The curse she had unravelled had left no mark, because the god's will had been pulled out of him, not shattered or completed. How had Inara described it? Like untangling colours?

'The god Aan drew it out,' said Skedi, his paws tightening on Elo's shoulder. Elo resisted putting his hand up to stroke him. The poor god was trying to make his power useful, but Yatho laughed bitterly.

'Lies,' she said and signed. 'All of it. Canovan is no demon summoner, all he can summon is a good hand at cards. Curses take more than a spat with a traveller.'

Telle, however, looked contemplative.

'He must have been protecting something,' said Inara. 'The rebellion, my mother was part of it. She wrote to him I think.'

Yatho and Telle shared a glance, but Yatho shook her head. 'He wouldn't have tried to hurt Kissen,' she said and signed. 'And he's no rebel.'

'You're wrong,' said Elo. 'He hated veiga, and knights, and he allowed innocents to die. A boy, an old woman. The curse was his.'

'It is *you* who brings death where you walk,' snapped Yatho. 'Don't lay the blame at another's door.'

Elo flinched, a tremor catching him across his chest and shooting down to his hands. A string of memories pulled through his mind: wading coldly through screams as the faithful lost their gods, holding a young girl of six who had been sacrificed to a wild god of wolves, tearing an old man back from the ruins knights had made of his shrine. Could he truly blame Canovan when he had also accepted the collateral of war? Kissen, too, had died so he could live.

Perhaps he should have never left his bakery.

Inara took hold of his hand and squeezed. 'Please,' she said to Yatho and Telle, who turned towards her more warmly. 'Let us prove it to you. Take us to this Canovan before this king finds other people to burn for his power.'

CHAPTER FIVE

Arren

YOU ARE NOTHING WITHOUT HER.

Hestra's bitter whispers were nothing worse than Arren's mind could conjure, though her voice was splinters in his head. He rubbed his eyes, carefully managing not to rub ink onto his brow. Two days since she had returned, and the hearth god spent every waking moment punishing him with sullen jibes. But, she had yet to leave, which meant she either had a reason to stay, or nowhere else to go.

Arren tried to focus on the map beneath his hands. A work of art, and true genius. His own. With information from his knights stationed across Middren, he had constructed it, piece by piece. As a squire he had been taught cartography; maps were useful, and detailed ones were rare. Usually the remit of knights, generals, not monarchs. But during Blenraden he had been both, and cross sections of the city had been essential. Now he had moved his secret planning from his chambers to his Smoke Room, he had enough space to thread together the pieces he had commissioned of each House's lands into one great tapestry of knowledge.

You are a failure, a puny human, Hestra added. Hestra was wallowing, pitying herself and the loss of Hseth. An ancient god reduced to a groan. *You were born a failure, as all humans are. I have seen them from my many hearths, dragged weak and squawking into the world. They live weak and squawking, and then they die much the same.*

'I have heard such things before,' said Arren, 'and yet still I am alive.'

His brothers had mocked him, his mother despised him, and even his sister's pity marked him out as least favoured of the Regna children. But where were they? All long dead. He had endured.

He leant over, reading a tiny scroll from a bird, and updated a fort's holding capacity in House Vittosk's land to the far east, then added a model of a ship to the Belhaven harbour in Restish, to mark another built. Well, that country had almost as much to recover from the god war as Middren, and Middren's reserves were all but empty. Or, they had noted Arren's shipbuilding in Middren and were trying to match boat for boat. His lands were more vulnerable than they had ever been, and the eyes of the world were on them. On him.

Talicia, to the north, had no reports. Everything he had known had been from Hseth. She had promised him godhood, the fealty of her government, dominance over the Trade Sea, but now there was nothing. No missives from her people, their priest-leaders, who had sent him written treaties. Enough. He no longer begged at other tables, and he would not wait on a dead god's promise. His position was too precarious.

He struck Talicia off with a daub of his brush, then paused and considered another black mark he had made. Right across central Middren, the heartlands of the Craiers.

You see, you are uncertain. Guilty. Your heart wavers.

He had been angry when Lessa Craier had presented a petition to the council, signed by some of the oldest and strongest Houses and traders in Middren, demanding that he reinstated gods to their lands. Hseth had told him how to show them all his strength, his conviction. Show that Lessa Craier could not usurp him with paper and make him a boy again.

Your knight said there were children killed, Hestra pressed him.

'People are pieces,' said Arren coolly. 'They roll off the board and clear the field for play. I mourn them, yes, but I do not regret it.'

Lessa Craier had no child. The records said her firstborn had passed in the chaos and sicknesses that plagued Middren during the war, and after. The others would have been servants' children.

A pity, but no more piteous than the bodies he had seen already. Elo, of all people, should understand that.

'That is the problem with fire gods,' Arren added. 'You think only in absolutes.'

The god hissed, her fire crackling and singeing Arren's shirt. He winced, but his shirt was only singed. He had chosen the Smoke Room not for its smoking fireplace, nor the incense placed in braziers by the great brass balcony doors and latticed stone, but for the black stains on the ceiling from a fire that had almost destroyed the Reach in Arren's great grandsire's time, and the scent that remained. No matter how much Hestra burned his shirts, she could make little difference. It also commanded a view of the supplicants' courtyard, where knights or courtiers knelt as punishment. It was good that they knew he was watching. Especially now the rumours were spreading that he had sacrificed his life in Blenraden, and that flame now occupied his heart. He had carefully mentioned nothing of the god. No one spoke that out loud. Not yet.

You are nothing, she spat, *nothing, nothing.*

Arren sighed. Hestra was born in hearthstones, from families wanting safe houses and full bushels. If insulted, she could spit flames, burn bread, turn a small fight into bloody anger. Her strongest curse kept a person cold for the rest of their lives. But she was not as cutting as Arren's mother, or as brutal as his brothers. But he needed her, and her power over his life was more than she had ever tasted.

'I would truly be nothing, my hearth, my heart, without you,' he reminded her gently, and felt her flame flicker.

Flattery will not win me to you.

And, like most fire gods, she really was not a good liar.

'You are not a prize to be won,' said Arren. 'It was you who chose to come back to me when you could have let me die.'

I had nowhere else to go. Her flame dimmed with mourning, and with regret. *My shrines are paltry few now.* So, as he suspected, she had not returned to him out of loyalty. How then to make her stay?

'And here you are,' said Arren, 'the king's life, my chest your hearth. You are safe with me.'

Hestra thought for a moment. Then: *Your safety means nothing. You kill what you love.*

That did hurt. He breathed out. Elo's face flashed again in his mind, the hurt, the betrayal; when Hestra had taken him to Blenraden in her twig form, he had seen it as clearly as if he had truly been standing before Elo and telling him he had to die. His 'knight', as Hestra called him, was now anything but, yet still he roamed so widely in his thoughts. 'I do what I must,' he said, 'so that I may keep my promises. To Hseth, while she lived. To you, now, in her stead.'

What have you except a bickering land of water and mud? You want to command the Trade Sea, but barely control your own subjects. She crackled again, and sparks burst out onto the map. *Hseth promised me a world on fire. Humans once more huddling around their hearths, praying to me to keep them safe.*

The embers almost caught this time on the precious map, and Arren slapped them out, his palms stinging with his haste. A few snaps of twigs between his ribs told him she was laughing.

'You are not the first to doubt me,' he said through gritted teeth. 'If you desire it so, then return to your little hearths and your littler dreams. But while you are here, I will live out mine.'

Whatever Hseth might have retorted was interrupted by the bells clanging out the new hour from the highest towers of the Reach. The other fortresses of Sakre soon followed – the Shield on the west coast, and the Forge to the south – and finally the city itself picked up the clamour, sending clouds of gulls flashing into the blushing pink sky. Beyond the fine trellises and pillars of his balcony, and the green stretch of the Reach gardens, the stinking, hilly, winding streets of Sakre looked almost beautiful. He couldn't see the Forge from this view west, but over the great harbour the flags of the Shield were flying, telling him that all was well.

It was time. Time to test their faith, before the whispered rumours turned to accusation, before this fomenting rebellion used the Craier destruction to retaliate.

He put down his brush and pushed his curling hair back from his circlet. If he still had a heart, it would be hammering, but all he could feel was Hseth's surly flame. Still, his hands shook, as if they remembered the rush of terror that would rattle his ribs when he had to speak to the queen, or if there was a grand event at court for which he was expected to perform.

The sound of spear-butts rapping twice onto the tiles outside his door announced his visitors.

'Enter,' Arren called.

The guards opened the doors, and Arren caught the scent of musk and sandalwood before its owner stepped in. The Gods Commander, Risiah. He had dark, wily eyes that darted from the ceiling to the fireplace, to the map, before he had set more than a foot inside the room. Since being elevated to this new post, commander of the Crown's godkillers, he had been cleanshaven. It really did nothing for his chin, which was rather too close to his neck, though the poorly stitched scar across it did give him some edge of authority. Risiah had not been Arren's first choice for commander, but he was one of the few well established veiga in Middren who had at least some connection to the nobility. Godkillers had once been the lowest of the low, and even with the king's approval, the profession was notoriously dangerous and disliked. But Risiah was the fifth son of a lesser House from near Fellic-Farne in the north, so his appointment had caused some flattery and no offence.

Behind him, however, was Commander General Antoc. The nephew of the present Lady Tiamh, whose wealth in the west made her a worthy ally. Arren had given him charge of the standing army of layfolk after the war, and he had proven himself a stern and conniving commander. Twice Arren's age, the pompous bastard wore each year as if it were his own circlet of gold. His hair was dappled silver, and he had the assured posture of a short man with a large weapon.

At least Peta was with them, and eyeing Antoc with clear dislike. Arren would have made her head of the king's army and its trained knights even if she hadn't been a cousin of the southern House Crolle. Her authority outstripped theirs, and this rankled Antoc in particular. Arren had no doubt he had found some gripe to accost her with before they came inside.

The three commanders made their salute. The new salute. Open palm, fingers splayed out on their chests like sunrays. Antoc a step behind the others, half-smiled as he did so, as if he found it amusing. Though, when his eyes found the dark hole of embers in Arren's chest, the expression faded.

Arren lifted his chin. He did not hide Hestra's flames now.

'Your majesty.' Peta spoke first. She had kept close by him since his incident two mornings before, like a shield on his back. Where Elo should have been.

'Thank you, commanders,' said Arren. 'I trust you are well.'

'Are we here to see what you have been planning then, my king?' said Antoc, three shades south of insolent. Risiah was scanning the map, his expression impassive. The work dominated the room, spread across a table fit for a dozen. 'Perhaps a way to feed the army you have twiddling their thumbs on barren fields,' Antoc added. 'Are the council's coffers still low?'

'Have you been much in council of late, Commander Antoc?' said Peta mildly as the bells of the three Sakrean fortresses pealed to a halt.

Antoc scowled. Only the leaders of the great Houses were permitted on the king's council: traditionally, commanders' advice was sought separately. Though, that was when there had been only one commander of the knights.

'The standing army were promised pensions,' Antoc said. 'By the king's *previous* knight commander.' He cast a glance at Arren. 'I see fewer ships, fewer stalls in the market, fewer delegates from our neighbour lands. I have eyes, and a mind to use them.'

'You also have a sharp tongue that likes wagging,' said Arren. 'Careful it doesn't cut your mouth.'

The silence that followed was full of daggers. Risiah's eyes glittered with amusement. As the youngest and poorest of the commanders, he was roundly ignored.

'I only mean, your majesty,' said Antoc, after a moment, 'that unpaid soldiers become angry. Angry, unpaid soldiers forget their loyalty.'

'Do you forget yours?' said Peta. She didn't need to move to suggest threat. She was like a boulder on a precipice, ready to fall.

Antoc sniffed, twisted his neck to crack it, then bowed his head just slightly. 'My apologies, your majesty.'

'Sunbringer,' said Arren. Oh, to gain this little victory. . .

Antoc's eye twitched, but he swallowed whatever he wanted to say. 'My apologies, Sunbringer.'

Arren smiled. He had often wished he could make Antoc kneel in the courtyard below, but this small capitulation tasted just as sweet.

Still, the man was right. He put a voice to fears that plagued Arren's dreams: a bored army full of rage, and only one way to point it. Towards the king who had promised them the world.

He needed to do something, something powerful to sharpen swords and minds and secure his standing.

'My friends,' Arren said, stepping forward to the map. 'Commanders. See what I see.'

Risiah didn't need to be told twice. He had clearly been itching to get near the parchment. 'This is quite magnificent,' he said, fingers tracing over the north coast. Peta was more reserved. Arren had showed her the small pieces of the map based on the information from her knights, but not all of it re-inked with meticulous detail and bound as one. 'Middren is so detailed, so beautifully coloured . . .'

'It is not a painting,' said Arren, annoyed. 'It's a battle plan.'

Risiah and Antoc shared a glance, then Antoc looked to Peta, who gazed stoically back. Arren let them sit with the idea, showing them he was not afraid of silence. Not afraid of anything.

'You understand what happened to the Craiers,' said Arren.

Only the slight paling of Antoc's neck over his stiff velvet collar suggested he had any idea what Arren was talking about. Risiah became very still, then cleared his throat. 'They were stoking rebellion, my king.'

So, the veiga was informed, but not smart enough to keep his mouth shut. Still, it showed he had a hankering for Arren's approval. Antoc, however, was waiting to see how the pieces would fall.

'Yes,' said Arren. 'And gathered the arms to fight it. The council did nothing. They do not understand action, not like *we* do.' He was admitting he had acted against a House without the consent of the council, the king's council. He was taking them into his and

Peta's confidence. Would Risiah and Antoc pull back, cowardly, or lean in and understand what he was offering them? A space in his inner circle, where even the Houses had no claim.

'The king meted out his justice swiftly,' said Peta. 'But most arms have not been recovered. The threat remains.'

Antoc cleared his throat. He would play this game, Arren had no doubt. But he would play it for himself. 'It was a bold choice . . . Sunbringer,' he said. 'But the Craiers have many friends.'

'Many of whom have spent the best of this month denouncing them,' said Arren, indicating four letters pinned to the map. 'Vittosk and Graiis, Geralfi and Tulenne.' Antoc blinked, and Risiah looked relieved, but Arren had not finished. 'Still, Vittosk and Tulenne have tripled their personal guard.' He touched the banners on the map. 'Lesscia suffers pamphleteering and pilgrimages, and the Geralfis have been consulting with godkind.' Risiah coughed, his eyebrows raised. Gods were his domain.

'How do we know this, your majesty?' he said.

'Because,' said Arren, 'strength is strength, but information is the lever.' That was a phrase from Elo, direct from his mothers. 'Information is what I have been sending our knights to gather.'

'The knights you have been sending as peacekeepers?' asked Antoc. 'I thought they were just . . .'

'Twiddling thumbs?' Arren interrupted, and Antoc fell silent. He was pleased to see the commander lost for words, for once. Arren had used his knights to lay out his lands like a game of chess, seeing its strengths, loyalties, weaknesses, as he and Elo had done during the war.

Elo always won at chess. But that was small scale. This was more ambition that Elo had dared to dream.

Your veiga hides his colours, Hestra whispered to Arren. *And your elder questions your authority.*

Arren took a breath. 'You are right to worry about paying our troops,' he said. 'But the money is there, the council simply won't release it. The Spurrisk lands to the north and Yesef to the south have had their biggest crop yields in a decade, yet our stores in Weild rot and in Sakre run low. I do not trust them to act in good faith. Not like I trust you.'

The implication was clear: choose him, and fuck the council. That at least made Antoc smile.

'So when you speak of battle . . .' said Antoc, stepping closer to the map. They were the only ones in the room, but he lowered his voice conspiratorially. Arren had him, he was sure. The man had a wearisome cockstand for power and influence, but it was something Arren could use. Risiah was harder to read, Hestra was right, but veiga rarely made headway if they were easy to manipulate.

'The battle is within,' said Arren. 'The loyalties of our lands are still split between our Houses. Our people desire certainty, they want to know where the power lies. With us.' His blood warmed with Hestra's interest.

'Commanders,' he said, 'we together hold the largest army ever gathered in Middren. We fought for our lands. The three of you stood at my side in the heat of war when half the nobles ran.' Arren could practically see the shine in Antoc's greedy eyes, he could certainly see the glow of pride in Peta's. This, he had never seen when he had faced his mother, this was light he never could conjure. His hands stopped shaking.

'We are the destroyers of gods, the bringers of light, of hope to our hearths. The people do not owe the Houses their safety: they owe us. It's been three years since Blenraden, let us remind them of what we achieved, march as victors back through our lands and show the might of our armies.'

Arren hoped Hestra was listening. Antoc's shoulders settled a little, he shifted his feet slightly apart, lifted his chin almost imperceptibly. A march. That sounded easier than a fight, would not necessarily risk as much.

Risiah's dark eyes had fallen back to Arren's chest, the chasm that was open there, would always be open. At last he nodded.

'Where?' the godkiller said. 'The Craier lands? The Geralfis'?' He pointed to the map, the straggling roads of the low and high lands, rarely better than cart paths. 'The ways are poor, the people suspicious. It would be . . .' He glanced at Antoc, then back at Arren, lowering his head. 'It would be expensive, your majesty. Even if we reclaimed their taxes and their fealty.'

'I agree,' said Arren. 'Those lands depend entirely on their connection with the coast.'

They all looked at Lesscia. The great inner port of Middren's fastest river: Daes. They had the wealth, the reach, the trade.

'Lesscia,' said Risiah. Peta had frowned slightly. Something about her stance, the set of her arms, or a narrowing of her eyes, suggested discomfort.

'Commander Peta?' said Arren.

Peta gave him half a smile that crooked the lines of her face. 'I worry that the Yethers are too powerful. Wealthy, with foreign connections. Even with our show of might, they may be difficult to sway.'

Arren smiled. 'We have no need to sway Lord Yether,' he said. 'I intend to break him. All I need is your faith.'

CHAPTER SIX

Kissen

KISSEN WAITED IN THE DARK FOR THE RAGE OF THE SEA to fade. She tucked herself in a stony corner, wrapped in her ragged leather cloak, and at some points between shivering, she slept.

Eventually, all was quiet. Silver moonlight filtered in through narrow channels cut in the walls, glancing off polished metal mirrors and casting the cavern in green light. As her eyes adjusted, all Kissen saw was memories of her childhood and old Talicia. This cave was Osidisen's shrine, and had been a haven for her and her brothers on the days the sea was too rough to work in. Its salt-encrusted pools were filled with treasure: golden chalices, strings of pearls, helmets, figureheads from model boats. Every new ship that was built had another made in miniature, offered to Osidisen's sea so he would bless their endeavours. Sometimes the small totems of other gods washed into these pools, prizes from the wreckages the sea raiders had made.

There were skulls here too. The bones of great families cast into the sea with their most prized possessions. Their ancestral lines were long broken, and Hseth's priests instead occupied their seats of power. Her incursion had been like a catching flame; little by little, then all at once.

Kissen swallowed and looked to the centre of the cavern. There stood a green figure, tangled in seaweed and adorned with fishbones, pearls, flashing mirrors and shells. Osidisen's totem, the man of

36

the sea. Every village, every town on the coast had gathered for the spring tides. They first built his bones using driftwood softened and mellowed by the waters, thickening it with green, budding branches and clay, tying together the riches of the land and sea with frayed hemp rope, ribbons and seaweed.

This totem must be over a decade old, since the fire god's followers had stamped out Osidisen's worship. Now, about the totem's feet were smaller dolls, made in secret by quiet hands, keeping the tradition.

The items were unbroken. Though the older green totem had faded - held together only by Osidisen's will, most likely - it had not exploded, or shattered. This cave, this shrine was still intact. That meant the god was still alive. Kissen's chest tightened, caught between annoyance and relief.

But he did not come. Which meant he had either forgotten her, or he could not.

Those briddite chains and cages must be keeping him from his shores. Why? A punishment for killing Hseth? How could they possibly know what she and Osidisen had done? No, this plan had been long laid, before Kissen had set foot in Blenraden, before Elo had called the wild god forth, before Hseth had died.

And her death had not deterred them.

The light was passing, the moon would not hold its position for long, and then she would be trapped in the dark and cold till dawn. Kissen groaned, unfolding herself out of her foetal position. Movement was pain. Movement had always been pain. But still she moved.

She shuffled to one of the rockpools and peered in, looking for something practical, usable. Among the useless gold and tarnished silver chains were blooded daggers, some bronze, some iron, remnants of the ages and offerings that had been made. Her eyes caught on a brighter edge. Steel. Workable, and she needed another weapon; the briddite of her cutlass would immediately mark her as a veiga in a land that lived by its god.

She plunged her hand in for the blade, thankfully free from rust, and tucked it, still dripping, into a loop on her leather girdle. As a child she would never have considered taking something from the sea god's shrine. It was the height of heresy. Now, Osidisen owed her one.

Or two.

She eyed the statue, considering its height. Yes, that might do just fine. She limped over, and took the measure of its legs against her body, disturbing some of the smaller totems to do it.

'I'm not sorry, you old bastard,' she said. 'But if you can survive a godkilling you can survive this.'

She dug her hands into the totem's flesh of seaweed and charms to find its wooden bones. Then, with a grunt and twist, pulled the driftwood away from the torso. The totem stayed standing, held up by the rest of its shape. She paused for a moment, half expecting the thing to move.

'If you've got something to say, then say it,' she said.

Something glimmered in its face, like eyes watching her, though it was likely drops of water that had fallen. A god's gifts held much of the original offerer, but over time became bound to the essence of the god themselves. The green man, however, remained as silent as the deeps.

And she needed a staff. This was how she remembered the totem's branches, curved at the top to hold the bow of his hip, or the pit of her arm. It was enough to help get her moving. A leg for her safety. He had taken that offering from her before.

Her turn.

Using the knife, she hacked at the stick until it was the right height, fitting snugly under her arm. Her damaged prosthesis felt springy and warped. If she could see it in the light she might be able to repair it, but not here. She needed balance, assurance, stability.

With the makeshift staff, she followed the shimmers of light into the recesses of the cave, careful with where she put her feet between the shadows. An arch of mother-pearl, just above her eye-height, marked a narrow passage upwards, the bright shells showing the path, gleaming in reflected moonlight. The same as Inara's buttons on her waistcoat.

Inara. That strange girl who could command gods. Kissen felt a wave of fear for the child she had left behind. She would be all right, she and Elo. The little god too. They had to be. There were no gods to pray to who could tell her that the risk she had taken had been worth it, that they had survived the city's chaos and made it back to Lesscia.

Though it was worth it, perhaps, to have heard Hseth scream as she had dragged her into the sea.

Kissen smiled grimly. Inara was tough, and Elo had too much pride to fail her. All Kissen had to do was get back to them. She followed the crevice as it curved and tightened. A mirror set between rocks lit a diagonal route skywards and Kissen grunted then turned herself sideways to fit into the narrow passageway that she had run up screeching, barefoot, with her brothers. Back then, everything had seemed so big, but now when clouds passed over the moon, darkness caught her between the stones, squeezing her tight.

Up and up. Kissen's arms shook as the staff and her hands took most of the weight of her aching body, moving as careful and quiet as she could. If the attackers from the cliffs had known about Osidisen's cove, they might also know about the shrine.

The crevice brightened, and chill air nipped her cheeks. The opening was a gap beneath a boulder of grassy rock that looked more like a badger's stay than a passage at the very top of the cliffs. Kissen peered out warily before extracting herself, ready to disappear back into the dark at the slightest sound, but no one appeared. No ships, no soldiers, no godkillers. She pulled herself up on the boulder and sat on it for a rest, looking out to the sea.

The moonlit water was brooding, disturbed, its waves small and scattering the light from the sky. Wind murmured over the cliff face, low and quiet, like a guest at a funeral afraid to make herself known.

'What the salt should I do now?' she asked the air. She wanted to go home. See Yatho and Telle and tell them all that had happened, that she had got her revenge. She wanted to wrap her arms around Inara and protect her from the world, and if that included Skedi so be it. She wanted to fuck some common sense into Elo before he made any more stupid mistakes without her to see them right. He'd appreciate that, she thought, as long as he didn't get all romantic. It felt as if Osidisen had brought her here just to spite her.

Not three miles to the south, beyond my reach from the shore.

That had been his reasoning to drag her into danger. Southwards, there were certainly fires warning the night sky, but there was no town there, at least there hadn't been when she was a child. Just some old ruins.

'Bah,' she muttered, pulling her cloak about her more tightly. What was it with water gods and muttering omens?

'Stupid, pissing, saltless fucker,' Kissen grumbled. 'Could have dropped me off at Lesscia with his warning then fucked off back to the sea.'

She would not have believed a word he told her. She still did not, but the briddite attack had dropped a stone of unease in her belly, weighing her down. So many ships for a coast that had all but abandoned its life on the sea.

South was the direction she would walk anyway. She would take just a look, to satisfy herself that Osidisen had cracked, and then keep on heading for the border.

Settled with that decision, she steeled herself to peer down at her prosthesis. Bent at it was, a good half-hand's span too short through twist and melt, it was still holding her. There were two missing plates, and one snapped joint near the ankle which was rattling.

'Oof,' she said. 'Sorry, Yatho.' The bridhid ore that made briddite when mixed with iron was in plenty supply. But since the war its price had risen to meet demand, and the time it took to cool it without cracking was what required training and patience. Each prosthesis Yatho made her was worth a small fortune.

She leaned down and pulled out the loose metal with a vicious wrench. If she left it it would rattle, and distract her. Then, she reached up for her ragged sleeves and yanked them off, one after the other, and tore them into strips to reinforce her leg, binding the metal so it would keep together.

That would do. The moon was almost at its peak, and she wanted to be a good distance from the barren shore before dawn. She hooked the crutch beneath her arm and stood, testing her weight, gritting her teeth, then headed south.

But as she travelled further, the evidence of people grew. She dodged more than one animal trap, some undergrowth beaten flat with passage, the sharp sap of recently felled pine, and patches of mud that smelled of piss and had been clumped by passing boots. The scent of smoke also floated by amidst a salted breeze. Coal smoke, bitter and hot.

Through it, Kissen caught the distant thrum of a *kithran*, a war drum or a waxing drum for wool makers, depending on who was playing.

She followed the sound back towards the coastline, careful now. Nearer the edges of the trees, flickering firelight danced in the upper boughs, staining their blooms and leaves to shades of blood and orange. There were voices too, raised in song. Worse: bells. Hseth's bells. Their chime sent shivers through Kissen's flesh.

Kissen crept forward, and through branches spied a ramshackle clifftop settlement; tents and cookpots, bowls, water barrels. A campfire flickered low, scattered with bones of whatever the evening meal had been, and a few lamps held back the night. This was not the source of the light in the treetops, nor the drums and music. There was no one moving about.

Kissen's nose twitched: horse manure. Something was moving, but it wasn't people. Half a herd of horses was tied against a long fence in a rickety stamping ground, disliking the close quarters they had been stuffed into.

'Poor sods,' Kissen muttered.

No guards, though a small hut just by them suggested some kind of stablemaster. Most of the horses were muddy, some still had their saddles on and bits in their mouths. An idiot stablemaster. Well, Talicians weren't known to be horse people, but these breeds were expensive. Usican, it looked like, or from the Curlish plains. If she met the master in different circumstances she'd have given them a hiding.

Nothing she could do for now. She moved past the horses, keeping out of the lamplight and creeping closer to the top of the cliff. All along its top were various winches and pulleys for lowering and raising goods, some large enough for timber, others small enough for fish and grain, and in the dark they looked like watchful birds peering down onto the flames and noise below. Not three hundred strides to the south again rose the walls of the ruins Kissen remembered. Some kerl's fortress, destroyed by Middrenite and Restish ships, blazing orange in the firelight.

Kissen crawled the last yards to the edge of the cliff and looked down.

Five great bonfires were lit on a great sand cove, enclosed by seawalls that hid it from the sea and protected it from high waves. The walls themselves were crossed with a chain, and Kissen did not have to see its dull metal sheen to know that it was briddite.

And no wonder they wanted the sea god out. The massive cove held twelve ships, bedded in and anchored just within the water. *Damn* Osidisen.

Four of the ships were Talician-made; she now recognised them as larger versions of the boat totems in Osidisen's shrine. Raiding ships, two-masted with a jib, thin-built for speed, and moved by oars and wind. The other eight were not Talician at all. The blunted sterns and figureless prows she had seen often in Blenraden on fatter ships, but these were huge and sleek. Three-masted, with cannons poking out of their sides. Restish.

What were Restish ships doing on Talician shores? The bonfires and the hive of activity was beneath the shadow of the ruins they had made of Talicia not three decades before. Restish was a great trading nation, almost as powerful as Middren, and had given aid to Blenraden. Their god of safe haven had lost his life to the wild hunt.

Kissen needed to be closer. There was something happening close to the ruins. This was the source of the drumming, the bells, the noise, and the largest fires. Upwards of a hundred folks were parading around something, too far to see.

She kept to the treeline, and then skirted around towards the wreckage of the castle. There were no lights within, and Kissen entered through long-broken gates, the shattered walls shaking with the sounds of below which had turned from singing to musical calls and bellowing, raucous answers.

'Hae dris sen-ga boretha med tolics?' They spoke in Talic. It had been so long since Kissen had heard highland Talic, but she could just piece the words together.

Who pushed the sea god back from our shores?
'Talic-i-a! Talic-i-a!'

The fortress was clearly used for storage. Barrels, tightly caulked against damp, filled the space that once would have held a guard-house. The other accessible room stank of excrement: a latrine. This, she avoided, but found half a staircase, a gaping hole from its foot to shoulder-height, that still stood at the door of the gate towers. Further up it, a window flickered orange where it overlooked the bay.

Kissen threw her staff up onto the lowest step, then pulled herself after it by her arms and shuffled up to the window. Here, she was hidden from the floor below and had a good view of the bonfires through the narrow slit. The folks in the cove were mostly dressed in vivid red, their marching and ringing was centred around what looked like a shattered bronze statue. Kissen could see the rafts from earlier, great barges more like, of heavy wood and, she assumed, Usican cork. They were being ceremonially burned to the sound of bells. Bile rose in Kissen's gullet, thick with salt and acid. That sound. The music the village had made when they sacrificed her family to the fire god.

'*Hae biret Hseth selika saolma?*'
Who will bring Hseth back to power?
'Talic-i-a! Talic-i-a!'

Kissen's heart plunged. The statue was almost unrecognisable, but now she understood: it was Hseth's. A totem. It had split in two with her death, and now was crudely wrapped in chains of metal, standing in a pool of coal and flame, fed and heated by the raging fire behind it. Beyond that, the shadows of the warships, the arms of the cove, and the unhappy, termagant sea.

The soldiers marched in a perfect, twisting square. A formal dance. And those in white were leading them, bells in their hair and ears, around their necks and wrists. Priests.

'*Hae obir béacen cerath kunin dwaeada medik?*'
Who will lead her war against the fool king's shores?
'Talic-i-a! Talic-i-a!'
'*Hae biret hsira Miden?*'
Who will bring the flame to Middren?

'Hseth! Hseth! Hseth!'

Chained to the statue were children, four of them, also in white. They were walking in slow, pained circles, looping closer to the pool of fire despite the burning heat. Binding Hseth back together. The chains would be burning hot, Kissen knew it by memory; tied to a flaming cage as her home burned, clinging to the bars as her flesh blistered, trying to free her father. In vain. One of the children was crying, but still they walked. As she watched, another who stumbled was shoved by a priest who kept them moving. Kissen caught on the breeze the smell of molten metal, burning coal, and charring flesh.

She clenched her jaw, a shiver of rage shaking her to her bones. Even in death, Hseth claimed blood and pain as her offering. Kissen wrapped her hand around her cutlass and dagger, but what could she do? How had they pulled together this ritual so quickly? It had barely been a day since Hseth was destroyed. Were these local children? Deckhands? Had they planned a sacrifice following the attack on Osidisen, and turned it into a resurrection?

A cry from one of the other bonfires. Two soldiers, their red jackets dark with ash and sweat, carried between them a pot on a set of bars. It glowed with molten metal, lifted from a furnace nearer the sea.

One of the priests rang a larger bell. Judging by its size, it had been pulled from one of the ships. Its deep tone resounded off the cliffs and over the waves. The small crowd fell silent, breaking their dance and forming lines before the statue.

'Hseth, Hseth, Hseth, Hseth,' the soldiers whispered, a susurration that stirred the air. This must be a common ritual for the god's faithful; it was too practised to be anything else.

A single priest stepped forward, and Kissen identified him as the leader of the cries. On his head was Hseth's bell symbol, daubed in blood. He spoke in Talic:

'It is time to act, and act as one as Hseth commands,' he said. 'Each of our coastal regiments has pushed Osidisen out to sea with guards of briddite, protecting our passage to Middren.'

Each coastal regiment? There were more soldiers? More ships? But Hseth had made a deal with Middren's king, that was why he had dragged Elo all the way to Blenraden. A heart for a heart. Elo's heart for the fire god's.

Then Kissen grasped it. Arren's heart would have been Hseth's. Hseth's will. And she could claim or kill him without a thought. Hseth didn't want to ally with King Arren, she had wanted to dominate him.

A lie. Elo had almost died for a lie. King Arren had been deceived.

'The foolish Middrenites thought they could kill our god like they killed theirs,' cried the priest. 'They thought it would save them from our might.' A few soldiers hissed, but the rest kept up the whispered chant.

'Hseth. Hseth. Hseth. Hseth.'

'Hseth may fall, but then she rises. Like Talicia from the ashes, our god will live again in war!'

The soldiers with the molten metal reached the priest, who rang the bell once more. This time, it signalled the younglings whose chains had bound the statue. They turned, taking hold of their metal with unflinching hands, and they *pulled*.

The chains tightened, and the children cried out as their hands burned, but they did not relent. Because pain was sacrifice, pain for gods was also love. Pain was an offering.

The halves of the statue came closer together, closer. One of the other priests approached the molten metal in the narrow cauldron. It had a dull sheen over its yellow brightness, oily and unusual. Kissen sniffed. Was that . . . bridhid in the mix? Were they trying to heal a god's totem with a godkilling metal?

The head priest and another hooked the cauldron onto a large staff and lifted it above the statue. Their hands havered, sweat poured into their robes, and then carefully, carefully, they poured.

The yellow metal splashed as it hit, clumsily striking the statue. A bead of it bounced away and struck a child who fell back, screaming and clutching their bare foot, and Kissen stuffed her hand in her mouth to keep from crying out. Another ball of glowing alloy spat onto the shoulder of the head priest who had spoken.

He screamed as the metal touched him, and his robe caught fire.

'*Hseth bleannat!*' Hseth blessed! he cried, then turned and ran, flaming for the ocean. 'God of fire! God of war! God who will reign over land and sea!'

He hit the water, the flames extinguished, but the rest of the soldiers flew into a fervour, screaming with noise that sounded somewhere between pain and ecstasy. More than one darted forward, running on hot coals while they drew their blades and pressed them to their hands. Blood sizzled as it hit the fire at the statue's feet. Offerings. Blood offerings.

Osidisen was right. Hseth's death was not some passing of a local god. Hseth had died while her faithful were at their highest strength.

She would not stay dead for long.

'*Cwel a Miden!*' came the next chanting cry, and the response was louder now, shaking the very stones of the bay.

Death to Middren.

'*Cwel a gaiet ni Hseth!*'

Death to all gods but Hseth!

'*Mailan Hsetha! Mailan telics!*'

The world is hers. The world is ours!

CHAPTER SEVEN

Inara

TELLE WAS HIDING SOMETHING. INARA COULD TELL. SKEDI
had taught her the tremor in a person's shades, the sly shifting of
hues that told of a lie.

They made a strange collection wending through the narrow and
winding city ways, led by Yatho with her grim expression and bare,
strong arms, Telle with her neat robes and quiet walk, Elo, limping
and ragged-cloaked. Inara little better with her tangled hair and
muddy clothes. She watched Elo's back, tapping the vial she had
tucked beneath her shirt which held the hair of Aan, the river god.
She had considered using it a number of times to try to call
the god and find some salve for his pain. But, despite it, Elo had
stopped her.

Do not take risks, he had said. Why? He had. Kissen had. She
was no different. Why did the world want to put her in a box and
hide her away? Yatho and Telle had even told her to stay put as
they went to seek out Canovan, but Inara was not about to let Elo
face Lethen and the rebel alone. This was her fight, her broken
heart, her grief. . . her revenge.

Skedi had elected not to return to the satchel, instead tucking
himself inside Elo's breast pocket for the journey. She had hurt
him, she knew that, but she was minded to let him sulk. He had
done worse to her than a sharp word.

At least they were not the most bedraggled travellers in the streets, nor the most interesting. Each corner in these narrow west-city ginnels was crowded with inns and patrons, strains of raucous music, and folk in mixtures of cloth and style: turbans ringed with coins that flashed in the light, urchins in rags dragging carts of travelling trunks that towered over their heads. Here, the sound of rushing water was constant, but the teetering sides of the buildings and their stilts only boasted narrow ways to the canals, too small for Yatho's chair, barely even wide enough for Inara to pass through while keeping all the skin on her elbows.

The Queen's Way was crammed up next to a brothel, judging by the lewd paintings across the neighbouring walls. Next to them, the inn looked understated, an afterthought. Its sign of pilgrims following a crowned woman was beaten by spring rain and cracked by more recent warm weather. Yatho entered without hesitation, but Telle lingered for a moment, flexing her fingers as if she wanted to talk, before they all followed.

They found Canovan smoking a pipe and contemplating a splintered gap in the inn's floor by the foot of the crooked stairs. Someone's boot must have gone straight through. The inn was empty, and mid-afternoon light shone crosswise through the back door that opened into a small courtyard, lighting up the dust motes that drifted gently in the air.

Canovan looked up. 'Yatho,' he said around his pipe, which dipped from his lip with surprise. Inara recognised the man, his crooked nose and lined skin she had marked out when he had gathered their pilgrim train at the fountain of faces, ready to send them all to their death. This time he wore a leather vest that showed his arms, chest and neck, all of which were thick with lean muscle and rippling with ink. 'I didn't—' He saw Telle, and froze, and then Elo.

Canovan's colours burst with emerald fear. He ran.

Elo moved before Inara took a breath. Despite a flare of pain in his colours, he leapt over a table and grabbed Canovan by the back of his vest before he reached the courtyard.

'Don't hurt him!' cried Yatho, but she needn't have worried. Canovan turned and slammed his arm down on Elo's elbow, breaking his grip. Elo scowled and rammed his left hand into Canovan's throat, shoving him back towards the bar in an explosion of strength Inara was surprised he had found. 'Stop!'

Canovan didn't stop, he clamped his mouth down on his pipe and blew on it, hard, throwing sparks and hot tobacco into Elo's eyes. Elo cried out, pulling away, and Canovan took the opportunity to kick him square in the chest.

'Elo!' cried Inara. *Skedi!*

Elo stumbled back, his grunt of pain turning into a wheeze. Skedi flew out of his pocket and into the air, unhurt. With a growl, Inara picked up a cup that had been left on the table and threw it with all her strength at Canovan, who threw up his hands to protect his face.

'Inara!' protested Yatho, but it gave Elo what he needed. The knight drew his sword.

Canovan reacted quickly, his hands flew up and a whirl of shadow appeared between his fingers, which he flung towards Inara and Elo. Elo bellowed, raising his sword. Telle and Yatho screamed, and Telle ran to grab Inara back.

But to Inara it was not just shadow, it was colour, light. Canovan's will. She stood still, and it washed over her and Telle, causing no harm.

An illusion! cried Skedi to Inara and Elo.

But Elo couldn't see that. He sprang back, his sword raised in defence, slashing at the shadow, and Canovan charged in through his distraction. He grabbed Elo by the wrists and *twisted*, wrenching Elo down to the side then aiming a knee for his groin.

But Elo had learned a thing or two from Kissen. He leaned in the direction Canovan had wrenched him, and moved his leg to counter Canovan's knee, then thrust his head up, hard, into the innkeeper's face. Canovan reeled back, mouth and nose bloody.

Elo took hold of his shirt once again and finally had him pinned, his sword across his chest. 'Stay still, won't you?' said Elo. Canovan bared his bloody teeth, putting his arm against the blade where he already had a crosshatch of scars.

'Go on,' said Elo. 'Call your god.'

Canovan's eyes flashed. He swiped his left arm along Elo's blade, adding another stripe to a hatch of scars on his forearm. Blood hit the ground. 'Lethen, help me!' he cried.

The inn flooded with the familiar scent of moss and blood, the scent of the demons when they came in the twilight. Shadow ran over Canovan's tattoos and for a moment the symbols shone to Inara's eyes, bursting with colour. Then, darkness flew out from his flesh, blasting into Elo's body and driving him back. Real this time. Yatho had moved protectively in front of Inara and Telle, her hands balled into fists.

Was Canovan a shrine, like Inara? But he used blood to summon Lethen; Inara didn't make a sacrifice for Skedi.

Elo gained his feet and brought his blade around, striking at the shadow. It shrieked as the briddite edge made contact, then the darkness thickened, and took form. From the shades manifested a pale woman with a black cloak and coarse grey hair tied with stones and glass beads. She carried a staff, with a will-o'-the-wisp lantern swinging from it. The same light that had shone from the shadow-demons' eyes.

This was Lethen of the Ways. God of lost travellers whom she led astray or guided home, depending on their offering or her mood. And her mood was sour. She raised her staff to strike, and Elo shifted into a defensive stance, but Inara was ready to attack.

She had not tried this in weeks. She gathered her will and focused it all on Lethen.

Inara, no! Skedi darted to her shoulder.

'Stop!' Inara commanded. She threw her will towards the god, wrapping it around her, and the divinity stilled, her staff in the air, frozen in place.

Elo glanced at Inara fearfully, knowing what she had done. Why was he afraid? He knew her power as much as she did.

But the others did not. What would Yatho and Telle think if they found out? What would Canovan and his god?

Lethen couldn't move her body, but she could move her eyes. And those eyes found Inara, pale and ageless.

Skedi landed on her shoulder, raising his wings and using his power too, not on Inara or Lethen, but on the others. *The god of white lies commands her to stop.*

The flickerings of suspicion in the others faded. Telle, Yatho, and Canovan turned away from Inara, focusing instead on the ancient god who had appeared in a city inn. Elo used this moment, and straightened, turning his sword in his hand and presenting it to the god, hilt-first.

'Be at peace,' he said, though Inara could tell by both his expression and the gleam of amber in his colours that he would like to punch Canovan a few more times. 'We are here for answers, not vengeance.'

Canovan was still leaning heavily against the bar. As the silence stretched the sounds that shaped it were his heavy panting breaths and the *drop, drop* of his blood hitting the floor. Lethen looked as if she was diminishing rapidly, her shadow barely touching where the sunlight gleamed from the door. She was a god of darkness: she did not belong in day.

'So, you did curse him,' said Yatho, breaking it. She was staring at the god, her voice cold and full of terror. 'Not just him. Kissen, Inara. The other pilgrims . . . the knight told the truth.'

Canovan didn't answer her. Instead, he looked from Lethen to Elo, clearly not understanding why his god had not ended him. 'You're supposed to be dead,' he said.

'I'm hard to kill,' said Elo, holding steady, 'and the curse was broken.'

Lethen hissed quietly through her teeth. They were white and sharp, like broken bones. Like the demons'.

'Our sister was on that trail,' Yatho snapped, her sign echoing her speech. Canovan clenched his fist, twisting with guilt and righteous anger.

'Your sister is a veiga,' he spat. 'A killer of gods.' He hawked and spat on the ground in Elo's direction. 'Knight, veiga, soldier, king. Everyone who has been stained with the blood of gods deserves whatever death comes for them.' A muscle worked in his jaw. 'I knew exactly what you were, Elogast of Sakre, the King's Lion, the moment you darkened my door.'

'So, when I asked you to take Kissen and Ina . . .' Yatho pressed her hands over her hair, her face filled with horror. She didn't sign, her grief-darkened colours writhed with pain. 'I trusted you,

Canovan. I defended you to my wife, my friends.' She looked at Telle, still by Inara, then turned her chair. 'I am calling the guard,' she said, signing with one hand.

Telle stiffened and shook her head. *No.*

His god is killing people! said Yatho back to her. *This is why the king outlawed them. This is why the laws are there to start with!*

You must not.

'If you bring the guard down here, Yatho,' growled Canovan, 'then I will give them your wife as well.'

Telle might not have heard him, but she understood what he said by the look Yatho gave her. A flush darkened the scars around her mouth. *I can explain,* she said.

You're part of this? Yatho signed back. *This . . . rebellion?*

Inara lowered her hands.

'Enough!' Lethen took advantage of Inara's distraction and snapped her will to pieces. She grew once more, moss spreading in an instant across the boards of the inn, darkness flying over the walls and choking out all light. One moment before they had been bathed in afternoon sun, now they were wrapped in the gloom of a forest at night.

The god charged, not towards Elo, but Inara, swinging her staff and lantern. Inara braced herself, raising her hands, but Skedi leapt down growing to a wolf's size and ducking his antlers. The staff cracked into them, and the lantern crushed into his wing, flinging him into the darkness.

'Skedi!' Inara cried, and pulled out her shortsword, ready to fight. Just then, her vial swung out of her shirt, the one containing the god Aan's hair.

Lethen's eyes widened, and she hesitated. *How many gods are your guardian, girl?* her voice came directly into Inara's head, only Inara's.

Elo stepped in. He moved between Inara and the god and caught Lethen's staff on the edge of his blade. Its briddite edge sliced straight through and the god cried out. Sunlight broke through the shadows of woodland, which thinned, and he swiped once more, pushing her back towards Canovan. 'If you kill us now,' he said through gritted teeth, 'you will lose your best possible chance at defeating the king.'

Elogast's colours were honest and true, steady as gold. Canovan's eyebrows flew up in surprise, rather than suspicion. He could see his colours too.

Lethen stepped back slowly, the darkness drawing back into her body. The boards of the floor hardened to their original state. An illusion: just an illusion. Like Canovan's, but more powerful. A bout of raucous laughter from the brothel cut into their silence, and a chorus of men burst into song.

Inara broke from behind Elo's back to find Skedi limping to his feet, his right wing bent and crooked.

'It's not healing,' he whispered, stretching and wincing, shrinking as he walked. He looked tired. Gods weren't supposed to get tired. Inara gathered him up in her hands.

She clutched him to her chest. 'It will,' she said, assuring herself as much as him.

He looked up at her, his whiskers twitching. She had told a white lie, to comfort him, as he had tried with her. 'Thank you,' he whispered.

'Thank you too.'

Elo lowered his sword slowly as Inara came back to his side, and Lethen backed away to Canovan's. Telle and Yatho were still beside each other, breath quick with terror.

'Good,' said Elo, and smiled as if they had not all come a breath from killing each other. 'This rebellion, you are its leader?'

Canovan laughed slightly, then put his pipe in his mouth to mask the shaking of his fingers.

'There are no leaders,' he said.

Lethen's darkness retreated to nothing, and she became a smaller version of herself, more shade than person, the light seeping through her.

He connects people, information, said Telle with her hands, then spoke the words quietly. Canovan scowled at her, and Yatho looked at her as if she was a stranger.

This man helped kill our sister, she signed.

I didn't know! I swear I didn't know. Telle glanced at Canovan with barely controlled anger. *I'm not a rebel, I'm just . . .* she made a sign so fast that Inara couldn't trace it, but by the way Telle gestured to her archivist's robe, it was connected to her work. Yatho was furious, it flared up in her colours; ashamed, hurt, and terribly, terribly sad.

Inara shivered, looking away from her. She didn't like seeing those colours. They were messy. They were too much. She had got all her own feelings in a grip, tight and contained.

'No leader, but I presume you have plans?' said Elo, sounding like he was discussing the weather. 'To fight back? Assassinate? Overthrow?'

No, said Telle before Canovan could speak, half to Yatho too. *To protect our communities. Our history.*

Canovan folded his arms, his colours disagreeing with Telle as he squared his shoulders.

'Tell us what our best chance is of king killing, briddite-wielder,' said Lethen to Elo. 'Then go. Our ways are not for you.'

'We need nothing from him,' growled Canovan. 'Let us beat out what he knows then leave his body to rot with the dog god of the canals.'

Elo raised a brow, unperturbed. It had never occurred to Inara that they might not *want* his help.

'Do you really think you could best me with pain?' said Elo. 'I am a knight, so you must know what that means. I have killed gods of vengeance and of nightmares. I have taken blades and terror and fire. I have left my home, my family and my king for my honour. I have no patience for empty threats.'

Not a word was a lie.

'I would speak to all of your rebels before I speak at all,' said Elo. 'Gather the people you connect, then perhaps when they hear the offer of my sword and my heart, we can discuss whose body belongs in the river.'

Inara swallowed, flexing her hands. 'And me,' she said. She was met with silence. She grabbed hold of Elo's hand. 'And me, Elo.'

Canovan had balled his big hands into fists. 'You say you have a use,' he said, then flicked his eyes to Inara. 'Does she?'

Inara held Elo's fingers tighter, but his colours were uncertain. He wavered.

'Absolutely the fuck not,' said Yatho. 'I'd not trust the either of you with a goat, let alone a child.'

Inara winced. Yatho just then had sounded exactly like Kissen. Elo clearly thought so too, because his colours sparkled with recognition in the colour of Kissen's auburn hair. 'Inara. . .' Elo began, his tone apologetic.

'No,' hissed Inara, her stomach plunging. 'Elo, no. You promised.'

'I said I'd be your protector,' said Elo. 'Not your commander.' He pulled his hand from hers, slowly, deliberately. 'I will not lead a child to war.'

'War came to me!' cried Inara. She looked at him, at Yatho, Telle. Any of them. They all looked away, apart from Lethen. 'I didn't do anything, and it came for me! For my mother. For Kissen.' She was trembling, her exhaustion rattling her down to her bones. Skedi nuzzled into her neck, feeling her grief. This was what she had kept moving for. The hope, the certainty that she could be useful, that she could help put it right. And they would turn her away? Now? After all she had done? 'What am I supposed to do?' she whispered.

Elo's expression wavered.

'Come home with us,' said Yatho. 'Rest. This is not your fight.'

'It's as much my fight as anyone's.'

Inara looked again at Elo, pleading with him. He hesitated. He was the only one of them who knew her, who knew what she could do.

'She's right, Inara,' he said softly. 'This isn't your fight.' He was leaving her, like Kissen did. He was sending her away. 'It never should have been.'

CHAPTER EIGHT

Kissen

IF HSETH REFUSED TO STAY DEAD, KISSEN WOULD JUST have to kill her again.

She waited, thinking, in her hiding space in the castle, opening an eye each time a soldier came too close in the dark as they defecated and gossiped. The tide went out, beaching the ships, then returned slowly, inch by inch. The sun would be rising soon, if Kissen was any judge. This was her last chance to run. Back to Middren and Lesscia, Yatoh and Telle, Inara, Skedi and Elo. They wouldn't know what happened to her if she stayed.

But she always chose the wild, the gods, her anger. Her vengeance. She would choose it again. She had to. They would understand why, if they knew. Hseth could not come back; one shrine at a time, Kissen would put out all her fires until they were gone.

And she would begin with the smelted brass statue by the sea.

Kissen whispered an apology to the air, the only sound near the camp that had settled into silence. Judging by the number of barrels they had cracked open, the quiet was deadened by alcohol as well as the still brooding water.

She looked further out to sea and frowned: instead of the greys of dawn, darkness was spreading, smothering the stars. A fret, some leagues out still. She hadn't seen a real one in years. A sea fog thick enough to blot out noon in midsummer, let alone a tentative sunrise.

Osidisen, cut off from the land, was showing his wrath, making his wrath known. Just like her.

And it gave her an opportunity.

Kissen cast a glance over the shore. The soldiers' victory fires had all gone cold. The children had all been released and taken away somewhere. She could do nothing for them, she knew that. If she tried to help, they would more likely call the priests than run for the hills; Kissen had seen it before in the faith-blind. Instead, it was better to target the faith itself.

She lowered herself down her perch on the broken castle stair using her arms, her staff tucked between her thighs; partly for silence, partly to test her strength. It would be enough, she hoped. Her wounds were not so deep, her body was resilient, and she was attuned to it.

She stole her way back across the sandstone cliffs to the pulleys that were erected on their edges like gallows. Most were huge, moved by winches and wound with hemp rope as thick as her arm. But one, closer to the poor horses, was smaller. Most likely for baskets of food, a keg or barrel, perhaps firewood.

Certainly big enough to carry a veiga.

There were two wheels. One winch at the ground with a lever and gears attached to a clamp. The other wheel swung at the top of the beam that hung over the cliff. The load tray was resting on the clifftop, luckily. Kissen released it from the heavy metal pulley hook; she wouldn't need it.

She went to the winch and released the clamp, then unwound the rope. The hemp was thicker than a bridle strap, but not the weight of some of those she had seen on the other machines. She pulled it out, hand over hand, and looped it carefully on the grass of the clifftop so it wouldn't tangle or catch, as her mother had taught her. The twisted fibre smelled like vegetables and wax over the other scents of salt and seaweed, charred wood and warm metal. Like her parents' boat, or the chandlers' huts in her village. Like the ties that she had broken her right tooth on trying to break her family free.

The rope was long enough. It could travel to the bottom of the cliff, which was about the height of a warship's main mast. She released almost all of it, then reclamped it at the other end. She would need it to get back up.

She tongued her gold replacement tooth thoughtfully. This might actually work. No one had stirred. The fog was thickening at the edges of the cove walls, but it had yet to reach the shore.

She shuffled to the cliff edge, put the hook under her left foot then wrapped the rope around her waist, around her calf, before threading her staff in as well so it would balance her. The loose rope from the other side of the pulley she held tight in her raggedly gloved hands as she moved to the precipice.

'This is a stupid idea,' she whispered.

She did it anyway, sliding off the edge of the cliff. A rush and swing, a sudden drop. The hemp around her tightened, the pull rope slipped a little, but she firmed her grip before she fell, thanking her own common sense for keeping the gloves; without them the hemp would surely have sliced through her palms. Her descent stopped, a patter of a few rocks hit the ground below, but the pulley held.

When she stopped swinging, Kissen braced herself, bent her left knee, then loosened her palms. The rope slid through the pulley wheels, unspooling from the nest she'd made on the ground, and lowered her down the cliff face. The gears squeaked, but no more than the sound of a distant gull or the nickering of the restless horses. She tightened her fists again, slowing her descent before she sped out of control.

Stupid, stupid idea. She should just sneak past, find a way home. Sit by a fire and close her eyes to this madness. Let kings and gods fight their own battles.

But those children, burning for Hseth because that was the fealty she and her priests demanded. What was it with people who thought children the bearers of their desires? If she went home to her family, how many more would burn?

She moved swiftly down the cliff, palm over palm, struggling to keep her weight centred. When she reached the ground she crouched as she landed, muffling the noise. No one moved. She held her breath, listening.

A whimpering sound came from a nearby tent, white sided and

set apart, daubed with Hseth's bell symbol. Priests. They could have chosen freedom in the wake of their god's death, but they chose flame. Why? She had never understood it, why humans chose, again and again, gods who abused their love, and demanded their pain.

Were gods and humans just as bad as each other?

'Saltless bastards,' Kissen muttered, spat in the direction of the white tent, then tugged her crutch out of the rope and pulled the rest of it, length after length, to loop it again on the ground.

'Stay there,' Kissen told it, then picked up the hook and wrapped it around her torso twice before hooking it to itself. Even this thinner hoisting rope was heavy, limiting her movement with the staff. She hauled herself forward over the sand, aiming for the statue.

The fret from the sea was moving quickly, thickening the air between the masts of the ships in the harbour. She didn't have much time before it completely enveloped the camp.

She planted her feet a step at a time, leaving drag-marks in the sand. Kissen could see the metal statue where it stood in the smouldering coals.

A step at a time, Kissen closed in on the god who had changed her life.

At last, she made it to the ashen firepit. The totem of bronze was seven foot tall and had cooled into a twisted version of the woman it had been. Still beautiful, streaked now with rivers of blackened metal. When polished, it would look as if she had been dipped in lightning.

'Stay dead, fire god,' Kissen whispered like a prayer, giving the rope another tug. She needed to be closer, and she had just enough, barely enough.

Kissen went over the coals, the end of her crutch blackening, smoking a little, but not catching light. Then, balancing precariously against her crutch, she drew out the hook, spun it, and threw it over the top of the god-statue's head. It cleared, the rope going over the shoulder, but the hook fell and clanged against the metal back.

Kissen froze, the hot coals warming the bottom of her leather boots.

Nothing. No yells. They were not expecting an attack. They felt safe. Imagine that; sleeping so soundly.

The fret was closer now. It clouded the waves at the edge of the shore, creeping up the sands. If the Talicians expected to set sail, they would struggle to navigate in the drear and looming mist.

Kissen unwound the rope and looped it around Hseth's waist, once, twice, then around one of the looser chains that bound her. Finally, she tied it back on itself and the hook. It would have to do.

Her next steps required haste more than silence. She moved swiftly back to the cliffs, tracing the path of the rope. She could see nothing of the water now, only the sand, the stone and the ruins. The edge of the shore was hidden.

A shuffle. A curse. The flap of a tent door. Kissen froze.

The sounds had come from nearer the water, and close to the statue. Kissen stayed very still, putting her hand on her cutlass, then moving it to Osidisen's dagger.

She didn't kill people. That was a promise she had made herself over and over. It was the gods' fault, not the people's. She was not a knight; she was a rat-catcher of the deities. Shrine-breaker, prayer-queller, briddite-wielder. Doubt gnawed at her heart. Kissen was not used to doubt.

A figure moved in the mist, grumbling quietly, their tone so muffled that she couldn't place their gender. They glanced up at the statue, but in the thickening dark they must not have seen the rope. They moved past it, closer to the water.

Kissen heard a couple of splashes of feet, in the sea, then a long, loud stream of urine. And a fart.

Kissen gripped her crutch. The stream of piss seemed to go on forever, splashing into the tiny waves.

The sky was lightening. Kissen could only tell by the sharpening of the edges of the cliffs, and the grey cast that fell over the sand. She could not tarry.

The pisser was swallowed by fog, then the statue. Whoever was awake wouldn't be able to see the end of their nose.

Kissen hurried forward again, quickly reaching the dangling rope that still hung from the pulley. She tested it: taut, ready to hold her. But she was less worried about the rope and more about the strength of her arms.

She flexed her fingers, rolled her shoulders, then tucked her staff into what was left of her breastplate to keep it out of the way. Her gloves, she tucked in there too. She needed grip. She needed to feel it.

Then she put her hands to the rope and began to climb. Her muscles strained at the shoulders, her upper back, her biceps. She couldn't stop: if she stopped she would slip, fall, and break her other leg. That would be the end of her: she'd take her own life before the priests used her for another of Hseth's little resurrections. She grinned through her clamped jaw, breathing in and out with each ache of her wrist and pinch of her bones.

There. So close. Just another stretch, another moment. The fret was creeping at her heels. If she lost sight of the clifftop she didn't know how she would manage to find it.

At last. She breached the cliff's edge and threw herself at it, sweating and half-laughing through tight breaths, though the crutch bruised her ribs as she landed. She had made it. Next time she lost an arm wrestle to Yatho, this would be the memory she'd rely on.

Kissen got to her feet, unclamped the rope from the base wheel and dragged it quickly back towards the horses. The fret was at her shoulders now, hanging about her like a cloak.

The horses scuffled and whinnied as she approached, uncertain about this strange-moving, salt-scented beast of a woman and the fog behind her.

'Shh,' Kissen hushed them, raising her hand so they could scent her. This was the second justice she could mete out. No one should keep horses all night like this, tightly bridled, poorly settled, standing in their own shit.

No time to waste. She marked out a big stallion with his saddle still on, and another gelding not far from him. They whinnied slightly as she came through the gate, leaving it open.

'*Hars. Set,*' she whispered in Talic. Quiet. Patience. She threaded the rope through their bridles, both of them, then a third, and bound it with a strong sailor's knot, like those her oldest brother had been so good at. The horses stamped but didn't bite or kick, though they might well have if they had more space. These Talicians deserved what they were getting.

Then she climbed over the front of the fence, took her cutlass, and sliced through the reins of each horse. They bucked their heads, moving back. The third she freed kicked up his front legs, thrilled, then whinnied loudly, earning a bellow in Talic from the nearby lean-to Kissen had spotted earlier. It was barely visible through the muffling fog. '*Shut it!*'

Kissen went on cutting. A few more were whinnying, hoofing around the pen, half ready to fight each other.

'*Set,*' Kissen whispered again. She just needed a few more moments, just a few.

She came to a saddled grey mare, which only huffed once when approached and allowed Kissen to stroke her nose. The poor thing still had a bit in her mouth.

'*Telic haar,*' said Kissen softly in Talic. Well met.

She climbed onto the mare's back, noting how the saddle had rubbed her skin. Kissen applied pressure to the bridle, guiding the mare back away from the fence and trying not to think of Legs. He must think she had abandoned him outside Blenraden. She only hoped the others had got to him before any thieves.

'Just a push, pal,' Kissen said to the grey. '*Sarethic mar.*' Come to me. '*Belik.*' Please. She decided to name her. '*Belik, Senfa.*'

Seafoam. She might be a Restish horse, but she had a Talician rider now. Senfa nickered, and wearily followed where she was told. The other horses were not so calm. They were free from their reins but still crowded. Two stallions rose up against each other, ears pinned back as they bellowed – a territorial warning.

'*What the fuck is going on?*' came a grumble from the shed. '*I'll skin you bastards and eat you if you keep me awake.*'

'*Sarethet mar,*' Kissen called to the others. She whistled low and guided Senfa towards the open gate. The others followed, and the stallions fell back, sensing freedom.

A board shifted by the hut, and Kissen heard the spark of flint, the hiss of flame. A halo of light barely glimmered through the murk.

Time was up.

Kissen lifted her staff. 'HAAAA!' she yelled, digging her heels into the mare's side and using the wood to smack one horse, then another on the rump. 'BE ON. BE OFF WITH YOU. BE ON, BE ON!'

Instant panic. The horses, disturbed, angry, stifled, all bolted in a riot of hooves, screaming as they went. The Talician began to yell.

'*Corsai.*' Thief. '*Belik mar!*' Help me!

Kissen ducked close to the mare's neck and held on for dear life as the silence of the fog was shattered into fragments.

She could not see it, but she heard the crack as the rope that bounded the statue went tight, and the scream of the stallions as they found themselves dragged back by the weight, fighting against the metal and height.

The horses won.

The brass shrieked and snapped. It made a sound like thunder as it dragged against the sand and coals, then clanged, discordant and broken, against the sand of the cliff face, then the wood of the pulley. Another snap. Kissen heard it as Senfa entered the forest. A splintering as the pulley broke. And still the rope came, the statue clanging across the cliff top till it too reached the treeline.

The sound of metal tearing gave Kissen great joy. It must have caught between some trees. But the horses no longer even paused; with a screech and a crumple they were free. They left behind a ragged piece of coppery ore, unrecognisable and thick with mud.

'Fuck you, fire god!' Kissen cried in triumph. One shrine down in Talicia. Thousands to go. She couldn't go back to Lesscia. She had to finish what she had started in Blenraden. She would rip Hseth out from Talician hearts one damned shrine at a time.

She was a godkiller still, after all.

CHAPTER NINE

Elogast

ELO SLEPT IN A BACK ROOM IN THE QUEEN'S WAY. Canovan had reluctantly accepted it as part of his terms, though perhaps only till he could find an easy way to be rid of him. Elo had slid the toilet pan – unwashed since the last guest, judging by the crust around the rim – right to the door. So, if Canovan did try to slit his throat in the night, he would at least have some warning.

When he woke, unmurdered, with the first glow of dawn, he realised how cold he was. The summers in Lesscia were wickedly hot, so Canovan's walls were thick and the windows narrow, but it was still spring and there was no fire, nor even a hearth.

Elo shivered and sat up, rubbing his arms. His fevers as he healed from the wound had left his body uncertain of itself, whether it was hot or cold, shivering or sweating.

He sighed and stood, carefully moving his arms back, and forward. He had seen burn scars before, not just on Kissen, on knights and the standing army when either people or gods had taken to fire. He remembered the advice of healers and one small healing god that had the shape of a snail: keep the bandages clean; wetness will ease the scarring but slow the healing; movement. Movement was key. It had to tug the skin but not tear it. And, despite the pain, he could not scratch. Where Canovan had kicked him, some of the healing skin had split. In places he could feel how tender it was; in others he had no feeling at all. His and Inara's careful work, so easy to undo.

Inara.

The thought of the way she had looked at him made him bury his head in his hands. It was the right thing. The only thing. But the fury and hurt, the rebellion in her eyes . . . He could only hope that Yatho and Telle would keep her from getting into further trouble, that she could have a chance to be looked after, to heal.

But the idea that she might not forgive him cut him to the marrow. She was a good lass, and sharp as a knife. If he was a more foolish man, he would imagine futures where he would teach her to fight, yes, but also to cook. He would take her to his mother-still-living and offer her his family's wealth and training till she was ready to reclaim her birthright. He would protect her and Skedi till his last breath.

But he was not a foolish man: he'd had that burned out of him. He was instigating a civil strife that he would likely not survive. He could not even write to his mother, lest the papers be intercepted and she or Inara brought to anyone's attention. Surely better to part with the girl, better to hurt her than destroy her.

There was no rest in him. Elo picked himself up, wrinkled his nose as he shifted the sloshing pan, then found his way back to the rickety stairs that led down to the inn. The bar and tables were empty, the hearths still unlit, but he could smell smoke, and a gentle waft of bread. And burning.

Elo followed his nose. The tables they had knocked over in their squabble had been put back and rearranged over the course of the night as the inn's patrons came and left. Other than the burning there was only the scent of the river and the vinegar top note of old ale.

Elo picked up his pace. The back door led to the courtyard and the river, but to the right was another. He pushed it open and found himself in a wooden outbuilding. An extension of the inn on stilts, reaching over the canal. Its front was open; a jetty thickly packed with pots of herbs and bones, and at the back was Canovan, sitting before a large fire and oven that had been built into the stonework of what had previously been the outside of the building. He was tossing fatty bits of meat and stone jars of pickles into a large stewpot while munching on the soft inside of a blackened roll. The stew, Elo recognised. An eastern vinegary hash in a base of beer and the previous year's pickled vegetables. Usually more of a snack than breakfast. The fire, however, was too high for the bread, and Canovan had let it burn. Three more blackened loaves were piled by his feet.

He glanced over at Elo. 'Piss off. I said you could stay the night because Lethen wanted it. You don't get a guests' breakfast.'

Over the way, there was another terrace on the water, this one filled with plants. Two naked folks were sleeping on a beaten sofa of old satin. A woman was sitting near them, drinking a mug of tea and reading a bound manuscript. She looked completely at peace.

'Can I help?' Elo said to Canovan, not knowing if she could hear them.

Canovan scowled. 'That sword useful for cutting brassic, is it?'

'I didn't lie when I said I was a baker,' said Elo archly. 'And it smells like you need one.' Canovan ran his tongue over his teeth, looked at the blackened bread in his hand, the stewpot, then back at Elo. Elo wondered what Kissen would have made of him. She'd have smacked him down and killed his god, probably. Then they'd be no further forward than they were when they left Blenraden. Would have been satisfying to watch though.

'Fine,' said Canovan. 'My cook broke his hand between boats, and I'm shit at beer bread. Five loaves, can you handle that?'

Elo shrugged. He had not made bread with beer before, but he had seen it done, and he missed the smell of the ovens, the bright sharpness of yeast in the air.

And Canovan. Elo needed to find a way to the heart of him, and a shared task was always how he calmed the tensions between unruly squires and knights. More than anything Elo needed allies, even allies like Canovan. If he wanted to even the playing field with Arren, he had to build some trust.

Canovan pointed him to nothing, but Elo had already spotted a bag of flour, a pail of milk, and a small churn with a healthy amount of fresh butter.

'Can I take some ale?' said Elo.

Canovan tossed his burned bread in the fire beneath the pot. 'Don't see how else you'll make it. I don't have leaven.'

No yeast. Elo went back to the bar and drew himself a tankard of ale from a spigot and barrel. Then, he mixed in flour and sugar, before adding butter he melted by the fire. The proportions, he judged by eye, attending to the coarseness of the flour and the scent of the beer as he added it cup by cup. Canovan watched him suspiciously, stirring his stew on occasion.

When the dough was ready, Elo waited for it to rise. The sun was slowly warming, shifting the breeze over the water, which might have been pleasant if it didn't carry with it the stink of the night's refuse. The couple from the brothel woke, chilled, and went indoors, but the woman finished her tea and continued reading. A pamphlet now.

As Canovan's stew began to bubble, Elo resisted telling him to add more salt; he forgot, sometimes, his own little luxuries. His mothers had never understood his self-imposed exile in Middren when he could have lived in wealth with them in Irisia, but they had still sent him desert salts, cooking pots and beautiful oils. Items many common cooks could not use, nor would use so liberally.

As soon as he dusted his hands with flour and took the risen dough into his palms, all else was forgotten. He felt calmer. He folded the bread to keep in the air and nurture some lightness to counter the wetness of the ale. It should crust well, if given the right attention.

'Don't,' he said to Canovan, who was about to add another log to the fire as Elo tucked the breads into well-oiled dishes.

'What?'

'They'll burn again if it's too hot.' Canovan grumbled, but he did put the log down.

Elo went to the jetty and plucked some sage leaves then, with a slightly smug flourish, tucked them into the bread to be baked.

'Too bitter,' said Canovan around his pipe.

'Not the young ones.'

As cloudless sunlight peered between the buildings, Elo brought the bread over the fire and used a poker to push the cooking grid-dles out on their pivot over the flames. Canovan reluctantly shifted his pot along on its hook so they would fit as Elo placed the loaves carefully down.

'They look doable,' muttered Canovan, then puffed his pipe and knocked it against the pot to shift the leaves. To Elo's irritation, a dusting of ash landed on one of the loaves. He said nothing, instead leaning against the fireplace. The silence for a moment was companionable. Or, at least not full of daggers. 'That girl,' said Canovan, speaking through a cloud of smoke. Elo tensed: a blade had been revealed. 'The one yesterday, who went with the veiga. Who is she?'

'A foundling,' said Elo, carefully, then smiled. 'And Lethen? What is she to you?'

Canovan didn't answer him. He had summoned a god from his flesh, had used her to plant a curse in Elo. The bond between them was not unlike Inara's and Skedi's, but Lethen had other shrines, other totems. Why bother with an innkeep from Blenraden? And he had some of his own power; when he had cast a hand towards Inara, Elo had been sure a shadow demon was about to bite her in two, but she had looked at it like it was no more than a gust of smoke.

After a moment, he said, 'It is hard to deceive a god, but not impossible. She said you should keep your life, and I agreed for now. But I will kill you if you pose a breath of threat against me and mine.'

Elo chuckled. 'And I'd kill you back, then we'd be nowhere.' Canovan grunted, a puff of smoke rising. 'So maybe let's be done with comparing the size of our cocks or the lengths of our loathing, and instead talk about tactics.'

Canovan tipped his ashes out on the hearth, put his pipe down then cracked his knuckles. The ink on his hands moved with his skin, but not with the strange shadow of Lethen's presence. This was a man that had set demons on Elo just for the suspicion of working for the king, had risked the lives of pilgrims and a child to do it. He courted violence, he enjoyed it. He was dangerous.

'We are are not all fighters, *commander*,' Canovan said, his tone curling with sarcasm. 'What makes you think Lesscia, the city of knowledge, is a place to find rebels?'

'You mean aside from you?' Elo hunkered down to Canovan's

level. They appraised each other like two cats, circling their territory.

'Lesscia is the king's weak point,' Elo said. 'That's why he has knights crowding out Yether's guards, that's why I knew this was the place to find the pilgrim ways. Yether has wealth to rival Sakre, protections, and connections too. This is where a fight will come.'

Elo saw the stir of excitement in Canovan' eyes, the twitch of a muscle in his jaw. If he was in the army Canovan would be a knight he put on healing duty, to ensure he knew the cost of violence.

'What makes you think that?' Canovan murmured, his eyes still alight. Did he know something?

'Because,' said Elo, 'that's what I would do.'

CHAPTER TEN

Skediceth

SKEDI'S WING STILL ACHED. HE HAD NOT TAKEN SO LONG to heal before, but then, he had rarely been injured, and he had rarely used so much of his power, so widely, so often. He was forced to remember he was not a god with endless love to rely on. He had Inara alone, Elo perhaps, and no offerings from them, no prayers. Gods lived on people's prayers. The only people who loved him at all were two people he had betrayed. No wonder he wasn't healing: their faith in him was still guarded.

I'm sorry, Inara, he thought to the girl, but as soon as Telle had brought her to Kissen's room and laid her head down, she had been asleep. As he watched, she stirred beneath Kissen's patched quilt, her brow knotted into a frown. She didn't used to sleep like this, tense and coiled, like a spring about to snap. But it had been so long since she slept at all. Skedi tucked his chin into his paws and waited.

The sun had long risen by the time Inara moved again. She blinked awake, then groaned. Skedi shrank to an amenable, squirrel-like size and jumped down to her chest. His wing had finally healed, twitching more than usual, yes, but no longer bent.

'At last!' he said.

'Ugh,' Inara murmured, rubbing her face with the backs of her hands. She sat up, instinctively holding Skedi to her chest so he wouldn't fall. It pained him that he might have lost her trust forever, her innocent, complete love. She looked around; her hair was wild, half-fallen out of its braid into the dark-briar tangles of a month on the road. Elo was probably right that she should cut it, it was so knotted, but Skedi knew she wouldn't. Her mother wore her hair long, and so did Ina.

'We're back,' she said quietly, stroking Skedi's ears. He allowed it, though some part of him wanted to remind her that he was a god, not a pet. She looked around the room, her colours heightening as she woke, remembering where she was.

'You got us here,' he said. 'Kissen would be so proud of you.'

Inara fingered Kissen's blanket, and then looked at the sparse trinkets on the edge of the small, glass-paned window.

'Tell that to Elo,' she whispered bitterly. A shiver of anger passing through her, and Skedi hopped to the windowsill as she remembered how she felt. 'Kissen would have . . . she wouldn't have.' Skedi knew a lie when he heard one: Kissen would have wanted her very far from whatever Elo had planned.

Inara's gaze landed on a writing tablet, cracked in two, tossed on the clothing chest. It was marked with wobbly, frustrated writing, and chunks of broken chalk. *Kissen*, it said, copied several times. *Telle, Yatho, home. Home. Home.* Kissen couldn't read or write, but she had been learning.

Inara sniffed, her colours rippling from her chest down her spine. This was the first time she had stopped, the first time she had nothing to do, nowhere to go, nothing to fight. Her face crumpled at the edges, buckling under sudden pressure, then her shoulders followed. She folded over and a sob wracked her small body to its core. Then another.

'Oh, Ina,' Skedi said. What could he do? What should he do?

Tears. They came in a wave of colour. Sorrow, frustration, and anger so great that Skedi felt it could wash him away. Inara had not cried in weeks; instead, he had watched her colours becoming more tense. Murkier. Closed. As a child, he had found her tears disconcerting; crying was wet and off-putting. But this was different. These were not the tears of childhood. They were more, bigger. She was being crushed by her heart and this was her only release.

Skedi hopped back onto her lap, placed his paws on her

shoulders. How could he soothe this grief, how could he make it go? 'Ina,' he murmured.

She placed her head against his antlers, pushing her fingers through his fur. 'Tell me it will be all right, Skedi,' she said, breathing through her sobs. 'Please, we're here now. Please lie to me.'

Skedi flattened his ears. 'You said you didn't want that,' he said. 'You made me promise.'

'Please.' She pulled up her knees into a ball, her colours crashing and spinning out of control. How could she hold this much in her? She had enough sorrow to tear the world apart. 'Please.'

Skedi hesitated a moment longer. He was still healing, weak. He had already overextended his powers, but he could not deny her. He pressed his will to hers gently, feeling her colours with his mind and trying to detangle them. He found the fear there, the isolation, abandonment, guilt – so much of it – then exhaustion and sorrow. He felt her emotions as if they were his own, and gasped with her pain.

It will be all right, he said, soothing her with his will, wrapping it around her colours, softening them. *All right. It will be all right. You have purpose, you will find a way. You can find your own way.* He became the size of a large cat, comforting, though he felt shaky, weary; frail. Still, what else was he for? Was this not the purpose of a god of white lies, to ease people's pain?

Inara slowly stopped shaking, and her breaths became gentler, and the murk of her colours soothed to crystalline once more. Finally, she picked herself up, pale and trembling, but calm. She shone with the lie she had asked for and wiped her face.

'I'll find my own way,' she echoed in a small voice. 'I'll show Elo. He can't send me away.' Skedi hoped he wouldn't have to find out what that meant, and she smiled at him before he asked. 'Thank you, Skedi.' She paused. 'Skediceth.' She looked at him as if seeing him for the first time as he reduced in size to a small rabbit.

He put up his ears, fluttered his wings. *Nothing to worry about.* She didn't look convinced. 'I'm all right,' he added out loud.

Inara's hand went to a button on her waistcoat. Her precious waistcoat that she had worn since she left home, the mother-of-pearl buttons from her grandmother's robes.

'Oh . . . no,' said Skedi, understanding what she meant by it.

'I asked you for a lie,' she said.

'No . . .' He wanted one. Oh, how he wanted one. He could see the colours in them, Inara's love, suffusing the pearlescence with her own precious shine. That could be his. 'I shouldn't. I couldn't. You're my shrine, Inara. I can't take payment from you.'

Inara wrinkled her nose, though a purple sheen that floated around her shoulders suggested that she was comforted.

'But I asked you for your help,' she said. 'And you're a god.' She twisted the button away. 'I've never offered you anything before. Maybe I should.' She pulled out the thread with it. 'To put a distance between what we are to each other. What we ask for, and what we give.'

A distance? Skedi had not asked for distance. He wanted Inara to love him. As he was.

She held out the button by its thread.

'I've nowhere to put it,' Skedi protested.

It shone in her hands with her energy, her essence that gave gods power. If he had it, her colours would become his.

Skedi flicked his wings uncertainly and felt his damaged one ache. That was what made him bow his head and accept her gift. Inara tied it around his right antler, wrapping the blue thread round and round. As she did so, Skedi felt its colours come into him; her love of her mother, her grief, her thanks to Skedi. They brightened his fur, brought him energy, strength. The ache fled from his wings, the fatigue from his body. It filled him up, brimful, and he knew for a moment what it felt like to be a true god.

He flapped his wings and turned to the window, growing as he did so. The button stayed clinging to his antler, still tightly bound. Now it was his, it was as much a part of his body as his wings were. He looked at himself in the glass, tipping his head to one side, then the other.

'It looks well,' said Inara softly, thoughtfully, thumbing her remaining buttons. 'I don't know why I didn't think of it sooner,' she added, her voice gaining strength. 'I gave one to Kelt before you.'

Kelt.

Skedi whipped around. That whisper. It had been so close, but more like an echo than a voice. Inara looked startled; she had heard it too. The tiny god of broken sandals, tied to a fading shrine in Blenraden. There was no way he could have followed them to Lesscia. Skedi shivered.

'Be wary of calling gods by their names,' he said. 'Even over long distances. They might feel it.'

A flurry of movement outside the window distracted them both. Telle and Yatho were standing outside, their hands moving quickly, speaking to each other. Their gestures were sharp, blunted. An argument.

This isn't about us, said Telle.

What else do we have in the world? Yatho looked rumpled. Skedi noted that through the open door of the smithy a cot had been set up of hay and some blankets. She had slept there. *Without Kissen, we're all we have left.*

Telle's brow creased in pain; her colours rippled with grief. Inara saw it too, her own colours radiating out in sympathy.

There is more than us, said Telle. They spoke so fast that Skedi realised they slowed their speech around everyone else. Between them, there was nothing to hold back. *There are people who the rebels help. They believe in teaching, in freedom. I believe in that too.*

I believed in you, said Yatho, then moved her chair back. *And then you lied. To me. Your wife. You lied and you kept on lying.*

Because I knew you wouldn't understand.

You're right, I don't. We have lost our sister to a god, we saw hundreds lose their lives to gods in our city, and you want to preserve them.

It cannot always be us and them, my heart, said Telle, pleadingly. *They are part of us.*

Yatho shook her head, still thinking of Kissen, judging by the grief that stained her colours indigo. *She would not want this*, she added.

Telle's hands hung in the air a moment. She clearly didn't know what to say to that. *I am my own person*, she added at last.

Clearly.

Telle stepped back, but Yatho didn't apologise. *You need to stop,* the smith said instead. *You're putting everything you've worked for at risk. Everything we've worked for. For a one woman fight against history.*

I'm trying to preserve our history!

Then do it legally, said Yatho, snapping her fingers in anger. *Speak to the archivists, tell them your concerns.*

Telle laughed and shook her head. *They will not listen.*

They are not Maimee, said Yatho.

Telle's colours flashed vivid white with anger, but all she did was clench her jaw. Maimee; the woman who had raised Yatho, Telle and Kissen collected children to abuse and force into thievery and beggary in Blenraden. Kissen had told them the poisonous woman had put the scars on Telle's face so she would be more sympathetic to rich merchants, but not pretty enough to be stolen away.

Maimee made you stay quiet, Yatho pressed. *Tried to stop you teaching sign. Made you doubt yourself, doubt everyone. Doubt me.* Her brow creased. *You always tried to fix everything in silence. You have a voice now, Telle. Use it.*

Telle dropped her hands. Yatho paused, staring at her, knowing she had cut her wife to the bone. Regret dimmed her colours for a moment, but she was too angry to retract. She turned her chair, heading straight for her smithy, and Telle watched her go. For a moment, the archivist's colours moved as if she would call her back, but instead she turned on her heel and stalked back to the house.

Skedi and Inara exchanged a look, Inara's thoughtful, then they winced as Yatho picked up whatever work she decided to do with a vicious clamour. Its sound was quickly followed by a loud growl from Inara's stomach. She sheepishly clutched her belly. 'Gods,' she said, 'I'm hungry.'

'You think we can go to the kitchen?' said Skedi

'They said to make ourselves at home . . . Though I don't know much about cooking anything but stew.'

Skedi had occasionally been glad he didn't eat on the road, judging by the smell of Inara's cooking and the colours Elo tried to hide when he ate it.

Inara swung her feet to the floor and stood like a newborn lamb, her legs shaky with sleep, then Skedi swooped down from the ledge and then hopped ahead of her to the kitchen. The hallway was as he remembered, its low beams hung with dried spring flowers and herbs. But, when he came to the kitchen door, he paused; Telle was sitting at the table, her hands laid flat on the surface as she stared at the wall. She didn't notice them immediately, but when Skedi made a move to retreat, she stirred and looked to the door then managed a smile.

Hungry? she signed, standing up and uncovering a bit of bread. *No butter, the goat didn't milk this morning, but there's honey.*

Skedi watched Telle's colours, which were still shivering with anger and some shame, dull emerald hues interspersed with blushing peppercorn grey. But clearly she had no intention of drawing Inara into her argument with Yatho and had no idea that they had witnessed it.

Thank you, said Inara, helping herself to a chunk of bread from the table and taking a long, luxurious moment to douse it in honey. Skedi kept his distance. He didn't like the idea of sticky fingers. It was strange how cold the room felt to Skedi without the little family together in it. As if the walls had lost their warmth.

Telle watched them both for a moment. *You need a bath,* she said. *I'll get some water.*

Wait, said Inara, still chewing as she signed. Telle paused. *What were you doing? With the . . .* Ina didn't know the sign for rebellion, she spelled out Canovan's name instead.

Telle grimaced, glancing out of the window to the yard. *I don't want to explain myself to you too.*

I don't need an explanation. I'm interested. Inara shrugged. *I can keep secrets, you know that.* She gestured to Skedi.

Telle lifted her shoulders, then sighed. She had no will to challenge her. *I have been smuggling texts from the cloche to be copied,* she said. *Then returning them.*

Inara frowned, chewing on her bread. *That doesn't sound so bad,* she said, voicing Skedi's thoughts. He didn't want to intrude with his voice into Telle's mind. In part, because it would hurt her, but also because her emotions were so deep and complex that they might hurt him.

They're texts about gods, she clarified. *The latest laws make taking them outside the cloche illegal. Copying them is illegal too.* She bit her lip. *My fear is that very soon it will be illegal to have them at all.*

Inara's colours flared with thought, and Skedi looked at her suspiciously. *What kinds of things about gods?*

Histories, stored knowledge, blessings, relations . . . she paused, and frowned at Inara, perhaps also sensing the intensity of her interest.

Inara smiled, and Skedi sensed a white lie coming, like a stirring in his feathers. *Canovan has been helping you?* Inara asked. *He doesn't strike me as much interested in texts.*

That was not the lie, it was a distraction. Skedi flicked his wings. What was she thinking?

He connected me with a woman who owns a printing press similar to Yatho's, said Telle, *I never thought he . . .* She closed her eyes for a moment. *He is more dangerous than I knew. Elo is right not to want you near him.*

Inara scowled, but quickly washed it from her face. When she next saw Elo, Skedi did not think it would go well.

I can understand why you take the risk, said Inara. *There is still so much we don't know about gods.*

Telle nodded slowly, tapping her fingers against her chin. Then she shook her head and smiled, clearly deciding it wasn't Inara's problem. *You have an accent you know*, she signed. *The way you sign reminds me of some of the more disreputable sailors in Blenraden.* She laughed. *It isn't what I expect of a noble girl. Even mine is not considered formal.*

My mother taught me, said Inara.

I know, said Telle, *She must have been somewhere she shouldn't have.* Telle was trying to be friendly, gentle. *Perhaps you are quite like her*, she added.

Inara smiled a little, but she didn't want gentle. She wanted action. It was with a flutter of disappointment that Skedi guessed what she wanted to ask before she moved her hands in sign.

Let me help you, Inara said.

Telle's brow furrowed.

It doesn't need to be dangerous, Inara added. *Just copying the god manuscripts. Or maybe I can go with you to the archives, help find the right ones . . .* All Inara desired was to be part of the rebellion, in any small way. And, a sweet addition: proving Elo wrong. It didn't matter whether Skedi thought it was a good idea or not.

Telle shook her head. *Yatho wants . . .* she began, then paused and touched her scars. *She wants me to speak to them,* she said thoughtfully. *Words they do not want to hear.*

Then let me come with you, said Inara, sensing an advantage. *I'll help you speak. We'll make them listen.*

Skedi settled a little. Talking to archivists, with Telle, did not sound too dangerous. But still, he sensed something else; an undercurrent of Inara's will. This was more than just being involved. There was something else she wanted. But what?

There is a forum, said Telle. *In three days. When I have tried to raise concerns with the head archivists she says to speak there but . . .* She looked at her hands. *Many there can sign, formally, but they don't understand me very well . . .* Her mouth twisted. *Or pretend not to.* She looked at Inara. *Could you? Come with me? It will be safe inside.*

Inara nodded. *Of course,* she said. *Whatever I can do.* Her face was calm, but Skedi watched her colours. They twisted with conflicting shines of generosity and deception, anxiety and certainty. Around their edges, they still glimmered with vengeful fire.

CHAPTER ELEVEN

Kissen

KISSEN STANK OF SMOKE AND DESPERATION. EIGHT MAJOR shrines and a hundred small ones down on her journey through western Talicia, countless to go.

Every town she had passed had already remade its totems, or were in the process of doing so by government edict. Their bells were recast in fire, the statues reforged in bloodied bronze. Most small ones had a sacrifice of a goat or fresh spring lamb, but one she had found had three bodies burned at the stake, old folk, she heard, from people's whispers. Another village she counted at least twelve women and girls with their hair burned down to the scalp, the skin on their heads still blistered and weeping.

Kissen had never seen anything like this. When gods died, people moved on. But Hseth had threaded her worship through every stone in this land, and brought the nation to the brink of war.

This she saw too, in each town. Evidence everywhere of garrisons leaving for the mountain borders, following the melting snow. Storehouses filled to the rafters with grain, ready to create supply lines as far as they could go. Oxen and asses loaded up by people, normal people, who laughed and joked and sang as they formed baying lines south. Two old forts had been rebuilt and hung with red banners daubed with a yellow bell. This was not just a raiding war by sea, this was an invasion.

It was so strange to feel both so at home and so alien in the land that had birthed her. The scents of the towns she passed; fermented fish, barley biscuits and spring vegetables with butter and oil. The sound of mothers' voices and fathers' calls, the riot of children bickering through the streets in babbling Talic. Even the colours of the homes, the washing that hung drying hopefully in the spring sun. Her heart ached in recognition for what she had lost. The home that could have been. The home she had made in Middren.

And then, the stranger things. The bell or woman charms worn by half the folk in the first almost-city she came to, carved out of quartz or cast in copper. The place – Poelt – had been a scratty town for big market days, and now was large enough to have several squares where wealthy merchant types gathered. Some of them had painted false burns in pink patterns on their faces, highlighting their cheeks or their noses and chins. She heard one woman arguing that she had sold three children to the marching soldiers for sacrifice, and therefore deserved discounted copper ore.

The cult of Hseth had spread so deeply into everyday life.

She had made a mistake, hunting through Talicia. She should have heeded Osidisen's warning.

Still, by force or trickery she had taken down every shrine she had found. One she broke by releasing barrels from an uphill store, sending them charging down the slope to shatter and burn on the altar and scatter its remaining figurines. One shrine was simply a cracked bell from which she stole the clapper, then threw it into a river. But who was to say what happened when she left again? Did they lose their faith, accept Hseth's loss, or did they forge it anew? Over and over again?

And soon, she would not have surprise on her side. Word would spread of shrines being taken down, and a burned and limping woman travelling alone on a war mare would eventually draw someone's attention.

Kissen went deeper into the mountains, hoping for something, anything, to fight against and win. They said that Hseth came down from the slopes in the hearts of the surviving kerls. The stories went that they sacrificed to an old god of wildfire who was previously invoked for faileseth, when the upland heather was burned. They had wanted to regain their strength, and so had turned to anything they could. But Kissen didn't know that for a truth. If the kerls had come out of hiding, then they were priests now, not lords of the sea. And there was no sign she was moving towards a central shrine. Most inland and highland holdings she saw were empty shells of buildings.

But she was committed now; she had to try. So, she pressed on. Her right leg felt as if it was clamped in a vice, enough to crush her bones. Spending too much time in her prosthesis was painful, spending days and days on a broken one was agony. Even her left leg was suffering, aching and bruised, as she struggled up the dark paths ascending the Bennites.

The slopes had been ravaged by winter and were now black with thaw and rotted bracken. Some still hid thick patches of frozen white, tucked into crevices and beneath rocks where no sunlight touched. The north wind bellowed and screeched through the budding trees, tearing at their roots and branches. More than one had come away, is roots weakened by the winter, and caused slippages that Kissen had to force a reluctant Senfa over.

At least the mare was faring better. Kissen had buried the saddle and replaced it with stolen blankets. Senfa did not like that, but she enjoyed her brushing down, and the evenness of her freshly-trimmed hooves. The beast seemed content, even happy, to be ridden. Even more so now she was given space at night to sleep and plenty of grazing on green buds. This was the life Kissen knew, deep in the wilderness, on her own. But she had never felt fear like this, fear that the world was bigger than she was, and far out of her control.

As they moved higher, into the twilight and rising mists, snow became more prevalent, and icier. They passed a shrine for Hseth made out of carved stones, marked as hers by the rune version of her bell symbol. Kissen and the horse pulled the stones down with ropes, leaving them aching and Kissen's hands bloody. She contented herself with thinking that by now Elo and Inara would be in Lesscia, safe. They would have worked out a way to break the curse. Inara was smart, and Elo had at least the makings of wisdom. If they found Legs, he would have walked them home himself.

Senfa, decidedly not Legs, whinnied as a gust of wind and sleet shook them both to their fatigued bones. Kissen hunkered down and swore, pulling her ragged cloak tighter around her shoulders before urging Senfa on. She remembered the name of this wind from her mother's stories: the Faera. It came roaring down with spring, strong enough to flatten pigs into their styes and tear thatch from the houses. The Faera was the breath that launched the old raiders from Talicia's coast, and had in her youth heralded the first big fishing hauls of spring. It moaned into her ears as she rounded a corner and saw the path narrowed, tugging at her hair and throwing leaves in her face. Senfa shied, disliking the noise and the rocky ground.

'Aye, all right, girl.' Kissen dismounted, tucked her staff under her arm and took her by the reins. 'Come now, petal. *Sareth.*'

Senfa huffed and shuffled on with her. The way was a narrow lip between cliff faces, stone rising solid and high to their right, and to the left was a steep dive down into icy blackness.

'Just a bit further today, hinny,' said Kissen gently, using an old term of endearment. 'Then I'll make you a fire, won't I? Some chestnut leaves, you'd like that, eh? You like the sweet fresh ones.'

She dug doggedly forward. The path was precarious, its edges loose. She shouldn't have brought Senfa here; she had thought it a wider road. Perhaps it had been, once. A strong gust would make short work of her as she edged around the arete, the wind in her ears so loud that she didn't even see the soldiers coming around the cliff face ahead.

A glimmer of red, a shout closer than the wind, then at once she was surrounded by bodies as if the Faera itself had blown them there.

'Who are you? What are you doing here?' They spoke such strongly accented Talic she could barely understand their words. Their lilt was from the grasslands, far to the north-east. Had they been lying in ambush, or coming around the corner ahead of her?

'Eh?' said Kissen, pressing Senfa back to the cliff and lowering her face, trying her best to look humble. She went for her thickest rendition of her childhood Talic. 'What do you want?' She hoped the soldiers would think she wouldn't understand their dialect.

They carried a Hseth idol with them, small, on a high pole, with two bells Kissen couldn't hear over the Faera. A rear scouting party, it looked like, either called back, or looping on the trails made by the soldiers moving west.

'They said what are you doing here?' This accent was south-western, closer to Kissen's.

A hand snapped out and grabbed Kissen by the cloak, pushing her back and off balance. Kissen's hair fell out of her face and she was confronted by a snub nose and pale-green eyes, wrinkled by wind and sun. A woman at least ten years the elder of the rest of them. The other scouts were no more than a gaggle of youths, not much older than Inara. Barely more than children. Soft-faced, ears sticking out, uniforms baggy and ill-fitting. Room to grow.

'Hseth-blessed,' said the woman who had Kissen, casting her eyes over the burn scars on her neck and chin, pausing for a moment on the top of her tattoo, and her lips twitched as she must have realised what the curling line meant: 'fuck you' in Talic. Then her eyes came to rest on the white curse broken on the side of Kissen's face, the spiderweb of script left there by a dead god of beauty. Kissen carefully put a hand to her knife. 'Middrenite spy,' the woman hissed, and shoved Kissen against the cliff wall.

Kissen let her: the wall would protect her back if it came to a fight. This must be some kind of krka; a squadron captain in Talicia. The youths stared at Kissen, at once fearful and fascinated.

'Spy?' said Kissen in Talic, keeping up the conversation. 'You think bad luck makes me a spy?'

'Only Middrenites play with other gods.'

Kissen took a breath. Senfa was hoofing the ground, unnerved. It would not take much more wind to send them all flying over the edge. 'I was a child,' Kissen tried. 'My parents took me.'

'You're a poor liar. And your Talic is stiff.'

Kissen's hand itched around her blade. She could gut the krka there and find a way through the others. She had a horse, and they were on foot, huddling together against the sleet.

But her rule: no killing people, just gods. Though now she had saved a god. More than one, if she counted not stabbing Skedi every chance she got.

'I'm just a traveller,' said Kissen. 'A poor one. I grew up in Senkørsa before it fell.' Fuck the krka, that wasn't a lie. 'Now give me some coin or let me be.'

'Senkørsa? I've never heard of Senkørsa. Nor of poor travellers with gold for a tooth.'

Kissen drew her knife, Osidisen's knife, and pressed it to the woman's belly, showing her that she had claws and could use them. The krka stiffened, but didn't draw back, she seemed to sense Kissen had no real desire to use her blade.

'I have heard reports of a traveller in these parts,' the krka added, more to her huddled and shivering squadron than Kissen. 'A limping woman, come begging, and Hseth's shrines falling the next day.'

Kissen didn't need to be a god to sense a human on the edge of violence.

Shit.

Kissen threw her left hand, the one without the dagger, over the crook of the krka's arm and shoved down, then twisted forward with her palm, slamming it into the woman's breastplate. The move broke the krka's grip and pushed her back into a dancing rip of wind. A boy caught her by the elbow as she stumbled and Kissen took hold of Senfa's reins again.

'I mean no harm to you,' said Kissen loudly, a last-ditch attempt. 'I'm passing through, nothing more.'

The krka straightened her uniform and spat. The air snatched her gob of saliva and dragged it over the precipice.

'This woman is a traitor to Talicia!' she bellowed. 'I can smell it on her. Traitor to our blood, to our land, to our war, and to Hseth. Show her what we do to traitors.' She grabbed the boy nearest her and thrust him forward. 'Show *me* your training.'

It didn't matter what Kissen said or what she had done, the krka just wanted to blood them. The lad put a hand on his sword. His fingers were blistered, his knuckles raw. And he was scared.

'You don't need to do this,' said Kissen.

'Come with us,' he replied. His voice trembled, not so long broken, gravel still grinding in his throat. 'We'll take you to the priests, and they will burn you for Hseth.'

The krka smiled tightly; that was not what she wanted. But

Kissen held her ground. She would burn for no one, even though she couldn't fight them all, not on her own.

'*Haetha!*' cried the krka. Attack.

The boy snapped into stance and drew his sword, dashing forward.

Kissen was ready. She dropped her dagger into her left hand, then swung the point of her crutch into his belly. He stumbled back, falling with a thud, but not before a girl darted around him to Kissen's right. Senfa, released, reared back several steps, unable to turn and bolt the way they had come. The girl flinched, and Kissen used the distraction to step forward and slam the end of her staff hard enough into her arm and to ram it and the sword into the cliff. The soldier's knuckles and blade scraped against the stone, releasing a shower of sparks.

Senfa squealed this time, ears going back. Kissen shoved the girl away as the mare reared and struck with her hooves, knocking Kissen to the ground.

Her advantage was gone. Kissen rolled to avoid the frightened horse but found instead that her arms were grabbed and wrenched to the side. She took a kick, hard, to the guts, and her knife arm was pinned back by another boy. Senfa at least had managed to buck herself into the other direction and she ran screaming back south for safer ground.

Lucky for some.

Kissen bucked up then pulled down her dagger hand with all her considerable strength, then threw herself bodily towards the kid who held it, headbutting him in the nose. But he did not let go.

The recruits pulled her upright. The girl with the sword had it again in her bloodied hands. Three more red-coated, redder-faced youths were advancing past the krka, gaining courage. The lot of them dragged Kissen back, and she yelled out in frustration as she lost a grip on her staff. Then, the cliff wall was at her back; they had slammed her against it.

Mistake. Theirs.

Kissen placed her left foot against the cliff then shoved forward, using it to spring a lunge towards the lad who still held her. Her teeth found their mark in his ear. She dragged him forward by it as he screamed and let go. Then Kissen leaned on her left leg and delivered him such a knee to the chest with her right that he barely made a sound as he fell. She brought her dagger hand around and slammed the back of her fist into a girl's jaw so her grip loosened. But then another charged and Kissen had to twist to parry a sword that went for her chest.

She couldn't win, not here. Not like this.

Sound up ahead. Kissen glanced up through sleet-stung eyes and saw the first lad she had sent sprawling. Still wheezing, ordered by the krka, he was drawing a bow and arrow. Smart arsehole. He yelled out to his friend who had gone to stab Kissen, and the girl drew her blade back then ducked as the bowstring sang.

Kissen ducked with her, and the arrow shattered against the cliff face. Its aim had been true; it should have caught her, but the wind lifted it away. Still, the boy was close enough that even the unpredictable Faera might turn a bad shot good. His next one could hit Kissen in the throat. The girl drew her sword back for another swing, and Kissen was forced to slice the blade up her arm. She shrieked, losing hold of her weapon.

'Get back!' the boy shouted in Talic to his comrades, the string taut. The others scattered. They trusted this one's aim.

Kissen ducked and turned. Almost fast enough. The arrowhead pierced the top of her arm rather than her belly. She grunted with the pain but used the moment to pick up her staff and run. The recruits scattered, surprised. She couldn't move fast, but if she forced enough distance she might be able to hide.

Too late: the krka was quick. A wrench on her cloak dragged Kissen by the throat and sent her sprawling. Then, a blade against her back. It dug deep, through cloak, leather, flesh, pressed hard enough to pierce her cuirass. She stilled, breathing hard as blood ran hot over her spine.

'Fuck,' Kissen hissed, tightening her grip on her knife, thinking fast. Her cutlass was beneath her, the knife barely in her hand. Boots appeared in front of her vision. The boy with the bow.

'Burning's too good for her,' said the krka from behind. 'Give her a coward's death.'

Kissen growled. Was that the sound of the bowline stretching, or the scream of the wind in the distance? Would she even hear her own death? No, she would not wait for that.

This was going to hurt.

She rolled, grunting as the blade scathed her back so she could put a hand on her cutlass, and rammed Osidisen's knife into the krka's boot. The woman howled.

And so did the wind.

The Faera rose up about them in a shriek that held a hurricane within. A scream from the path, and Senfa came charging back up the slope as if demons were chasing her, behind her a blizzard as thick as cloud, a wave on the wind. The krka's blade was ripped away, and Kissen felt a tug on her knife as the boot pulled free. A moment! A moment to escape. Ice dug into her eyes like nails, her skin stung as the snow raked across it.

Kissen leapt to her feet, drawing her cutlass, and spinning to face where the krka had been. The blade met flesh.

The wind faded. She blinked the grit from her eyes and found herself looking into a face. Not of the krka, nor even a god. The boy with the bow. Her sword was buried in his gut. He must have moved to save his commander, who was nowhere to be seen.

'No,' whispered Kissen.

The boy was staring at her, surprised. He looked down slowly, and saw the sword, and yelped. Then his knees gave way. Kissen caught him. A sound half of pain, half gurgling came from his mouth, his breath rising in gulps.

'No, no, no, no,' Kissen hissed. 'I'm so sorry. I don't . . . I've never.' She hadn't meant this. She had felt her sword in flesh, smelled the scent of blood, but god's blood, god's flesh. This was just a boy.

'*Loebh, falr . . . resais . . .*' He was trying to speak, but she couldn't understand his dialect. He gripped her arm. '*Failr.*' Failure? Father? Faith? His face was grey. Blood was on her hands. Her own, and his.

His breath stopped, his eyes stilled. Dead. The boy was dead.

The first person she had killed was barely more than a child, barely older than Inara.

Kissen lowered him gently, her hands shaking, and looked up.

The soldiers were scattered, only three left on the path, clinging to the ground, the walls, whimpering with fear. The others must have gone over the edge. Senfa was still there, pressed flat against the cliff, her sides swelling with panic. But she went no further. Up the path was a wall of raging air.

That was no ordinary wind.

The air that touched her neck now was soft, calm again. Teasing.

'Come out you coward,' Kissen growled. 'Show yourself, Faer!'

She called the wind by its name, the name of its god. It tugged at her ears, nipping at them as it rushed along the pathway and the cliff's edge, slamming the remaining soldiers back down. Then, it thickened once more and whirled into itself, sleet marking its edges as it whistled into a tornado that became a laughing stone face, cheeks big and bellowing, hair wild, white like streams of cloud.

Faer. Snow-shifter, ship-launcher, skin-parcher, the god of the mountain wind. The deity appeared for a moment then slipped into the air again, screaming into the ears of the fallen recruits with cold breath.

'Leave them be!' cried Kissen. She tried to move, but the injuries in her back, shoulder and ribs lanced her through with pain.

You're welcome, veiga, the wind said.

The Faer sprang through different forms. They were an ancient god, wilderness manifest, whose voice pierced Kissen's mind with words like teeth. Goat legs danced out of the wind and the god's face again appeared, this time masked and with a feminine slant, and she kicked the fallen pole with Hseth's figurine and the bells on top, sending it tumbling over the mountain where the krka went. Kissen glanced over the edge, and saw prone forms red and broken against the trees in the dark below.

A whirl, and Faer stood before her, manifesting into silver fur and flesh like light through cloud. *Aan says you must come. Go to her.* In a flick, the stone mast showed a carved and toothy grin. *They will send more after you, shrine-breaker. You are known to them now.*

With that, the wind god tipped themselves over the side of the mountain and roared down the slopes, leaving softer air in their wake.

Those who had survived the fall below were crying out. The god was right; they had known her. The krka had been looking for her. She needed to leave, and fast, before they found other soldiers to rally.

Kissen sheathed her cutlass, then her knife and, grunting with pain, tugged the bow and arrows from the boy's body, then his satchel for good measure, and went to the mare that the Faer had redelivered her. Senfa was pinned in place, paralysed with fear.

'Sareth mar,' said Kissen. Come to me. Her voice ground in her throat, she was covered in blood, but the horse heard her, her ears twitching forward. In all this madness, Kissen was stable, familiar. 'Senfa, come.'

The mare let her take her reins and pull on them, though she protested crossly as Kissen dragged her blood-soaked self, her staff and her looted satchel onto her back. A god had saved her, again, and passing a message from another. Since when had gods spoken to each other? What was changing in the world?

At least now she knew where she must go to find out: the shrine of the river god.

'Ruen,' she whispered to Senfa.

Run.

CHAPTER TWELVE

Elogast

ELO SPENT ANOTHER TWO DAYS OF WAITING, BAKING FOR his keep, before Canovan came to his cramped room while he was running through his sword flows, testing his strength and the stretch of his burn. Canovan didn't knock, just pushed open the door and gave Elo's bandages a disgusted glance before turning.

'Today,' he said. 'Follow me.'

Against Elo's better judgement, he threw on his shirt and followed the man into the narrow Lesscian streets.

This western quarter of the city was old and measlybuilt, with little space for horses or carts. A quarter for working people, the makers' districts and factories selling some of the city's main exports: paper, ink, and tile. Some corners in these areas had faces carved into them, or symbols and runes, though most were sanded away. Likely for gods of smugglers or secret keepers. Elo couldn't know.

In silence, Canovan led him over rickety, makeshift bridges, and stepped from boat to boat to cross canals before darting up winding, narrow towers of steps. They passed two lost-looking knights in king's blue sashes who eyed them suspiciously. Shortly afterwards they found a guard in yellow, sitting on a stoop by the waters and reading a few leaves of paper. Another pamphlet. She nodded at them both, looking quite at home.

'I don't remember Yether guards being so prominent with their colours before the war,' said Elo when they'd passed.

Canovan glanced back. He had not warmed much to Elo, but at least he was past pure ice. 'It's new,' he said. 'Since the king's reinforcements started pissing on their territory.'

They turned closer to one of the main canals, crossing a bridge made of stone rather than planks and barrels, then along the water-front to a series of warehouses all with boats tied haphazardly outside their jetties and slipways. The canal was west-facing, and sunlight glanced off the water, blinding Elo with its sudden brightness.

Canovan took a shortcut to one of the buildings, across six boats and then up a ramp to wide open wooden doors. Smoke curled up from behind them and into the bright sky and as Elo followed the innkeep he smelled hot spices, boiling liquids. His chest twinged from the memory of heat.

Just within the mouth of the warehouse, six workers were fanning flames that heated large drums of liquid dye. Beyond them, two men and a woman with strong arms were pounding half-dried ink, folding it, flattening, slapping it down like dough. Their hands were blue, black and orange with the different colours.

Canovan led him past them, further inside, and they were not spared more than a glance. Within, the light dimmed only to the sunshine coming through strips raised out of the ceiling. Twenty-odd workers were cutting and stamping the dry ink with rhythmic precision, marking its colour. Each table had its own hues from yellows to reds, purples to inky blacks.

Then, at the next stage, the blocks of ink were folded into paper, loaded into boxes, then carts, then presumably taken away for inspection before they were sold. Solid inks were easier to transport than liquid dyes, just a drop of water and a thousand parchments could be illuminated, a hundred writs could be signed across lands from east and west, beyond even the fulcrum of the Trade Sea.

They went to the back of the warehouse, and through another set of doors to a storeroom, filled with equipment. Canovan lifted a hatch, revealing stairs down to canal-scented dark.

'Ser,' he said to Elo, waving a mocking hand into the shadows.

'After you,' said Elo, resisting the urge to draw his sword or run. He felt the pommel with his thumb, missing the lion's figurine that had once adorned it, lost now. For Arren.

Canovan cackled, enjoying his discomfort, and jumped down the stairs.

Elo followed him cautiously, and smelled incense: pomegranate, beet and rose; used for red dye as well as scent. There was a shrine, just visible in the light from the trapdoor, and a lamp in the far corner, the glimmer of which also revealed that there was a large channel of water that ran right under the warehouse and a small barge tied up in it.

The shrine itself was a plinth with a totem in the shape of a gleaming bronze snake, polished almost to gold from decades of touch. Its scales were imprinted like the inkers' stamps, each one a different shape; an inker god. The offerings around the shrine were mostly small bits of paper and cloth, strips of wood. Some bore beautiful calligraphy, others simply new and fresh markings of dye. There were so many layers of writing built around the pillar that it looked as if it were blooming paper petals. Some had fallen to the ground, but were left undisturbed, even when they dampened and rotted into the flagstones.

'So, this is the knight?' A soft voice.

Elo looked up to see that they were not alone. A woman was waiting in the corner by the other lamp. She was dark-skinned, darker than Elo, and the lamplight gilded her cheekbones and the fold of her arms. Her hair was in braids, back from her face and down her back, banded at intervals in silver wire.

'Elogast,' said Elo, and took a wild guess that she was Irisian. Something about the tilt of her chin made him think of his mothers. 'Of Ellac and Bahba.' He held out his hand. 'Call me Elo.'

Elo wasn't sure what he saw in the woman's face, amusement combined with suspicion perhaps, but she took his hand. 'Naiala of Yanik and Allemni.' He was right, Irisian by blood, though her accent was Middrenite like his. 'Call me Naia.'

Elo smiled. He hadn't met another Irisian in a fair while. Footsteps on the stairs behind them told them another had joined.

An inker, this one; his bare, muscled arms were stained blue to the elbows. When he set his feet, he looked Elo from foot to crown, and folded his arms. He wore a conspicuous purple sash, denoting some kind of authority.

'You trust him?' the man said to Canovan.

'No,' Canovan said.

'I am hoping you will,' said Elo, looking further into the gloom. Now his eyes had adjusted, he could see more of what they kept here. A printing press, of all things, and beside it a wooden box filled with paper pamphlets like those he had seen in the city. A desk too, with some scrolls neatly stacked above it in dry wood containers. And then there was a collection of woebegone swords, daggers, axes and poorly maintained bows, arrows arranged in buckets. Some were Middrenite, and Elo felt a pang as he saw the styles that were common in Blenraden. Others were from further afield, beaten back into shape from whatever rents and dents had killed their owners.

'Is this everyone?' said Elo. 'Everything?'

Canovan folded his arms.

'There are many others,' said Naia. 'Some heads of guilds who let us distribute, teachers and other workers and unions. But in Lesscia we are the most active.' She gestured to the newcomer. 'This is Ariam, head of the inkers' union.'

'I don't like him,' said the inker, leaning back against the ladders, standing to his maximum height. He was broad, but didn't have Canovan's wary, balanced stance.

Canovan put his pipe in his mouth and used his flint to light it. 'Neither do I.'

Naia sighed. She was finely dressed from what Elo could tell in the gloom, and her hands were open and relaxed. Elo realised he had seen her before, when he had first come to The Queen's Way: she had been writing letters in lemon juice. Secret missives, similar to those Inara had seen her mother reading.

'And yet your god Lethen let me live for a reason,' said Elo. 'She is not known for her kind heart, nor for forgiving those who break her curses.'

Canovan scowled as Naia and Ariam looked at him sharply.

'You had Lethen curse someone?' said Naia. His silence was admission. 'Canovan, we're trying to remind people of the good gods can do.'

'He was a knight in our business,' he said around his pipe. 'It seemed wise.'

Ariam shook his head. 'Gods, how many times have I told you, Canovan, that your haste will return to trip you?'

'And how many times have I told you that if you are always waiting for finer weather, you'll eventually come to rain?'

Canovan spoke the adage with a slight smile. Ah, they were friends. Good friends. Naia stood slightly apart from them. Newer, perhaps, to their circle.

'I'm not here to trip anyone,' said Elo, though he had enjoyed bloodying Canovan's nose. It was still swollen. 'I'm here to help you take action against the king.'

It was easier to call Arren 'king'. Despite Elo's anger, when he thought about Arren, he still saw him laughing at a joke over a campfire. Losing a game with a smile. Arren, hungover, sleeping in his bed.

Naia and Ariam looked at each other. 'What have you told him, Canovan?' Ariam asked.

'I told him you aren't fighters. But he says he has information.'

Naia looked at Elo. 'He's right. We have no intention of making war.'

'Your collection here suggests otherwise,' said Elo, gesturing to the closest bucket of chipped swords.

'We're prepared to protect ourselves,' she replied, with a look of distaste at the weapons. 'But not against an army. Even a petition to the king by one of our allies was met with burning.'

'Lady Craier,' said Elo. Inara's mother. Naia looked surprised, but nodded. 'You wrote to her.'

'It wasn't just for the petition,' said Canovan. 'She had weapons supplies and plans, good ones, should the king reject a peaceable resolution.'

'They burned her alive, Canovan,' snapped Naia. 'Her whole House was destroyed.'

'So you intend to let him continue burning?' Elo interrupted.

Naia bristled.

'We *intend* to survive,' said Ariam, thumbing the sash he wore; it was printed with a snake on the end. 'If we educate, keep our gods safe, things will change. The king is just a man.'

Oh, so recently Elo might have been relieved to hear such a thing. That they had been patient, as he had been, hoping the king would ease.

'He is not a man,' Elo said. 'And no longer intends to be.' He put his hands to the buttons of his shirt and began to undo them. 'The king has more thirst for power than even I knew, and I have been his friend since we were boys.'

His shirt opened to his bandages, and he unpinned them next. When the gauze came away Naia put her hands to her throat and chest, wincing in sympathy. Ariam looked as if he was about to be sick. The surface of Elo's wound was much healed, but its mark was still clear. In places, his skin was pale and pink, in others still yellow, in twisted patches, clearly a palm and five fingers and bigger than any human's hand. Most of the blackened skin had fallen away, but still the wound smelled foul, and was sticky with blood where he had taken a hit the day before.

'Arren was mortally wounded in Blenraden,' said Elo. 'He took the god Hestra's offer to save his life, and she replaced his heart with her power. He now bargains with Hseth.'

'The Talician god?' said Naia, unable to draw her eyes away from Elo's burned flesh.

'She promised him more power, immortality, and dominance over Talicia. Middren. Then the seas, and the other coasts. He offered my life in exchange, and she almost took it. I barely escaped with the help of a godkiller, who sent me here to find you and stop him.'

Naia frowned, and Canovan almost choked on his pipe.

'So what will you do,' said Elo, 'when his laws now are his laws forever? When he cuts away all faith, like Hseth, till one remains from shore to shore? One god, one rule, one king. Because he will do it, if he can.'

Silence fell, heavy with uncertain horror. Elo pinned the gauze back again, his fingers trembling, almost numbed to the tips. His

95

chest didn't hurt as much as his lungs did, his shoulder, his belly, an ache like a ball of tension. He had let Arren take Hestra's offer all those years before. He had abandoned Arren to mire himself in Hseth's promises. He let all of this happen.

Naia hadn't stopped looking at Elo's chest. 'And what was he to you,' she said, 'that he could offer your life for such power?'

'Comrades,' said Elo.

Naia looked sceptical.

You are the last thing Arren loves, and he has chosen to lose you.

'This man has killed gods,' said Canovan. 'Whatever he says, we can't trust him.' Ariam nodded his agreement.

'I killed people too,' said Elo. 'I am not here to apologise for my actions, I am here to offer my sword.'

Ariam stared at him, his light eyes shining in the lamplight, then he glanced at the shrine and shook his head. 'We have enough trouble with this one stealing or gambling weapons from knights who come through his inn.' He thrust his thumb at Canovan, who did his best to look innocent. Unsuccessfully. 'You're just spoiling for a fight, and I'll bet it's more for yourself than it is for us, or Middren.'

Elo tensed. 'Everything I have done, I have done for Middren,' he said. 'Everything I have sacrificed, I have sacrificed for these lands and its people.' Was it for Middren, or for Arren? Had he led the army to save his lands, or his friend? Had he left Arren to make Middren better, or because he could not stomach contradicting the king at every turn? The pain in Elo's chest tightened. He had not expected this wall of defiance. Even Kissen, even *Inara*, did not balk from the idea of resistance. Was he so out of touch with the people he wanted to protect? 'And I will not stop because you are fearful of action. I mean to help the rebellion take the king down.'

'You mean to frighten us into a fight,' said Naia.

Elo looked at Canovan, who met his eyes, his face impassive. He would have no help there. 'You should be frightened,' Elo said to Naia instead. 'If you do not ally against him he will scatter you to the winds like the Craiers.'

'I am a teacher, not a soldier,' said Naia severely. 'If you want to help us, help us educate people on the good things gods have done for us.'

'Teachers burn as fast as soldiers,' said Elo, losing patience. He had come all this way, hoping, for nothing. 'Faster, with paper in their pockets.'

Ariam clicked his tongue in the darkness, and Naia sucked her teeth, biting down on her reply. For someone who was so against violence, she looked in the dark as if she wanted to slap him.

'You thought you could walk in here and raise us like an army so you can go back to playing war,' said Ariam. 'You were wrong. Perhaps Canovan was right to lay a curse on you. Perhaps I'm starting to wish it had worked.'

Elo ground his teeth. 'War is already here,' he said. 'A noble House has been burned, its people killed. The king's knights are inside your city's walls, wearing the king's colours and claiming the king's justice on Yether land. I don't know how, but the king will come for Lesscia soon, and he will crush any resistance he finds here. What will it take for you to act?'

After a moment, Canovan spoke. 'He's not wrong,' he said reluctantly. 'Word from Sakre is the king is preparing a victory march.'

Ariam scoffed. 'For what victory?'

'Blenraden,' said Canovan. 'Our counterparts in Sakre say he's moving his forces. The city has been in uproar with preparations for the last few weeks, and half the towns coming this way have been told to feed an army.'

'Who told you this?' said Naia. 'I've heard nothing since the Craiers.'

'Who doesn't matter. I hate to admit it, but the knight's instincts are right. They'll come straight through Lesscia across the south coast. If they set off tomorrow as planned, it will take them eight days.'

Elo's mind was moving fast. Arren was moving his pieces more quickly than he had expected, but then he had always been rash. 'You need an alliance,' he said.

Canovan sneered. 'With you? You're nothing but a broken man with a sword.'

Elo squared his shoulders. He was not broken. He was never broken. Kissen had taught him that.

'No,' he said dryly. This thought was only half-formed, since he had seen the yellow and blue colours, clashing on each street. The game board was tipped in Arren's favour. Elo needed to tip it back. 'You need the city on your side.'

CHAPTER THIRTEEN

Inara

INARA'S SKIN WAS SCRUBBED RAW, AND STILL THREE DAYS later she had dirt between her knuckles. She had shed her travel clothes, even her waistcoat, and given them to Telle, who promised to take them to be washed, and was instead dressed in grey cotton robes that were so pale they were a shade away from snow.

Back in Kissen's home, Yatho and Telle were barely speaking. Telle had tried to tell her their plan, but Yatho had turned her eyes away from her attempts to make peace. The grief and tension in their colours was seeping into the walls, the rooms, into Skedi and Inara. It was like walking through spiderwebs of hurt; intricate and clinging.

So it was a relief to follow Telle away from the house and into the city, with Skediceth stashed in her robes, the iridescent jewel of her button still swinging from his antlers. Inara toyed with the fine ends of her plait, thankful that Telle had spent a long, patient evening untangling it, piece by piece, with oil and a comb. When she was out riding, Inara's mother always wore a long braid down her back, though her thick, straight, shining hair always looked finer than Inara's brown curls.

You do look like her, Skedi spoke to her. *Your hair looks tidy.*

Inara flung her plait back over her shoulder, frowning at her thoughts having been so obvious, even to Skedi.

Thank you, said Inara. Despite the time that had passed since he had taken her over against her will, she couldn't shake the memory of it. Speechless, helpless. His gentle voice in her head still reminded her of his trickery. She was trying to forgive him, but she could not lose herself again.

Too hard to think about. She looked at the buildings instead. How strange now to be in stone avenues full of people. In these central streets there were small shops selling soaps and dried flowers, coloured tiles and reams and reams of paper next to wavering towers of coloured ink. Lesscian food traders had to keep their wares outside the city walls to reduce paper-eating pests, but it seemed there were still thriving markets inside for those who could afford it.

The city air was cool with the morning and a slight scent of rain, but sunlight fingered down the sides of the great white buildings, and Inara was soon sweating trying to keep up with Telle's light, quick steps. The weeks in the forest had accustomed her to the green smells of spring: damp earth and sap. Here, she breathed in stone and canal water, faint and steaming, laced with the sweet smell of charcoal from ovens and the crisping of morning bread.

Elo. What would he think of her plans? She could not help but miss him and his quiet humour, the vastness of his patience. She would prove how useful she could be to him, and he would want her back instead of Canovan.

First, she needed to find out what made her useful: her power, her connection to Skedi, what it all meant. Where better than the archives that held all the nation's knowledge?

The ways through Lesscia dipped them in and out of quiet. People argued in porticos over cups of tea and almond milk, or hurried into doorways of workshops, their chatter cut into silence as they disappeared within.

Knights and guards too were common sightings on the streets, most wearing yellow, but here and there a dart of blue. They did not mingle at all, and Inara saw more than one cross the street to avoid walking the same way.

She was about to comment on this to Telle, but her hands were caught halfway into speech by the scent of roses. Inara looked up, surprised. She knew enough of plant life to know roses were far from in season. Telle had led them beneath an arch covered with them vivid reds and pinks, and bright as if in high summer.

They're like that every year, said Telle. *Wealthy archivists, seniors, live in these buildings, they must know a trick.* She pointed ahead, and Inara forgot all about the blooms.

A circular plaza widened beyond the rose arch. It had several entrances, each at different points like spokes on a wheel, though none of them filled with blooms like the one through which they had entered.

At the centre of the plaza were the archives themselves; a towering pillar of white with colourfully tiled windows, topped with the copper dome that gave the building its name: the cloche. The copper had turned blue with age, which contrasted beautifully with the ring of gold leaf around its base.

Not a full dome; the tower was open at the top, and the windows that spiralled up it gleamed with inner light. Either side of the tower, the rest of the archives stretched long wings of monastic stone, reaching around the plaza as if to embrace it.

Telle smiled, radiating pride, her soft colours of grey and green intensifying, though tourmaline shades of grief still clung to its edges.

Inara felt Skedi raise his head out of her collar, as small as a mouse, and look up at the arch behind them.

There is a god in those roses, making them grow, he said, using his sharp eyes. *Its shrine is hidden by the balcony, a few sweets and a bowl of mead.*

Inara didn't follow his line of sight: if she looked, someone else might see, and then there would be no more roses in early spring. She ran instead after Telle, who was heading for the gates into the cloche. All the doors along the wings were shut, and the one in the central tower was guarded by knights in blue and gold. King's colours. Their sashes were ornate in a way Inara hadn't yet seen and pinned in place by a stag's head on their left shoulders. From that point a pattern of gold-threaded sunrays flashed out, gleaming down their backs.

They moved their spears across the gate as they noted Telle's approach. Inara paused, grabbing her wrist. Did they know?

Don't worry, Telle signed with one hand. Her green shades had shifted again, intensifying into the colour of a forest canopy with light filtering through it. It gathered around her shoulders, like a cloud forming in the shape of a shield. *It's always like this.*

Inara swallowed her nerves, hoping Telle was right. She was using Telle's desire to speak in front of the day's archivist's forum to get inside, where the knights were not yet allowed. But if what Telle was doing was dangerous, what Inara wanted – access to the god archives – was treasonous. She might be jailed, whipped or executed. Just like her mother.

At least she would then feel like her mother's daughter.

'Papers,' demanded one of the knights as they came close. A tall man with a black beard cropped close to his chin.

Telle pulled a leather case from her pocket and passed it to him with an open palm. He grabbed it, spear still tipped in his other hand.

'Name?' he asked.

Telle gestured to her ears, signalling that she was deaf, though Inara suspected that she did understand what he was saying, she just didn't want to work for him.

He leaned in and shouted louder. 'What. Is. Your. Name?'

'Her name is Telle,' said Inara. 'I'm her assistant, Ina.'

Telle pointed at the papers, indicating the stamp she had put on them the day before; a day pass for Inara. Her shades intensified as she asserted herself, and pointed next to all the stamps further up the page. 'I am here every day,' she said.

'Oh, *now* you talk,' he said, lowering the papers. 'Are you deaf or aren't you? I note your scars don't reach your ears.'

Telle kept herself still. 'I am deaf, not dumb,' she said out loud. 'Ask anyone inside.'

'You're a bit plainly dressed for an archivist,' he said. 'I take it you're one of their charity cases? Some commoner's whelp with her hands dipped in ink.'

The man's colours were a similar bright steel as his blade, and he lowered the latter to Telle's shoulder, edge first.

Inara froze. Unlike gods, she couldn't stay the man's blade. He smiled, as if he had put his hand on her shoulder instead of the edge of a spear. Telle didn't move, her eyes on him, defiant.

Can you do something, Skedi? Inara asked in her mind.

I don't know, Skedi replied. *His will is strong, a lie won't sooth it. The other . . .*

Inara felt Skedi move his will to the other guard, who was pretending not to see his companion, instead looking blithely at the sky. After a moment, his shades turned turquoise with anxiety.

'You really should learn some manners,' said the bearded one, still bearing over Telle and tipping his spearblade right and left, only just shy of fraying her shoulder. 'We are the knights of the king.'

The other knight cleared his throat. 'Are their papers in order?' he said. 'I think I just saw our captain.'

The first knight lifted his blade and glanced down at the papers. 'I suppose so,' he said, and looked back up at Telle. 'Watch your back, charity,' he told her. 'We know it's the forum today. The slightest step out of line, and we will come.'

She gave him quizzical eyes. 'I'm sorry,' she said, feigning innocence, 'could you repeat that?' When he didn't, she held out her hands for the papers, and he thrust them back to her.

Tell them thank you, said Skedi.

Inara almost slapped him down. *You're joking.*

Just do it, Inara.

Inara swallowed her pride. 'Thank you, sers,' she said. 'May we . . .?'

The spears pulled back; the gate was free. Telle folded the pages with tense fingers, but that slight movement was nothing compared to the colours that bristled like a riot around her shoulders. She took Inara's hand and walked her past the knights and into a tunnel beneath the cloche walls. Only when they were three steps in did Inara hear the two men laughing.

They did not speak in the corridor. Telle was seething, and shaken, Inara could tell.

What will they do if the forum doesn't go as planned? said Skedi just to Inara. *Telle is making a big bet on her safety, our safety, to satisfy the expectations of her wife.*

Inara frowned. *She said there are rules.*

Rules change, Inara. What if she's wrong?

It doesn't matter. This might be our best chance.

Best chance at what?

Inara hadn't told him what she intended. She knew he would advise against it, to be patient. Inara was sick of patience.

Be brave, Skedi, she said instead of answering.

The length of the tunnel suggested to Inara that the walls of the cloche were thicker than she had suspected. Its vaulted arches held small alcoves at intervals which reminded Inara of the great hall in Blenraden's palace, built to house the shrines of various gods. The friezes above them had been carefully sanded down and plastered over, and within the alcoves were no longer shrines, but brass castings. Inara peered at them in the gloom, half-lit as they were by torchlight. The king was in the first, with a gathered host outside a city. Blenraden. Inara recognised it by its walls. In the next, he was watching ships in a harbour, torn apart beneath a cloud of faces. Wild gods. These were etchings depicting the war, each significant moment, Inara noted them by the stories Elo and Kissen told.

Until they reached the innermost arches. Inara stopped in a cloud of incense, and Telle paused too. Here, there was a fresh cast plate of metal, so polished that it gleamed as bright as the morning, in the final arch. The king stood crowned, holding up a stag's head, a sun rising behind him. This, Inara had seen before. What was new was the gold leaf marking out a rent in his chest and shining rays of gold radiating like a blazon across it, joining the dawn.

This is new, said Telle.

Inara nodded slowly. At the foot of the cast was a bottle of barley wine, two cups and a ring carved with flames. Beneath it hung a little trough with six sticks of incense, all burning, and the stubs of others. Inara was reminded of something Kissen had said when warning Elo about Arren. *They put all their hopes in a saviour; they raise his pictures on the walls.*

This was a new shrine where old shrines had been. In a land that had banned worship of gods, the king was filling their spaces. This was the man who had killed her mother, who had ruined her life. Loved. Venerated.

Do not linger, Skedi whispered to her, and Telle pulled her along, clearly thinking the same thing.

What did you say to him? Inara said to Skedi. *The knight at the door.*

I told him he would get in trouble if anything happened, said Skedi. *He did nothing to stop the other.*

Some people aren't as brave as you, Inara.

That felt pointed. They stepped into a cloistered courtyard echoing with the trickle of a small fountain and the hum of cicadas. Old fig trees grew out of carefully tended circles in the stone of the open centre of the cloche, supported by trellises. Two youths sat gossiping by the fountain, their robes a few shades darker than Inara's but lighter than Telle's. They stood as Telle came through and nodded their respect.

This was the consulting courtyard, said Telle. She gestured at the tables arranged between the trees and beneath the colonnade that ringed the yard, providing shade from sun or rain. Inara looked up to see a circle of sky within the roofless dome. A line of bells ran across on a beam.

I saw the courtyard used only for a year or so before they stopped public access to the cloche, she added. *Now only archivists and their novices can come inside.* Her hands trembled as she signed, though she tried not to show it. *The guards aren't allowed in either,* she said. *No matter what they say. They have to keep by their own rules.*

Inara thought about what Skedi said: rules can change. But she said nothing as Telle led her to the door to the right of an arch. In front of it were rows of outdoor shoes, boots and clogs, and a box of indoor sandals that they both changed into. Inside, they followed spiral stairs up the cloche, their sandals clapping softly against the worn centre of the steps, smoothed into a dip by centuries of slippered feet.

The first door they passed opened into one of the wings of the archives; a long corridor, and on the other side a landing that became a balcony ringing the inner courtyard like the colonnade. Up the next flight of stairs was a reading room, almost empty, with a rope barrier in place. Only a couple of dark-robed archivists were poring over manuscripts on a large desk, taking notes in silence. The third floor that followed was only an arch onto another balcony, and at the fourth they stopped.

Here, Telle opened a thick wooden door into hush. Not silence; the air breathed with muted voices, the rustle of parchment, ink brushes scratching.

'Aman is looking for the translated philosophies of mathematics . . .'

'The travel tales of the Burja seas vary . . .'

'The Stone manuscript, the only real scholarship of the far west worth reading . . .'

'Ectura of Usic wants to know which divinity blessed his—'

'Shh.'

The last voice was quickly silenced. The long thin windows on this floor, which looked so bright from the outside, were inside tinted yellow and green, muting the light that slid through at sharp angles and creating cage bars across the shelves of scrolls, codexes, and tiny labelled drawers.

Telle strode on. Each of the shelves they passed was carefully stocked, arranged and labelled. Not like Inara's mother's library; all bright windows, bound books and parchments pinned to tables with glass balls. Lady Craier had encouraged her household staff to send their children for reading lessons and to use the library as often as they pleased, and Inara too. But here, the archivists in darker shades of grey handled crumbling parchment with soft white gloves, delicately rifling through the past. Their colours moved like the light through the stained glass, soft and radiant, content.

This is the seeker's floor, Telle signed to Inara. When I first came to Lesscia, we took out a loan to afford the kid leather gloves. Next floor up with the poetry are the copiers and preservers, they have all sorts of instruments and things, even weapons. Most novices begin at the top, the twelfth, and work their way down based on skills and talent.

Is there a map? Inara asked, and Telle smiled. She turned along a set of shelves and brought Inara to a flat table set with glass. Not an ordinary table: a diagram of needle-thin lines. It showed the cloche in a cutaway diagram, fine writing labelling each floor, what each room was for, and what was stored in it. On the fourth she could find geographical records, maps, and philosophies of numbers, thought and time. Sixth floor were Houses, their lineages, histories on the rise and fall of nations, then seventh were important texts from other languages. At the very top of the dome, weather maps, star charts, and the looking glasses for finding them above Lesscia.

Some archivists are still permitted to travel, said Telle. *They look for the newest thinking in the farthest lands, bring them back and store them here in the right category. Some return only after many years.* She paused. *Some who have come back more recently have been . . . surprised by what has changed since the war.*

In ink, flying over the tower, was a symbol of a veiled woman, her arms outstretched over the sky, just like the wings of the archives. Her arms were painted in whorls, pieces of writing so abstract and archaic that they could not be read. Scian, the patron god of the city. Outdated now. Everywhere, Scian's images had been removed or destroyed. At least in ink she still shone.

Inara traced down the cloche. The diagram went further down than the courtyard, into the foundations and the vaults, which were shown with intricate arches and lanterns. Lower still, what looked like a canal that went right beneath the building, and a tomb built in stone within it.

The god archives are stored down there now, said Telle before Inara could ask, following her line of sight. *Histories of gods, their gifts, or the knowledge they bestowed. Before, they were just history.* She gave Inara a meaningful look.

So, to take the god texts, Telle had to get down into the vaults and smuggle the scripts back up. She had told her where she stored them: hand-sewn pockets she had secreted in her robes. Inara hadn't asked for pockets. It would have made Telle aware of what she had planned, and as much as she liked Telle, she wasn't sure what to trust her with. At least not till she understood her own power better.

Inara looked up at the sound of quick steps, and a finely robed archivist was hurrying towards them, signing awkwardly. *Old Restish? You can read it?* he asked Telle.

She nodded. *A little.*

I need your help, there's some . . . He fumbled the words, tried again, then flung his hands up in frustration and looked at Inara.

'Lindis Godspels,' he said aloud as if she would know what he meant. 'Bastard to read, but there's a note I need.' He shrugged at

Telle, who looked mildly amused. 'Sorry, Telle, I'm still so bad at sign. I know they offer teachings but . . .' He frowned at Inara again. 'They let you have a day novice? I thought they were banned?'

Telle shrugged and gestured quickly to Inara.

I will help him, she said. *You can look around, just keep out of trouble. This place . . .* she smiled. *It's sacred to me.* Inara swallowed her guilt down. She could see how precious the archives were to Telle, her work here, her value. She shone with it. *When the bells ring, find me in the courtyard.*

Inara nodded, then watched as the two archivists disappeared into the stacks.

I like it here, said Skedi quietly. *So many secrets, so many interpretations. So many little lies.* Inara looked around and breathed in the scent of paper, bark, wood and parchment. Like a thousand autumns packed into the curving room.

So many truths too, she said.

Some truths are too bright to look at directly, that is why they couch them in paper. Skedi poked his head out from beneath the robes at her neck as she walked down the bright shelves and into the shaded areas where the air turned cool and thick, and the ruffle of robes and ink dimmed. They passed only one archivist, more junior than Telle, judging by the pale greys of their tunic. They were turning a handle attached to one of the shelves, and above them a gleaming mirror hanging from the ceiling moved, reflecting light from the windows onto the required patch texts.

Speaking of lies, said Skedi, *why have we really come here, Inara?*

She had to tell him eventually. *What else?* said Inara. *We're going to find out more about us. About gods.*

Skedi popped his head out of her collar again when they were alone once more. *She said it was restricted.*

Inara was looking for the nearest staircase. *When has that ever stopped us?*

Ina, we're finally safe and Elo . . .

She stopped in the shadows. She knew it, this was why she had not told him. *Safe?*

Skedi batted an ear at her, then shrank a bit when they heard sandalled footsteps approaching, but they passed.

We're not safe, Inara said to Skedi. *Elo thinks he can fight a war with people who tried to kill him. Kissen died to give us a chance, Elo a chance, and he's going to ruin it. We need to know who and what we are, what we can do, and* make *him listen.*

But . . . we agreed. You are my home. I don't need to know anything else. I don't want to be anything else.

Was he lying to her, or to himself? It didn't matter. *What about what I want?* she said. *What about who my father is, and if he holds the key to us? What about our future, the future of my House? Does that not matter too?*

Of course it does.

Then help me get down to the god archives, and let's see what future we can find.

CHAPTER FOURTEEN

Elogast

FOOLS. FOOLS AND COWARDS. THE REBELS HAD OPTED instead for their ink and paper and frightened hole.

Elo would not be deterred. Even if he had only his sword and mind to offer Lord Yether. Even if he was arrested at the gate and sent to Arren to be beheaded for treason. He would not sit still with Kissen's life weighing down on his shoulders.

At one time, Elogast would have had no fear of walking into a lord's halls. He would have been a prince's guard, even if a lesser prince. His clothes would have been fine quality silk and cotton, gifts from his mothers, silver bracelets on his wrists and the occasional wink of lapis. He would be standing proud, Irisian and Middrenite, a knight and a good man.

He had at least bartered for a bed and a new shirt in another inn, suspecting that if he returned to Canovan's, the innkeep would make good on his promise to finish the curse's work. In the morning, he borrowed a razor and finally shaved his beard and hair down to the skin, and felt the lighter for it. But even now, as he approached House Yether's Lesscian manor, he felt small. And vulnerable.

The manor was much as he remembered, sequestered behind a long pavilion and a terraced garden where old folks played games of guards and stones. The orange trees were in full fruit, and smelling of spring, and beds of flowers were blooming as if they had been commanded to the day before. Elo remembered that Yether kept glasshouses, then had the flowers planted fresh each month if he wanted more colour in season. The paths closest to the grand property were filled with gardeners clearing the beds.

The manor itself was enclosed by a long wall trailing with ivy, yellow-eyed vines, but its gate was open. Before it, there had once been a statue of Scian standing in a marble pool. The statue was gone, and the pool had been replaced with an extravagant fountain.

Beside that fountain, stood Naia.

She looked different in the light, taller, more striking; and older. Perhaps seven years Elo's senior. Her braids shone, perfectly neat and oiled to tapered points. She was wearing an elegant white jacket that bared her arms, showing silver bracelets on both, and a blue tunic beneath that came down to her knees over wide trousers that were tucked into fine leather boots.

'Canovan said I would find you here this morning,' she said as he approached, looking him up and down with mild appreciation for his efforts. Elo ran a hand over his bare head and came to join her by the fountain. There were guards at the gate to the manor proper. One was drinking from a wine gourd, though it was still early. They would not hear them over the water.

'Are you here to stop me?' said Elo.

Naia twisted her mouth at his blunt manner and looked beyond the gate and the fountain towards the Yether house. Unlike most coastal towns or cities, Lesscia had no fort. The seat of the Yethers' power was beautiful, made for entertaining and show, not for defence.

'This manor is panelled in west Irisian marble,' said Naia, pointing to the pale walls of the house as they passed under the flowers. 'My great-grandparents shipped in the tiles all the way from southern Usic. Then the yolkstone friezes, can you see? They were from over the Westersea. At the time, my grandparents did not know the local peoples were exploited to mine the stone. When they found out, they brought weapons to help them fight back.' She sighed. 'Retribution on both sides was bloody, and cruel. Many innocents were killed.' She cast her eyes at Elo. 'If we commit to violence, when will it stop?'

'If we do not,' countered Elo, 'will anything change?'

Naia clicked her tongue at this line of argument, though she had started it. 'We have principles, knight, Ariam and I, and the teachers, archivists, printers and artisans I represent. They will not turn at your moral convenience.'

Elo laughed. Her tone was softer, her delivery more eloquent, but in her words he heard Kissen, and the way she had no fear of her own voice. A wave of sorrow rushed into him. He missed Kissen. He missed her deeply. Her laugh, her freckles, the way she looked at him when she didn't like a thing he was saying. Kissen would have come in growling and shaken the lot of them to their bones.

'Then what are these principles?' Elo entertained her for a moment, gathering his courage for the conversation to come with Yether. What was she doing waiting for him? Where they stood, when the breeze blew, a fine spray misted them from the fountain, refreshing in the warming morning. 'What keeps safe your love for the gods?'

'The belief that need is not a sin,' she said certainly. 'That our gods are not unlawful, and our faith is not a failure.' Elo sensed there was more. She threw her braids over her shoulder, and he caught the sweet scent of almond oil.

'When I was young,' she continued, 'my family thought me a boy until I told them I was a woman. They were joyous, but I did not find joy. My body didn't . . . feel right. The god of new beginnings helped me accept what I wanted to keep and change what I wanted to change. Without her, the powders I needed would have cost a small fortune.' She looked up at the manor. 'Gods balance our access to power. They belong to everyone, not just the wealthy. Like our lands belong to everyone, not just the king.'

Elo understood why she was here: she had changed her mind.

'And you are willing to fight for that?' he asked.

She hesitated, then nodded. 'We are agreed,' she said. 'Ariam took some convincing, but Canovan talked him around. He does not want to put his union at risk, but if Yether gives support he will work with you. If I act as your steady hand to stop the flow of blood, he will help.'

'Why would Canovan speak on my behalf?' Elo said. It was unexpected, and *deeply* suspicious.

Naia shrugged. 'Seemed to have a fury in his cap yesterday evening.' She appraised Elo. 'So, what of you?' said Naia. 'What do you believe?'

He believed he shouldn't question too hard any help he could get, but he suspected that wasn't what Naia wanted to hear. He had believed in Arren, and that failed him. He had believed in his honour, and it led him astray. He had believed in Kissen, and she was gone.

'The best of people comes with their freedom,' he said. 'If that is what Arren will destroy, that is what I will stop.'

Naia appraised him carefully, then nodded. 'Then I will come with you,' she said, 'and represent the others.'

'Why you?'

She tipped her chin. 'Am I not good enough for you?'

'Just curious.'

She shrugged. 'Because those two like the sounds of their own voices, and it's time they listened to mine.' She glanced at the gate beyond the fountain, then up at the sky. 'Canovan said you were a dawn riser, but we are still early for his consultation hours.'

'I don't intend to wait for a consultation like cattle with a squabble to settle,' said Elo, glancing back down the garden ways. Others were climbing the pathway to the manor, some wearing formal robes, some carrying papers. There was even a couple bedecked in red marriage beads for some kind of alliance. They all wanted Yether's ear, and they all wanted it before the others.

Elo turned and approached the gate. One of the guards stoppered her gourd.

'Consultations wait beyond the fountain,' she said.

Elo smiled, Naia came to his side curiously, but seemed as like to drag him away as have his back. 'Please,' he said. 'Tell Lord Yether that Knight Commander Elogast requires an immediate audience.'

The other guard paused, looking at Elo more closely. 'Elogast . . . of Sakre? The king's lion?'

Would he ever outrun that title? 'Yes,' he said. 'Once.'

After a long moment, the guard nodded. 'Stay here,' he said. Then growled, 'Watch them,' at the other before turning for the manor. He started at a walk, but when he picked up to a run the first guard put both her hands on her weapon.

Naia crossed her arms. 'Did you have any intention of warning me before naming yourself?' she muttered.

Elo lifted his shoulders, then regretted it as his chest shot with pain. He hadn't stretched enough that morning. 'You asked to join me, remember?' he said. 'If they arrest me or invite me in, it tells us something.'

Naia scowled. 'Did you not feel like giving me a chance to decide if *I* wanted to be arrested?'

Elo cast her a grin. 'You can decide now,' he said. 'Rebels should be quick runners.'

Naia puffed out her cheeks but didn't move. 'If this goes wrong I shall kick you in the shins first,' she said.

'I thought you weren't a violent woman.'

'I can make an exception.'

The guard reappeared, followed by someone in a neatly tied, emerald-velvet waistcoat. Likely a steward. Behind her was a knight in full armour and a sweeping, yellow-lined cape. The mark of the Yether eagle was etched onto his breastplate. The woman guarding the gate stood to attention and stuffed her wine gourd behind her. The knight, Elo suspected, was her captain.

'Fine of you to end a rebellion before it's begun,' hissed Naia.

'Wait,' said Elo.

The steward caught Elo's eye and made a hurried beckoning motion towards the manor while the captain looked them over, his face impassive. He was the same height as the steward, and well-built, with a wide frame and a longsword like Elo's that he looked more than comfortable carrying. Likely half a noble himself. Most senior guards were. Elo wondered where his allegiances were; to House Yether, to his king, or to his own?

It seemed he would soon find out.

CHAPTER FIFTEEN

Kissen

KISSEN STRUGGLED UP THE PATHWAY THAT MARKED HER trail through the Bennites. Pieces of slate had been hammered in at intervals, giving her a measly grip on the damp and frosty slopes. She wasn't sure if it was morning or evening, so blasted churning was the air with storm and cloud. Since she and Senfa had passed the snowline, the slopes had gone from the black and green to pure white sheets of ice. As they climbed higher, they were wading through fresh, wet spring snow, and some powder. The raging winds of the peaks were tearing them to pieces.

The ragged tops of the Bennites bit into the belly of the sky, and it bled: snow, hail and mist would soon swallow them whole. There was no light to guide them, no map, and Kissen regretted bringing the mare even this far, knowing it may be the death of them both. In the moments the clouds cleared enough to see them, Kissen was following the lines and shapes of peaks she had seen before only from the west looking east. Her trust that she was going in the right direction wavered day by day.

She couldn't go much further. Her hands were cracked and bleeding, her wounds beginning to seethe with infection and her right knee was bloody, blistered and weeping. She would die soon, and Senfa, and another innocent's blood would be on her hands.

Last time she had come this far, the way had been hard. It had been a wet autumn, but her master, Pato, had been there to guide her, had packed the right provisions, had a pony more suited to the slopes. His ankles had been cursed by a god of old age that had slipped away from their net, and had swollen to twice their size. He went to Aan for a remedy.

Kissen had hated it then, a godkiller like Pato gone to ask favours of the gods. She was seventeen and had barely achieved his acknow-ledgement after running away from Blenraden and chasing him till he accepted that she would be his ward and apprentice. He did not hold with her arguments that it was wrong for a godkiller to ask for help from gods. That people shouldn't need gods for anything.

'I have no desire to suffer for your anger,' Pato had said. 'This is the nearest shrine with a god strong enough and wise enough to help me. Either you come with me, or you can go back to the city you hate.'

It seemed history was hers to repeat. Summoned by Aan, so soon after speaking to her in Blenraden; the river god of Talicia and Middren had finally developed a desire to meddle.

Kissen crested another slope. Her gold tooth that had given her away would surely have a dent in it from clenching her jaw with the pain. At least it was one of the few parts of her body that wouldn't get eaten up here in the wilds.

Was she still bleeding? She couldn't tell anymore through the fever and the cold. She could see nothing from this height, only trails of mist skirting over ice, cloud roiling in the upper winds like the skirts of a fighter. Senfa whinnied nervously, sensing something was amiss. Kissen had covered the horse's head with a blanket, leading her blindly on to stop her panicking and protect her eyes. She was right to be nervous.

No. Kissen had to make it, if only for the damned horse. She had abandoned one to fate and she couldn't leave another, no matter how tired she was.

'Move,' she whispered to herself. Staff first, left leg, right, then pulled the horse with her. Her body did not always do what she wanted it to, but this time it must. Staff first, then her body, then the horse. Staff. Body. Horse.

Her left foot broke through snow and into water. She gasped as it soaked her through and looked down. A stream. And beside it, deer marks, hare-patterns, criss-crossing the slope, spindrift chasing over them like the ghosts of the creatures who had been there. This could be a river in the summer months. Could be.

There was hope. Kissen forged her way up the water, sinking sometimes to her thighs, her elbows, and Senfa huffing with the chill while forging through behind her. The sky and ground looked the same; tipping whiteness, grey, nothing. Only the slight dip of the stream and the sounds of the mountain oriented her. The boom and shake of an avalanche, the cries of wolves and the cackling of jackals carried on the hands of the wind to nip at her ears.

She would not stop. This had to be right. She would not die here. Worse things than this had not killed her, worse things had tried.

The ground was sloping up, just slightly, and the shadow of a cliff rose before it. It stood like a guard, watching her approach. Kissen hauled herself on through the pain.

Finally, another sound over the wind and death: water again, louder than the trickle beneath the snow. And flags.

The sting of the fine, wet snow lessened, then stopped. The wind fell away to nothing, and she was standing not on snow, but on stone. Flat, grey pebbles, and through them: running water.

Behind her, the snow stopped in a straight, stark line, cut through as if it had met a threshold it dared not cross. The mist, wind and sting were there still, breaths away, but across her numbed face the air barely stirred. Senfa lurched forward, shaking her head with irritation, and nickered as she felt the wind die.

Trembling, Kissen turned and saw a small lake surrounded by cliffs on three sides. At their crests, the wind screeched and tore the mists apart, but on the water there were three silk pennants on high, wooden poles, and they twisted gently. The water of the pool was as still and clear as glass.

Kissen fell to her knees.

The source: she had found it. Aan's source. A deep pool gathered from meltwater and tiny rivulets, filtering through ice, mud and stone before the lake was filled. The great river wound from this very spot across two different lands, mingling with streams and lakes, hot springs, royal gardens and commoners' wells.

A light flickered on the other side of the river. Kissen blinked at it, unable to move. She was frozen to the bone, to her very soul. She was lost, and uncertain. A murderer. Guilty, and vulnerable.

A crunch of stone, a step.

It was not Aan who appeared, but a man, old and bent, his long beard unevenly plaited and thick with grey.

'Come, pilgrim,' he said, opening his hands to her. Beneath his hood, two bright eyes glittered.

Kissen opened her cracked lips. She had broken her promise to herself that she would never kill a person. She would not let fate make her a liar too. 'I am no pilgrim,' she said. Her voice creaked with frost and misuse.

'I know who you are, godkiller.'

Kissen let out a shuddering breath, and the world went dark.

CHAPTER SIXTEEN

Skediceth

SKEDI HAD TO ADMIT IT WAS USUALLY HIM ENCOURAGING Inara to break the rules, but she was three steps ahead of him this time. She had lied to Telle, and he had known it, but this? Break into the god archives, so soon after their lives had been threatened for entering the cloche at all? The king had rewritten her life by burning it down, and now she had nothing left to lose.

Well, to get in trouble, they would need to get caught. He wouldn't let them get caught. And he could not deny that he was curious about what they would find.

Inara moved surely through the shelves towards the next set of stairs, nodding respectfully at the archivists she happened across. Skedi crouched, the size of a baby mouse, at the top of her shoulder beneath her robes, nudging his will at anyone they passed, soothing their colours.

She's always been here, no one interesting, you've met her before.

Thanks to Inara and her button, he felt more solid than he had in days, his power more real. The gift on his antler glinted in his eyeline at this size, and he tried not to grow too happy and large every time he saw it.

They reached the level of the courtyard, but instead of going out they went down another flight of stairs. There were archivists already gathering under the fig trees, but with Skedi's whispering they didn't spare them a glance, seeming more interested in the clouds rolling in above them in shades of grey much like their robes. It appeared that the spring sun was short-lived.

Further down into the darkness, the light faded to pinprick holes dug through the flat cobbles above, flashing in time with people's footsteps over the thick glass that protected them. This was enough to illuminate the first basement they passed through, but in the next level down the light was replaced by globe lanterns glass wrapped in filigree metal petals, stretched on springs so that if the glass broke the metal would close, extinguishing the flame in a moment.

Down again. They reached the foot of the stairs. There were no further steps down to the strange tomb beneath the foundations, but here was indeed the great vaulted space that the map had shown. It was as large as the Craier hall, with thick pillars of marble in the same positions as the entrances to the plaza. Between them, metal gates formed a locked wall around the archives in the centre.

A snore shattered the silence, and Inara and Skedi both jumped.

I knew that was too easy, said Skedi.

Telle said knights weren't allowed inside the archives.

It wasn't a knight. Barely fifteen steps away, in front of the entrance from another stairwell, an old archivist was asleep on a stool, his head back against a gate, locked like the others, but with a key set into it.

Skedi took off from Inara's shoulders, feeling the dip of chill air, and the catch of it as he beat his wings and flew in a swift circle around the inner gates. No, no other guards, but no other entrances either. Strange, he felt as if they were being watched, but this archivist was definitely asleep.

The archivist stirred, grumbled, and Skedi flew back to Inara's shoulder like a dart. Perhaps the man had felt a breath of air from Skedi's wings, or some shade of warmth they had brought down with them from the upper levels.

Run before he sees us, said Skedi, crawling into her collar to hide.

We might not get another chance, said Inara, starting off towards the man. *Aren't you a liar? Think of a good one.*

Inara! But was this a mote of trust? She put on a smile, and walked over to the archivist, who sniffed and looked up, immediately suspicious. Well, Skedi had no choice now.

'Good morning,' Inara said and signed, just in case.

'What do you want?' he replied, embarrassment playing around his cheeks in a pink flutter. 'You're not allowed down here.'

Skedi's fur stood on end, but embarrassment was good: the archivist would be more likely to listen to a lie that painted him in a better light. Skedi started with his first: *You've seen her before, she's familiar to you.* He pressed his will towards the man, who relaxed a mote, his shoulders descending. Then Skedi whispered a good lie directly to Inara.

'I've been sent to check a fact about a dead god called Aia,' she said at his prompting. 'The readers' floor want to copy down the knowledge but leave the record of the god. I thought that was what we were doing now?'

The archivist stood. His robes were dark, gleaming grey. A few ranks higher than Telle, judging by the shade.

An apprentice, Skedi pressed towards him. He suspected 'day novices' as Inara had been called were not allowed into this inner sanctum. *She might report you for sleeping if you refuse her, but she can do no harm if you let her in.*

'When did you swear in?' he asked, looking her up and down, still bleary-eyed from his nap. Luckily Inara's robes looked slightly darker in the dim light. 'You've no brush and pen?'

Two months, said Skedi to Ina. Believable, but would explain his uncertainty. *It's illegal to keep the words of gods.*

'Not two months ago,' Inara echoed. 'And as the words of the god aren't lawful, I was advised to memorise them.'

The archivist clicked his tongue, his colours softening; that had been a test. Skedi relaxed a little.

'Good, good,' he said. 'Who are you working with?'

Inara cleared her throat, flushing. She didn't know any other names, and nor did Skedi.

Be quick, Ina, said Skedi.

'Telle,' she said.

'Godsblood, one of the head's pets?'

The guard had said something similar. Telle had said how hard she had worked to be in the archives, but Inara hadn't even suspected how hard. How many white lies did she tell to Yatho and Kissen, to assure them that her work was easy, her time respected? Skedi was starting to realise that there were many more layers to Kissen's sisters than he had thought.

'Poor you,' the archivist continued, 'you look like a proper noble but her, with her scars? Just unsightly.' He lifted his shoulders in a mock shudder, and Skedi felt Inara's whole body tense.

Let it pass.

'Good with translations I suppose,' the man continued. 'You know they let a cousin of the Brahims work here too? I don't know what's worse, a disgraced House or a scarred street urchin with no blood to speak of.'

Smile, Skedi shot into Inara's head. *Smile and reassure him.*

She managed it, a slight upward creep of the corners of her mouth. It wouldn't have fooled anyone on a bright day, but in the lamplight it was enough.

'As you say,' she told him stiffly, though Skedi was pretty sure she would have liked to smack him in the mouth. 'I'm afraid I am not in a position to speak on it.' She bowed a little, deferential, and he was pleased. 'May I go in please? I will be straight out.'

'Ah, yes, you may enter.' He turned the key with an unnecessary flourish. 'I'm supposed to follow you, but you look like a good girl, and I need the lav. Don't tell anyone I was sleeping, yes?'

'Of course not,' said Inara, looking suitably abashed.

'Ah, good. It's important work, the king's laws give it reason, but a little dull.'

He ushered her in and closed the gate behind her.

'Mind the bells,' he added. 'The forum will be soon.' He dusted himself down and headed for the stairs. The lies had worked well. Almost too well. The man left, whistling, trusting Inara where she shouldn't even set foot. Inara's offering had made him stronger.

Skedi poked his head out again, his ears following, and he turned them to listen. 'No one else is here,' he said. 'Your gamble paid off.'

She cast him a sharp glance, catching the dryness of his tone. 'Do I owe you anything for the lie?' she asked.

Skedi blinked at her. 'No,' he said, pulling himself fully out of her sleeve and shaking out his wings. 'Some things are done out of love.'

Inara smiled, a little more gently, then went to the lectern at the fulcrum of the shelves, which were laid out like a star. It was lit by several of the same glass globes wrapped in metal petals, but these were on short poles slid into bases.

Ina stepped up to the ledger, and Skedi jumped onto its pages. It was open against categories: *War*, *Wardens*, *Waste*, *Wastrels*, *Water*, some of which had extended beyond the original page and been added on with thin pieces of paper that lifted out like ribbons. Above the ledger was a key to the book, which was arranged in several sections. Categories of gods was where they had found it.

'We don't have long,' said Skedi. 'Where do we even start?'

'With you,' said Inara, taking hold of the thick pages. She had to use her knees and all of her strength to lift and turn them.

'Me?'

'You had to come from somewhere. Aan said a promise bound us. What if it was my father's promise?'

Skedi swallowed. Aan also said the water knew him. He remembered it, just. More like a dream of a memory. Sea and chaos, sinking ships and him flying between them in an attempt to calm the dying. The massacre at Blenraden harbour, a fight between the wild gods and the refugee ships. He was sure that was where he had been before Inara.

'Let's search by your name,' whispered Inara, finding the right section as marked by the lectern.

She paused as she found the pages. The section was as thick as her arm. There were thousands of names, thousands upon thousands. Gods, stretching back into centuries. This was not even all the gods, only those mentioned in the archives. Some references Skedi saw as Inara passed through were dated and linked to an older ledger. Some of the writing was marked in a clear hand, others scrawled.

'Inara what if I'm not in there?' said Skedi as she traced her finger down 's', 'sk', 'ske'. He was half-listening for footsteps on the stairs. What would happen if they were caught? Would Telle's smuggling be discovered? Would they undo everything? 'I'm a small god of small power.' Most gods lived and died for only a village, or a tree, or a well, only loved by few and mourned by fewer.

'Skediceth,' whispered Inara.

He fluffed up his fur as she pointed at the page.

Skediceth.

Skedi crept closer. He could hardly believe it. There he was, on ink and paper. Only one reference. But still . . . 'I'm here,' he murmured. He looked up at her. 'I'm real.'

'Of course you're real,' said Inara, frowning at him.

Skedi flicked a wing. He had begun to doubt, somehow, of his existence beyond Inara.

'Let's find you.'

She closed the ledger and hefted a lamp out of its holder, wrestling it under her arm and looking for shelves that matched the numbers next to his name. Most of the scripts that Skedi could see were in scrolls, carefully packed in wooden cases on the shelves, or were written on strips of wood themselves. These must be the ones Telle had been stealing, there was no way she would be able to smuggle up the thick codexes that filled up the bottom shelves.

But the worries about the forum, being caught, everything, slipped slowly from Skedi's mind as it reeled with the discovery that he was real. He was known.

He took to the air like a hawk, swooping over the shelves and beneath them in the quiet, nosing at the books. This was like the old days, back in Inara's home, when they had sneaked around and hid together, each other's friend when they had no one else. He had felt resentful then, that he was stuck in farmland with nothing to entertain except childish tricks. Now, he sank into the moment, remembering how good those days had been.

'Here!' he said, finding numbers that matched.

Inara came and put the lamp in a slot made for the purpose between the shelves, then extracted the slim scroll. It was a collection of papers in a thin leather case, handwritten and tied with a fine silver thread. Skedi flitted to the shelf beside her, then to the lamp, then back around her head.

'You're distracting me,' warned Inara.

'I can't help it.' He was too excited.

Inara unravelled the scroll. Within the leather protection, a thin bar of metal had been sewn that contained the reference number and the title.

'*Abridged Tales of Boro the Traveller*,' whispered Inara, reading it aloud. She turned the thin pages carefully.

'These are barely tales,' said Skedi as Inara searched for him. Each page had a paragraph scratched in ink, dated about a century before. These were just excerpts from Boro's accounts combined from several other journals based on key dates, meetings, and references to gods.

'Here,' said Inara. A short account, no more than four lines.

An audience with Yusef, the god of safe haven, on the great ship Moonswake. *It was a long journey to the west, docking at Sakre last, and he introduced me to his companion, Skediceth. Many ship shrines to Yusef have a space put aside for this god of white lies, for each traveller knows the lie they tell themselves: I will be safe, there is nothing to fear, I will come home. How else could we bear to set our barks on these unpeaceful seas? He gave me his blessing, for my own telling of tales.*

Skedi felt a flutter in his core. He had given a blessing? He had been loved by a god? Not just any god, a great god, one of the greatest new gods that were born beyond the wild. Yusef of safe haven. The same god killed in the massacre of Skedi's last memory.

'The god of safe haven,' whispered Inara, and looked at Skedi. 'Do you think . . .' She paled with fear. 'Do you think that could be my father? Aan said I might be my father's daughter.'

Skedi's mind raced through the implications, the shade of fear in Inara's colours. 'Gods do not have children,' he said quickly. The idea was absurd. And if gods were outlawed, what did that make Inara? Would she then be hunted? By people like Kissen? 'We do not have the appetites of humans.'

'But Kissen said her father loved a sea god. Canovan can summon Lethen without a shrine.'

'I . . .' Every part of Skedi found the idea too strange. Gods were made from emotions. Could emotions bear a child? When gods bled, they bled the blood they had taken not blood they had made themselves. 'A blessing, Inara. Your mother travelled in her youth, there are stories about it. Perhaps he blessed you.'

'His blessing would have broken as he died. And why then would she hide me away? Halfling, Hseth called me.'

'Unraveller, Aan called you too,' said Skedi. 'Perhaps your mother found a way to make a blessing stick, so you could fight gods.'

Inara frowned and put the scroll back. 'But she wanted gods to live. She died for that.' She stood up. 'We have to find out more.'

Skedi fluttered his wings and looked up. There was no way to tell how long they had been there. The archivist had not come back. 'We don't have time, Ina.'

She was already by the lectern, flipping hurriedly through the gods' names. But its pages slipped, ruffling of their own accord through her fingers. She lifted her hands, startled, as they kept moving even when she stopped. Skedi dropped like a stone to the ground, but there had been no sounds of doors opening, no footsteps on the stairs, nor even the bells.

The pages continued turning, and the ink on them began to bleed and run. Skedi loped up to Inara and she picked him up, moving slowly back from the ledger as the colours of the ink changed to vivid indigos, bloody reds and forest greens. The air around them thickened, the lamplight darkening.

A god was near.

Voices came out of the dark, a wave of whispers, then hushes that quelled the sound. The sound of paper, scratching, quills, the click of beads on calculators, the gasp of discovery. Shadow descended around the columns, hiding the bars that enclosed them.

The voices intensified, combining into one sound, into words: *What are you seeking what are you seeking what are you—*

Skedi grew to a larger size, the size of a hare. He was not as weak as when he had faced Lethen. He might be a small god, but he was Inara's protector.

A woman's voice came through the others, clear and strong. 'What are you seeking, little girl, and little god?'

The running ink on the ledger pages sprang into the air like ribbons, dust billowing up with them then twisting together into a veiled woman, her bare arms painted with swirls and eddies of words.

Skedi recognised her instantly. The woman on the map, the

woman for whom the city was named. 'Scian,' he said, then managed a bow. Inara quickly followed. 'Lady of learning.'

Scian smiled, her face moving beneath her veil. 'You come here seeking, when so few do these days.' She drifted closer to the ledger. 'They come and peer at the scripts as if looking were sinful. Or, stranger, they take them away and return them smelling of fear.' Her presence in the room thickened the air, but Skedi didn't feel threatened. More . . . comforted, enclosed. Secret. 'My blessings are said so rarely now, little prayers that barely sustain me. Fewer and fewer.' She looked up at the vaulted ceiling. 'I have a day and night of celebration soon. I wonder if anyone will remember.'

Skedi flattened his ears in pity. He had seen what would happen to Scian when no one prayed to her anymore. She would become a ghost of what she had been; no shape, only aimless will and power, slowly diminishing until she was nothing but a dream.

Scian looked back down and settled on the ground. As her feet touched she became the size of a small woman wearing plain white robes. 'For a candle lit on Scian's day, and a prayer in my name, I can help you find what you seek, little girl. Even though you carry other gods' gifts with you.'

Inara felt for Aan's vial on her neck. 'Is that all?' she said, and Skedi knew she was thinking of Kissen. Scian sighed.

'I can ask for precious little,' she said. 'Only my tomb beneath these vaults keeps the love of me alive.'

Tomb. Not shrine. 'You have a grave?' said Skedi, surprised.

'This shape belonged once to a human,' she said. 'In a time like this one she was hunted, killed, then buried here. For pity, and admiration, people brought flowers, prayers, books. They read to her their thoughts, new ideas.' Her voice grew distant, fading, and her robes darkened with grey dust and darker patches. Blood. 'And in her place, I took shape. A different being in her form. A symbol of truth against all brutality. It is a pity, that such things come around again.'

She did not seem all there. Through her edges Skedi could still see the shelves, and her mind was wandering.

'Great Scian,' said Inara, trying to call her back. That wouldn't work, it didn't give her purpose.

'We are seeking,' said Skedi.

Scian sharpened again, her robes white once more.

'We are looking for our history,' Skedi continued, 'a connection between House Craier and the god Yusef. And . . .' Skedi looked at Inara. Did they ask what Inara was? But Scian's focus had sharpened on him, pleased.

'Yusef,' she said. 'First formed of travelling communities in the east who found their way to the Restican plains, looking for green valleys and safe pastures. A small god, a lone statue on sailing boats and caravans. Then, the trade routes formed for silk, salt and spices. People explored further east, further west, the oceans beyond the oceans. They took Yusef with them over land and water.' She waved her palm over the ledger, and its pages turned, filling with ink once again in drops from her arm like blood.

Skedi hopped up and bent over the pages. Yusef had many references, too many, hundreds to go through. But Scian pointed to one line: Yusef and the Houses of Middren. Beneath were noted the Brahims, the Vittosks, Benins, Yesef's. No Craier.

Scian drifted, her body fading.

'No, wait,' said Inara. 'Please, Scian.'

Scian looked at her again, eyes faint and confused, as if unsure why she was there. Her robes were darkening, unravelling.

'I need to know what powers I have and how to use them,' said Inara desperately. 'How and why my mother made me, and whether a god can be my father. I need to know who I am.'

'So many questions,' said Scian. 'I have not read of such a thing in centuries, though blood records are rarely kept. Who you are is not a matter for the archives yet, little one.'

A ring of a bell cut through the quiet, then several more clanging even through the thick ceilings of the vaults. Scian disappeared more softly than she came, fading at once into shadow. The lights brightened, and the darkness and hush that had cocooned them lifted. Beyond it, the bells clamoured for the forum.

They were late.

CHAPTER SEVENTEEN

Elogast

THE STEWARD USHERED THEM THROUGH A DOOR IN THE side of the manor, which led to a busy kitchen. Piles of sweets were drying in cool air coming in from the open windows: blood-orange tarts, cardamom and honey crispels, and almond biscuits drizzled in pomegranate molasses.

Then, nearer the oven, were savouries. A shaker filled with corint, green spice, lemon zest and seeds was being so liberally used to dust sheep cheese and onion pies that Naia sneezed and received a sharp elbow for her trouble. Elo was reminded of the kitchens in the Forge. He and Arren had stolen a tart each when they were nine years old and received a thorough beating with a broom handle from the line cook. Arren's younger brother had taken a plate of cakes the day before and had not received a single smack. He was instead baked two batches more.

Next, they were taken up a passage and flight of stairs, through a dining hall and down into a wide study. The surly looking captain followed behind them, close enough to Elo to stir the hairs on his neck.

The fire was lit in the study, the windows open, and chairs artfully placed across fine mosaic floor. This, Elo remembered vividly: a broad-winged eagle with a vine and flower in its claws, dominating the room. The walls were painted vivid blues, darted through with roiling sea and pretty, delicate clouds, and above them the ceiling boasted polished brass, inlaid with silver that reflected the tiles, the wings, the petals of the flower.

Elo peered through the door they had not come through. This led out into the receiving hall at the front of the manor, which was being bedecked with flowers in preparation for the lord's formal consultation. The mosaic from the study ran through there too, unchanged from Elo's memory and barely legal. The floor was laden with gods; most dead now. Agni, the god of fortune whose death had started the war, Tet the wild god of sex and wine, and Bela too, his Curlish counterpart, near the entrance to the dining room. Scian of Lesscia, of course, graced the door to the study, and triumphant Mertagh the dead god of war, his antlers jutting into the god of safe haven's feet. Some of the mosaics had been altered slightly; perhaps damaged and reset, as if someone had taken a hammer to them.

'Wait here,' said the steward, gesturing to the prim loungers that sat by the eagle's head near the open fireplace, then she disappeared into the hall and made for the stairs.

'Elogast?' said Naia, her voice nervous. Elo turned back, and she nodded pointedly at the captain, whose hand had alighted on his sword, his eyes fixed on Elo as he nosed into the house proper. He must have looked like he was scouting for an exit. 'Don't quake on me now.'

Elo stepped back from the door. Naia's eyes in the light of the large windows were amber brown, darkening as the clouds grew in, and narrowed with anxiety. He had taken a risk to be here, and she to come with him.

'Apologies,' said Elo, coming towards the others and nodding at the captain, the steward had called him. 'I came here once or twice, briefly, when I was young, I was curious to see what had changed.' He smiled in what he hoped was a disarming manner. 'The house is one of the most beautiful in the country.'

The guard's hand relaxed a little.

'I feel we have met before,' Elo added, stepping carefully. 'I didn't catch your name, Captain . . .?'

The guard smiled slightly. 'Captain Faroch of Yesef.' he said. A cousin of the Yesef House, denoted by his 'of' rather than adopting the name as his own. 'I remember you . . . Commander Elogast, but I was only a second at the time. You sparred with my friend Maia.'

'Ah, I remember Maia. She almost bested me with her long knives. Where is she now?'

'She died,' said Faroch. 'In the war.'

Elo's heart sank. 'I am sorry.'

'Don't be. She was proud to follow you, Commander.'

Commander, from a captain. A compliment, possibly. It made Elo his senior. 'Please,' said Elo, 'I have no rank now, Captain. Elo is fine, if you prefer.'

Faroch hesitated. 'I would rather Ser Elogast,' he said.

Elo nodded, he would take that token. Yesef House was, like Yether's, fed by the River Daes. Elo drew the potential alliances together in his mind, tucking away that information.

A door opened in the wall, and Lord Yether swept through in an indigo doublet and gold-printed breeches, embroidered slippers on his feet. Naia and Elo bowed, and Faroch dropped to his knees.

'Up, up,' said Yether. He had the powerful stature Elo remembered, but his beard was more grey than brown, though his brows were still very dark over bright blue eyes. His gaze had ever been direct and shrewd.

'Lord Yether,' said Elo as Captain Faroch stood again.

'Young Elogast,' the lord replied with a nod. He was out of breath, red in the face, and angry. But not, Elo thought, at him. 'It has been a long time, my boy. Last you were here you were begging for soldiers, I thought that was repayment enough. I was generous.' He came and clapped Elo on the arm, a little too hard. 'No bowing, no bowing, I'm not wearing shoes for looking at.'

The silk slippers looked as if they were worth more than everything Elo was wearing, except his sword. 'I have told you before, my lord, you owe me nothing.'

Yether blew out his cheeks. 'Everyone wants something. Thought you had gone back to Irisia with your mothers and the rest of them.' He nodded at Naia, who had also straightened. 'Taking good manuscripts and good trade with them too.'

Elo felt rather than saw Naia stiffen with annoyance at 'them.'

He also sensed her curiosity about what Yether thought he owed him.

'My lord,' chided Elo gently, 'we are Middrenite by birth and raising.'

'And the blood you shed for us in Blenraden, I suppose,' said Yether. His piercing eyes explored Elo's face, and Elo met his gaze, his hands behind his back disguising the tremor in them.

'Yes,' Elo said simply. 'Blood I gave for you, blood I am still willing to give.'

'So,' Lord Yether went to one of the loungers by the fire and sat down. 'You've come barging in before my consultation hours, invoking an age-old debt—'

Elo opened his mouth to protest.

'To tell me the king is marching on my city,' Yether went on. 'This, I already know. The sod has told me to drain the Daes of fish and water to feed them all.'

Elo closed his mouth.

'And I suppose you are come to apologise for your brother-in-arms, thick as thieves as you were, and tell me he means no harm to me and mine?' Yether steepled his fingers and looked over them from Elo, to Naia, then back. 'Tell me to open my arms and halls to him and his many-mouthed army he doesn't know how to feed?'

Elo almost laughed. Yether hadn't changed one bit, still liked to keep people on the back foot, attack with words sideways, disrupt their thoughts and fluster them. Judging by the thin line of Faroch's mouth, he was very used to this. By the annoyance on Naia's face, Elo suspected she had not been face to face with the lord before.

'I am come,' said Elo, 'to advise that you lock the gates.'

Yether regarded him. A word, a look, and Faroch would draw his sword, the steward would summon any number of soldiers from the manor and its lands. Elo wondered if they would be wearing Yether yellow or Regna blue.

'So, it's true,' said Yether. 'You have turned against your king.'

'He is not my king. Not anymore.'

Faroch shifted his feet, moving onto his front foot. More relaxed? Naia took the opportunity to step forward. 'My lord, I am Naiala of Yanik and Allemni, an old trading family here in Lesscia.'

'I am aware of your parents. Your mother's father built my house, no?' Naia inclined her head. 'I am also aware of the pamphlets you have been spreading,' he added. 'Interesting reading. Passionate. Naïve too.' Naia didn't look sure whether to puff with pride or shrink with shame.

'You know?' she said, shaken.

'Not many families own their own small press, young lady, I am old, not stupid.' He shrugged. 'Our business in this city is pieces of paper, among other things, I like to know what's written on them and by who. Your distribution is impressive, you must have connections in the ginnels.'

'I—' Naia began.

'My lord, this is not the most pressing matter,' said Faroch, before Elo could. If Faroch was now the captain of the guard, overlooking Naia's activities was his domain. Elo found a shred of confidence. He should have known that Yether was not so quick to lean to the whims of whatever monarch ruled.

Yether tutted. 'Well,' he said, 'so what if the king wants to come in all his pomp and splendour, show me what a man he is?' He put his feet up on a footstool of silk and rosewood. Its cushion was fragranced with lissom flowers and just a hint of relaxing sless seeds. 'Who could refuse such a popular man?' He nodded at Naia. 'For every leaflet she gives out, ten more are filled with songs of praise. It isn't wise to swing dicks against a man whose cock is crowned with gold. It would hurt.'

Elo barely blinked. He had spent two weeks with Kissen, the crudest, foulest mouthed person he had met. 'Nor is it wise,' he responded, 'to keep an army that owes you no fealty within your own gates.'

Faroch grunted with approval, his back straightening with what looked like vindication. Of course, he would not like knights splitting loyalties in the city he captained. Elo suspected he had argued this point with Yether before. A suspicion confirmed when Yether gave him a sharp look.

'I don't pick fights with kings,' the lord said. 'Even upstart boys like the one you put on the throne. Do you pick fights with lords, Elogast?'

The air tightened.

'I have no quarrels with you, my lord,' said Elogast. 'In fact, Naiala is here to counsel against it. But this isn't a *show* of power, my lord. King Arren means to seize yours. Entirely.'

Yether scoffed. 'He would not make war on his own land,' he said. His blistering joviality had dissipated, cooling into a sternness that suited him better.

'This isn't about war,' said Elo, 'it's about faith. Who will people believe in? The king who saved Blenraden? Or the lord who rolled over when he marched an army up to his walls, and let them run amok within them?' Yether's faced hardened, and Faroch caught Elo's eye. It was risky to threaten his honour, but they had eight days or less, if Canovan was right. He couldn't waste time pandering.

'You think this country can afford a war?' the lord asked. 'Do you know how much Blenraden lost us? While you were hiding, Ser Elogast, you did not see the plagues that came with the refugees. You did not see the ships that stopped at Talicia, Usic, Irisia, instead of Middren. We are weak, even in Lesscia. What you see is show, and pomp, and splendour, but beneath is grind, and work, and sickness. We are not warriors here: we are archivists and traders. We cannot close up our gates like a clam on ice.'

'And do you think the king means to let us continue as we are?' said Naia. 'To leave you with floors like this,' she pointed at the mosaic on the ground, the gods out towards the hall. 'It has been three years since you allowed him to stand outside our gates and tear down the statues of our patron god Scian, who blessed your line. She allowed herself to be defiled for you, for this city. The archivists of Lesscia, once the silver of your city, now whisper behind closed walls and hide their own texts while the king's knights harass them at their work. What if he has come to cut it all down? Rip out the gods, root and stem? What ships would come here then, when Middren is proved just as bloody and mad as they thought three years ago?'

Elo hid his smile. He knew Naia was sharp-tongued, but this was more than that. Bold, decisive. A leader. Yether ran his tongue over his teeth and took his feet off the stool.

'What would you have me do?' he said, then looked to Elo. 'One decent knight and a mouthy teacher does not an army make. And I do not want to end up like the Craiers.'

Elo and Naia shared a glance.

'A mere letter,' Yether continued. 'A petition, and now their lady is gone, her manor and steadings burned, sinking into the earth, her family in disarray. If the king can burn down the House at the belly of Middren, he could burn mine too.'

'How long would that House last, my lord,' said Naia, 'if you bend your knees at a boy's first swing of a sword?' She lifted her chin. 'Apologies, no. What did you say? At the first swing of his cock?'

Yether's face darkened, and Faroch's fingers flexed. Their reactions were aligned more than Lord and his captain. They were friends. Elo's mind raced.

'You signed it, didn't you?' he said, leaping to a conclusion. 'Craier's petition.' Yether had attended some of the dead queen's god parties in Blenraden; he had loved gods before the war.

Yether swallowed. 'I withdrew,' he said.

'It isn't enough,' said Elo. 'You are a threat to him, and so he will take you down. We do not ask for war, only that you claim what is yours. This city.'

After a long moment of silence, the door Yether had come through slammed open, cracking against the wall, and a man of middle age came striding through. Beloris Yether. Elo hadn't seen him since he was a well-favoured man who wanted to prove it by picking a fight with a boar. He was the spit of his father, though with a full head of wavy brown hair and the shine of a stag over a rising sun on his lapel. With him was a young guard who wore two sashes; yellow and blue.

'I knew it,' Beloris spat. 'Ser Elogast the Great returns to spread lies and falsehoods. Hafil, arrest them.'

His guard nodded, stepping forward and drawing his blade.

'Hafil, stand down,' Lord Yether snapped. 'Beloris, I asked you to remain upstairs.'

'I am not a child.'

'And yet you listen at doors in my house.'

Beloris bristled. 'You are entertaining rebels and dissenters against our saviour,' he said. 'In *our* house, Father.'

'Saviour?' Yether tipped back his shoulders, then threw his head up to laugh. 'He is a lucky man who won half a war through rabble-rousing and treachery. Ser Elogast is as much Blenraden's victor, and more your saviour than he.'

Beloris glared at Elo. 'If he had let me have that damn hunt . . .'

'You would have been dead, and your sisters would have mourned you.'

Elo's last visit to the Yethers had been before Blenraden. Lady Yether still lived, and the queen's court and the Yethers' went to hunt in the woods on her birthday. When Beloris had attempted the boar in fury, he had been gored across the thigh and was about to be trampled before Elo put a spear through its head. Beloris had never forgiven him for claiming his victory.

'The king wants stability,' said Beloris. 'Not rebels and dissidents.' He spat on the floor at Naia's feet and turned to his father. 'I would have them arrested, Father, as the king commands.'

Yether's smile was again gone, all humour dashed away. 'You are no lord of these lands yet, Beloris,' he said. 'This is *my* House. My city. My lands. And I can take them from you as quickly as I gave you life in the womb.'

Beloris went white. 'Hafil!' he cried.

His guard stepped towards Naia and made a grab for her arm. Faroch drew his sword, but Elo caught Hafil's wrist and pushed him stumbling back from Naia. Beloris did not take this well; he pulled out his own dagger, and Naia grabbed Elo's arm, tightly, before it could go for his sword. He looked at her, and she shook her head once, slightly. Violence. The one thing she wanted to control. Elo hesitated, then put his hands forward, palms out, showing them empty.

'If Lord Yether commands, I will go peacefully,' he said. But he knew that zeal in Beloris's eye. He had seen it in the people who had fought for the old gods of Blenraden, who had burned their own homes down just to set the next district on fire. This time for Arren.

'Boy.' Anyone with a parent knew Lord Yether's tone. The tone that made children out of adults no matter what age they reached. 'Remove yourself and your dog or Faroch will have you removed.'

Beloris's lip twitched. Hafil did not shift, but then Faroch spoke. 'If you bare your blade any longer in this hall without Lord Yether's permission, Second Hafil, I will have the hand that holds it removed.'

Hafil swallowed, then stepped back and sheathed his sword, bowing his head. Naia released her hold of Elo, her breath quick.

'The king,' said Beloris, 'can march his army as he wills. This land is his. We should welcome him with celebration, as he asks.'

'The land is ours,' said Naia angrily. 'The king rules by consent of his people. If dominance is what you want, then go to Talicia where a god rules instead of kings.'

Beloris shook his head. 'You don't know him like I do.'

'From your three turns at court?' said Yether, standing. 'Excuse me if I don't swoon.' He made a generous bow to Naia and Elo. 'Apologies. He has been struck with . . . king-fever, I call it. I've had a few of the Houses and tradespersons wandering through with it. It's almost like . . .'

'Worship,' said Elo, and was treated to another glare by Beloris. But it was Lord Yether's House, Lord Yether's city, and the understanding he saw in the older man's eyes was what he needed. That, and the little touch of fear.

Yether snapped his head around to his son. 'Beloris, you ungrateful wretch,' he said. 'If you love the king so much tell him I expect him to halve his force and send a herald with his intentions before entering Yether lands. And wrap it in as much grovelling as you see fit.' He drew himself up proudly, his dark brows furrowed. 'When you return, I hope you have developed a spine and with it a mote of sense. We once were kings too. We fought for this jewel, this city, and we allowed it to adorn the crown of Middren. We do not show our bellies to tyrants.'

CHAPTER EIGHTEEN

Inara

THE ECHO OF THE BELLS SHOOK THE DUST FROM THE stairs as Inara took them two at a time. Skedi flew back into her sleeve as she broke into the light of the courtyard, dusting off her face and slowing down as she noted that she was surrounded by over a hundred archivists.

The warm, damp air was a relief after the chill, still stone down below. Inara tried not to think of Scian's look of longing as she thought about leaving the vaults.

Inara looked for Telle's colours in the crowd and spotted them, olive and grey like washed stone, close to her skin again like armour. Her shades changed so little, true to her certain nature, and it stood out among the murmuring archivists, all of them floods of change-able moods, clashing and chaotic. Her clothing was also simpler than most, cottons rather than silk or quilted muslin, not trimmed with velvet or silver brocade. Most of the darker-robed archivists were pushing beneath colonnades as heavy clouds rolled in above them, pushing the lighter shades out to deal with the rain that had just begun to fall. But Telle avoided the shelter entirely, standing instead in the middle where the water drops stained their robes more senior, darkening their colour.

The bells were slowing. Inara tapped Telle on the arm, and she smiled distractedly, then signed. *Where?* instead of the full *Where have you been?* Informal, but nervous. Her grey had deepened with concern.

Nowhere, said Inara quickly. *Are you ready?*

Telle took a breath, then nodded. The green deepened now, richer, vibrant. She was thinking of Yatho. *It is not unlawful,* she said, assuring both herself and Inara, signing small so they wouldn't be easily seen. *Not here. These walls are for free talk. It is how it's always been.* She hesitated. *If you don't want to, Inara, we can still leave.*

No, I want to. She still wanted to help Telle if she could. It was a pity Scian had been next to useless.

Telle asked nothing further as the crowd quietened. Three archivists, well into their winter years, had ascended a dais, their gleaming robes were so dark they were almost black.

'Yes, yes,' said one of them, a short woman with grey hair braided out of her face in a circlet. She wore a fine pair of spectacles on the end of her nose. 'It's just a bit of rain, and we must dry off before we touch the texts again, but this is the space we must use now. Even in inclement weather . . .' She gestured for space to open around her, causing a few more junior archivists to be displaced, and one stepped forward. A young man in a mid-grey shade, just lighter than Telle's, took a place in front of the dais.

'That's the Brahim boy,' said one of the archivists behind Inara.

'A cousin of the House that was broken.'

'I thought any of them who survived Blenraden were stripped of status?'

'Is he allowed to be here?'

'No law against it.'

'First order of calling!' the senior archivist said loudly. Within the shelter at the courtyard's edge, a junior archivist was hastily unrolling a blank manuscript and filling her brush-quill. 'Year four of the reign of King Arren, and the fourth month of this year.'

The youth in front of her, this 'Brahim boy' took to signing what she said, for archivists too far away to hear, or anyone who was deaf like Telle. It seemed an honoured job, and the Brahim apprentice did it proudly. Several of the older folk looked more at the signing boy than the speaker. Telle was right, his 'accent' was different, more formal, his gestures precise, his expressions carefully worked to match. Interestingly, Inara could barely see his colours, only if she focused. He had learned to hide them like Kissen.

Inara cast her eyes over the other archivists, wondering what else she could learn. Most colours were difficult to distinguish, almost bleeding together between people. There were a few who stood out. One in particular was a bright tower of purple: challenging, fierce. The man stood under the shelter, his skin brown and weather-worn, and his samite robes the colour of thunderclouds before lightning.

'Please,' said the head archivist. 'As you know, we have increased our numbers by opening our selection processes. To great success, may I add.' She said the last bit loudly, pointedly, as if expecting rebuke. 'Make room for others.'

So, this was the woman who had allowed Telle to enter the archives, and a disgraced House too. There must be others, and in the forum there was some half-hearted shuffling. Still, the space was packed in, far too tight with people corralled together, nudging and pushing and griping. Several appeared on the first- and second-floor balconies rather than brave the crowd.

'All right,' said the head wearily. 'Come forward with any new acquirements since the last dark moon, their storage and treatment.'

A dulled silence stretched between the tapping of the rain on stone, cloth and the copper of the roof.

'I received some trade records,' someone piped up, a mid-grey archivist with bright red hair tied in bunches down their back. 'New breeds of Curlish horses traded with Restish. Corroborated by sales records and anecdote.'

'Where stored?'

'First level. Modern trade goods and Curliu. Animals and livestock breeding.'

'Good, fine. Anyone else?'

The man with the challenging colour stepped forward. 'Record of two gods in Restish spreading across localities.' The signer's mouth thinned but he translated anyway, and Telle's colours brightened with curiosity. She leaned to see who had spoken.

That is Solom, she said to Inara. *He returned two weeks ago after seven years away.*

'They have shrines now in Belhaven,' Solom pressed on when no one responded. The other archivists murmured. 'A god of silver, and another of worksmithing.'

'Store it below, Solom,' said the chief archivist, her eyes skittering to the tunnel and the gate beyond it, where the guards must still be standing.

'I have another,' said Solom.

The colours in the courtyard were fracturing. Some archivists shrivelled with fear, others sparked with excitement, or anger, or flat disapproval. But several auras shot with blue, a tinge of gold. The king's colours. One of them the senior man who had let them into the vaults. Still, more were craning to look at Solom, and Inara sensed anxiety building in Telle.

The head archivist closed her eyes for a moment, glanced at the gate again, then back at Solom. At last she nodded.

'The great shrine to the god of safe haven has now been fully restored in Restish,' said Solom. 'Twelve white cows, six black horses and an anointed goat were sacrificed at its base.'

The archivists erupted into gossip. Even those shining with the king's colours warmed. Yusef. Inara tried not to reach for Skedi.

But ... even if Yusef came back, he would know nothing of Skedi, of the Craiers, of his past. Of her. What could he really tell her?

'Do I store this under architecture?' Solom asked brightly. 'Or below, with the other signs of his return?'

'What signs?' someone asked from far underneath the dome.

The Brahim boy's colours were less guarded now, fluttering out in chiffony streams of proud lilac and irritated mauve. He made a gesture in the direction of the asker and repeated the question. The head archivist scowled, and Solom looked her in the eye as he responded.

'Pomegranates fruited out of season on the western harbour by one of his broken shrines,' he said. 'Swallows blackened the sky between the Irisian coast and Middren on his holy day. Two Restish ships he had been on and been scuppered grew branches and leaves ...'

'We have no need to record the works of foreign gods,' snapped a middle-aged archivist beneath one of the fig trees. 'Gods have no place in these archives: we are not their worshippers.'

'Oh, pipe down,' said someone else by the stairs.

'We no longer abide by such idolatry.'

The Brahim boy's hands faltered. He couldn't move quickly enough between voices.

'We are archivists,' said one of the trio on the dais. 'Gods still live, we keep their record. That is our law.'

'The king's law is our law,' said the old archivist who had let Inara into the records below. The signer stopped completely, but Inara saw a glance pass between him and Solom. The Brahim boy was annoyed, but Solom was smug. They knew each other.

The woman on the podium clapped her hands once and the courtyard fell silent.

'Debates of the law belong in the street or the home, not in this forum,' she said. 'Store the new information below, Solom. That is where it belongs.'

Solom nodded, his purple defiance still flaming bright. Satisfied. Certain. But then, the blue and golds of the archivist under the tree were just as bright, their fury as potent.

What is it, Inara asked Skedi, knowing he would have found a way to peep out, *that brings them out in fire like this?*

Faith, said Skedi. Inara felt the longing in his thought.

'Are there any more new records of note?' said the head archivist. 'Anyone?'

Out of nervousness, or the oppression of dissent, no one else spoke.

'Fine,' the head heaved a sigh. 'Then the floor is open. Do we have discussions to be raised?' She said it tentatively, doing her best not to look at Solom, who had folded his arms.

Telle tensed and Inara almost put a hand out to stop her. Even for Yatho's forgiveness, there was too much danger here. She couldn't see the colours, the tension strung between the archivists like wires.

But Inara couldn't tell her to stop, not in this moment, not without risking everything.

Telle stepped forward.

'Ah, Telle of the third.' The head looked relieved, though Inara heard a tut or two from others that Inara hoped Telle didn't hear.

'That's another one,' someone near them whispered. 'Not even related to a House. She lets anyone take the exams these days.'

Ignore them, Inara, said Skedi.

Telle gestured Inara forward. *My day novice will speak for me,* she said, signing. The colours of the crowd moved back in motion with each other, like a calming sea, and Inara tried not to look in the direction of the archivist she had lied to in the god vaults.

Telle locked eyes with Inara, who swallowed dryly. This was all Telle had asked of her, to represent her voice without frills or interpretation, so they would listen. Inara had used her need to get close to the archives but hadn't till now understood just how alone Telle was in these crowds. Yatho hadn't understood either.

Friends, Telle said, and Inara spoke her words out loud. *Our archives are not safe.*

A frisson of surprise stirred the robes. The sea would not be calm for long. Solom, who had been staring down the head, looked at them.

When once this was a place where people could walk freely, now we are threatened with blades at our own gates.

Telle's speech and Inara's voice overlapped, like the ripples and echoes of a stone dropped in a pool. The Brahim boy echoed them again, signing back to the walls.

Our trade was once in knowledge, said Telle, *but now it is in secrets we hoard. We once had two hundred texts announced and discussed at each forum; today we are afraid to speak of barely three.*

'Tell her to be quiet,' hissed someone to the head on the podium, who was staring at Telle in surprise, as if she had grown a third eye.

Someone gestured at Telle to be silent, but another shouted, 'Let her speak!'

I believe, continued Telle, *that these are signs of a greater threat against our way of life. Our archives, our precious manuscripts. I believe it is our duty to protect them from anyone who might do them harm.*

A shower of water drops hit the stones of the plaza as someone scaled a fig tree to get a look at who was speaking. Another stood on one of the stone tables. Inara wished she was bigger, like Kissen, so she could be intimidating. Kissen should be here, not her. She would know what to do.

I fear, Telle continued, *we should protect the archives most under threat, the records of the gods that lived in these lands. At very least we should copy them and secure their storage. At best* . . . she paused, letting Inara catch up, and taking a breath herself, *move them out of Middren entirely.*

The crowd erupted in colour and sound before Inara had finished speaking. Members of all factions, the king's and otherwise, struck through with horror at the very idea.

'These archives have been developed over centuries,' said someone from between the pillars in iron-grey. 'You want us to disband them?'

'Gods are dangerous,' someone else broke in. 'They are not bound by human laws. King Arren's rules have been made for a reason.'

'They are protected here. You think our king won't protect them?'

'Who are you to demand such things?'

'A Blenraden rat, come thieving.'

'Once a thief, always a thief.'

Telle didn't look around at the speakers, or hear their voices layering on top of each other, but she could see their faces. More people butted in and jostled forward to get a look at them. Telle looked suddenly very small and vulnerable.

Inara signed to Telle as they restrained themselves. *They're saying they want the archives protected here, that the king's rules are here for a reason.*

'Quiet!' said the head. 'Quiet! Respect is due to our speakers.'

Telle controlled her expression, but for the first time her colours changed; a glaze of red fear bloomed around them. Still, she moved her hand soothingly.

Of course, I would not speak against the king here, she said. White lies. To soothe and gentle. Inara felt Skedi creep down her sleeve and press his will to them. *I dare not trouble with the politics of the great Houses, nor the thoughts of the king. I am no noble blood like so many of you.*

Telle's words tasted bitter in Inara's mouth, but Skedi's will spread over the crowd, and the archivists delighted in it. Colours settled like cats' fur stroked back to sleekness; by diminishing herself, Telle made them feel bigger.

I speak against the fearful who might misrepresent the king's intent,

Telle added as they settled. *The king holds us in his heart, is that not true? He would never do us harm, would he?*

She turned the question back on itself, twisting its power. It was working, the archivists were listening. The noise dimmed. How much of this was Skedi's power after her gift? Should she be proud, or concerned?

All I ask, said Telle and Inara, *is for us to consider how best to protect our centuries of work, and the work of those who have gone before us.*

She almost had them, they were listening. The head waited.

'Protect?'

Skedi twitched, and Inara turned, not signing. She recognised that voice.

'Protect how?'

The senior archivist who had let them into the vaults spoke from the columns, indignation filling his face and colours with ruddy shades. He spoke in sign and speech, and Inara couldn't hide it as he gestured curtly to Telle. 'You protect us by allowing your "day novice" to run rampant about the archives, lying to her betters and entering "protected" areas?'

Shit, Inara thought, clamping her mouth shut.

'You don't speak against the king, yet a girl under *your* protection sneaks into the records of the gods, breaking his laws?'

A mutter passed through the crowd, and the mood turned in an instant. The blue and gold from before came back, bright and vehement. Inara looked at Telle, who was staring at the speaker. *My day novice would do no such thing,* she said surely, then looked at Inara and gave her a nod. Trusting. Could Inara lie? But it wouldn't be a white lie, something so self-serving, it wasn't within Skedi's power. Inara just looked back at Telle, speechless.

Telle's eyes widened, understanding. Her colours changed, and the fear came back, stronger now, shifting with bitter grey betrayal.

The old archivist glowered, seeing that they had no response. 'Knights of the king!' he barked.

'Betrom!' cried the head archivist, casting a frightened glance to the gate. 'This forum has rules! Free speaking rules that have been here for centuries.'

Shots of blue were shimmering up everywhere. Gold-edged. More than there had been before.

'You have been too lenient, Perell,' said Betrom. 'You have opened up our doors when they should be closed fast. You allow dissent when you should hold to our king!'

A clatter of feet on stone echoed from the tunnel. The two guards from the gate appeared, halberds already lowered. The one with the beard looked practically sick with glee, though he had not yet spotted Telle and Inara.

Ina, said Skedi into her mind, panicked. If the guards found him, he would certainly be killed.

Stay hidden, said Inara. *If they get us, fly into the sky.*

I won't leave you.

You must!

'This is insanity!' cried Solom, stepping forward, his voice ringing with command. 'Blades in our archives! Guards at the gate? For the love of Scian, are we to live her days again?'

Betrom ignored him. 'Arrest that woman!' he bellowed, pointing at Telle. 'The child too. Dissidents!'

Two of the archivists started to applaud, and the bearded one's eyes landed on Telle. His face lit up further.

'How dare you?' one of the others on the dais shouted, their face puce with rage. 'You should be stripped of your dust robes, Betrom. Out. Out! Knights out!'

Some of the archivists picked up her order, pressing forward and gesticulating to the guards, shooing them away. The crowd rippled like two currents of water, dragging against each other. The younger one nervously lowered his spear.

They had to leave. Inara took Telle's wrist and pulled her away. The archivist's face was pale, her colours turbulent.

Is there another route out? Inara asked. Telle looked at her, dazed, hurt. There was no time to apologise. She had not thought . . .

Or she had. Just of herself.

The king's colours caught in the forum like smokeless flames, spreading and filling the stones with fear and faith. Most were more distracted by the activity at the gate, the intrusion of the guards, than Telle and Inara. Some fighting to let them in, others trying to push them out. At once the crowd was churning, shoving, stamping, threatening to catch them all up in it. Ink was thrown from above, and the mayhem intensified near the tunnel. Someone screamed, then several, but she couldn't see why.

Inara felt a hand land on her arm. She turned, teeth bared, ready to fight, but it was the Brahim boy. His colours firing, panicked, but not deceptive.

'Come,' he said, 'quickly!'

He dragged them through the battling edges of the crowd, feet slipping, wet on the rain-soaked pavement, then through a door. There, Solom was waiting. He pressed a bundle of keys into Telle's hands, and the Brahim boy signed to both of them.

Out the east wing, this key opens the doors. He touched one with a yellow tie, then another, red. *This one lets you in the back of the house by the roses. Hide there.*

Telle nodded. Behind them was a chaos of moving bodies, but Inara could only see the clashing maelstrom of their beliefs. Terror in blue and gold.

For love or fear, they were thinking one thought: the king, the king, the king.

CHAPTER NINETEEN

Kissen

KISSEN WOKE WITH A SPLITTING HEADACHE. JUDGING BY the state of her vision, the darkness outside, and the dulled sting of her skin and wounds, she had slept a full day and into the following evening. She had never slept so long or so deep, not in a decade or more. She must have been close to death.

And yet not dead. She sat up slowly, careful to stay quiet, which meant stifling her groan of pain as her entire body reminded her of what she had been doing to it. Her left leg cramped with muscular aches, her knee twinged from overuse, and her right felt as if it had sunk through the bed into the floor and was trapped there, clamped in the teeth of the cave she was in.

The cave. Two rooms deep. She remembered it faintly. A stove burned near its entrance; a rough thing of worked clay with a pipe of a chimney slid up through the roof of the cavern. This must have been the light she had seen over the breadth of Aan's lake.

The bed that held her was just furs and woven wool. Most of the layers were threadbare with use but piled together so thickly that their age didn't matter. Above the bed hung pine branches, but deeper into the cavern the decoration was dried fish and drying rabbit, suspended with a forest of crumpled mushrooms and cloves of garlic threaded through with strings.

Kissen propped herself up on her elbows, wrinkling her nose as she caught sight of a mess of bloodied rags, used and discarded, on the floor beside her. She could smell something of herbs, salt and meat, and after a moment realised it was a waxy salve that had been smeared liberally on her frostbitten skin; nose, cheeks and knuckles.

Her right leg wouldn't shift, frozen as it felt within the bed, instead her whole ghost limb shot with pain. Closing her eyes, she breathed out, then pulled the blankets off, scooped her hands beneath the air where her flesh had been. She lifted high, higher, as if pulling the limb out of the ground, then imagined laying it out flat on the bed.

The pain lessened, her leg was freed, lying on the bed just like her left leg of flesh. She opened her eyes to consider the damage. Her right knee had been pasted with a poultice of moss and leaves that stuck to it like a bandage, her arm and shoulder too. Her left foot also stung with blisters, and she could feel the crack of the same poultice pasted around her toes, but whoever had taken care of her had wrapped them in cloth before tucking them beneath the covers, to make sure they didn't get cold.

Where were her weapons? She was sure she was in no danger – if someone wanted to hurt her they would have done it while she was sleeping – but she wanted them all the same.

Thankfully, the blade she had taken from Osidisen's lair, along with her cutlass and staff, were not far from her reach. She picked up her cutlass but left it in its sheath. She had washed the blood from it, but she still felt like she could see it when she looked at the blade. Next, Osidisen's knife. The stones flashed at her.

'Look what a mess you've got me into,' she said to the blade.

A crunch of stone. Kissen switched her grip to defensive and tried to move to her feet, but a wave of dizziness sent her back to her arse. A man appeared at the cave's entrance.

'Ah,' he said. 'Kissenna, I'm glad you're awake.'

Kissen got a better look at him as he brought down his hood. He was worn thin, like a tree that had stood out too long in storms, and as pale as one that had been stripped of its bark. His grey-streaked beard hung to his waist, but he looked hale and healthy; his eyes bright and his smile quick, though he was missing a few teeth. This was not a god. Gods touched the earth with purpose, humans because they belonged to the ground.

'Aan told you my name,' said Kissen, but the man laughed.

'We met before,' he said, 'though you were smaller then. Angry little thing, some level of youth. Sixteen? Seventeen?'

Kissen sat up properly, still holding her knife. 'Not so little now,' she said, 'and still angry.' She looked him up and down. 'Doric,' she said at last, finding the memory. 'You're the nutter who lives here. Pato brought you wine.'

Doric smiled, lifted a bag from the hook by the door and chucked it onto the blankets, as he might to a cat or a dog he thought might bite. He went back to the fire, pulling a piece of dried meat from the ceiling as he went, and sat on the low stool with his knees up and his elbows on them. He gnawed a chunk off the meat and chewed loudly as Kissen opened the bag. Inside was a wineskin, cooled in the outside air, hard cheeses and biscuits.

'It's from a more recent visitor than your veiga,' said Doric. 'And there's a pot of fresh water to your right.'

Kissen looked, realising she was terribly thirsty. The water she all but inhaled before unstoppering the wine and taking a long draught.

'I was sorry to hear about Pato,' said Doric, looking at the fire again. His voice creaked with lack of use. 'He was a good man.'

'He was a crabby git,' said Kissen. 'And smelled bad, to boot. Where's my horse?'

Doric huffed out a laugh. 'Well,' he said. 'You've taken after him nicely.'

Kissen looked up, her mouth half stuffed with the cheese and dried grapes from the bag and snorted. He wasn't wrong. She stank to the sky of poultice, old blood and sweat.

'Your horse is much happier,' Doric added. 'Roaming loose. It's lucky I had some spare straw for her.'

Kissen swallowed. 'Thank you,' she said, meaning it. Senfa deserved better.

Doric clicked his tongue. 'You show more gratitude for some straw for a horse than for me saving your own sorry life,' he said.

'The horse didn't make my choices.'

He thought about that and swallowed. 'Fair,' he said. 'You know, it always surprised me that Pato ever took an apprentice. He was a solitary fellow. You are similar there, too, it seems.'

'He didn't have much of an option,' said Kissen. 'I cut all ties and tracked him out into the wilds. If he sent me back, it would have been to death. Even he couldn't stomach that.'

When she had followed Pato out of Blenraden, she had reneged on the debt Maimee, her buyer, had been drawing up for years. Everything was added to it; her food even when she starved, her clothes even when they were rags; her crutch, even the splintering peg she had to strap to her knee, worse than nothing. Maimee even added the ring she broke when she had beaten her. None of the children Maimee had bought or bartered for were ever intended to be free.

So, when Kissen ran, smuggled out of the locked house by Yatho and Telle, she knew she couldn't come back. Maimee made examples of runaways, and the ones she couldn't break she destroyed.

'He got used to me, after a while,' said Kissen, then thought of Inara. 'And now I know how it feels.'

'You picked up a brat?'

'She picked up *me*.' Kissen pushed her hair back from her face, feeling every ache of her body.

Doric chuckled and took another bite of his meat. 'Where is she now?' he asked.

'Getting into trouble I suspect.' She glanced out of the front of Doric's cave at the pool before it. Aan's source, the heart of her power. It was perfectly still in the evening, darker somehow than the sky, and untouched by frost, though the mountains and the paths beyond were white and tipped with silver. Aan would know what was happening with Inara, they had exchanged hair. Even a small piece, a lock, was a good offering.

'That's your past come back to bite you,' Doric said. 'You were trouble enough last time you were here. Headed for the border in a blizzard to summon the fire god.'

Kissen tongued her gold tooth and took another gulp of wine. 'It seemed too good a chance to miss,' she said. There hadn't been shrines to Hseth in Middren, not outside of Blenraden, but in

Talicia . . . even just over the border, she had found a bell on a pile of twigs and stones, Hseth's symbol carved on the bronze. She had rung it, howling for the god to face her and her small bag of tricks.

'She didn't come,' said Doric, a statement not a question.

'No,' said Kissen.

'Killed her anyway, didn't you?'

Kissen looked at him sharply, but he was still chewing at his meat, completely relaxed and staring absently at the fire. He could be anywhere between fifty and a hundred, Aan's hermit who tended the source of the waters. How many years had he spent here? How much did Aan speak to him, and tell him the ways of the world beyond his sight?

'What am I doing here, Doric?' she said.

'That is for Aan to say.'

Kissen rolled her eyes. The fucking faithful; they got through a few bare sentences before straying into blether. 'Then where is she? I hope she didn't drag me here to wait at her pleasure.'

'You dragged yourself here,' Doric pointed out while scratching his ear. 'How do you feel?'

'Like shit.'

Good.

Aan's voice struck into both of their heads with all the joy of a needle through the eyeball. Kissen winced, but Doric smiled as if he had been kissed.

'You'd better have good reason for calling me, Aan,' snapped Kissen, earning herself a disapproving clearing of the throat from her hermit.

And yet you made it all this way on a god's whisper, said Aan. *An unexpected pitch of confidence. Perhaps your time with the lying god and his guardian was good for you after all.*

Kissen did not like the smugness in her voice. She steeled herself for the ache of rising, then reached for her staff and stood, dragging some of Doric's bed-furs about her shoulders as she did so. She was largely naked, shivering with pain and fatigue, and everything ached. Not just her body, but her heart; it was heavy with what she had seen, what she had done. She had been sipping water from a breach in a dam. It wouldn't stop the flood. War was inevitable, a tide already rising. Hseth . . . inevitable too.

She lodged the staff beneath her armpit, picked up her briddite cutlass, and limped over to the cave's entrance. Doric turned to eye her as she passed, his skinny ankles sticking out from his trews. They were marked, Kissen noted, by old scars; chains that had been fastened around both ankles, making a twisted tattoo of his skin. A prisoner, he had been once, or a slave.

Kissen dragged her eyes away. The god was waiting.

When she stepped outside the cave, Aan was sitting cross-legged on the waters of her perfectly still pool. This was the first time she had appeared to Kissen clothed. Previously, she had always appealed to Kissen's desires; a big, powerful woman, radiant with curves: a round belly, soft arms, and hair dark as a raven's wing along her legs, and sex. Now, as thick as a river from her regal head, her hair drifted out in the water before becoming one with its darkness, but the rest of her was covered with a mantle of fur. White as a wolf's pelt, long and brilliant, gleaming in the first light of the stars.

No, not fur. It was ice. She bristled with fine needles of it, spines that prickled like the furs of a great beast of myth, glistening and deadly. Anyone who embraced her would be impaled. This was not Aan in a gaming mood.

Kissen tightened her hand on her cutlass. Could she use it, would she? Half-naked and devastated before one of the wild gods of old? Here, in Aan's domain, without any of her tools, she didn't stand a chance.

Instead, she sat down on the stones before the pool. They were cool, but not icy. A nicker in the distance, and Kissen looked up. Senfa was lying by Aan's waters, de-saddled and healthier than Kissen had seen her. Kissen sighed.

'What do you want from me?' she asked Aan, moving her staff so it was across her knees, and putting her knife and cutlass on top of it. 'I'm batted between gods these days like a plaything. I hope it is for something better than boredom.'

Aan looked at her steadily. Her eyes were almost black; liquid and shining. It was an insult, to bear a briddite weapon in Aan's shrine, like bringing a noose into a family home. Aan's follower had nursed her to health, and Aan herself was now protecting her from the cold of the mountainside. Kissen could see snow spinning up from the ground, and thin strips of cloud streaking across the sky like arrows.

'You've been watching me,' said Kissen.

'You carry a god's gift on your person,' said Aan. 'It was not I who was watching you.'

The dagger. Osidisen's dagger. Kissen had been right, Osidisen was keeping an eye on her. But why involve Aan? Her water did not even flow into his seas.

Water speaks to water. Aan had said as much in Blenraden. Kissen pulled Doric's furs higher on her back, bitterness rising in her throat.

'You were fighting a losing battle against a dead god.' Hearing that out loud tasted foul. 'She sits in Talician hearts on a throne of war, and you cannot unseat her.'

Kissen shook her head, frustration sending a shiver down her spine, despite the fur.

'So I called you here,' said Aan, 'and you came.'

Kissen scowled. 'You gave me a living god to pursue instead,' she bit back. 'Faer killed those lilns, barely weaned from their mothers' tit, and he came at *your* bidding.'

Aan lifted her chin. The air cooled just enough to nip at Kissen's skin, reminding her that she was no threat to Aan. The god could crush her if she wished. Kissen's breath came out in fog.

'Children are not innocent,' said Aan.

'Well, they fucking should be,' Kissen spat.

Maimee should never have been allowed near children, let alone vulnerable children. Inara should never have had to see her home burn. That young boy should not have died. None of them should have.

'They are not the last to die, Kissenna,' said Aan after a moment. 'You know this already. You feel it in your heart.' She turned her head, looking south towards Middren. 'I have seen nations here rise and fall. Gods too, lifted high and then dashed to the ground. And yet . . .' Her eyes came back, deep and unyielding, 'This is the first time I have seen godhood and nationhood so deeply entwined. It frightens me. Hseth frightens me.'

Kissen blinked. She expected many things from Aan, but not honesty, not weakness. 'Hseth is dead,' she said sourly. Finally, she had killed the god who had destroyed her family, and it had made the barest mote of difference. Even worse, Kissen felt that by killing Hseth, she had inflamed her followers.

'She returns to us with each breath you take,' said Aan. 'Dragged back to life in a world where she will not die, will not change, will not soften.' The air warmed a little, as if Aan wanted to prove that she could again be gentle. 'Once Hseth was a fire god that warmed people on the coldest night,' she said, 'and cleared the slopes of heather for grazing cattle. Near my waters, I would hear people telling stories by her light. In her brightness was industry, imagination, safety. Gods are power, made real by faith, but the faith that makes her now is death-bent. Osidisen was right, she will invade Middren faster than she even came through Talicia.'

Kissen closed her eyes, panic tightening her chest. 'This is what you've brought me here to tell me?' she said. 'I understand. I've seen this. I am trying.'

'You're failing.'

Kissen bared her teeth, incensed. 'And what's it to you? Your waters will run no matter who fishes in them.'

Aan laughed, tipping her head back to expose her throat, but the smile did not reach her eyes. 'Is it just gods you think so little of?' she asked, 'Or is it all speaking beings?'

'Fuck you. Answer the question.'

Kissen was pretty sure she heard Doric make a great intake of breath behind her. Aan's icy furs bristled, extending like a shroud of knives. Her black eyes bored into Kissen's, and her skin took on the quality of stones like those surrounding the pool. Kissen stared right back, refusing to be afraid. Aan moved her hand, and Kissen gripped her sword, but it was not an attack. The water of her pool shifted into the shape of mountains, their sloping peaks rippling with water and storms, and an army. Not small groups like the children she had fought; phalanxes, marching in unison, carrying poles bearing the fire god's figure, dragging shrines with them on the roads.

'They march with the meltwater,' said Aan, 'They carry grain, drive oxen, and slaughter the first stirrings of goatherds as they go. But this is a distraction.'

The view changed again, to the shores of Talicia, to waves and then to fleets. The pool moved and Kissen noted a different shore, one she recognised only vaguely from maps Telle had insisted on showing her. Restish. With over thirty warboats.

'Talicia has used briddite to enclose Osidisen out at sea, and they have set sail. A passage of safety to Middren's waters. Restish waits for the tide to turn, and they will come too. Both have gods on their side of flame and ruin, while Middren has none. From sea and sword, your lands, our lands, are on the brink of destruction.'

They were a beast with clipped wings, ripe for the slaying.

'This is what the rain and snow tell me,' said Aan, 'come up from the oceans to fall in my waters. Many sea gods would have Middren fall, and Restish wishes to sit fat and rich in your harbours. But they do not see what I do. The threat of Hseth, her barbaric balance of wealth and terror. They only see a puny king, a drop in the ocean of time, screaming at the waves. But when Hseth is reborn in the heat of war, at the heart of a nation, centuries of blood will follow in her wake.'

'You cannot know this for certain,' said Kissen. 'So what of shores and land and rulers? One king is much like another.'

'I know that the rivers carry the Talician soldiers' voices, their tales of raids and scourges, burned earth and dead gods. The water they piss into the ground stinks of violence and blood, their sweat and spit of power and faith. Their tears are the tears of zealots. We must undo it, King Arren must undo it.'

Kissen twisted her mouth. 'That bastard king. What's he going to do about it?'

'Only a power greater than Hseth's will be able to counter her.'

'Hah. Well, he'd be happy to hear you say that, seeing as he wants godhead so badly. Why don't you bother him and leave me alone?'

'His eyes look only inwards, it seems, and he marches on his own people.'

The waters changed again, to a broad city of concentric canals across a large river that flowed down to the sea.

Lesscia. Kissen knew it well, from the cloche down to the tower towns that guarded the harbour miles south. She looked up at the god. This was manipulation, Aan was tugging on her heart, and she knew it. She was hiding something.

Guilt.

'Why didn't you tell me this in Blenraden?' said Kissen.

The water fell again to flatness. Aan's ice-fur bristled. 'I offered what I was asked for.'

'And now you are offering what was not asked for,' pushed Kissen. 'Why? What changed?' They stared at each other in silence broken only by the wind whistling over the mountains and dancing around the circle of Aan's shrine.

'You thought I would kill the knight,' said Kissen at last, threading their encounter together. 'Didn't you?'

Aan pouted. 'Yes. When the little god told you, I thought you would end the knight, the king would die, and all would go back to what it was. Only after the chaos at the wild gods' shrines did I note Hseth's hand in Middren. How she communed with fire as I do with water, through hearths and light. I had blinded myself to Osidisen's glowering, the muttering of the rivers and the rain, for far too long.' She twisted her mouth. 'You took an unexpected path and showed me I was . . . wrong.'

Kissen tried not to laugh. The river god looked as if she had sucked a lemon.

'I don't kill people,' said Kissen, then added bitterly, 'or I didn't used to.'

Aan sighed. 'It is well you did not. This war is a long time coming, I have simply been too long in my own currents to understand it. However, your decision has another cost.'

The water rippled, then showed a man Kissen immediately recognised. Elogast. Alive. She knew he would survive, but seeing proof was a stone lifted from her chest that she didn't know had been there. But gone was his wry smile, his calm, his satchel of flour and herbs. He was haggard, gaunt, with danger in his stance and a hand on his sword. This wasn't Elo the baker, this was Elogast the knight.

'He wants to kill the king,' said Aan.

Kissen shrugged. 'Tit for tat,' she said. 'The king tried to kill him.'

Aan hissed through her teeth and the water fell. She stood up, the mantle of ice falling around her shoulders, turning into water near her feet. 'This is not a game, veiga,' said the god. 'You did not heed Osidisen's warning, and now you will not countenance mine?'

'What does it matter?' shrugged Kissen. She turned the staff carefully in her hands, preparing herself. 'What love have you for a boy-king who has turned you into a backwater god drinking the piss of mumbling soldiers?'

Aan's expression froze into one of rage, her eyes widening as if they were deepening pools of liquid, black to their edges now.

'Do you not understand what I have been saying?' said Aan. 'What do you think happens when the last of the line of Regna dies and each noble with half a wish squabbles for his crown? When you petty humans eat yourselves for the fun of it and torch your own beds? Who will watch your borders then for fire and ash?' Her voice shook the stones around them and Kissen leapt up on her staff, ready to move, or fight. She had provoked Aan to get a reaction, and a reaction she was getting.

'You and your knight would tear out Middren's heart and leave it for the vultures,' said Aan, pointing an accusing finger towards Kissen, her body hardening into slate and shadow while the lake at her feet turned rough and churning. 'With little tools you make battle with gods, but you still cannot fight faith. If you break your king, you will break the last thing your lands have faith in, and a broken country cannot defend itself.'

Aan now was more stone, ice and water than flesh. Only the river of her hair remained her link with humanity. 'You are a petty mortal, who thinks killing ancient things for the price of coin is a right you have earned. A few paltry years of small pains and sad little feuds, and you think you can put out a fire by spitting at it.'

She stopped: she had seen that Kissen was smiling. Well, Aan was difficult to anger. Kissen had tried before, to no avail, but this time it had been as easy as poking a wasp nest. Kissen's smile faded. Her eyelashes were thick with ice. Her breath froze in the air and fell. Aan was serious. No, more than that, she was truly terrified. A god had to be frightened to call on a veiga for help.

'I am only a godkiller,' said Kissen quietly, her breath coming out in fog between her lips. 'I killed the god already. What do you want me to do now?'

'Save one,' said Aan. 'Save the king who would be a god. Fight fire with fire.'

CHAPTER TWENTY

Arren

ARREN WATCHED A ROARING CROWD THROUGH THE SLIT in his helm.

The sky was noonday bright, though he could not feel its warmth. He could only see it gleaming on the blue velvet cloaks and freshly polished armour of his commanders and generals. It lit up his pennants, striking out across the stag's head and its rays. Mertagh's head. Arren smiled. The god of war had tried to kill him, almost succeeded, but now Arren was replacing every memory of the war god with himself. The stag was his now. Mertagh would never live again.

He knew much of the crowd that cheered him had been gathered by House Crolle, his most ardent supporter after one of their own had tried to poison his wine. The Elemnis, Sakre's closest southern neighbour with an abundance of textile makers, had also spread blue-dipped cottons, leftovers from the soldiers' uniforms, to be waved as he passed. Court bards were already preparing their lyrics, painters their ink, historians their paper, to keep record of this show of glory for which Arren had ransacked the treasury.

And the standing army. Fresh coats made by half a city of seamsters walked down the king's parade, wending their way from the fields, through the Forge, and out the eastern gate in a river of blue. They jeered and clapped, more joyous than Arren had seen the host since they won the war, and some danced with the drummers that walked along with them, to keep them in rhythm as they headed east.

This was a victory parade. It had to be. Hseth was nothing to him, he didn't need her. Why did he ever think he would? That was the old Arren, waiting for approval, waiting for help. He didn't need it anymore. Not from Hseth, not from Elogast, not from anyone. Look what he could command before him. A shining city of blue and gold, cheering for him. Loving him.

His own armour he had adjusted specifically. His helm bore antlers tied by a circlet, with a closed grille over his face. His chestplate he'd had cracked in two over the sunrays and reset so it had a schism within it, over his chest, his flaming heart.

He would show he was not afraid of death.

Peta, at his side, was watching the crowd. Sakre was the largest Middrenite city, so their departure was the most likely to suffer attack. Arren was almost begging for it, his heart exposed as it was.

None came. Not even a thrown tomato, nor a yell of discontent.

You see, Hestra? Arren thought to his god.

I see it, the god said to him, her voice soft. She had never had such crows, such adulation. Not even with Hseth. *The brightness, the faith, the fervour.* She laughed. *Perhaps I was wrong, kingling.* She prickled, a spark flew out of his chest, drawing a gasp from the crowds, then applause. *Perhaps.*

The march moved towards the city gates down the main street under a carefully curated shower of flowers. Cherry blossoms, plum and hawthorn. Anemones, spinning as people tossed them from their windows. Some lilac, sweetly scented. Elo's favourite.

Arren proved them all wrong in the end.

CHAPTER TWENTY-ONE

Elogast

IT HAD BEEN A LONG TIME SINCE ELO HAD PREPARED FOR war. The fear tasted sour and familiar. The loneliness felt strange.

The plan he had made with Yether was simple. Even Naia had been impressed. But it would take timing and a show of force. He needed every person the rebellion could offer. For that, he had to show them what some tactics could do.

He and Faroch left Yether's house together with Naia, who led them to an old theatre, closed weeks before for hosting a play that mocked the king and his armies. There, she had told them, the others were waiting for their return.

She knocked once, twice, then twice again in quick succession. Ariam opened the door and nodded his welcome before closing it quickly behind them.

'He was right,' said Naia as they entered, giving Ariam's arm a squeeze of assurance. 'Lord Yether offers his support to Elogast's plan. Captain Faroch here too.'

'Well,' said Canovan, from where he sat on the stage. His arms were covered, his pipe was nowhere to be seen. His eyes flashed as he looked over Faroch and Elo. 'Yether has some steel in him after all.'

The theatre was damp with the smell of the rain that had been and gone, and they were not alone. Eleven more stood around the stalls, and two were sitting in the shaded seats, clearly deep in conversation before Elo had come in. Those were wearing leather apron dusted with scales. Dock filleters. There were weapons too, not in their hands, but piled as they had been in the inkers' cellar, against walls, dumped in chairs, tucked beside the stage. Still, Elo tensed. These were not his allies yet.

'Be wary of your mouth, ser,' said Faroch stiffly to Canovan. 'I represent my lord's interests. His *best* interests.' The message was clear, Faroch would not stand for any jibes towards Yether, nor anything that threatened him.

'And we his city's,' said Canovan, leaping off the stage and landing carefully on his feet. On its boards had been carved the words *Death to the tyrant*.

Elo read it with mixed emotions, but guarded his expression. It was what he was here for. To kill a king. 'Why did you change your mind?' he said to Canovan.

The innkeep smiled, showing crooked teeth. 'I want to be where the action is,' he said.

'That isn't an explanation.'

'And *I* wanted to see if you were all talk,' said Ariam.

'Ah,' said Faroch, 'Ariam of the Inkers. I remember you from guild meetings last year. Quite the rabble-rouser, weren't you?' He looked around at the others and corrected himself. 'Aren't you?' His hand twitched, and Elo knew he wanted to put it on his blade. Wisely, he did not. They were very much outnumbered, and Elo noted that most of the other people in the theatre had ink-stained hands. Working people. Some of those Ariam could call on. His respect for the man increased.

'So, you have a plan?' said Ariam, ignoring him.

'We mean to clear out the king's knights,' said Elogast. 'Before the armies arrive. Most knights are nobility of some ilk; we can use them for ransom and fortify the city against him.'

'There are a hundred and fifty knights in Lesscia at last count,' said Faroch. 'Their number has increased by a few each month. We'll need the entire guard, and more, to catch them.' He looked at Elo. 'So, how many dissidents are there? How many can you lead?'

'Lead?' said Ariam, then chuckled darkly. 'What makes you think we'll follow a knight?'

Laughter echoed around the theatre, and Canovan smirked. Naia had warned Elo about this, that they would not take orders well. And certainly not his. From that comment alone, Elo understood much about the rebellion. They were like cats, each following their own lead. Naia as well.

'The way I see it, knight,' Ariam continued, 'you've used your connections, you've had your big ideas. But I've seen your wound. You're a half-healed man who doesn't know us. You couldn't even hold your own in a fight. Why should I trust my folks with you?' He squared his shoulders, and Elo understood.

'Ariam . . .' Canovan warned, to Elo's surprise. Perhaps his face still smarted from Elo's head.

'Is that what you want, Ariam?' Elo said lightly. 'A fight? Seems a poor way to prove a leader. I've known good leaders who could not beat me at swords, and good fighters who loathed strategy. Are you either?'

Ariam was built like the side of a house, thick and broad, and shorter than Elo. His equilibrium was lower, and he would certainly be stronger if he knew how to land a blow. Elo had dismissed him as no real fighter, but there was a chance he just did not wear the threat of violence as proudly as Canovan.

'Please,' said Naia. 'This is ridiculous.' When Ariam continued to stare down Elo, Naia appealed instead to the nearest inker in the stalls. 'Paritha, talk him down?'

'I'm not following someone who don't work beside us,' Paritha said, putting her hands in the pockets of her apron. 'That's what nobles do, isn't it? Bark orders from the soft seats at the back. If we fight, what's he going to do?'

'I'm not a noble,' said Elo. 'And I will fight beside you.'

'Then prove your salt, not-noble,' said Ariam. 'That's what the Talicians say.' He grinned, confident, cocky. 'Show us if you have a backbone in you, or if you were just born lucky.'

Elo laughed. He *was* born lucky. His mothers were wealthy, he was able to train with nobles and knights, he had been heartsworn to a prince and then won a war.

Then he had lost it all.

'Very well,' said Elo. He tipped his neck to one side, then the other, and breathed deep. He felt the stretch of his burned skin, the ache of his limbs, the muscles along his back, waist, legs.

'Oh please,' said Naia. She rolled her eyes and looked at Faroch, who had made no move to stop them. 'You too?'

The captain shrugged. Elo suspected Faroch, too, wanted to see if Elo was still who he once had been. Perhaps Elo wanted to know the same.

'Do you use a weapon?' he said to Ariam.

'Staff,' replied Ariam, then shrugged. 'I'm not one for stabbing folk.'

'Staffs then,' Elo agreed, unbuckling his belt and blade, then his jacket. He handed both to Faroch, who took them without comment.

'You mean you can fight without your big sword?' Ariam smiled.

Elo attended to his movements. His breath the most important. Breath steadied the heart and heightened the senses, dulled pain and shifted the blood. He cracked his knuckles too, for good measure, though he hoped that unlike with Kissen and Canovan, this wouldn't come close to a brawl.

'It's not the weapon,' he said, and allowed himself a smirk. 'It's how you use it.'

A few of the rebels snickered, though Naia did not look impressed. She muttered something that sounded very much like 'Gods save us from bloody men.'

Ariam went to a clutter of staves by the wall, grabbed one and threw the other to Elo, who caught it.

And Ariam lunged for him as his fingers closed.

The inker wielded the staff like a sword and went straight for Elo's side. Elo stepped back and met the staff with a crack of his own, the sound loud enough to set a wave of doves flying off the rafters. The man was strong, even stronger than Elo had expected, and it stung his hands and wrists to meet the blow. His chest, too, wrenched with the effort, agony shivering across his seared flesh and muscle. Hard work had made Ariam's upper body powerful, and he knew how to use it, stepping forward in a loose stance and coming sideways at Elo.

Elo moved back, bearing the brunt of Ariam's assaults, shifting the blows with his staff and defending as they crossed the stalls. The reverberation hurt his chest, more than just the surface: it went deep into his muscles, troubled his bones, his lungs. Each turn drove an ache into his sternum and across his back.

Ariam pressed his presumed advantage, driving Elo another step back then making a heavy stab for his chest as Paritha let out a cheer. He was decent, definitely fast. If he was younger he would be a good squire. Elo deflected it carefully, testing his backhand which was hard to measure when going through flows of his sword on his own. Needed more power, he was being too wary of his wounds.

Ariam thought he had him, but Elo had let the man show enough strength. Had taken it at some cost while the inker's people were watching. Enough was enough.

Elo turned to the side, letting the next blow pass, then hooked his own staff between Ariam's outstretched arms and swiped it underneath, tearing his opponent's weapon neatly out of his hands. In the same movement, Elo turned and kicked into Ariam's loose stance, striking his knee and sending him sprawling.

Ariam rolled on his back, more surprised than hurt. He glared at Elo, who smiled and stretched out his hand.

After a long moment, Ariam took it.

'I'm not even sure I know what happened there,' he said. Then understanding dawned in his eyes. 'You could've felled me outright, couldn't you?'

Elo didn't say yes. 'You're very strong,' he said instead. 'But your guard is weak from your belly down, and your stance is too short.' He stepped aback. 'Look, strike my leg from the inside.'

He presented his knee, and Ariam picked up his staff and did as he was instructed, more gently than before, both of them completely forgetting they had an audience. Elo bent his thigh into the strike, twisting his heel into the ground and turning it into a forward step, his staff aimed at Ariam's chest.

'Stance is your safety,' said Elo. 'You have power, but not balance. You need both.'

The theatre was silent. Canovan was watching them intently. Faroch looked pleased, while Naia was still annoyed.

'So, you are actually good at this,' said Ariam, stepping back.

Elo smiled. 'Fighting is my trade as much as inking is yours,' he said. 'Though our unions are not quite as strong.'

Ariam straightened his robes and looked to the others. Paritha nodded. 'So, you want to purge the knights, prepare for a siege. That's your plan?'

'We ask your help for the strike,' said Elo. 'That is all. A siege will not last, but it will force the king to negotiate or stand down. He won't risk an all-out war.'

Ariam looked impressed. 'Do you believe you can win?' he asked.

Elo put his staff on the ground, standing straight and sure. 'What makes you think I don't?'

The man shrugged and exchanged a glance with Naia. This was something they had discussed, it seemed. 'The look in your eyes when you talk about the king,' he said. 'You fought together, worked together. If you stood blade to blade, think you could beat him?'

'I can beat him,' Elo said certainly.

'Could you kill him?' said Canovan.

Elo tightened his grip on the staff and heard a light intake of breath from Faroch.

It had to happen. Him and Arren. He knew it as surely as there was a god's hand scarred on his chest. Arren had gone too far.

But Yether did not want the king's head, he wanted to bring him to heel. Elo would have to tread carefully to achieve an end to Arren's borrowed life.

'If it came to it,' Canovan added, clearly catching Faroch's unease.

Elo gritted his teeth. Could he do it? Kill the man he had cared for most in the world?

A rattle at the door saved him an answer. Someone burst through, a woman in archivist's robes. She was sweaty and covered in dust.

'Naia,' she said, rushing over. 'There's been a riot at the cloche. Someone was killed.'

'A riot?' said Naia, taking her hands. The archivist rubbed her face, her breaths hot and fast. They were far from the cloche: she must have run half the way.

'What do you mean a riot?' said Faroch. 'When?'

'Morwen, calm down,' said Naia, throwing him a glance that told him to be quiet. 'Breathe.'

'It was Telle,' said the newcomer. 'The one who brings you scripts. She must have changed her mind. Naia, she spoke against the king at forum. The fucking knights tried to have her arrested!'

'Shit,' said Faroch. 'I'll be back, Ser Elogast.' He went straight for the door at a run.

'Was it Telle, you said?' said Canovan. Elo was surprised. Telle hadn't seemed like someone who would instigate a riot.

'Yes,' said Morwen, her breath slowing now. 'Telle from Blenraden. And a little girl—'

Elo's heart stopped.

Inara.

CHAPTER TWENTY-TWO

Elogast

ELO HAMMERED ON YATHO AND TELLE'S FRONT DOOR, HIS hand wet with the paint that had been daubed on the gate to their yard. Clouds had covered the sky, thick and oppressive, but no rain came to wash the words away.

Die with your gods
Go back to Blenraden.

Knocking on the gate had gained him no answer. That and the door were damaged, but not broken. Whoever had gone to the house had left without breaking in. One of the building's windows was smashed, but was boarded up from the inside with what looked like the top of a barrel. Someone must still be home.

'Yatho!' Canovan had come with him, and finally spoken up. An unexpected level of compassion. 'Yatho, it's us!'

'Who the fuck is "us"?' came a voice at last from inside.

'It's Canovan,' he said.

The door rattled with the noise of a bolt shifting, then slid open on its rails. Yatho was standing, a hammer in her hand, its tip bloody. Behind her was Bea, cloth pressed to a split lip with one hand while the other balled and unballed from a fist. He was looking at the floor but had the air of a man about to charge into battle.

'Where is my wife, Canovan?' Yatho snarled, then caught sight of Elogast.

'Where is Inara?' he countered.

'She went with Telle to the archives,' said Yatho. 'They . . .' Her face stirred with fear, and she looked outside the door, fearful of the street.

'Come in.' She moved aside to let them pass. Bea took one or two steps back, fist tightening.

'What's wrong with the boy?' said Canovan, striding in.

'Give him space,' snapped Yatho, forcefully, as Bea shrank back. Canovan stopped, and Elo closed the door behind them.

'It's too much for him,' said Yatho, turning to sit in her chair, then moving between them and Bea. 'He doesn't like to be touched, he doesn't like noise, and he's just had all of it, so he's fucking scared. Leave him alone.' She looked at the lad then said in a firm, soothing voice. 'Bea, I told you, no fighting. Whatever you need to be calm, do that instead.'

Bea shook his head, jaw flexed, then glanced at Canovan and Elo suspiciously and muttered something.

'You recognise them?' asked Yatho. 'You've seen them before?'

Bea nodded.

'They're safe. I know they are, I promise you I don't need protection. Now, what's your job?'

His shoulders settled a little. 'Worksmith apprentice,' he said.

'Are you good at it?' She was doing her best to keep her voice steady.

Bea nodded.

'Then go do your job, make some good metal noise, and when it's safe you can go home to your brother.'

Bea's face twisted and he put his hands over his ears, wracked with indecision.

'I'm safe,' said Yatho, her voice breaking. 'I promise. No more fighting. Please, for me. Stoke the fires, the horse will like it. He'll be frightened too.'

That gave Bea pause, and he looked at the door. He lowered his hands, and Elo realised the boy's knuckles were bloody. He must have tried to fight off whoever had attacked. Bea took a breath, then another.

'And if there's loudness at the gate,' said Yatho, 'what will you do this time?'

Yatho, too, looked ragged and worse for wear. Whatever riot Telle had begun, it had come to find them.

'Come inside,' said Bea. 'Lock the door. Shut the shutters.'

'Do you promise? If I am here or not?'

Bea scoffed, then paused. 'Promise,' he said at last.

'Good. Now go to your work, I'll come into the yard.'

Bea closed his eyes for a moment, and Elo watched Yatho's face almost break with worry. At last the boy nodded once, then turned back down the corridor to the yard. His hands were still flexing, but less violently.

'What happened?' said Elo, following Yatho as she followed him.

'Quiet voices please,' she said.

Elo took a breath, and tried to soften his tone. 'She was supposed to be safe with you.'

'You think I don't know that?' snapped Yatho. The yard was littered with smashed bottles. 'Bea is supposed to be safe with me too. I'm supposed to look after him after so many smithies turned him away.' Her voice tightened. She had blood on her shirt, over her forearm. Beneath it her arm was badly scraped. She had another hammer tucked down the side of her chair with a head the size of his fist.

'They left this morning,' she said. 'For the archives. It was quiet all day . . . then . . .' Her voice tightened. 'Then about six people came running this afternoon. Three in archivists' robes, a knight I think, and a couple of locals. They were yelling for Telle to come out. But she's not—' Yatho put a hand to her head. 'But she's not here.' Her voice cracked. 'I tried to tell them, but then they started throwing things, Bea ran out and I couldn't. Couldn't let him be hurt.' Her knuckles were bloody too. They had put up a good fight.

Elo cast his eyes about for some water, spying a quenching bucket and some rags. He went to fetch them.

'I broke one of their arms, kept them off the gate. Then they ran away as Yether's guards came.'

Elo knelt by Yatho. She frowned as he took her arm but let him clean the wound.

A clanking from the smithy. Bea was sorting out some iron and bridhid rods that had fallen. Legs, to Elo's relief, was in his stable, huffing but not stamping.

'Archivists rioting?' said Canovan, looking half-impressed, but then began to pace. 'Did Telle tell you what she was doing? What she planned?'

'Didn't she tell *you?*' Yatho said, bitterness in her voice.

Canovan stopped and sighed, then shook his head. 'Yath, I'm just the go-between. I connected her with Naia and that was it.'

'Don't call me that,' said Yatho. 'Your wife called me that, and Kissen. You've lost the right.'

Canovan held up his hands and looked to Elo, before remembering that they weren't friends either.

'Tell me anything you know,' said Elo to Yatho instead. 'I'll go and find them.' He should have known Inara wasn't going to sit back politely when he asked her to. But he hadn't expected her to get into trouble quite so quickly.

'She . . .' Yatho shook her head. 'She's supposed to tell me everything. But we had a fight. I didn't think anything when she and Inara went to the archives. I don't know what happened.'

'Then the archives is where I'll start,' said Elo, and Yatho put her hand on his where it held the cloth in place.

Canovan clicked his tongue. 'Don't you have a job to do?' he said.

Elo stood up. 'I'll play your games only so long as it suits me, Canovan,' he said. 'Now I'm delegating. Isn't it time you showed what you're good for, other than casting curses from the sidelines?'

The innkeeper narrowed his eyes. 'I did not stick my neck out for you only for you to get arrested chasing after a girl,' said Canovan.

'You still haven't said why you stuck your neck out for me with the rebels,' said Elo. 'But I think it's because you want a fight.' He went to the stable and opened the door. Legs nickered a greeting. 'Go make it happen, Canovan. Scian's Day is in six days, just before the armies arrive. Naia is printing pamphlets, that's her work. Faroch will be busy keeping the city calm. *You* need to gather your weapons and your people with Ariam. I will join you when I'm sure Ina, and Telle, are safe.'

'I'm coming with you,' said Yatho, putting on her brakes.

Elo shook his head. 'Legs can't take the chair.'

'I'm not an idiot.' Yatho winced as she stood, picking up both of her hammers. 'But nothing is going to stop me finding my wife.'

CHAPTER TWENTY-THREE

Skediceth

SOLOM'S HOME WAS ALL BUT EMPTY. THEY HAD ENTERED
through a narrow door as the chaos of the archives spilled out onto
the plaza, and locked it fast behind them.

Up on the second floor, his furniture was mainly covered in dust
sheets and cobwebs, except for cabinets that displayed all manner of
items from far beyond the Trade Sea. All of them were freshly dusted
and polished: a gaming board from an emperor labelled with a note
of parchment, a piece of embroidered art preserved in glass, a bracelet
of shells, each as blue as a dragonfly and, dangling from it, the
preserved body of a tiny coloured bird the size of Inara's thumbnail.

Telle was standing at the corner windows by the blooming roses,
looking over the cobbles, tense and still. There was a bloodstain at
the gate where a body in pale robes had been taken out and covered
in sheets. There were still two knights in blue guarding it, and six
in yellow who were attempting to get near. Archivists were milling
around the square in small groups, gesticulating and arguing, or
being questioned by the Yether guard. Skedi was sure that if he
and the others attempted to leave they would be spotted, arrested
most likely. They were trapped.

Telle couldn't keep her eyes off the blood, and the body beneath
the sheet. She stood like a statue as the sun fell, and Inara alter-
nated between peering around the room and crouching on one of
the sheeted chairs, silent and guilty.

Skedi, however, had grown impatient with the doleful silence. For the first time, it wasn't his fault at all.

'Elo will come for us,' he said certainly as the shadows lengthened. 'When he finds out, he will come.'

'No, he won't,' said Inara softly. 'He doesn't want us.'

Skedi batted out his wings. How wearisome that Inara wanted to be both a rebellious grown-up and a petulant child at once.

'You know that's not true,' he said.

The doorhandle shook. Someone was coming. Inara looked up, scared and leapt to her feet.

'Skedi, they'll see you.'

Telle turned, perhaps feeling the vibration of Inara landing, and Skedi shrank. Too late to hide.

Solom came through, looking haggard. Behind him was the boy who had saved them from the forum, the signer from Blenraden. The former looked around, relieved to see everything still in order, and Skedi stayed very still, gathering up his will for a lie that might pass him off as another of Solom's trinkets.

But Solom spotted him almost immediately, and his eyes widened.

'You're not mine,' he said.

The Brahim boy looked up and flinched, his colours immediately wrapping tight to his skin as he recognised a god. Skedi tentatively grew in size to a hare.

'No,' he said, then nodded at Inara. 'I am hers.'

Inara held out her arm, and Skedi flew to her and landed, creeping closer to her hair. Solom stared, curious. 'I don't understand,' he said. 'Where is your shrine?'

Though Skedi had never stopped yearning for a shrine, Inara and the others were so used to it he had almost forgotten it was strange not to have one. Like a person without a face. He was relieved when Telle interrupted.

Why did you help us? she said. *Who was killed?* Her hands darted from one question to the next, dancing through movement in stark contrast with her stillness before.

'It was an accident,' said Solom and signed, though his gestures were stilted and clumsy. 'Too many people pushing, a lowered spear.'

Who?

An apprentice called Gia, signed the Brahim boy, still casting Skedi suspicious looks. Now Skedi was closer to him, he could see that he was not so much a boy as a young man, at least six years older than Inara. He was getting better at telling human ages. *Her fathers have been told. She was examined last month.*

Telle put her hand to her mouth, her brow creasing. After a moment, she folded, slowly, to her knees and made a soft, distressed noise.

'Come now,' said Solom, clearing his throat. 'No need for that. You couldn't have known.'

Telle couldn't hear him. Her hands went to her eyes now, as if she could hold herself in, but she could not. Her colours spilled out, stricken with grief. Inara hesitated briefly, then went to her, putting her hands on her back.

'She's deaf, Solom,' said the boy.

When Telle felt Inara's touch, she startled, shaking off her hand as if it burned. Skedi didn't need to tell Inara what the sharp edges of her colours meant, steel and storm: Telle was angry. Though she tried to contain it, standing and turning to the window to take deep breaths.

Inara looked at the floor. 'It's not Telle's fault,' she said. 'It's mine. She didn't know I went down to the vaults. I broke her trust.'

Solom lifted his shoulders in a shrug. 'The pot boiled over because it was already hot,' he said, then threaded his hand into his thick silver hair. 'Yes, any novice worth half a brush would have known not to provoke Betrom, but when I was last here you might have been set to cleaning quills, not arrested. Though I'd love you to tell me how you got past the fool in the first place.'

Telle had gathered herself, her colours calmed, she turned again. *I'm sorry,* she said. *Thank you for sheltering us. We have to go home.*

Telle looked at Inara, then held out her hand. *Come, let's go.*

Inara stared at her, surprised to be invited.

'You can't go,' said the Brahim boy, and signed. *The guards are looking for you, the knights. They still want you arrested, and half the archives. You have to stay here.* He looked at Solom. 'They can't go out there,' he said out loud.

'I know, Cal,' said Solom.

The archives want me arrested? said Telle slowly, baffled. *For speaking? It is our right.*

Inara held tightly to Skedi. 'She didn't do anything wrong. I was the only one who broke a rule.'

They're saying you both caused a riot, said Cal.

Telle's hands hung in the air for a moment. *Have they gone to my home?* she said, her colours blooming with love and fear. She stepped forward furiously. *Have they gone for my wife?*

Inara's pulse quickened, Skedi could feel it through her neck. Yatho was a well-known worksmith, they had been there for hours, and Telle hadn't been able to tell her what they had planned. What would she do if knights came to their house?

Why did Skedi miss Kissen so much?

'I'm sure your wife is fine, Telle,' said Solom, soothingly. 'We have more serious matters to discuss. Your fears for the archives are correct, and what happened today shows me that—'

It doesn't matter, said Telle. *They didn't listen.*

'It does matter!' said Solom fiercely, signing as well. *It matters more.*

He wants to rescue the texts, Cal explained. Telle laughed harshly, shaking her head.

Do what you want, she said. *My wife is my priority.*

She went for the door, and Cal moved to block her. 'You don't understand,' he said, then signed. *If Yether's guards find you, they might offer some protection. If others do . . . if the knights . . .* He shivered, swallowed. *I don't know. I've seen it before. They might want to make an example of you.*

I don't care.

'Let me go,' said Skedi suddenly. *Let me go,* he said to Telle. She winced at his voice in her head, but he could not sign, and he could make some amends for he and Inara's transgression. And, perhaps as a sweet addition, Solom would stop looking at him less like an artefact out of place and more like a god.

Perhaps even a god worth trusting.

I will look around, said Skedi to all of them. *See if there are any pathways out.* Solom looked about to protest, but Skedi reared up on his hind legs and he closed his mouth.

Inara tentatively touched Skedi on his back. 'Is it safe?' she said to him alone.

'I still have flight,' he said, 'if white lies can't carry me.' He flexed his wings. They both looked to Telle, asking her permission, and she folded her arms around herself, then nodded.

'Come straight back,' said Inara. 'Don't be seen. Please.'

'I'll be small as a bird,' Skedi assured her.

She swallowed, then went and unbolted the window door onto the small balcony. A flood of rose-scent and petrichor stirred them both, and he hopped off her shoulder and took to the sky, flitting smaller than a sparrow into the air.

And then he flew. Up and up, he went, to the height of the townhouses, enjoying the freedom just like any other creature, human, god, or animal. Before they had met Kissen, Skedi had never been able to go more than ten feet from Inara without a wrenching ache on his heart. Now, Inara stood at the window, watching him, her face pale as he darted past the chimneys, up through the smoke, to the walls of the cloche.

As he ascended, he looked down, and saw a sea of colour. Not just the city, its tiles and goods, its flags and clothes, but the people. They busied their streets with the radiance of their feelings in all possible hues; love and anger, fear and hope, for each a different gleam, a different meaning. Each street was a river of beauty and light, some clashed, in conflict, some radiated in harmony, like flame. So much feeling, so much potential, so much faith to give. To give to him. No wonder humans made gods: everything they desired and feared just spilled out of them, staining everything they touched.

Skedi had just reached the roof of the cloche when he felt it: the tug, the aching chain. The bond between him and Inara, it was still there. It still hurt.

He dropped a few feet, then tipped his wings, circling back, his fur on end. Though he could see the vibrant roses, he could not see Ina. His strange, angry, frightened girl. He loved her, of course he did. If he was human, his love would be the dark shades of her hair, the brightness of her joy, but he couldn't help the sink of disappointment as he felt the tie that bound him to the earth, to her. He had been known once, far beyond Middren. Would they raise his shrines again if the god of safe haven was remade? In Restish? Could he possibly be who he was before? Without Inara, would he be more real? More himself?

Such thoughts had led him wrong before. He had hurt the person who loved him most, and she still had not all forgiven him. In fact, she had pushed him harder. Into the vaults, when he said he didn't want to go. Into lying, when he said they should run. Now, he supposed, he knew something of how she had felt. He didn't like it.

Skedi flapped his wings, dipping down towards the plaza again now he knew the distance he could move from her.

He circled around the cloche, where guards in yellow were bickering viciously with knights in blue, but they had finally been given access to the body which was being carried away on a stretcher. Archivists were washing blood from the stones with buckets of water filled with pumps inside the square. But Cal was right, there were surly-looking folk grouped in corners, watching the yellows and blues while nursing violence in their own colours. Guards and knights were positioned at all the gates, swords drawn.

We cannot leave now, said Skedi to Inara. *We have to wait at least till dark.*

He paused. A rattle of hooves, a shimmer of colour he recognised, back from the street behind the roses. Skedi flew up and over the archway.

Elo.

Elo had come.

CHAPTER TWENTY-FOUR

Inara

INARA COULDN'T BEAR TO BE BESIDE TELLE. IT HAD SEEMED so simple, just sneaking into the archives as she would her mother's study. She had just wanted to know.

But Telle's colours still trembled with hurt and betrayal, even though she hadn't thought twice about offering to bring Inara home. That was almost worse, Telle's kindness compounding Inara's guilt.

So, when Telle, Solom and Cal entered into quick conversation, talking about the godscripts, the books, how to protect them, Inara moved away. They didn't need her, and she'd already lost sight of Skedi, flitting about the rooftops. The wrench on her heart didn't last long, but she knew what it meant. He had tried to get further away but had not succeeded.

No one really wanted her now; they kept her out of obligation. Her mother had lied and kept her at home. Elo had stayed with her only as long as it was convenient for him. Telle felt obliged to look after her, and Skedi tried to fly the first chance he got. Only Kissen had really chosen her.

Inara stayed at the window with the roses, the thin balcony allowing her to sit just outside, out of sight from the plaza. She had taken off her robes, and now just wore her shirt and leggings. She sat, holding her long braid in her hands, thoughtfully running her fingers down its curls. It was messy again. She no longer looked like her mother.

Evening was closing in, the sun shining across the street and through the blooms, soft and gilded with warmth.

Her skin prickled. A god was near, and it had noted her presence. Looking to the right, she saw what Skedi had pointed out that morning: tucked into the corner of the ledge, half-hidden by thorns, was a pile of sweets and a bowl of mead. No totem, other than a single dried rose.

She didn't want to speak out loud and draw attention, to herself or the god. Could she speak in her mind as she did with Skedi, even if she couldn't see the god? She directed her attention towards the shrine, giving it her sole focus, the centre of her mind.

What is your name? she thought hard.

The dried rose flushed for a moment with life, red and bright.

I am Makioron, said a voice, little more than a whisper, a creak like the twist of branches growing. *Who are you who speaks?*

Inara, she said.

You are not a god.

No, she said uncertainly. She was born of flesh. She looked like her mother, though not as much as she wanted. *How long have you lived here?*

One hundred and twelve years, I have been god here.

Inara blinked. *But you have no form?*

The roses rustled.

Gods come before form, said Makioron. *Only through people do we take shape in their desires. What is a rose but a rose? I have no need of shape, little one, and it has saved me, these recent years. No one has noticed me since they pulled out the offerings at my roots except those who already know I am here.* The voice paused, then said fondly, *Not till Solom returned and refreshed my offerings has anyone spoken to me, but I feel their love as they pass below.*

Unlike Blenraden, where all the people were gone, there were people still in Lesscia who loved their gods, even silently.

So, more gods remain in Lesscia? asked Inara. *Other than Scian?*

Makioron's presence made the roses more vivid, red as blood.

Poor Scian. The heart of the city built on her bones, and as such the target of all their fear. A small bud burst into bloom, its scent heady and rich. *Yes,* the god said. *There are others. The god of paper and the god of wells, the god of inkers and the Geniv Canal. So many, still, forgotten as they watch.*

Small gods, living in corners. Like the god of broken sandals.

Kelt, thought Inara, casting her mind further, over mountains, river and sea. Then, the echo of his voice came back:

Kelt.

The gods were still there. She could still hear them. She was so used to Skedi that she had rarely thought to cast her mind further. If she could hold back a god, could she call them too?

What had Scian said? *Who you are is yet to be written.*

A rush of cool air, and Skedi landed on the balcony beside her.

They need to open the back door, he said, his wing still fluttering. *I led them away from the guards, but it won't be long before they draw attention.*

Inara stood up. *Who?*

Who do you think?

Inara felt her heart lift, then resented it. Elo. She turned back to the room. 'Solom, you need to open your back door.'

'Back door?' he said. 'To the courtyard? It's shared.'

Inara signed to Telle. *It's Elogast.*

Telle nodded at Solom. 'Let him in,' she said out loud.

Solom looked at Cal, who rolled his eyes and disappeared through the door. Inara had gleaned that they were related by marriage. Solom nodded after him, then to Telle. 'I was worried today would be . . . difficult for the lad.'

Telle frowned. *I have heard about him,* she signed, perhaps reminding him to do so as well. He took the hint.

He was in the queen's palace, he said. *When the war began. The madness . . .*

Inara winced, knowing of what he spoke. The curse from the god Tet that had forced half the palace to tear itself apart. She had seen the ruins, the blood staining the great hall.

But, Solom added, *he survived, and saved many of their texts from burning. The archive . . .* He made a gesture out of the window.

They didn't want a cousin of the Brahim name, but I and Perell convinced the others to take him.

Telle half-smiled. *The head took many from Blenraden into the fold,* she said. She had slowed and formalised her speech to make it easier for him to understand.

I know, said Solom. *She tries.*

The stairs creaked and the door burst open. Skedi flew in, followed by Elo and Yatho, who looked pale and uncomfortable without her chair, though ready to fight with two hammers in her belt.

Telle cried out and flew to her. Yatho let out a small 'oof', but she wrapped her arms around Telle, holding her tightly as tears of relief flooded her eyes. Telle buried her face in her neck, her hands going around her waist, and their bodies knotted so close they looked like joined branches of a vine. They didn't speak. Words didn't seem to matter.

Elo stepped away, his eyes finding Inara.

'You're all right,' he said, coming closer, but she stepped back. What was she supposed to feel? Anger? Relief? Abandonment? She felt it all and didn't know what to do. Pain passed over Elo's face and colours, the latter silvery bright. 'I'm sorry,' he said. 'I came as quickly as I could.'

Telle and Yatho broke apart. *My love,* Telle was signing. *You're in pain, where's your chair?*

I rode a horse, said Yatho, with an additional sign that looked not too dissimilar to a swear. Their hands danced, their colours softening as their emotions aligned. *Are you all right?* Yatho asked. *Did they hurt you?*

Telle shook her head, directing her wife to a chair and helping her sit. Then she sat beside her, heavily. *We're not hurt,* she said, then hesitated before adding. *But I'm not all right. I was . . . so scared.*

You tried to speak to them, Yatho said, *didn't you?* Telle hesitated, then nodded. *You did what I asked.* Yatho rubbed her face, which was already marked with white streaks and dirt. She was hurt, her arm gashed and bruised. *It's my fault.*

It isn't. I should never have lied to you.

Solom had no chance of following their speech, so he shook his head and looked at Elo. 'So, if that's her wife, who are you and why are you in my house?'

'He *was* Knight Commander Elogast.' Cal had just come in, and leaned back against the doorframe.

If Solom was surprised by Skedi, he was appalled by Elo. 'You're the one who sacked Blenraden?'

Elo raised an eyebrow. 'Sacked is a bit strong,' he said stiffly. 'Liberated is what we said at the time.'

Cal laughed, his voice a little high and hysterical. Elo ignored him. There was something different in him since Inara had seen him last, only days ago. He looked . . . bigger. More frightening. 'Yatho,' he said, his voice solemn.

Yatho paused in her conversation, then nodded. *The king is coming,* she said to Telle. *To Lesscia. It's sudden, we only have a few days.*

'What?' said Solom. 'King what?'

'She says the king is coming to Lesscia,' Cal whispered, dread in his voice.

Elo says we should leave, Yatho continued. *With Inara and Bea, maybe his brother. There's nothing good for us here.*

'No!' said Inara. She looked defiantly at Elo. 'We can't leave. I won't.'

'Ina . . .'

Inara, please, said Skedi. *Elo says he's bringing an army.*

'Leave?' said Solom, frowning at Telle. 'We have work to do. We have important work to do.'

'What work?' said Yatho dismissively, but Telle grasped her hands, and looked at her pleadingly till she softened.

My work, said Telle. *Everything I've fought for. Everything I believe in. I can't let him destroy it all.*

Yatho stared at her for a moment. *You're more like Kissen every day,* she said. *You want to fuck them all over.*

Telle laughed, leaned over to put her head against Yatho's knee, then looked up and nodded. *We want to save the manuscripts,* she said. *Take them away. As many as we can. To Daesmouth. Further, maybe.*

'I don't know what you're discussing,' said Elo suspiciously, 'but whatever it is, I would advise against it.'

'We are going to rescue the endangered books,' said Solom.

Elo looked incredulous. 'Books?' he said. 'This city is about to be under siege. On Scian's Day we will fight back, before the king arrives. If you already have guards after you you won't want to be here if anything goes wrong.'

'They want to *do* something,' snapped Inara. 'They don't want to be patted on the head and told to go away.'

Elo looked about to protest, then ran his hand over his head and glanced at Skedi. The god had jumped back onto one of the cabinets and preened his wing. Inara scowled. What had they been saying to each other?

'I only want to protect you, Ina,' said Elo gently.

'I didn't ask for your protection. I asked you for vengeance.'

'You will have it! By my blade, I promise you will have it.'

Inara half-laughed. Despite the power in his stance, Inara could see something in his colours, some uncertainty. Love, still there, a sneaking, silver-tinged blue: Arren. 'I don't believe you,' she said, and he sucked his teeth in frustration. 'You need me,' she pressed.

Inara, please, said Skedi suddenly, directly into her mind. He stood up on his hind legs, looking down on her from the cabinet. He batted his wings for her. *For me too.*

Inara looked around. All the adults were looking at her, some with pity. Even Telle. She found what she wanted to say catching in her throat stoppered by Skedi's pleading eyes. None of them were on her side. They didn't want her; they didn't need her. Again.

Help us, said Telle, to Inara's surprise. Yatho had been keeping her informed of their conversation. *We need to get into the archives and out again,* she said. *They're occupied most nights and are always under guard. We'll need all the hands we can get to get them to Daesmouth. And . . .*

She looked at Skedi, who stretched a little, picking up his antlers. She had wondered for a moment why Telle would have asked for her help when she had betrayed her trust only hours before, and didn't even know the extent of Inara's power, but now it made sense: Skedi.

'What do you mean?' said Cal.

Skedi gazed at Inara a moment longer, before answering. 'I am Skediceth, god of white lies,' he said. 'It sounds like you may need them.'

CHAPTER TWENTY-FIVE

Kissen

DAWN BROKE ORANGE OVER THE BENNITES, TURNING ALL the shining snows as vivid as mirrors in a brothel. Aan's pool, untouched by the wild air outside, gleamed as the sun spilled across it. It half-blinded Kissen where she sat at the edge of Doric's cave, contemplating Osidisen's dagger in her hands. The gems in it were the dark, shining grey of his eyes, like water-washed stone.

'You should rest some more,' said Doric, coming to sit beside her. He was sucking on a long old pipe that smelled of Curlish herbs. A long way for such things to travel: they must have been brought as an offering for Aan.

The god and her hermit lived in strange peace. She did not appear to pay him much attention, but he was content to tend her stones and flags and turn whatever she was offered into her waters. If she cared to peer beneath the surface of the lake, Kissen knew she would see gold and jewels, woven tapestries and banners. Perhaps even, like Osidisen, the standards of fallen enemies, their bloodied mail, their weapons. But whose enemies? Her river passed through many lands. How many sides had she taken?

'I'll rest when I'm dead,' said Kissen. She couldn't deny that Doric's company was pleasant. He needed nothing from her and had no fear of a war which would take an age to make a difference at Aan's source. If his god died, Kissen did not think he would long outlast her. Senfa also seemed happy enough, even without grass. She was drinking directly from Aan's waters, her tail swishing gently. Kissen sometimes wondered about animals and gods, whether horses could love a deity. Certainly, there were gods of cattle, gods of wild things, gods of birds. Were they shaped by humans alone, or did animals also pray for love and safety? Did they also fear war?

War. Kissen had seen too much to doubt what Hseth would become. She knew how gods were made and remade. No wonder Aan was scared. Hseth was worse than a hundred godkillers, a thousand; she sucked the love and life from other gods. Even Arren she had used for an invasion of his land, body, heart and mind. Kissen wondered if the king yet realised what had been plotted against his ambition.

What of Arren? If Middren's king fell now, he would leave chaos behind him. And Hseth would fill it, just as she had done in Talicia.

But this king wanted to be a god himself. He already had his own designs on power and war. If he lived, what would he become? Would it be better than Hseth, as Aan thought, or worse?

She couldn't know.

Kissen groaned and put her head on her left knee. No path was certain. She wasn't a politician to play at games of land and power. All she knew was that all her loves were in Middren. Loves she wanted to protect. What would hurt them more? An army from the land and sea, or a mad king within?

'Tea?' said Doric, kicking a kettle at his foot closer to her.

Kissen lifted her head to gaze at it, then sighed and took a long swig to wet her throat. Barley tea, toasted. It tasted like childhood.

'Not a bad thing,' said Doric into her silence, 'this, every morning.' He nodded at the bright water, the ragged mountains.

'Even when it hails?'

Doric cast her a side eye. 'When it hails,' he said, 'I sit further back.'

Kissen snorted and took another drink from the spout before passing the kettle back.

'Why do you live here, anyway?' she said. 'What's in it for you?'

'Peace and quiet, usually,' he said dryly. Kissen just looked at him, and he chuckled. 'The source of Aan's river has been here since long before these lands were tamed,' he said. 'Living here is like living in time, speaking to the centuries, and the god Aan is the centuries speaking back. All the haggling, the squabbling, petty scraps and pointless deaths of the world . . . they fade away under a broad sky and clear water.'

'And Aan would pay as much heed to your passing as you would a tick in your bed,' said Kissen. 'Gods that live long forget the value of human lives.'

Doric shrugged. 'You're telling me you've never met a god who still loves humans?'

Kissen twirled the dagger in her hand again. To her surprise, Osidisen had remembered her father, and her family. 'Veiga are rarely called to gods that are well liked.'

'So, you don't have faith in anything?' said Doric, somehow baffled.

A question she had been asked endless times. She rolled her eyes. 'Faith does not fill the lungs, the belly or the sky,' Kissen said. 'Faith doesn't bring fruit from the boughs, or put water in the sea, or flame in the fire.'

'I've never met a person who believes in nothing at all.'

'I believe in myself.'

He laughed in a puff of smoke, then choked on it and spluttered, coughing until Kissen gave him a pat on the back and he took a swig of his tea.

'The self can only see what the eyes give it,' said Doric. 'You don't know how many cubs are being born in the valleys. Or which side of the mountain will be next to fall.'

'I can guess,' said Kissen.

'With the experience of a paltry thirty or so years,' said Doric. 'How many years has Aan's water known? How many centuries of memory does she hold? If you do not know yourself what will happen next, who do you trust to guess better than a god?'

Kissen rubbed her tongue against her gold tooth. Two months before, she would have told him to go fuck himself. But, since then, a little girl and a god had come to her aid, and she had seen a king sacrifice his friend for power. Had killed a god, then found them ready to live again within a moon's rise.

'She's giving you a chance to change the world, godkiller,' said Doric.

'People like me don't change the world,' said Kissen. 'We just survive it.'

The hermit scoffed. 'Tell that to a girl with one leg who picked a fight with a fire god and won because she hasn't a single bending bone in her body.' She laughed, but when he looked over, he wasn't smiling. 'Just be careful, godkiller. If you do not bend to the world, it might snap you.'

'I know that,' said Kissen. 'More than most.' She looked down at her hands. Scarred and worn, hard-working hands. Unpretty hands. They served her well, as her body served her, her mind did her will. She had two choices, really. Move, or hide.

And she had never been one for hiding.

She hooked the staff under her arm and stood up, stiffly. Then looked at the knife. 'If you're still watching me, rat-drowner,' she said to it, 'I might still have a use for you.'

But it was another god she needed first.

'Come on then, Aan,' Kissen said to the waters of the river god. 'I know you're listening.'

Aan's head slid up through the water, her dark hair draped around her shoulders and her cheeks pink as if nipped by cold.

'You are ready to listen?' the god asked.

'My family first. Are they well? Are they safe?'

Aan paused. 'I cannot find what is not near water.'

'I know you watch the girl,' said Kissen. 'I know she is with them.' Well, she had guessed, had hoped, but Aan's annoyed expression told her she was right.

'They are hale and healthy,' said Aan. 'But they are on the edge of trouble. The girl begins to understand that their paths cannot continue as one.'

'We'll see,' said Kissen. Whatever great interest Aan had in Inara, Kissen wouldn't let the girl become a god's new toy. 'And you'll watch the horse?'

'She is free to stay till the melt reaches here, then she is free to go,' said Aan.

At least that was one thing Kissen had done right by. Senfa deserved a turn at freedom.

'All right.' Kissen steeled herself. 'So how do you propose to get me to the king?'

Aan raised her shoulders out of the water. Its surface did not change or ripple. 'You don't want me to heal your wounds?' she said. 'Fix your leg? Your scars? Give you a shining shield of ice . . .' she paused and looked Kissen up and down. 'Clean you?'

Kissen looked down, surprised. 'No,' she said. 'Why? Yatho will fit me a better leg and relying on magic is a fool's game. As for healing, I'm pretty sure whatever poultice Doric used has some of your blessing in it.'

'You'd be hard pressed to find anything around here that doesn't,' said Doric, tipping his pipe out onto the ground.

'So,' said Kissen. 'Tell me.'

'You won't like it,' said Aan, rising out of the pool. Shoulders, breasts, round belly, rippling thighs, the water clinging to her like silk. It grazed her skin in drifts and eddies, less clothing, more adornment. It barely hid the dark of her nipples or her sex, and Kissen's mouth went immediately dry.

Now, Aan was toying with her. That meant she *really* wasn't going to like it.

'Only one thing other than fire can get you to Middren faster than water.'

'What?'

'Air.'

Kissen stared at her. 'Fuck,' she said.

'Indeed.'

'No.'

Aan flicked out her silks and stopped at the shore. 'I thought trust was no longer an issue.'

'You, I trust as far as I can throw you and no further.' Which was not, in fact, very far. 'But that bastard, I wouldn't . . .'

'Be careful,' said Aan. 'They have been waiting, and time, my veiga, is running out.'

Kissen glared at the edge of Aan's shrine where the wind tore about its merry way. That wind that had killed several Talicians in a moment, had helped Kissen bloody her blade with a boy's life. She shivered. The wind and its wild god: Faer.

'Shit,' she said. Was she going to back out now? No. She balled her fists. Her blade had killed the boy, it was her responsibility. She had to accept that. Did blood sit as sourly in Elo's gut, or was it just her it seemed to burn?

'Call him then, river god,' said Kissen. 'You'd better be right about this, or I'll come back and kill you myself.'

Aan laughed softly. 'You can try.'

Kissen didn't move from where she stood, but the water behind Aan curdled. A moment of rippling, then eruption: a column of foam speared the sky. It struck the air and hissed out sideways like a banner in the wind before falling back to earth. A wave of cold, chill air rolled into the sheltered valley, and Kissen suppressed a shiver.

'Godkiller.' Doric was behind her. She turned, and he was holding out a thick cloak in long soft leather, dyed a deep red and lined with fur. Kissen stared at it, so he pressed it into her hands.

'I have no use for such things here,' he said. 'Nor Aan, and its owner did not care for it.'

Kissen closed her hand on it. She had never held something so fine. 'Thank you,' she said to Doric, meaning it, and held out her hand. He clasped her wrist.

'Pato would be proud of you,' he said.

Kissen allowed herself a small smile. 'If there's a next time,' she said, 'I'll bring you better wine.'

Doric grinned and stepped back so Kissen could throw the cloak around her. Her shoulder still ached where it had taken Senfa's hoof and the arrow, but it wasn't excruciating, and the weight of the leather was a comfort. She buttoned it carefully as the air beyond the shrine screamed.

The wind arrived. Pieces of leaves, snow, earth and twigs skittered around the edges of the rocks, circling Kissen in a twist of gale but not daring to touch the water. Aan's white flags snapped out, stretched horizontal for a few moments, the edges fraying, before they fell still once more, and a god stood between them: Faer.

He had taken a masculine form. His horns were a goat's, and his legs too, thick and matted, with leaves tangled in the powerful flanks and the wool on his aggressively large balls. Above them, his chest was bare and hairy, human-like, with long pale arms that ended in silver claws. Those looked as if they would strip a pine of its bark.

Instead of a face, the god bore a stone mask of white, with great carved cheeks rounded as if they were ready to blow. The eyes cut into it were dark and curved as if smiling, but Kissen had no doubt that could change in an instant. She had killed a wind god once, caught her in a net of briddite wires; they were fast little fuckers, and liked a good trick better than anything.

'So,' said Faer loudly from where he stood. 'Your pet project has heeded you, great Aan of the mountain water.'

Kissen shifted on her legs, testing her balance. If she closed her eyes, she could feel both of her ankles squeezing, her calves aching. She ignored Faer, knowing it would annoy him. He kept his wind to a respectful level, but still its presence rattled the items in Doric's cave. She wasn't going to be intimidated by a blustery old bastard, barely tethered to the shrines that still stood for them. Anyone who spoke and remembered the name of their wind, the Faera, spoke the name of the god. It slipped into their mouths, on their tongue, bringing the wind on their breath.

'Be welcome to my waters, Faer of the mountain wind,' said Aan. 'The veiga has heeded our warnings. It is time to take her to the king.'

'Does the veiga make an offering?' The god's eyes had tipped and turned downwards into his distended cheeks, angry.

Kissen had never made an offering at a shrine. Never. Even when she had tried to summon Hseth she had offered only her anger. 'I have little,' she said. 'Only my blood.'

She placed Osidisen's knife on the back of her arm, but hesitated. She had to, for her family, for Inara. There was no way Faer could carry her to Lesscia on his own.

Faer cackled and the laugh ricocheted around the pool, their face changing before Kissen's eyes. Wind stung her skin, played at her hair.

'Your blood, reluctantly given, is not enough,' he said. 'You have bled for friends, for family, for strangers you do not know. You part with your blood for love and rage: it is not for me.'

Aan cast Kissen her dark, shining gaze. The two gods were so different, but their age was alike. Faer was asking a lot, an offering in Aan's shrine, an offering from a godkiller no less. But Aan's look told Kissen that it was necessary.

It had to be something she didn't want to part with. Kissen swore under her breath, thinking of the knife again. No, that was an offering for Osidisen, and she suspected she was going to have use of it.

The only other option was her cutlass. Her last briddite weapon. To be without it, travelling at the whim of a wild god, was not how she had hoped to spend her day. She pulled it out, and the gods both flinched. The air cooled a little.

Another stupid idea. But it would be enough, more than enough, to satisfy them both.

'Then I offer you both my last defence, my protection,' said Kissen, turning the sword so that she was holding it by the blade in her left hand, and dropped the pommel to the ground. 'Aan, to break the blade that could have hurt you. Faer, to scatter the shards.'

Aan smiled. The wind stirred her watery silks and her pool brightened. 'I accept your offering,' she said, before Faer could respond. 'It will rust to nothing on our mountainside, hurting nothing, not even the deer who step on it. May this shared gift between us seal our pact to save these lands from fire.'

Faer's stone face drifted, becoming not stone but silver air for a moment as they considered. Then: 'I accept,' they said, their words whispering in Kissen's ears with a sting.

Aan gestured, and her water leapt out of the pool and seized the sword. With a flick of her fingers the water froze into ice for a blisteringly cold moment, then she *twisted*.

The blade shattered into fragments as Faer spread his hands wide. Wind howled through the valley and screeched across the water, catching up all the fragments of the sword and ripping them into the air, up, over the peak above Aan's shrine and glinting as they scattered.

Kissen braced herself. Faer's chest puffed up, bigger, and wider. The air around him intensified, and the hairs on Kissen's arms stood on end as clouds welled up behind them into a wall of thick grey, rising over the peaks like the front of a helm.

'Good luck, godkiller,' said Aan, then Faer launched himself at Kissen with a howl, the wind raging at their sides, their back, their heels, slamming into her with all his might, ripping her off the ground and away into the sky.

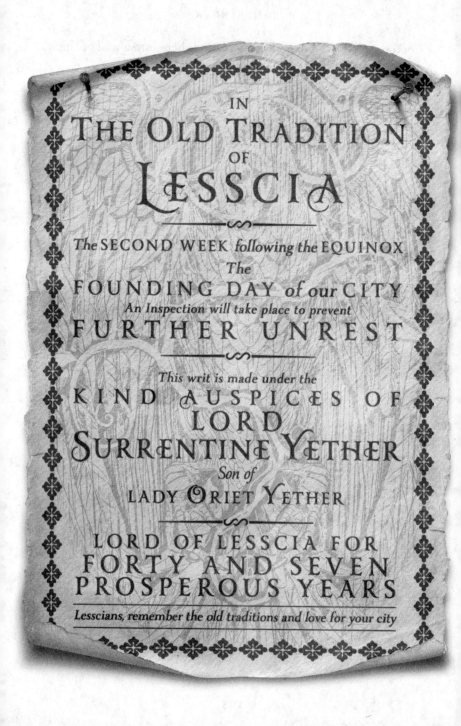

IN

THE OLD TRADITION
OF
LESSCIA

The SECOND WEEK *following the* EQUINOX
The
FOUNDING DAY *of our* CITY
An Inspection will take place to prevent
FURTHER UNREST

This writ is made under the
KIND AUSPICES OF
LORD
SURRENTINE YETHER
Son of
LADY ORIET YETHER

LORD OF LESSCIA FOR
FORTY AND SEVEN
PROSPEROUS YEARS

Lesscians, remember the old traditions and love for your city

CHAPTER TWENTY-SIX

Elogast

Elo sat in the theatre, waiting, beside him a basket of baked nameen. He hadn't intended to make it, but he had not slept, back again in Canovan's inn, and he had nothing to do except wait for the evening. The pamphlets had been distributed, spread as wide as they could through the inkers' networks, the archives, the sex-workers' guild, the merchants' guild, the boaters, the paper-makers, the worksmiths, the carters. Anyone they had a connection to, no matter how slight, had pasted them to walls, daubed them in yellow ink. Naia had her own network of students, teachers, archivists, pacifists. Elo held one in his hand. He had read and reread it.

Yether had given it his eagle and vine sigil, but only the night would tell if anyone had listened. Every day brought Arren and his march nearer. Every day was a step closer to standing before him with a sword in his hand.

If he could just hold the walls for long enough, force Arren to negotiate, to get him close enough to his blade. If he could just get Inara out before things went wrong . . .

Too many ifs. Too many possibilities. Too little time.

Gods, please let him save just one girl. Whether she wanted him to or not.

The way she had looked at him, with more anger than he had

thought possible. Elo wished he could work with her to understand her strength, to control it, but Yatho and Telle would help her. He had to do this grim, brutal work of playing war.

The theatre door opened, a square of brightness into a rich and golden evening; though where he sat he was mainly in shade as the sun slipped beyond the walls, dragging time with it.

Faroch came in. He had twelve guards with him, sidling in one after the other, looking uncomfortable, nervous, but determined. It had been a hard week for the vanguard, quelling squabbles and riots across the city. But most were ready to bring a fight back to the knights that had killed a Lesscian. Elo would take five of them.

Soon after, Ariam entered. 'What have you got there?' he said immediately, nodding at the basket.

Elo looked at it. 'Nameen,' he said.

'Supper?'

'If you want it.'

Ariam had brought more people. Twenty folks came piling in in twos and threes, one after the other.

'The knight brought bread!' the inker leader said with a grin, coming to the basket. The tension in the air softened, and several approached, eager for food. Elo nodded at Faroch, who sent over his own guards. It had been a long day, and he had made a lot. It was not as fluffy as he would have liked, the sides not as evenly crisped as they would have been in his own ovens or his mothers' pot-sided sand pit.

Still, it smelled familiar as the gathered rebels broke open their pieces, mumbling approvingly. He'd been able to purchase some of the less expensive herbs quite easily outside the city when he had gone out with Naia's pamphlets. Guards stood next to inkers, dissidents all of them, eating together. When Naia came in, a heavy bag weighing down her shoulder, she looked pleasantly surprised.

Last time Elo had baked nameen, Arren had been with him. He had lied to his face and sent him to die.

I don't believe you, Inara had said.

Not Arren. He needed to stop thinking of him as Arren. As the boy he grew up with, the man he had protected. King.

But it was still too close to King Arren. Too close for comfort.

Elo stood as Naia came over to him. 'I have a present for you,' she said. Her bag landed with a clunk as she put it down. Then she took one of the remaining pieces of nameen from the basket and took a bite. She frowned. 'The herbs are wrong.'

'It's what I could afford,' said Elo. He leaned over to the bag and opened it. Right at the top he found a breastplate, beautifully designed and inlaid with a lion of lapis and gold, its etched fur waving as it moved.

'Why are you giving me . . . this?' he said, touching the buckles, almost in awe. The leather was freshly oiled, and the armour exquisitely made. Irisian, or a good approximation. The patterns in the beading, the embellishment, were classic scrollwork from the art of his mothers' land.

'They were my great grandfather's,' said Naia. 'Passed down to me over my sisters. Little did he know they would never quite . . . fit.' She smiled, looking from the plate to Elo. 'Not a perfect fit for you either, but it's better than an old shirt and jacket. And if you want to lead, best to look like a leader.'

Elo pulled out a pauldron, also detailed with scrolls and waves. The Irisian god of change was often compared to clouds and tides. 'I can't wear this,' he said. His shoulder ached, and in his mind he saw a flash of blood and gold. The god of war. That was the last time he had worn armour. Real armour. His heart rattled, and his hands shook as he lowered the plate. 'It's an heirloom.' It should be something she passed to siblings, children. Not to strangers. 'And the lion is the king's symbol, not mine.'

'Was,' she said, taking another bite of her flatbread. It made a satisfying cracking sound. 'He has a new symbol now. Anyway, lions were Irisian first, not Middrenite.' She took the breastplate from him and held it up to his chest, tutting. She had dark bags under her eyes from lack of sleep, and her bottom lip she had chewed to pieces. Her hands, too, were rough from late nights arranging press letters and helping teams print and pick up page after page.

'If you look at me too closely you'll go blind,' said Naia, and Elo blushed.

'I'm sorry,' he said, and she smiled.

'No fear, it's looking at you that made me bring this.' She pressed it into his chest. 'How likely are people to follow your orders if you look like some ruffian out of a ditch?' Elo laughed, but Naia didn't. She regarded him sternly now and stepped in close. 'The better this works, the less fighting there will be. That's all I want, *Ser* Elogast.' She used his title. 'Bring me peace.'

Elo took a careful breath. She was right. This was it. He had chosen this, to pick up his sword again. And now, to put on his armour. 'Thank you,' he said. No more protests. No more uncertainty. He would be his own lion now.

'Good. There's quilting in there too, Faroch can help you put it on.'

Faroch looked up at his name. He also looked worse for wear, managing both the choice of guards to help with the rebellion, while keeping the city in one piece. No surprise that Yether had promoted him to captain.

'Are you and your people prepared?' Elo asked him.

He nodded. 'We are ready.'

'And yours?' Elo said to Ariam.

The inker looked at the others and a few nods were exchanged. Nerves came out in the inkers' bodies; they tapped their fingers, cleared their throats, blinked at the sky. Like Faroch, Ariam had not brought his whole force, but someone Elo had expected was still missing.

'Where's Canovan?'

Ariam shrugged. He had braided his hair back from his neck and wore his purple sash still. 'Praying, I think. Last I saw he'd bought a goat.'

Praying or summoning? Lethen's demons had always attacked them when the sun went down. Elo had not asked him to use his connection with Lethen – the evening they had chosen belonged to a different god.

But it was evening, when the god of the ways was at her most powerful.

'Now?' said Faroch, not comprehending.

'We could do with gods on our side tonight, captain,' said Ariam.

Faroch grunted, discomfited. Elo had gathered that the captain thought gods were better not seen and not heard. He wanted the city back, that was all.

'Don't worry, captain,' Ariam added. 'Canovan's with me. He's a good arm in a fight, has saved me from a spat or two. I trust him.'

Elo didn't. Canovan wanted to fight more than he wanted to win. If he was making a sacrifice . . . Elo didn't want to think what he would get up to.

'I'll go check on him,' said Naia, sounding almost as suspicious as Elo felt. She gave him a long glance. 'Good luck,' she added.

'We'll be fine, Naia,' said Ariam, nudging her. 'It's going to be fun.' She rolled her eyes but managed a smile as she went for the door.

Elo rubbed his brow, then cleared his throat. 'Lesscians,' he said, his voice carrying through the room. He spoke with his belly, drawing up power from his breath and his gut. He was a tall man, he knew it, so he stood to his full height and command. They all fell silent. 'Tonight is ours. The dark of the day of Scian, the founder of Lesscia, this great city.'

A stir of anticipation ran through them. Elo had seen it before. A setting of the shoulders, a shift of the feet, a stirring of the heart. He hoped if they had gods to pray to, they had already given their offerings.

'It's time for us to take it back.'

CHAPTER TWENTY-SEVEN

Skediceth

THE COBBLES AROUND THE CLOCHE WERE SILENT. EVEN Skedi, knowing why most of the city folk had disappeared into their homes, found it eerie.

Two guards again kept watch at the front gate of the archive, their colours showing dull: weariness and boredom. It had been a week since the riots, and it had taken two days for the city to calm enough again for Telle and Inara to make it back to the smithy to prepare. But even now, the city felt quelled and oppressive. Yellow-sashed guards made frequent rounds, and most of the king's knights had been advised to keep to their barracks, save those at the archives, the gates and the docks.

If anything, the riot had done Elo and his rebels a favour.

But still, there were blue sashes before the cloche, and Skedi and Inara were waiting with the Brahim boy, Cal, on Solom's little window balcony as darkness deepened. One by one, the lights in the surrounding houses winked on, flickering and warm.

'I've been told I'm a bad liar,' Cal murmured, gazing down at the gates. He frequented the archives at night as routine, so he would cause the least suspicion. Skedi wondered if that was for the hush after the bells of quiet ended, or because there would be fewer prying eyes and whispers of 'Blenraden'.

'A white lie is not a bad lie,' Skedi whispered back from where he sat, the size of a mouse, in Inara's collar, his antlers and nose poking out. He could feel the god of the roses watching them, watching her, curious. It annoyed him. 'It's more like a . . . softening of the truth. White lies are to protect, to encourage, not to hurt.'

'Most of the time,' said Inara pointedly. She had been quieter than usual, her colours contained and careful. He shouldn't have encouraged her to give up her dream of vengeance and battle, but what could she truly do to a king? Better to grow, to wait, to let Elo take the sword. For a moment, he had been tempted to try to will her into it. He still was. Day by day, he could feel them growing further apart, wanting different things.

Skedi fluffed up his fur and peered at Cal. The lad had light brown hair, cropped neatly to his ears, a warm olive tint to his skin, and the hint of a scar on his left wrist and around his lip. He was chewing at his thumbnail, watching the guards.

'Why do they call you Brahim boy?' said Skedi.

Cal looked at him with surprise. 'I'm a cousin of the Brahim family,' he said as if it were obvious.

'But you're not a boy.'

Cal's colours stirred above his skin for a moment, a complex twist of cerulean and jade, gone too quickly for Skedi to understand their meaning. 'They want to make me feel small,' he said. 'Most blame my family for what happened, so when I came here . . . well, they didn't like it.'

'Like Telle,' said Inara.

'Not like Telle,' he scoffed. 'They don't like her because she's nobody. They don't like me because I'm somebody they hate.'

Inara tutted much like Elo did when he was exasperated. 'Telle isn't nobody,' she said.

'You wouldn't understand, you're like her.'

Skedi revised his understanding. Cal was *definitely* a boy. Inara looked as if she was about to slap him. *You are from a House,* Skedi said to her, just in her mind. *As powerful as his.*

It shouldn't matter, she fired back.

'Why are you helping her then?' she whispered to Cal. He sniffed.

'I'm helping Solom,' he corrected. 'And some of those manuscripts are all that remains of my family library.'

'Telle wants them because it's the right thing to do,' said Inara. 'You want them for a stupid legacy.'

'It's not stupid,' said Cal quietly. 'They're all that's left.'

Inara stiffened, and Skedi felt a wave of colour wash over him Grief, unexpected in her anger. Ah, she had thought of her own home, her own library, her own family.

'Not all,' said Skedi, he directed it at Cal, but spoke to Inara. 'There's you.'

Her jaw tightened, and she looked away, down at the plaza, then straightened up. 'He's leaving,' she said. 'Let's go.'

It was what they had been waiting for. One of the guards clapped the other on the back in a friendly way, though from all the way at the rose arch they heard the slap of it. Maybe not all friendly. He then walked away from his post, heading west, oblivious to the tense, waiting silence of the street. Cal said the man always went to gamble for a few hours after dusk. The inn he frequented was already prepared. Skedi wondered which of Elo's rebels would catch him.

The remaining guard stared around the square for a moment, then leaned against the wall. The yellow annoyance that had flared as his companion walked away faded, leaving his shades in muted russet. After a while, he pulled an old shirtsleeve from his pocket, and a needle and thread, then began darning.

Inara, Cal and Skedi slipped down Solom's stairs and out into the courtyard. Skedi was well hidden within Inara's hair, which was loose now and tucked around him. They stepped out into the street, and around, under the rose arch before walking quietly towards the remaining guard. Cal was in his darker grey uniform of a junior archivist, and had found Inara the greys of a senior apprentice.

'Ruki!' Cal called, waving at the guard.

'What now?' Ruki said, lifting his chin to see who was intruding on his solitude. Suspicion stained him the colour of white marble.

Skedi already knew his task. As soon as Cal called his name, Skedi wrapped his will around the knight, ready to press lies in among the truths.

'What do you mean, "what"?' said Cal, laughing disarmingly, and nervously enough for it to feel appropriate. Perhaps, Skedi thought, he was a better liar than he had suspected. 'I'm here most nights, though this time I'm lumbered with this one.' He nodded at Inara, who folded her arms and looked irritated. She didn't need to put much effort into it. 'Idiot translated the wrong passage, and did a shit job anyway, so she's been told to sit with me and do it again by morning.'

The lie took, easily. The guard barely hesitated. 'Unlucky sod,' he said to Inara. No recognition in his colours, though Skedi's soothing might have seen to that.

'They say midnight oil burns brightest,' Cal added, and Ruki laughed.

'Yes, my commander said much the same thing.' He scratched his chin where he had an unsettlingly purple rash. 'Got your papers?'

Cal and Inara produced them, his legal, hers forged by another archivist Solom had pressed to their cause. Ruki gave them a cursory glance, then shrugged. 'Go on then,' he said. 'No one else in there I think.' He stopped scratching. 'Quiet tonight. What's this founding day about?'

Cal hesitated. It would not be long before this knight was in gaol with his fellows, or dead if he tried too hard to resist.

Let it be, said Skedi to Cal, who managed to cover the ache of Skedi piercing his mind by rubbing his temple. *Tell him it's just an old tradition.*

Cal swallowed. 'Just an old thing,' he said. 'They'd usually have a parade in the day, and feasts indoors in the evening, the idea is to leave the place peaceful.' He shrugged. 'Basically an early curfew, it looks like, to stop any more fighting.' For someone who said he wasn't a good liar, Skedi had met worse. Kissen, for example.

Skedi increased the hold of his will on the guard, who nodded.

'Aye. That was a bad business. Didn't think a bunch of paper-turners would get so rowdy.' He leaned back against the wall.

'Same here.'

'Can we go in please?' said Inara, tired of the chit chat. 'I've got thirty-odd pages to redo and I'd like to be home before noon tomorrow.'

Now *that* was a liar. Skedi felt a little proud.

'Sure,' said Ruki. 'Just don't do anything I wouldn't do.'

'What, you mean reading?' said Cal.

'Ha ha.'

Cal ushered Inara after him into the tunnel, which must have been pitch-black to the humans, other than the scent and glow of dying incense that guided them to the opening by the forum. On the other side, the fig trees barely moved in the stillness of the night. The archives, too, were mostly unlit, save for some lamplight on the second floor and another flicker of a few candles at the very top.

Cal breathed out, his relief palpable, even if Skedi couldn't see it hanging on the air around him.

'Is it usually busier than this?' said Inara.

Cal nodded. 'Much,' he said. 'I was expecting some like Betrom to stay in protest against Scian, but what happened to Gia must have scared them off. Come on.' He hurried beneath the colonnades to a door that would take them down to the vaults. The doors to the stairs were open, but the passage down to the vaults was closed. He produced a key from his pocket and put it carefully to the lock.

'They lock it now?' said Inara.

'Yes, thank you for that,' said Cal with some sting. 'This is Balefor's. He's one of the few still allowed one. He hates gods, but texts to him are sacred.'

The bolt clicked as it turned, abominably loud in the courtyard, and the door itself groaned as Cal pulled it open, as if in pain. Skedi was already whispering: *Nothing is heard, nothing is seen, all is well, nothing has changed.*

There was no movement, no shout, just quiet.

Inara and Cal slipped inside, swinging the door shut behind them and locking it, enclosing them in darkness. This time even Skedi's night vision failed him. He hopped off Inara's shoulder and to the ground, growing to his hare's size.

'Well done,' he said.

'I could hear your power,' said Cal. 'Like a buzzing at my ears. I'm glad it worked.'

'Flattered,' said Skedi, with some sarcasm. He didn't like the sound of 'buzzing', nor that he had not thought it would work.

'You can't blame me for my surprise,' Cal added. 'You shouldn't exist, you and the girl. I lived in Blenraden most of my life and I never saw a god without a shrine.'

'That is not the first time we have heard such a thing.'

'Come on,' hissed Inara, already walking down the stairs.

Skedi hopped after her steps, the echoes of her feet, the soft brush of her fingers against the wall, captured in the close, thick dark of the stairwell. When they reached the vaults, the sound of their breath, their movement rushed away from them, arching and echoing up the walls.

'There has to be a lamp here somewhere,' said Cal, blindly feeling the wall.

Inara rustled in her pocket. A click, scrape, and a spark flew into the air like starshine in the darkness. Flint. Kissen's flint and striker: she had kept it with her. Perhaps remembering the last time they had broken into a place in darkness.

Cal saw a lamp and grabbed hold of it, lifting it out.

'Pass it closer,' said Inara with another flash showing her location.

Skedi heard hands and fingers touching glass, then metal twisted and pulled out of place, working together without another harsh word. At last, another strike. A spark. The shine of Inara's eyes. Then it caught on the wick of the lantern that Cal was holding. He turned it up into the glass bulb that enclosed it, and its glow shone warmth on the vault walls, picking out the shape of the arches and the bars that enclosed the texts. Cal carefully closed the metal petals around the glass to ensure the safety of the flame and lifted it to show the gate into the god vaults.

'Gods' piss,' he muttered. Now they had light, they could see that the bars weren't just locked; they were chained shut, too.

CHAPTER TWENTY-EIGHT

Kissen

THE WIND BATTERED KISSEN'S EARS. IT TORE AT HER BODY, her hands, even as she rode it. The cold breath of Faer screamed through her and froze her to the bone, stinging her skull and thieving the breath from her lungs.

She had tumbled from the god's arms onto their back, clinging onto stinking, matted fur. The world roared past at breakneck pace, the slopes of the Bennites quickly giving way to the wild, green forest she had passed through weeks before. Then, down to the greening fields of central Middren. Craier lands, Inara's lands, striped with rivers and clear roads. All of it passing in each blink of her eyes.

She couldn't take it, the spinning of the world, the blinding sun, the clouds roiling as the wind blasted them apart. Kissen screwed her eyes shut and waited for her stomach to stop churning.

As the sun sank, the wind's strength lessened, faded, died. She could feel herself drifting down from the heights, the air dragging her lush cloak out in a flag that wrestled with her neck. The temperature changed from frozen, to tepid, to warm, and the gale ceased its screaming. Kissen cracked open her streaming eyes to see a gloaming sky and the dim golden lights of a city and its walls rising ahead as night fell.

As if sensing her attention, Faer's descent turned into a plummet. Kissen barely had time to tighten her swollen hands on the god's fur before she was yanked from her seat and had to hold on for dear life.

'Hey!' she yelled as Faer tumbled towards the earth and lights. The flags at the edge of the city below them twisted from a gentle courting with a westerly breeze to snap-straight at their arrival from the north, fraying as they descended in a tornado. 'Howay, you salt-sucking demon!' bellowed Kissen. 'Do you intend to kill me now?'

At last, they slowed, skirting just barely over the city walls before landing with a thump in a mound of hay.

CHAPTER TWENTY-NINE

Elogast

ELO LED A GROUP OF FIVE YETHER GUARDS DRESSED IN thick cloaks and scarves of vivid yellow.

His contingent wore soft boots that scuffed gently over flat cobblestone as they edged along the canal in the twilight. Elo had memorised this route, a little-known way in the city. He had never led from behind.

He walked tall and sure, catching in the windows they passed a glimpse of Yether's yellow ribbon flicking out from the band he had tied on his arm beneath Naia's armour. It felt strange to wear another lord's colour. Unsettling. Factional. He had always thought he looked good in blue.

Stranger still was the weight of the armour. Or, not strange: both painful, and satisfying, like braiding his hair when it was long. He felt contained, anchored in his bracers, tassets, pauldrons and greaves, though the cuirass was too tight in the shoulders and too thick in the belly. The cuisses for his thighs he had to abandon completely lest they cut off his circulation. Naia had cared for it well; the plates barely squeaked as they moved through the city.

The pamphlets had brought something out of Lesscia Elo hadn't seen before. Naia had told him the traditions, but he had not expected to see the candles lit in the windows, spring herbs arranged around the sills. Little scrolls of paper, with hopes and wishes written on them, Elo spied tucked into shutters, pinned under stones, some even under tiny statuettes of Arren. Nothing incriminating, no shrines, but Lesscians still remembered what once had been.

The king's knights barracked in the south of the city, closest to dockworkers, less wealthy travellers, and small stall traders from the outermarket. Elo had stayed there before, with Arren; when the manor had been full. They were the first to be moved away from the court.

Elo raised his hand, and Faroch's guard obediently stopped behind him on the precarious lip over the water they had been secretly following. They were excited, nervous, their breath fast in the quiet night.

The lip over the water had led them down the side of the barrack building over its closest canal, one of the small ones, barely two strides across, that had several names in slang and Middric. A right turn at the end of the building and they would be in the barracks square.

They could hear the off-duty knights drinking and eating, lit all around by braziers. And, as Elo paused, he heard the percussion of dice, the click of a tile and a round of cheers that suggested a gambling game.

Thirty, at least, outside, more in the barracks. As expected. The rebels held their nerve where they stood in shadow, ready, waiting.

A clatter from the other side of the river. Elo pressed himself hard against the wall as a pair of shutters opened, releasing a billow of steam into the night air as a man tipped out a bucket of water. The fellow peered across at the guards' activities and, in a heartbeat, he found Elo. His eyes widened as he caught sight of the Yether guards, and Elo steeled himself. But, after a moment of silence, the man retreated back inside and drew the shutters behind him with a click.

Elogast breathed out.

A rattle of horse hooves on cobblestones. The king's knights quietened as Faroch emerged from a main street in full armour, mounted on horseback, his helmet visor open. Around him were knights on foot, more formally dressed than Elo's guard, in velvet tabards stitched with eagles.

'Is this part of the inspection we've been hearing about?' laughed one of the guards, stepping forward. His hand, though, was on his sword. 'Bit much, no?'

The other soldiers laughed. Faroch too, allowed him a smile.

'Perhaps, Captain Graiis,' he said. 'But it's our city's history.'

Elo's cue. He drew his sword as the Yether knights spread out, forming a line around the edge of the square. Elo ghosted forward, his own contingent blocking the entrance to the barracks and the side of the river. The king's knights were neatly surrounded, penned in, cut off before they had a chance to swear.

'What is this fuckery?' said Graiis, standing and taking his chance now he had it.

'Lay down your weapons,' said Faroch. 'Lesscia is not a playground for knights of the king.'

Graiis snarled and drew his sword, but Elo was ready, and faster than he was. He charged before Graiis completed the draw. Surprised, the captain swung loose and Elo caught his blade on his own, tipping it back. Using the movement, Elo grabbed Graiis's wrist and tilted the point of the blade in toward his throat, close enough to shave his beard from his chin.

'Attack!' Graiis cried, but half the knights were unarmed. One woman was still holding her dice. From inside the barracks, there was a shriek, and one squeal of metal, then silence. No one answered Graiis's command.

'You'll be getting no reinforcements,' said Elo. 'Our third team came through the roof.'

Graiis stared at Elo. After a few moments, recognition widened his eyes. 'Ser Elogast,' he said, his voice catching. 'It's . . . it's true. I heard you'd turned traitor.' He growled. 'You were the king's brother-in-arms. You swore an oath!'

'I swore to fight for Middren,' said Elo, keeping his voice low, but the sound carried. 'I keep to that. Lay down your weapons.'

Those who had them had half-drawn their swords, but they still hesitated, looking to their captain with the sword at his throat. But then the barrack door opened and the third group of rebels appeared, pushing unarmed, startled looking knights ahead of them into the light, arrows trained on their backs.

The first sword hit the cobbles. Another, and another.

'Arrest them,' said Faroch, and the knights. 'Take their names, confiscate their arms. The gaols are ready.'

'We'll have your head for this, Elogast,' snarled Graiis. 'The king will know this is your doing. He will see it so.'

Elo let go of Graiis as a soldier took him from behind and twisted the sword out of his hand. 'He had my heart and lost it,' said Elo calmly. 'My head is not on offer.'

CHAPTER THIRTY

Inara

'HOLD IT STILL,' SAID INARA, PEERING AT THE CHAIN THAT held the gate shut in the light of the lantern. Padlocked. They had no key.

Cal did what she asked. 'If we can't open it . . .' he warned.

'We can,' said Ina. She reached beneath her robe for her satchel and pulled out a hammer and a tough conical stake that Yatho had given her 'just in case'. Smart. Used for shaping small metal links or rings, it slotted easily into the top of the padlock. Inara lifted the hammer, then brought it down as Yatho had shown her.

The sound was loud, as loud as a ringing bell, and it ricocheted around the walls, sharp and brutal in the silence. The air tensed, or was that her imagination? Inara tried again. High, then down. Again.

Skedi took off, flying up first one stairwell, then another in the dark, hopefully to ensure no doors were open, no one was listening.

No humans, anyway.

The hammer stung her hands. She wasn't strong enough and was reminded of when she had tried to string Kissen's much larger bow and failed miserably.

'You have a go,' she said, passing the hammer to Cal. 'You're bigger.'

He took it, and she the lantern. He lifted the hammer high, brought it down with a clang, a creak. Skedi swooped back, and

Cal slammed the head again into the wedge, driving it further into the padlock. Its shackle lifted, twisting slightly.

She's watching us, said Skedi. *Scian. She doesn't like it.*

Inara nodded. Scian's attention felt like a weight, the boards of a codex pressing them down.

She'll understand, said Inara back to him. 'One more go, Cal.'

Cal nodded, held onto the wedge, and slammed it down. The shackle snapped at the bolt. He dropped the hammer and twisted open the chain, then unlocked the door with his key.

'Nice work,' Cal said to Inara.

'Thanks,' she said, though she had no intention of forgiving him for dismissing Telle. 'Let's find the trapdoor Balefor promised.'

Skedi winged his way over the shelves, scouring the flagstones with Inara as Cal lit the lanterns around the lecterns. All the stones of the floor looked much the same in the dark, their edges chipped and dancing in the wavering light. The air rushed above them as Skedi crossed, forward, back, darting like a bat after mayflies.

Then, 'Found it!' he called out loud, and dived straight down.

Inara rushed toward him, and saw, half-hidden beneath a griddle for stacking lanterns, a trapdoor bolted but not locked. Skedi was sitting on it, his fur and feathers settling slightly, proud or relieved, but only slightly. Scian's presence was all around them, deep with suspicion. Intruders in her archives, her ultimate sanctum. And she knew they were not there to read.

Cal helped Inara push the griddle, grunting with the weight of it, and Inara pulled the bolt, lifting the trapdoor. Several faces looked up at them, carrying their own light. Telle, Solom, and the others he had gathered to help them. Ertha, an older woman with fair skin, dark eyes and thick mahogany hair that she had netted in silver wire. Balefor, a shrewd looking old man with gold front teeth and dark hands constantly spattered with green ink. There were others too, more junior, one even the fellow who had asked Telle for help with the godspels before the forum. They had two barges between them, carefully guided into the canal that ran below the vaults.

Skedi peered through. *Scian's tomb,* he said.

Inara looked down with him and spied the stone lip of the box she had seen in Telle's map, just breaking the surface of the water. If there had ever been writing on it, it had worn down to nothing. Inara wondered how long before the stone wore down to bones, then down to nothing but water.

'Well done,' said Solom as Telle climbed up the ladder. They were none of them wearing their archivist clothes, but instead trews and tunics, boots and jackets, the better to move quickly and remain undetected.

Telle met eyes with Inara, her colours still uncertain, but she managed a smile, and Inara smiled back. Ertha directed the others to begin bringing boxes out of the water while Solom went to the lectern. The boxes were Yatho's, stamped with her worksmith's mark, but she and Bea had quickly made up false bottoms for them. Inara helped Cal tip and open the boxes as Solom pored through the ledger. Balefor and Telle went to join him, pointing out some texts and writing quick, decisive notes.

Inara felt the air draw closer still. Their voices did not echo as her feet first had when they entered the vaults. It was as if a hand were pressing their sounds down, squeezing them out. The others had not noticed

Can you feel that, Skedi? she asked.

Skedi's fur was sticking up, his ears twitching. *I feel it.*

'Cal, your texts are here,' said Balefor, handing him one of Telle's notes. 'Be sparing, we haven't space for all of them.'

Cal thanked him and looked at Inara, by the boxes.

'Can you help?' he asked.

Inara hesitated, tempted to tell him no out of spite. But her wilfulness had hurt Telle, and certainly wouldn't help her now. She nodded and picked up a crate with him, carrying it through the shelves. Skedi landed on the side of the box, the size of a kitten so he wouldn't weigh it down.

We should ask her, he said to Inara. *We should ask her now.*

The lamps, too, were dimming even as Ertha lit them. Inara could feel Scian's suspicion in her bones. He was right. She paused. 'Cal, we need to stop.'

'We don't have time.' He was already pulling texts off the shelves and packing them.

What are you doing? Scian's voice came as a whisper, a thread of ink through the dark.

The lanterns flickered. Inara and Skedi jumped, they all did. She wasn't speaking only to them. '*What are you doing? What are you DOING? WHAT ARE YOU DOING?*'

CHAPTER THIRTY-ONE

Elogast

PENNING IN THE BARRACKS WAS THE FIRST STRIKE, BUT not the hardest. It had scuppered almost half their numbers, but there were still many of the king's knights about the city. The next moves would be fast and vicious; the knights had stations at the walls, the gates, the docks and the archives.

The west gates were Elo's, with Faroch going south. Sparks flew from the cobbles as Elo and his small command raced towards them, the yellow ribbons of Yether flying out behind as they went. Elo caught a glimpse of faces in windows, lit by candlelight, staring as they charged past. No need for secrecy now, only speed. Over the noise of hoofbeats on cobbles, Elo wondered if he would hear people praying.

He did not pray. He had not prayed since Blenraden. When he and Arren had seen the walls shadowed by wild gods who spent their days circling and firing death and fury down on any who resisted; then, he had prayed. To gods of healing, gods of safety, even the great god of war. The god of change, his mothers' god, he had prayed to them too.

But when they entered the city and saw what the gods had made of its people; when he saw the wild divinities massacre fleeing refugees along with Arren's sister; when the Houses abandoned them with barely a scattering of their guard; when he felled his first shrine, to the maddened shrieks of its priests, their hands red with the blood of a street urchin mixed with wine . . . his prayers had diminished, faltered. Then they had stopped.

The time for praying was long gone. This was time for action.

Elo spurred on his horse, racing down the streets to the east of the larger canal and the larger thoroughfare. Scian's Way, it had been called. Victory Way, now. They were close; he could see the wall.

A strike of metal on metal.

Fighting had already begun. A shiver of energy ran through Elo, tingling down his spine, across his chest. His body remembered this. The breathlessness, the terror. He thought he saw gold flash before his eyes, the colour of his fears, but it was just another candle in a window.

Elogast spurred on the horse. 'Follow me!' he cried, clattering onto the main street.

The west gate. They flew into the square where he had first met Kissen, Inara and, unknown to him, Skedi. He had already been cursed, on a mission for a friend who wanted him dead.

But he had also been alone, in a cage of his own trauma and isolation. The trauma was still there, but the cage was open. This was what he had been trained to do. Everything else faded. All he needed was the narrow focus of his eyes, his breath, the horse, the night.

They charged first past the grand fountain depicting Blenraden's victories, then the smaller, older fountain of faces. The stairs near the gate flashed with metal: two of Yether's guards had fallen, marked by their yellow sashes. It was a wide plaza, giving little room for surprise, and the Lesscians were aiming to arrest, not kill. Arren's knights had received no such orders.

Three in blue were up the steps to the wall, directing their bows into the fray. Beneath, the remaining eight of Yether's guard were outnumbered and expertly surrounded by twelve of Arren's. A few of the yellows held shields, raised to stave off the arrows, but as soon as one of them left cover enough to swing, they were felled from above. One of Arren's broke from the melee and ran for the horses, ready to spread the message of attack.

'Spread out!' cried Elo. 'Flank them. Arrows to the wall. No one escapes!'

Three obeyed his order, breaking from his side and spreading across the empty square. One of his archers dismounted and took careful aim. The other stayed on horseback, levelling their bow, but hesitated. Naia's disapproving gaze skittered across Elo's vision. He blinked it away. He knew how this game must be played. One death now might save hundreds later.

'Release!' yelled Elo, driving forward.

They did not. Twenty paces, fifteen, ten. Still no arrows. Another of Yether's guard fell from their attempt to climb the steps. The odds were turning, and not in their favour. Elo squeezed the sides of the horse.

'Release!'

The archers on the wall turned to this new attack, one called out a warning and two of the king's knights twisted to face outwards, their swords bared. Elo ducked beneath an arrow and dragged the horse's reins to the side before another struck her flank.

Yether's guard weren't going to shoot first. They were not warriors. He was.

Drawing his sword, Elo dived straight into the fray, plunging his blade into the gap between the helm and throat of one of the king's guard. Blood shot into the night. Red and gold flashed before his eyes, Arren's blood on his hands, Mertagh's armour, the screams of his friends.

He shut it all away, closed it down, pushed it deep.

'Release for your city!' Elo yelled.

The mounted archer did, the woman by the horses fell back, a bolt buried in her chest. The standing archer took courage, taking one of the others on the wall in the shoulder, sending them tumbling to the ground.

'Break!' cried the blue commander as Elo's flanks came flying in, knowing they would suffer badly against cavalry. Elo kicked another blue cloaked knight to the side as they attempted a blade for his ribs and made directly for their commander as he came down the steps. Had they fought together before? Elo would not let himself know. The king's knight raised his sword, fear rising in his eyes, smart enough to see he was outmatched. He opened his mouth again as he met death: 'Flee!'

Elo's next swing removed his head before he finished yelling, and the second archer on the wall fell to Elo's mounted guard with the bow.

The knights in blue split into groups and ran, following their final command. Three made for the horses and another eight racing across the plaza.

'Chase them!' Elo bellowed. 'Take them down! Kill the horses if you must!'

His flanking guards did as commanded, sending their horses galloping after the blues on foot while the archers took down the ones running for the horses, one after the other. One of the knights fell, tripping over her own legs, and the others abandoned her as she was caught and arrested. Two more blues fell to the charge of a horse and a sword through the shoulder as Elo reached the fountain of faces, and there he caught another and sliced straight through their back. Blood spattered across the people carved into the fountain's ancient plinth; closed, open, screaming, scared. Four got away into the streets.

'Litha,' said Elo, to one of Yether's guards who had manged the first assault, she was breathing heavily, a great gash in her forearm. 'Hold the gate and recover the injured.'

She nodded.

'Usian!' He called to the standing archer who had failed to release. 'Round them up and take them to the gaol, there are healers there. Count the dead and take their names too.'

'Yes, commander,' Usian said quickly.

The guards that had chased the fleeing knights disappeared into the cobbled streets after them, and Elo kicked his horse to follow. The gate was claimed, the blood already washing from the fountain, but the streets were for routing; a single knight free could cause havoc. He had already proved that much himself. Ariam and Canovan were patrolling the ginnels and alleys, catching the stragglers, but Elo wouldn't leave it to chance.

'The rest of you!' he called. 'With me!'

CHAPTER THIRTY-TWO

Inara

SCIAN ERUPTED INTO THE DARKNESS IN A CLOUD OF VEILS. She took over the vaults, huge and full of fury, her arms stretching across the length of the ceiling. The archivists cried out, and a splash echoed from below as one of those in the canal fell below the water, struck by the god's rage.

How dare you?

Her voice shook the walls and their minds, deadly as an avalanche. Dust and cobwebs fell from the highest vaults. The other archivists put their hands to their ears, their heads splitting with the pain of her voice. Even Inara caught the echo of it, a pressure on her skull. The god's wrath was focused on her and Skedi, she could feel it, as if anger alone could shatter her ribs.

I gave you sanctuary, little girl, looking for a future, and you come thieving.

Inara held her ground, even as Skedi leapt defensively to her shoulder. They both tried not to cower beneath the ferocity of the god.

You handle my paper, my self, in my last sanctuary, my place of safety . . .

'Please, Scian,' Inara protested, raising her hands. 'We're trying to help you!' She tried her mind as well, as she did with Skedi and Makioron: *I lit the candle for you, all the windows in the city are lit. Can't you see?*

Help? Scian laughed. *You gut me. You steal me. You strip my skin to bone.*

The veils lifted. Scian's face had changed with her anger. It was skull-like, full of death. The bones and ragged flesh of a dead woman who had been murdered then celebrated into godhood. The air thickened, stinking of dead skin, leather, cold charcoal, hot ink. She reached towards Inara, her hand growing.

'I see you little people,' she whispered, out loud this time. 'You, little girl, nursing anger in your heart.' She looked at the others. 'All of you.' She tossed her head around, her gaze finding Solom. 'You. Vainglorious, belligerent, desperate for relevance as your body ages. You,' to Telle, 'trying to cling onto the first importance the world has given you, hiding it beneath your robes and coddling resentment that it is still your lot . . . and *you*,' she cast at Cal, who shrank in terror against the cases. 'Your blood-soaked records preserving the legacy of dead kin. You do not do this for *me*.'

'Please,' said Skedi, rising on Inara's shoulder. 'They are only trying to do good . . . to protect your work.'

'Liar!' snapped Scian. Her dark hair was falling out of her skull, turning grey as it fell. Shadow curled around her skin, and the paper on the shelves trembled. Two scrolls leapt from the box Cal had just packed and he whimpered.

Skedi jumped down to the flagstones before Inara, widening his wings, unnerved.

'Lies are in your nature, little god,' said Scian. 'I am a god of truths. Truths that change us. Truths that kill us. Truths that save us.'

Paper flew off the shelves, skittering into the air, unravelling in scrolls. The ones stacked in the boxes did the same, and one codex in Solom's palms drew blood as its metal clasps sliced through them.

Inara held out her shaking fingers, pointing them at Scian. But the god had a right to be angry, she was right to be afraid. 'Stop,' she said, uncertainly, trying to dredge up her will, her power. Her voice shook. 'I promise we mean you no harm.'

Scian drew her hand back, ready to strike. A glass lantern smashed, its cage closing on its flame, and a crack ran up the stones of two pillars. The bars of the vaults bent inwards. Inara didn't know what to do.

'Stop!' she tried again, as cracks spread to the ceiling. This was what she was good for, if nothing else. But didn't she wish she could have done this? That she could have been there when her home was burned, her family murdered? Didn't she wish for vengeance? Wasn't Scian's rage just like her own?

Your will doesn't work if it is shaken, said Skedi, shifting his feet, growing to the size of a wolf and ready to fight.

Inara grabbed him to stop him. But Telle was there first. She stepped in front of Inara, her arms wide. Her scars stood out starkly on her skin with fear, but her colours were bright, like sunshine through green water, unwavering. Protective. Like Kissen.

Scian hesitated, the glamour of Telle's ardour capturing her attention. This was the energy that could be given in prayers.

Telle took advantage of it and signed up to her. *This was my idea,* she said bravely. *Do not punish them for it. Punish me.*

Scian looked down at the archivist. Her skull eyes were dark, endless pits of ink and age. But she didn't move. Telle carefully went to her knee in a gesture of supplication.

We should have begged your leave, she said. *God of the archives, god of the city. Great Scian, in our fear we did not think.*

'What leave could I give, diminished as I am?' Scian snarled. She grew bigger still as if to deny her own words. 'Not even forgotten, as is the natural way. Ignored!' Her ire was growing once more. 'After all that I have done for creatures like you. Gave you history, purpose!'

Solom had recovered himself enough to go to his knees, Ertha too, Balefor and the others. Scian was not soothed. She barely deigned to look. More books were rising from the shelves. The ground split along the centre, drawing a scream from the boats below. The archives groaned over Inara and Telle. Scian was ready to bring it all down in her rage, and she raised her fingers to the vaults to do so. Cal slid to the floor, gasping with fright.

Inara balled her fists. No one else would die. Not Skedi, not Telle, not Elogast, not even Cal. She could do this. This was her purpose. This was her power. She could speak to gods, unravel their wills, stop them in their rage. If Scian was too furious to listen, Inara would make her.

Her will would not be shaken.

No, Inara thought it at the god, sending her will with it, imagining it wrapping around Scian like a net, pinning her arms, her fury, her magic, in place. 'Stop. We are not your enemies.' *Stop. Stay back.*

Scian blinked in surprise, her body frozen. She did not move, but her eyes changed. A glimmer in them, a light not of fury, but of interest, soft as a lamp in the darkness.

The king is coming to the city, said Inara into her mind. *These people believe he will destroy this archive and burn the books of other gods. Up there, rebels are moving, people are praying. This is the last of our chances.*

Scian gazed at Inara, then her eyes went distant. Elsewhere. The lamps gained some brightness. The air in the room lifted, its thickness unwinding. Tentatively, Inara released the god, who looked up at the ceiling of the vaults. Her skull held no expression, but after a moment her veils settled.

'They are praying,' she whispered, surprise in her voice. 'On my day.' Her eyes shone. 'Scian's Day.'

She diminished in size, just a little, but then her eyes darkened once more.

'If you take the last remnants of me,' she said after a moment. 'I will die again.' The scrolls in the air shivered, one crumpled. She changed more, flesh coming onto her bones, flush passing over it. 'Slowly, inevitably,' she said, 'fading into the air and dust the world made of my body.' She was a woman, her skin inked, her expression torn.

'Why does it always come to this?' she said. 'That power changes, and knowledge burns?'

Telle looked up from where she knelt. *We want to save what you built*, she signed. *Please, I tell no lies, I have no power. You are right about me. This work. It is everything to me. The first thing I have had that is my own. A commoner, like you were, daring to dream.*

Scian turned her attention back to the archivist, whose shoulders were tense, though her colours still gleamed emerald and silver-grey. Bright, true.

The god saw it too, her truth, and settled, shrinking to human size.

In fire you will be lost, said Telle. *In ink, you live forever.*

Scian smiled. *Perhaps*, she signed, then looked up at the vaults again.

'Very well,' she said. Her skin was brightening as Inara watched, the ink on her flesh moved slowly, as if it were being freshly drawn. The prayers, the candles in the city windows, were filling her with brightness. With colour.

'Take what you can,' she said out loud. 'My shrine, my lanterns, my heart of hearts, and carry my memory with them. But raise no more shrines for me. This city they built on my bones, and I cannot leave it.' She looked up to the ceiling and was her true self again; a woman of middle age, her hair fresh brown but greying, her skin bright with ink that glowed.

Prayers. She was filling with prayers.

'Instead, I will walk its streets tonight,' she said. 'And soothe those of my faithful who remain.' Her feet left the floor, and she rose. 'One last time.'

CHAPTER THIRTY-THREE

Kissen

KISSEN GROANED, SPITTING STRAW OUT OF HER MOUTH and rolling to her feet. She could hear pigs and smell them too. She pulled the staff close and used it as a lever to shift her shivering body upright. Her eyes stung, and she felt daggers in every bone.

'You fuck,' she snarled. Pigshit. She was covered in it. The pigs whose sty Faer had flung her into were squealing in fright. 'You did that on purpose.'

Faer had dwindled in size and stood before her now only reaching the height of her knee. He still presented male, but his mask was chipped, his fur bedraggled, and flesh hung off his bones. It had taken great power to bring her here. He looked almost cute.

'And what will you do about it?' he smirked. 'No briddite, no tricks.' His eyes tipped to smiling. 'You're just an ordinary—'

Kissen slammed her right leg into him, her shin making contact with his side. He went flying, howling with pain, into the fence of the pigsty.

Yatho had made the bones and plates of her prosthesis out of briddite, and no matter how twisted it was, no matter how she limped, it could still hurt gods.

'Still got some tricks,' she said, shrugging her cloak back on her shoulders as Faer picked himself up, his thin arms and legs shaking. His power was spent. He was too far from his home.

Kissen looked around them. The pigs were still shrieking, either at her or the god or both. Strange. Lesscia didn't allow livestock in the city. She glanced up at the buildings, sniffed the air. The streets around her were close-built, paved with dirt.

'This isn't right,' she said.

The sky was dark, but there were lights around, noise coming a few streets over, some kind of clattering or family brawl. The walls, too, were more timber and limestone than sandstone. The scent was of dung and food waste, not piss and canal water. Her heart plunged. This was horribly wrong.

This city wasn't Lesscia.

It was Sakre.

'Why have you brought me here?' Kissen demanded, striding towards Faer. But, even before her eyes, the wind god was fading. His feet were not substantial, turning to ghostly tufts of silver air that spread upwards through the god's body as they faded from the city, going back to where they belonged.

Kissen growled, and made a grab for him, but he disappeared.

You're where you need to be, godkiller, said Faer, cutting into her mind with the thought, adding a bit of extra pain for spite.

Sakre. The capital. Days' ride from Lesscia at horse-breaking speed. But Elo had been in Lesscia. Inara and her family were in Lesscia.

'Take me back,' said Kissen. 'Take me back!'

The god didn't answer.

CHAPTER THIRTY-FOUR

Elogast

THE KNIGHTS AHEAD WERE GAINING GROUND: THESE
streets were not built for horses. Lanterns stuck out at odd angles
along the twisting alleys, which were cramped and close, ready to
strike riders from their seats. Each corner deepened in shadow.

'Stay low, stay close,' said Elo. The air smelled strange, but he
shook away the thought. Now there was only the hunt.

Another corner. Lesscian streets were a labyrinth, seeming to
move around them, the shadows twisting in the night light,
stretching out like the arms of trees. Footsteps echoed in several
directions, sideways, behind them, onward. Elo saw the tail of a
blue cloak going around the corner, licked by the light of a candle
which was hazy, pale. Oddly white.

The scent was still strange, tugging at his memory. Moss. No,
moss and blood.

'Wait.'

He reined in his horse, and the others stopped. Elo looked
around.

'What is it?' asked one of the guards, Cardra, to his right. Her
horse was breathing heavily, spittle flecking his mouth, as if they
had run for miles though Elo thought they had only been minutes
within the streets. 'We're losing them!'

She didn't feel it, the shift of hair on the back of her neck. Elo
raised a finger to his lips, looking around for something, some sign.

There. A chalk scratching, so light it was almost invisible. A runic fork in the road. The curse that had been pinned on his shoulder. He focused his mind, listening carefully. Since Lethen had cursed him and Skedi manipulated him, he had reminded himself of the way to hear gods' voices when they didn't want to be heard, when they wrapped their will about a person instead of piercing their mind.

The faintest whisper. He heard it.

Follow me.

The candle wasn't a candle. As he focused, it changed into just a glimmer of light, a will-o'-the-wisp. It drifted around the corner the king's knight had turned. The walls around them havered in shadow, as if seen through high heat. If he had not been looking for it, Elo and the knights might have kept running into the dark, chasing after cloaks just out of reach. Lethen's will had taken hold of the streets, but they were simply at the edges of her illusion.

This way, the god whispered. *Safe this way. Follow me.*

Whatever Canovan had done, it had given Lethen enough power to bring her wild magic to the city. Pieces were moving on Elo's playing board of their own volition. Dangerous. The worst warriors weren't those who pissed themselves or ran away, they were the people who ran in to the fray with madness in their eyes and got other people killed.

'Follow me,' said Elo, Lethen's echo, 'and be careful. There is gods' work about.'

The god of nightmares had employed similar illusions in Blenraden. The Gwyn Mare, a bone horse bedecked with ribbons, had lured some of Elo's companions into an ambush of arrows and rabid people with pitchforks.

Spurring his horse, Elo followed the sound of Lethen's voice, careful now. He saw no shadow demons. Not yet. But he did catch sight of another wisp, floating above them.

Follow.

A scream. Feet running through the dark, and a bellow. They passed a prone knight in Arren's blues, their throat slit and bleeding out, a horse pawing the cobbles nearby. A horse? None of those they were chasing had a horse. This knight had come from somewhere else.

Follow, follow.

A bellow, a strike of wood on metal, the sound of a body hitting earth. Elo bared his teeth. They turned left, then right; the narrows twisted and moved around them.

That mark again. The chalk on the wall. The wisp-candle, a flick of cloak around the corner.

'We've gone in a circle,' said Cardra. She looked back, then forward. 'That's not . . . I've lived here all my life, we couldn't—'

Lethen knew they were there. She was trying to keep them out.

'Close your eyes,' Elo ordered. 'Trust the horses.'

'What—'

'Just do it.'

Blinding himself, Elo urged his mount onwards. Gods rarely toyed with animals; sparking an animal's feral nature was one thing, but manipulating it? Much harder.

The gelding went forward beneath him, then turned where before Elo had seen no path. He felt the air clearing as he walked, brightening, as if he could feel the moonlight on his skin. The moss-scent faded, and instead he could smell the canals.

A thud, skin on skin, close at hand, and the sing of a sword. Fighting.

Elo opened his eyes and looked behind him. The others had followed, breaking the illusion by walking through it, and saw the streets as they were. The sky was brighter, the shadows contained.

'Draw weapons,' said Elo, spurring on. 'Be ready.'

A scuffle. They passed another body in blue. Not dead, breathing. Another. A narrow arch, it too daubed with chalk, marked the entrance to a crossroads square with a bridge, a water pump, and a canal drifting by it.

This was where Lethen had been leading the knights. Bodies in blue were strewn along the walls, called by a god to a slaughter.

Because what met them were fifteen fighters, inkers mostly, their eyes wild, their bodies slick with sweat, screaming as they wielded clubs filled with nails, rusted old swords, barely registering their own weeping wounds. Ariam, wilder than Elo had ever seen him . . . and Naia.

'Stop!' cried Elo.

They didn't hear him. Naia, almost unrecognisable, brought a kitchen hatchet round onto a knight's helm and embedded it in their neck, yelling as she dragged it out and struck, again and again. A knight was backing away from Ariam, hands raised, and Ariam slammed his halberd, not a staff, into their belly, their chest. They went down, and he kicked them.

Elo had seen this before. His body went cold as he recognised humans consumed by a god's illusions. The god of war had driven an army to madness with darkness and fear, the Gwyn Mare had willed a man Elo had known for ten years into turning on his wife and putting his hands on her throat. Lethen hadn't summoned her shadow demons. She didn't need to. This was Blenraden, over again. These were the horrors that shook Elo's hands each waking moment, that put their teeth into his dreams.

What had he unleashed?

At the centre of it all was Canovan. Shirtless, his arms dripping with blood, a hatchet in each hand. On his chest, his belly, he had carved Lethen's rune into his skin with a knife. His trews were dripping red, but the carving was dark with her power. Around his neck were two goats' horns, still bloody at the stump from a recent sacrifice. Their powers had combined, illusion, fear, shadows and blood. This connection to his god was bone deep, blood deep. Like Inara's.

If this was what Canovan would do for vengeance and fury, what could Inara also become?

CHAPTER THIRTY-FIVE

Inara

'I THOUGHT SHE WAS GOING TO KILL US,' SOLOM SAID, then signed, then hesitantly rose from his knees, wiping his bloody hands on his robes.

The others were also stirring. A sound of splashing and wood from below the trapdoor suggested that whoever had fallen had managed to get back in the barge.

Inara looked at Telle, who was staring at her. She couldn't understand her colours. Gratitude? Love? Fear?

Solom glanced at Inara, but then his eyes landed on Skedi, who had come back onto Ina's shoulder. 'Was it you?' he asked. 'God of white lies, she was going to bring the building down. Did you speak to her, convince her?'

Skedi's ears sprang up with surprise, his wings flicked. Inara tried not to look at him as he nodded.

'Yes,' he said, his whiskers standing out, his head proud. A white lie, of course. It was easy to believe: the others were relieved. A god against a god, and theirs had won out. 'It was me.'

Inara hid her pang of injustice, for herself and Telle, but Telle raised her fingers, catching her eye. She knew what Skedi was capable of, knew what a god of white lies should do. The archivist shook her head, very slightly, and Inara kept her mouth shut. Telle had just risked her life to save her, Skedi had been ready to do the same, people could believe what they wanted. That didn't change the truth.

'Thank you,' Solom said to Skedi, casting him a low bow. His colours changed, a warm indigo respect passing through them, like a gleam on velvet. Cal, who was still seated, panicked by the shelves, also bowed, muttering a prayer. 'You saved our lives, our endeavour,' Solom continued, touching his wrist and undoing a bracelet of fine green beads and tiny drops of gold. He held it out to Skedi, his hands glowing with that shine of appreciation. The colours infused the bangle, filling it with meaning, love. Prayer.

'I offer this in thanks, god of white lies,' said Solom, 'Skediceth, if you will take it.'

Skedi blinked at it, his whiskers twitching, but he spoke directly into Inara's mind. *It should not be mine*, he said.

But Solom's faith was in Skedi, not Inara. She bit back her pride. 'Take it,' she said. 'It's yours.'

Tentatively, Skedi grew again, his wings rising, and Inara held out her arm. He hopped along it, then flew to Solom and met him at the ledger before bending his antlers forward. Solom draped the bracelet on his left antler where it looked grander than the button Inara had tied on a broken thread. Skedi stretched out his dappled wings. Did he brighten? It looked like it, his feathers glowing with light from within, like Scian.

Telle touched Inara's shoulder, took her by the wrist, and pulled her away into the shelves, leaving the others behind. Inara let herself be led away from Skedi, the love he was getting from others, the strength. How much more would it take before their connection was gone?

They rounded a corner, sheltered by scrolls, and Telle let go, and turned around. She and Inara regarded each other.

Thank y—Inara began. Telle had stood between her and an angry god, but Telle shook her head.

It was you, she said. *You stopped her, not the god. You saved us.*

Inara clenched her fists. Skedi didn't want her to tell, thought it was dangerous. But Skedi was doing his own work, finding his own power. Inara needed help.

You saved me first, she said at last. It was as much an admission as anything.

Telle almost laughed, stuffing her hand to her mouth, then

putting it on her heart. Inara watched her colours for fear. There was some, jagged-edged, but the light of them was otherwise softer, calmer than it had been since Inara's betrayal.

This was why you came to the vaults, Telle said. *You wanted answers.*

Inara nodded slowly. *I have power,* she said. *I don't understand it. With my mother dead, I have no one left to ask.* They both paused as Ertha walked past, directing the godspells archivist to one of the shelves. *I should have spoken to you,* Inara added. *But I was afraid.*

Did Kissen know?

Inara shook her head, then paused. *I'm not sure.*

Telle chewed her lip for a moment, thinking. *I have not read of this . . . magic,* she said, and Inara's heart sank. *But I saw what Canovan did, making shadows, passing curses. There is precedent, which means something will be found.*

Scian said that what I was couldn't be found here. I just . . . Inara clenched her fists, not sure what to say. *I just want to help,* she said. *I want to know what to do.*

History is for guidance, said Telle. *Threads from different cloths that we stitch together. It is not instruction.* Her fingers drifted towards the scars on her face, then she added: *Knowledge can bring pain in place of ignorance, terror in place of hope. Whatever place your strength has come from, it is still yours. You choose what to do with it.*

CHAPTER THIRTY-SIX

Elogast

CANOVAN MOVED AS IF HE WERE MADE OF FURY AND shadow. Darkness crawled along his back, bristling like the fur of shadow demons. He struck to kill: throat, belly, chest, head.

'Stop!' bellowed Elo, swinging down from the horse, flicking his hands to the others, telling them to circle the plaza.

Naia didn't hear him, couldn't. Ariam too. The other rebels had no qualms about bloodshed. One woman whooped as she swung a club fitted with nails, slamming it into the back of a dazed knight's head as if he were a straw man in a game of striking. Ariam slammed the butt of his halberd into a fallen knight's chest, over and over.

They couldn't see what they were doing. They couldn't feel it. Whatever Canovan had done, it had locked some part of them away, and given free rein to their rage.

Elo stepped in to the innkeeper as he prepared another swing. He broke the axe's arc with his sword, whirling his blade around and down, forcing Canovan to duck forward. With a grunt, he slammed a kick into the man's belly, knocking him back. Naia cried out and charged wildly towards Elo with her hatchet, her eyes clouded white and glowing. The edge came around, but Elo caught her wrist with his hand and twisted it out of her grip.

'Naia! Listen to me!' Naia bared her teeth, but Elo grabbed her by the tunic and shook her. 'Naiala!'

She recognised her name at last. Her eyes darkened, back to her colour.

'Elo?' she said, her brow creasing.

Canovan snarled behind him, lifting his axes again. But he ran past Elo, back towards a knight.

Elo let him go. Canovan had chosen this, Naia had not. 'Look around you!' Elo snapped at Naia. 'Do you not see what you have done?'

Naia stepped back and looked down. Her hands were red. Blood, everywhere blood. Across the cobbles, seeping into the waters. One of the inkers had two fingers hanging off their hand, Paritha. Elo recognised her, but she was still fighting. Another was lying choking on the floor, a gash across their stomach. Ariam was still crushing a man's chest.

Then there were the knights. Led there in confusion, including the ones from the west gate. They lay dead, dying, or gravely injured, beaten bloody. One was weeping in shock.

'Stop!' Naia cried hoarsely, turning to the others who were still fighting. She grabbed Ariam by his shoulder, dragging him back. 'Stop!'

Ariam stumbled.

'Cardra, give us fire!' said Elo.

The woman pulled an oiled wood torch from the horse's saddle and, with a spark of flint, set it alight. The flare cut through the night, lighting the canal, flaring up the walls, chasing the shadows away.

The noise and the light was enough. Ariam found his feet, stopped, and stared at Naia, then back at the others. The inkers faltered, the madness falling from them. Paritha shrieked, dropping her weapon and clutching her injured hand to her chest. She keened with pain.

'Knights of Middren, surrender!' Elo roared.

The knights had been fighting for their lives, not their honour. They faltered, exhausted, and their swords dropped quickly. One of them leaned over and vomited.

But Canovan did not stop.

'Please,' said the knight he was fighting, who kept his sword only to defend himself. 'Please stop. I'll surrender!'

'Canovan!' Elo leapt towards him. 'Stop!'

Too late. Canovan's axe made contact with the side of the man's chest, beneath his armpit, with a bloody blow that sounded like broken earth and water. Elo grabbed the innkeeper by the neck and threw him back, but the knight fell.

'I told you to stop!' said Elo as Canovan's opponent hit the floor to a cry from his comrades.

'I am not one of your knights,' spat Canovan. 'I stop when I want to stop.' He wrenched himself out of Elo's grip. 'They did not stop with my wife. They dragged her from her shrine. They threw her to the ground!'

Elogast shoved him back, and Canovan stumbled over a corpse.

'And what of your friends?' Elo growled. 'Did they stop when they wanted to or when *you* gave them leave?'

Guilt passed over Canovan's face, for the merest moment, and his eyes flicked to Ariam, who was staring at his hands, to Naia.

'I . . . didn't see the blood,' she murmured, and looked up at Canovan. Tears came to her eyes. 'Why did . . . I just came to check on you . . . I . . .'

'You got caught up in it,' said Canovan, breathing heavily, his stomach slick with sweat. He looked to Ariam, who stared at him like a stranger. 'Ari, it was to make you stronger. To make us stronger.'

'What did you do?' said Ariam, but then his eyes widened. 'Stop!' he shouted, running towards Canovan.

Elo twisted. One of Arren's knights had picked up her sword and was running for the innkeeper, yelling.

'Begone, gods!' she screamed. 'With Blenraden!'

Ariam held out his hands, dashing between her and his friend.

'Ariam, no!' said Elo.

The point went straight through the inker's unarmoured chest. Naia screamed.

The knight dragged her sword out of Ariam's chest, giving Elo just enough time to leap and swing his blade through her neck. Her head dropped into the night with a spray of blood, and, for a fractured moment, Elo thought he recognised her. A knight from Blenraden. Had he commanded her? Only to kill her in another city?

Her head rolled towards the inkers, and her body clattered to the floor. Ariam choked, red spattering his lips. He crumpled to his knees and Canovan caught him.

'Enough!' said Elo. There was blood on his face, he could feel it, hot and wet. He shook his sword down. 'Enough.'

The square fell silent, except for Paritha, who was stifling sobs while staring at Ariam in Canovan's arms. His body had stilled, his eyes open and glazing. Death had taken him quickly.

Naia put her bloody hands over her ears, while Cardra still sat on her horse, torch burning, her face a mask of horror.

Elo pointed his sword at the king's knights. No mourning, no hesitation. If the knights detected weakness, they might regain their will to fight, might decide vengeance was the way to die.

'Move away from your weapons,' Elo said. 'Kneel, and you will not be harmed.'

Some hesitated, but they followed his order. Elo nodded at his cavalry, and they dismounted, pulling rope down from their packs.

'This is why the king has banned the gods,' hissed one of the knights. 'This is treason.'

'I know,' said Elo.

He walked over to Canovan. Ariam's head was cradled in the innkeeper's lap, eyes still open. The shadows had retreated from Canovan's skin, his tattoos were still. Whatever summoning he had wrought, it fell from him with his will to fight.

He had done this. Elo swallowed his rage. Hot rage was no good. He must control it, like the temperature of flames in an oven, or he might burn everything down. Like Canovan wanted. Inara too.

He would not permit madness and blood.

'Put out your hands,' said Elo through gritted teeth.

The innkeep slowly turned his gaze to Elo. The light had gone from his eyes: he looked hollowed out, only skin and bone.

'He was having a child,' he whispered. 'His husband ... his husband is waiting for him.'

'You should have thought of that before,' said Elo. 'If you had stopped, he might have lived.'

'I didn't—'

'Elo ...' said Naia, shakily.

'*You* did this,' snarled Elo over both of them. *You did this*, he heard his voice in his own mind. He had started this. He had allied with Canovan *knowing* that he wanted blood. 'We fight as one. We stop as one. We do not kill for play or pleasure, or they will think that is our game and play it back. Better.'

Canovan winced, his face slack with shock, gently, he lifted Ariam's head off his lap. The blood from Lethen's symbol had begun to dry and flake. The others were watching.

'Put out your hands,' said Elo, 'or I will remove your head. Lethen be damned.' The air stirred with moss, but it was faint now. The blood and water were stronger.

Canovan swallowed. He looked at the others, for succour, for support. They looked away. Then, dazed, he put his hands on the cobbles out flat, moving his shaking fingers out into the blood. 'Mother . . .' he whispered, as if in prayer.

'Elo . . . please,' said Naia, but Elo lifted his sword once more and, without hesitation, brought down the point of his blade. He was precise, not cruel. He severed the fourth finger from Canovan's right hand, straight at the knuckle.

Canovan screamed, snatching his flesh away and tearing it from the blade. He grabbed his hand to his chest, eyes wide with shock. 'Mother!' he cried again. 'Help me!'

Elo raised his sword, ready to face his own consequences, ready for the god, for she could be the only one that Canovan called. He waited for the blood to crust over into moss, for shadows to rise on the wall and whispers to drill into his head.

Nothing.

No . . . there was something. Something different.

Instead of darkness, the stones of the buildings brightened, lit as if from within, by lamplight.

Ink-writer, paper-mover, land-walker, to you we pray.

The whispers he heard were not Lethen's. The scent on the breeze was of paper and air, dust and ink, lamp oil. They ached in Elo's mind, but not in agony. More like a muscle after use, or eyes after staring at scribbles too long.

All things end, all things change, all things begin again.

The blood on the cobbles ran black, then gold, then green,

brightening as it seeped towards the canals. Elo twisted around, looking into the streets.

Curious dreamer, star-counter, bridge-builder.

A glow, beyond the crossroads, from the east. A woman, small, about Telle's size, walked within it, her head covered in veils. Down the street across the bridge, she passed by window ledges with candles and berries in them, and the candlelight glowed brighter, the fruit shining as she passed. She wore white, like a novice archivist, and plain robes that trailed along the ground. Ink swirled across her arms, from her feet, up the walls. No wonder Lethen could not come. This was another god's city now.

Do not forget your voice. Do not forget your wisdom.

She came over the bridge slowly, her light glittering in the canals, and then she walked into the square. She did not mind the death and destruction. The green blood turned clear, to water, rushing over the cobbles. The god turned to look at them, and through her veil, her face was full of sadness.

Do not forget.

Her whisper faded, and she moved on. The blood-water and canal water mingled, washing away. Elo saw that the sky had turned pale. The sun was rising.

Elo lowered his sword. The Lesscians with him were praying, most of them on their knees. The god of their city was walking its streets.

Do not forget.

CHAPTER THIRTY-SEVEN

Kissen

KISSEN MANAGED TO RELEASE HERSELF FROM THE PIG PEN, much to the relief of the pigs, and took stock of her situation. She was somewhere in downtown Sakre. From where she stood, she could see towards the Forge and the Reach fortresses. Their flag-poles were bare. Strange. She had never seen them without some gaudy colours. But then, she tried not to spend too much time in Sakre: too big, too smelly. Refuse and animals everywhere, and that wasn't even counting the livestock running rampant within the town. The humans were just as bad. It reminded her of the worst parts of Blenraden, but colder and windier.

Her first temptation was to find an inn and a horse and either steal it or bargain for a quick run out of the city. She had one or two friends, a third of whom owed her money, but she didn't have time for pleasantries. Sakrean veiga were ten a copper, employed by the king, and the gods miserable, sewer-dwelling rats living on the offerings of thieves and murderers.

She had one job: find someone who had a direct bird to the fool-king and warn him they were about to be invaded. Then home by horse, raft or ship.

Reluctantly, she calculated that she was about a half mile closer to the Reach than the Forge. She felt half-sick and sweaty with disorientation; from blistering cold to the drizzly warm of western Middren, from early evening to the moon-sunk hours before dawn.

Still, her stomach grumbled, and she hoped the king gave food to messengers.

It was a hard way going up the cobbled streets: the hills were murder on the knees. The path she followed went from the cattle keeps through butcheries, the greasers' district, and candlemakers' square, then over the big river that split the city in two and fed the port. Sea air cut across it, salt-laden and stinking of fish guts and kelp. There was no one about, which was odd. One or two faces peered out the shutters, then quickly slammed them closed at the sight of Kissen.

Over the bridge should have been the first of the night markets that picked up from spring through summer, but the first eel and grain stalls she found were abandoned, bowls burned and blackened at the bottom near the embers of their fires with no one to turn them. Minted coins had been scattered across the nasty, round Sakrean cobbles, and no one had yet picked them up, and the other covered tables of food and trinkets were half emptied. In a rush. One stall had been tipped over, and its clumps of briddite carved in the shapes of stags and suns and little kingly figurines had been stamped into the ground.

Kissen passed a hot pot bar, its pots still bubbling, a few half-cleared fruit and vegetable stalls. After a while, she picked up an orange from the filthy floor and peeled it while looking around. Something was going on in Sakre, but that made no sense. Elo was in Lesscia, starting his little rebellion. The king was marching there. She had seen it.

'Psst.'

Kissen turned, a piece of orange half to her mouth, and looked up. A dark-haired woman was peering out from between her shutters on the second floor, two children at her side.

'The fuck is going on here?' said Kissen.

'The fuck are you doing, nicking my fruit, eh? Took me three days to drag those up from Weild.'

'It was on the pissing ground,' said Kissen. 'Didn't think you'd want it.'

'Well, I do want *paid* for it. Floor or not.'

Kissen contemplated throwing it at her. 'Why've you all run in a hurry?' she said instead.

One of the kids stepped up, perhaps five years old. 'There's knights all fighting—'

The woman put her hand on their head and about turned them back into the safety of the room. 'That's one copper,' she snapped at Kissen. 'Leave it on the table.'

'Who's fighting?' said Kissen.

'It's passed by here, up to the Reach,' said someone else. Another pair of shutters opened, and an older person stuck their head out.

'The king left,' they said, 'sun bless him, then night before last, madness broke loose, and keeps breaking. We're just trying to get on.' They looked around nervously. 'Is it safe, yeah?' Their accent was so western Kissen could barely comprehend it.

'How the salt should I know?' she said.

'All right fire-top, keep your head on.'

Hooves on cobbles, the squeak of wheels making a terrible racket on the uneven ground. Kissen dropped the orange and put her hand to her cutlass . . . then remembered it wasn't there and cursed Faer with every stinking swear she could think of.

Three rounded the corner on cobbles back from where she came, dragging some kind of metal cart behind them. They weren't wearing armour, at least not the fancy knights' armour Kissen had seen on the king's favourites. More formal leather cuirasses, thigh- and shin-plates, shoulder- and neck-guards and leather caps. She couldn't see their cloth colours in the dark, but she noted no stags or suns.

'You!' they yelled at her. 'Halt!'

'Halt?' said Kissen. 'I'm not moving.'

She heard shutters close, and held her palms out. Or, one palm, the other she still had on her staff.

'Get inside then,' snapped the soldiers.

'I've got no inside to go to,' she replied, only then considering that she probably should have run.

They came closer, trundling through the market, and peered at her. She stayed still as the leader dismounted. 'Who are you?' he asked.

Kissen got a better look at the cart. Not a cart. A cage. With a few people inside. 'I'm a messenger,' she said warily, 'a veiga.' That usually gleaned some respect.

The leader came closer, their expression unmoving.

'I have important information,' she added, 'for the king.'

From the sudden silence, Kissen suspected this wasn't the right thing to say.

A fist landed in her sternum, crushing the breath from her. She buckled with surprise, and felt a hand on her neck, forcing her down to her knees. 'Peace!' she said. Not again. The man kicked her staff away. 'Oh, for fuck's sa—'

'Quiet, messenger, or your head is next.'

Her hands were roughly bundled behind her back.

'I'm serious,' she said, struggling. 'This is important. Let me just send a bird to the king then I'll be on my way.'

Her face was shoved into the dirt and stones. She hadn't been expecting a fight. Osidisen's dagger was down the side of her boot, but she couldn't reach it and didn't want to do any more stabbing of people. Shit. Her hands were being bound with rope, elbow-snapping tight, and then when she was trussed the knight picked her up by her hair and hissed:

'The king is no master here.'

CHAPTER THIRTY-EIGHT

Elogast

ELO STOOD ON LESSCIA'S WALLS AS THE MORNING BRIGHT-ened pink and fresh over a changed city. He was heavy with fatigue, but it was too soon to sleep. He watched instead for the army he knew would be coming. The king's banner still hung to the side of the western gates below him, but only one. The rest gleamed in Yether-yellow, adorned with eagles, bright and triumphant.

Below was a steady flow of people from the outer city and its marshy streets, through the empty stalls of the food markets. Yether's edict had temporarily permitted them shelter within the city walls, with their paltry belongings, for the first time enabling food trade over the canals. However, the southern roads were also full of people carrying their homes and families away from danger, unwilling to be captured by another war.

'Commander Elogast?'

Captain Faroch had come to find him. Somehow, Elo had slipped back into his earlier title, and he felt its weight. After the success of Scian's Day, he had also heard more than one person mutter 'The Lion of Lesscia.' Naia was to blame, his armour stood out too grandly.

Naia. He dreaded seeing her.

'Captain,' Elo said with a bow. 'What can I do for you?'

'The city is full,' said Faroch, nodding at the activity below. 'We can take no more. We can't feed them.'

Elo looked towards the outermarket; there were still many coming towards the gates. Progress was slow; they were checked cursorily for weapons as they entered. 'I see,' he said.

'You don't agree?'

Faroch was a dangerous man to cross. He seemed happy enough to follow Elo's direction, more so after the success of the night, if they could call it that. Elo wasn't certain if it was genuine respect or because, whatever happened, Elo would take the blame. Elo carefully sorted through his thoughts. With Ariam's death, he had lost a strong potential ally not affiliated with Yether; it would take a lot to convince the inkers to fight again, let alone with him. Canovan, Elo suspected, would be plotting some level of terrible revenge and Naia . . . He had not seen her since she left to wash the blood away. The playing board might be more level with Arren, but he had lost some key pieces. His position was precarious, and he needed Faroch on his side.

'I understand your concern,' said Elo evenly. 'Mine is that leaving them outside gives a besieging army free access to foot soldiers, food, tools and weapons.'

Faroch considered this. 'Lord Yether does not expect it to come to a battle,' he said.

Elo nodded. His intention was still to kill Arren, but if Yether and Faroch caught wind of that they would likely send him to the gaols as well.

'The fewer resources they have,' Elo added, 'the quicker they might be to negotiate.'

Faroch tugged on his beard, then grunted and lowered his voice. 'We could disperse them with cavalry, make them seek homes elsewhere.'

Elo could not deny, he had considered it.

'I did always enjoy the outermarket,' added Faroch, 'even its queasier parts, but the shanties spread like a rash in the last few years: it's an eyesore, and full of crime. Most people here will think good riddance.'

Elo sucked his teeth. 'The king wants to be a saviour,' he said after a moment. 'Do you really want to give people a reason to think they need saving?'

Faroch released his beard, then sighed. 'I was never very interested in politics,' he said. 'Good pay, a good cup, and good land. That's me. It took me a year to realise the king's knights matched us in number. They'd just been trickling in, one by one, each with their own reason.'

'You had no reason to suspect them,' said Elo generously. Faroch knew it was generous. He had let the city almost be taken from under him as he watched.

'But you think like Lord Yether,' the captain added. 'Three moves ahead, all the time.' He smiled. 'The lord does like to beat me at chess. Ruthlessly.'

Elo matched his smile. 'We are not lords or kings,' he said. 'We can't afford to be ruthless.'

A woman's voice broke in from the stairs behind them. 'You seem pretty ruthless to me, Elogast.'

Naia, and no 'Ser' this time. Her face drawn tight with grief, and her skin wan. She stood at the top of the stairs of the parapet tower.

Faroch cleared his throat and stepped aside. 'Very well,' he said. 'We'll continue to the evening bells, and I'll check when the supplies from Daesmouth will arrive.'

'Thank you, Faroch,' said Elo. 'Lord Yether . . .'

'He'll be along this afternoon to speak to the guard,' he said. 'He's impressed with you, you know. And I don't often see him impressed, the old grouch.'

Faroch liked Yether. That was his loyalty, not just his pay and pride. If Elo could stay on Yether's side, he'd still have Faroch. Piece connecting to piece. The captain clapped Elo on the shoulder in a genial way, then turned and sidled past Naia, who barely acknowledged him. She was glaring at Elo as if her gaze alone could extract a confession of sin.

'Do you think Canovan did not deserve punishment?' said Elo. Naia's mouth pinched, and she swallowed.

'Ariam was a good man,' she said instead of answering. She wore a wool jacket, tied at the panelled waist with a ribbon of pale blue, an Irisian mourning colour. 'Passionate, intelligent, kind.'

'I did not kill him,' said Elo.

'You might as well have done,' she said. 'We were doing fine before you came, running rebellion into the city. Now one of us is dead. We should never have listened to you. I should—' Her voice broke, she tightened her hands on her sleeves. They were raw with scrubbing. 'I should never . . .'

'What would you have done instead?' he said. 'Sat quietly and written pamphlets?'

She expected too much of him, everyone expected too much of him. He had been lucky in Blenraden, had managed a win out of theory and luck and Arren. He had been lucky with Hseth, and now bore the weight of Kissen's life. He was weary, and in pain, and guilty, and he was just trying to do his best. Best by Inara, best by Kissen, best by Middren. It was never enough. Like his best by Arren hadn't been enough.

'Then,' he pressed, 'when the king came marching through the gates, you would write another.' Naia flinched, but Elo wouldn't stop. 'As he burned your archives and your paper, you would write another. Start a war, and break your presses, and you'd write. Built an empire on blood and faith and you'd—'

'Enough,' said Naia, flush with anger, which at least brought some colour to her face. Her brow creased and she pushed her braids back from her shoulder, taking a breath to calm herself. Elo marvelled at it, how quickly she recentred. He put his hand on the broken pommel of his sword and tried to do the same. He breathed in, imagined flour under his hands, then nodded towards the west.

'Do you see that?' he said.

Naia frowned at him but did turn to look. The sky was pale above them, but where it reached the hills westward, a grey haze was rising, dark and murky.

'That's smoke,' said Elo, 'from campfires.'

'The king's army,' she said. Elo nodded.

'An army that has order, training, pay. A cause and commitment to it. An army like that is not powerful because of its size, but because of its discipline. Like pieces on a chessboard, we are not much until we act as one.'

Naia's dark eyes followed the rising smoke, then turned to him.

'People are not pieces,' she said. 'This is not a game, and we're not soldiers. We were never yours to lead to our deaths.'

'I did not lead you astray,' said Elo.

'This all began when you came to us!'

'What would you have me do?' He turned to her, holding out his chafed hands. 'Lie down and wait to die?'

She opened her mouth, then closed it. Her eyes were bright with a wash of tears. She didn't answer. She couldn't answer.

'Don't think I'm someone I'm not, Naia,' Elo continued. 'I have led people to death before. Over and over, I called them away from their homes to a burning city. Some of them were scared . . .' His voice caught, and Naia closed her eyes, tears dropping down her face. 'But fear, I could not allow them. So, if they left their post once they would lose a finger. Twice, they would lose a hand. I scared some more than the gods, and so they fought. And we won. And we lost as well.'

She stared at him as if seeing him for the first time. He wished he could say something kinder, softer, but Skedi wasn't here, and he was who he was. Kissen had understood that, but Naia was unused to the worst parts of herself. The place where a god of war could be born out of humans' desire for power and death, where a god of the ways could bring out blind terror and make them use it.

'Then when does it stop?' she said at last.

'I don't know,' said Elo honestly. Cruelly. 'I just know we cannot let a king drag us into darkness without fighting back.'

'No matter how much we lose?'

'It does matter,' said Elo. 'It matters what we lose. But that doesn't stop it.'

A cry from the wall. Elo turned, and in the distance he saw, not an army, but a single rider flying a blue-and-gold flag, moving at speed through the outer city and its dismantled market, scattering people as they blew their horn, which glinted with gems. Elo recognised that horn: he had borne it himself when recruiting common folk for the war. Either Arren knew he was here, or he had forgotten entirely. Elo didn't know what was worse.

A guard mounted the steps two at a time. Cardra. 'Should we close the gate, commander?' she asked Elo.

'It's one rider,' said Elo quickly. There were still so many queuing to get in, dragging ponies, horses, goats and pigs with them. 'Let them in.'

Elo leapt down the stairs as the rider reached the gate, Naia following close on his heels. The rider was proudly turned out, his chainmail polished to a perfect gleam beneath his brocaded cloak. Covering it, too, was a tabard of brilliant blue, hemmed in gold, which boasted the king's sun blazon at its centre, with the stag's head stitched over it in jet-black silk.

Elo recognised him: Antoc, who had been put in charge of the standing army, a nod to the number of them who had come from the lands of Tiamh, Artemi and Farne. Interesting that Arren had sent a commander instead of a herald.

'People of Lesscia!' he bellowed, wasting no time. His cry ricocheted up the walls and around the square. Perhaps that was why: he had the loudest voice and liked to use it. People stopped to listen.

'Our king and saviour, Arren the Great, Sunbringer, the rising light of the west, brings his glory to you, last jewel of the south.'

'Sunbringer?' Naia mouthed at Elo.

'He comes with reverence, to parade through your streets and cast his blessings.' Antoc looked around, seeing no one in blue. 'He comes . . . to admire your city and purge it of troubles. Our sunbringer—'

'Sunbringer?' Elo interrupted. There it was again. Arren couldn't be serious. 'Does the man who broke the gods think himself one now, Antoc?'

Antoc backed up his horse, his eyes scanning the wall till he saw Elo. He sneered, recognising him immediately.

'Elogast the Irisian,' the commander said, fingering the jewels on his horn. 'You question our saviour of Blenraden? Who brings the hundreds of his armies victorious through his lands?'

The man had all the delicacy of a blunt axe.

'So, "Sunbringer" he calls himself,' said Elo. He could play too. 'I'll credit him some poetry. Have you checked if it shines out his arse?'

A snicker passed around the gate. Some of Elo's contingent

HANNAH KANER

looked uncertain, sheepish, as if they had been caught in a schoolish trick and didn't know if they were about to get in trouble.

Antoc growled. He had a short fuse, Elo remembered, and didn't like to be laughed at. 'Who the fuck do you think you are, Elogast?' he snapped. 'You're just a fairweather fighter and traitor. A two-country turncoat. You think you can deny a king peaceful access to his own lands?'

Elo tipped his head, keeping his smile. Another piece come to his side of the board. How should he move it?

'I am only a knight,' he said, 'who bled for this land I call home. And now I know it was just for a pompous, shiny-shouldered fool to come blasting a horn at Lesscian walls and expecting them to fall.'

Antoc's face brightened with anger as the gathered crowd laughed, at him. 'You would do well to watch your tongue,' he snapped, and lifted the horn. 'Pick fights you can win, Elogast, or go back to putting your head in your ovens.'

Elo grinned. 'At least the light from there smells pleasant,' he said, to another round of laughter. Then he turned to the Yether guard: 'Seize him.'

He spoke softly, but the guards were ready and listening. Two started forward, grabbing Antoc's horse by the reins.

'Stop!' Antoc cried. 'I am commander general of six thousand soldiers. I will have you all slaughtered!' When they did not stop, he reached for his sword.

Elo lifted his hand, and the bowstrings of three archers stretched above him.

Antoc at least had some instinct. He turned, saw the archers, and balked, somehow surprised. 'This is treachery, you fools!'

One arrow struck his sword, and he dropped it, then growled as one of the guards below him grabbed him by his chainmail and dragged him bodily from his seat. 'I am the king's commander,' he said. 'You . . . you must not touch me!'

'Elo,' Naia said, her grip tightening. 'You won't . . .'

'I won't kill him,' said Elo, watching as his hands were bound. 'But I will play him.'

CHAPTER THIRTY-NINE

Skediceth

SKEDI FLITTED OVER THE BOATS, WHICH THEY HAD managed to get through the canals to the inkers' basement. There, they packed and padded the precious texts, covered them again with the false lids and stuffed down straw and items from Yatho and Telle's home; iron and briddite ore, hammers, tools, pots, pans, food and grain.

He swooped inside the dark of the basement and then out into the bright morning, the size of a jay, and no one took note. The water was a hive of activity. Food and livestock were being sold inside the city for the first time in decades, and hawkers cried out their wares from water to shore. Longboats were passing, guarded by soldiers with yellow scarves, filled with stocks of dried meats and grain, and small, narrow boats stuffed with belongings: books and scripts, a rocking chair, a chest of spices, pushed by harried-looking families down the water. Everywhere were colours of panic, uncertainty, fear.

Skedi swooped back in, landing on Inara's shoulder as she packed in some of Yatho's heavier equipment.

'Can you stop that?' she said, sweat standing out on her brow as she pushed down bags of coal and coke. She had plaited her hair again, but it had come loose, her curls falling around her neck and face.

Skedi hopped off again, fluttering his wings, uncertain where to land. He settled for the edge of the box. 'What's wrong?' he asked. Inara had hidden her colours, unusually.

'Nothing,' said Inara.

Skedi batted an ear, annoyed. 'Lies of omission are still lies,' he said.

She didn't respond, her gaze distant.

'You're talking to the inker god, aren't you?' he said. The inker god's plinth was quiescent, but he still felt their presence. When Inara had mentioned her conversation with Makioron, he wasn't sure he liked it, her talking to other gods in a way he couldn't hear. When had she discovered this?

'She's sad,' she said, meeting his eyes with a frown. 'One of her faithful died in the night.'

Are you angry with me? he asked into her mind. That was theirs alone. Private. But Inara looked away. After a few moments, he lifted his wings and took off again, clearing the barges then flying low through the dark tunnel. The gate that barred access and reduced the influx of debris from the canals into their cellar loading point was still closed, but Skedi tipped himself through the bars with thoughtless ease and into the bright sunshine. He whispered as he flew up over the crowded waters; *you can't see me you can't see me you can't see me*; but he was part tempted to let them see, show them that the god of white lies was here.

He could go further now, from Inara. The beads from Solom's bracelet rattled against his antlers beside Inara's button, and he felt the bright energy of the archivist's gift. Each hour he felt freer, more himself, as if he and Inara were equals, not that he depended on her kindness and waning patience for his life.

A gust of cool wind pushed him higher than the rooftops, and he darted back down to beneath the eaves, scouring the streets for signs of trouble. The colours of people's emotions were big and bright, hard to distinguish, full of conflict and frantic worry. But then he saw robes of grey through the brightness. Archivists. They were grouped close together, looking around with nervous eyes.

Skedi dropped closer, landing on a gutter to watch them go past. *You can't see me you can't see me—*

'Inkers were part of the brutality in the night.' Skedi recognised the man they had lied to in the vaults. 'This is their district.'

'We have no weapons, Betrom. What do we do if we find them?'

'We just need to find the others and stop them leaving,' the woman with them said.

Betrom nodded. His failure to guard the godscripts had clearly cut him deeply. 'The king will break through, he has to, and then we'll deliver them up for execution. It's that Telle who was stirring up trouble, and Solom.'

Skedi fluttered his wings in agitation, and one of the archivists looked up with a frown, sharp as a dagger, suffused with maroon suspicion. Betrom followed their gaze, glowering. Skedi ducked down into the gutter, hiding his antlers.

'Be careful,' Betrom said. 'I swear the only way they could have got to those scripts was with the help of gods.'

You can't see me you can't see me . . .

They passed quickly, thankfully not turning down towards their warehouses, not yet. But how long would it take them to notice the one with the least activity? How long would it take to surround them and stop them leaving?

Inara! he called in his mind to her, and its urgency summoned her attention from wherever it had gone. *We need to leave. Now.*

CHAPTER FORTY

Arren

DAYS OF MOVING, SAKRE TO LESSCIA, THROUGH EACH town a celebration of flowers and wine, fish or game and grain, whatever they had to offer. When they had passed through Elo's old village of Estfjor, Arren had tried not to look towards the little bakery, still locked tight, the first of the spring's returning swifts already nesting beneath its eaves. None of the villagers recognised him, for he did not once remove his helm. Not the whole way to Lesscia.

The rest of his army shone as they moved, as a narrow flank four abreast to hide their sheer number from the front. The Lesscians should not be overwhelmed too quickly. He must show a kinder face, and keep his true power hidden.

Ahead rose the city of knowledge, like the petals of a white rose rising from marshy riverland against a blue sky. Its cloche shone like a second sunrise of copper-blue.

Are you ready? Arren asked Hestra in his mind.

She was quiet for a moment. Then, *I am ready,* she said, her voice still sharp enough to sting.

Arren smiled. No weakness, no frailty. No hesitation.

They soon entered the outermarket, which was quieter than he had expected. There were few people about, and those that were gazed at the moving army with baleful eyes. Many of the little houses stood empty. Odd. He had still been expecting people to come out to sing and run with the pipers or bring them sweet treats and food.

The gates ahead were shut, and the blue banner Arren had seen flying from the walls was solitary. The rest of them were bannered in yellow.

The message was clear: Yether would not be easily bent.

And Elogast had made it to Lesscia.

It did not matter. Must not. If Elo insisted on remaining a thorn in his side, Arren would suck it out and spit it away. But he could not help but wonder if his chest still hurt from Hseth's burn. If he would forgive him, knowing that Hseth was no longer a problem. Would he be proud at what Arren had achieved despite her? Or angry?

'My king,' said Commander Risiah, spurring his horse beside him. 'The day looks warm, and you have worn that helm since Sakre. I worry for your health.'

'My health is fine, thank you, commander,' said Arren.

'But—'

'Sunbringer.' Commander Peta came clattering up beside him on her horse, her voice deep with warning, but Arren had already seen what she would rather he hadn't.

Commander Risiah looked ahead, distracted from Arren for once, and made a gulping sound as he swallowed a laugh.

Commander Antoc was sitting in front of the closed city gate on the back of his horse, which was roped in place. His greying head was bowed, as if that could hide who he was, but his face and neck were beet-red, and he was shivering despite being still wrapped in his shining cloak. This was because he had been stripped naked to the balls, his hands tied in front of him to the saddle of his horse. Around his neck, the Regna horn was tied with ribbons of Yether yellow. Otherwise, he was unharmed.

A snort of laughter came from Arren's personal guard and it rippled through his host, preceded by a whisper as the spectacle of Commander Antoc was passed back along the lines.

Antoc had requested, no, demanded, the honour of riding first to the city. He had insisted that the leader of the largest army should be the first one to speak in the city walls, and now he had been made a fool. A middle-aged man, balls out in front of Arren's intended victory.

Arren held back a growl in his throat. 'Elogast,' he muttered.

His friend always did have a wry sense of humour hidden beneath his sanctimonious exterior. Even for him, this was low. He wanted to make a mockery of him, for nothing could disarm a leader's power faster than laughter. Did he have no respect? For everything Arren had done?

Well. Perhaps this was an opportunity. To show Elo he wasn't as clever as he thought, and Antoc that he wasn't as important.

'Cut the rope,' he said to Peta.

'My king?'

Arren looked at her. 'Your best archer,' he repeated. 'Cut the rope. No commander of ours should have allowed themselves to be made so ridiculous, do you not think?'

Peta paused, then her mouth twitched in a smile, and she gestured one of Arren's mounted guards forward. They raised their eyebrows as she repeated the order but did as they were told and lifted the bow. Well trained, they stretched the string back, back. Listening for the wind, directing the arrow up, to the side. Whispers and muttering rose around them, but Arren did not look back.

'Loose,' barked Peta.

The arrow flew, whistling over the abandoned outermarket, and struck, snapping the rope that bound the horse, and startling it. Antoc yelled, helpless and clinging to the beast as it reared and set off at a run, clattering through empty huts and tables, washing lines, fences, bolting for freedom. If Antoc held on, he might survive.

He fell as he struck a clothesline. The horse dived to the side, and Antoc was dragged by the beast over the marshy ground, his cloak torn off, his back and sides bloody, his mouth wide. If the drums weren't still playing, perhaps they would have heard him scream.

Arren lifted his chin, looking at the walls. He wondered which of the shining helms on the ramparts was Elo's. Would his friend be surprised? Appalled? Scared, maybe?

'The gates have not opened,' said Peta. She did not bat an eye at the Antoc's fate. If anything, she rather looked as if she approved, her golden faith unmarred. 'What do you want us to do?'

Arren smiled, though she would not see it. 'We wait,' he said.

CHAPTER FORTY-ONE

Kissen

AT LEAST THE PRISONERS' CART MEANT SHE DIDN'T HAVE to walk. Through the night they were dragged around the east side of the city, every so often breaching a melee between knights in blue and uncoloured soldiers, after which another person or two were dragged into the cart. Then, when Kissen was backed against the bars of the cage by bodies and the sun was brushing the night from the roofs, they were taken up through the wider ways near the Reach. The seamsters' district, then the merchants' houses and the nobles', for the very few that did not stay outside the stinking city's walls. Finally, to the gardens surrounding the fortress walls.

Here, Kissen saw the full extent of what Faer had dropped her into.

Instead of wide garden spaces filled with fancy-footed noble children taking a turn around the herb beds and shrubbery, there were campfires and tents. The foliage was in the process of being trampled, and guards were stationed at regular intervals stinking of sweat and a long wait. Most of them were archers, though some bore pikes and bows.

It seemed someone had the guts to besiege a fortress that had never before been claimed from the Regna Line. So far, they had not succeeded; the heights of the walls were hung with shreds of burned banners and more than one end of a swinging grapple that had been cut off or snapped. But Kissen half wanted to applaud the sheer gall of the attempt.

The others in the cage were all in blue – king's knights or soldiers. Two had been beaten senseless, and a third looked to be faking it, judging by the constant flicker of his eyes. They were under guard, but not strictly, for they could all barely move for the shifting of other bodies. Kissen was grateful for Doric's cloak.

'Oi,' said Kissen quietly to a man closest to her. 'What's happening here? I thought the fight was in Lesscia?'

'Lesscia?' he mumbled. 'Lesscia nothing.'

'Be quiet,' hissed one of their guards, rattling his scabbard against the bars. Kissen narrowed her eyes at him.

'I need to piss,' she told him.

'Piss where you stand. You already stink.'

'Pigshit washes off,' said Kissen. 'What are you going to do about your face?' A cheap shot. The guard scowled.

'If you don't shut up, I'll shut you up.'

'Ooh, very scary.'

She didn't push him further, though he would be hard pressed to reach her through the bars. She would have to wait, for answers as well as a piss.

When the sun was high, two soldiers barked orders and they were hitched to a horse and moving again. Not as far this time. Kissen twisted, eliciting some groans and complaints, to look at the besieged castle. What was the point, if the king was in Lesscia? All they would get out of it was a castle they would then have to defend. It was clear as they passed the wrecked gardens that who-ever's occupation this was, it was thin, perhaps a thousand strong, and with no clear allegiances. When the king came back there would be a reckoning, and they would lose.

The cart pulled to a halt outside a clean, well-made tent with flags standing out the front. Here, at least, she recognised the colours of the Vittosks, red and yellow, gaudy and warlike, and the purples she thought belonged to the Benins, but it could have been the Spurrisks. Finally, green and silver, faintly familiar.

The bar on their cage was drawn across, the door opened.

'Out. Kneel on the ground.'

The one who had been faking leapt to his feet and threw himself at the door of the cart, only to be grabbed by his blue cloak and thrown to someone else, who slapped him before tossing him down. Another guard reached in and grabbed Kissen by the collar. She smacked his hand away, then swung her legs out of the cart. This was perhaps the first time they noted the sheen and wraps of her bent metal leg.

'You took my staff,' said Kissen pointedly. 'Any of you going to give me a hand?'

One of them took her by the arm and helped lift her out. Her hands were still bound, and she was pretty sure if someone shoved her a shoulder would pop out of its socket. The one who had her gave her a shove, and she let him, going knees-down into the mud. Still, she winced as her prosthesis badly twisted her knee. The other prisoners followed.

A woman stepped out of the tent wearing a tabard of the green and silver, her hair cut to her shoulders. She cast an eye over Kissen and the other prisoners.

'Anyone interesting?' she said, her hands on a pair of twin blades.

'We're here for the lady,' said the one who had arrested Kissen.

'The lady is resting,' said the woman. 'I speak for her.'

The man hawked, but didn't spit, then shrugged. 'That one is a son of House Farne,' he said, pointing to the one that Kissen had tried to speak to. The woman nodded.

'Hostage,' she said, then nodded at others in her colours, standing nearby. They came to grab him, but as they did the escapee leapt up again to his feet. He dodged the swipe of the guard and sprinted away from the gathered soldiers.

'Get him!' the woman shouted.

'For the king!' screamed the running man. 'Sunbringer. Sunbringer!'

Another figure, taller and slighter than the first, stepped out of the tent with a bow in her hand, took aim and released. The arrow caught the man in the back. He grunted, fell, and did not get up again.

Kissen took a shaking breath, looking back at the shooter. The soldiers all bowed in quick succession.

'My lady.'

'My lady.'

'Great leader.'

She had long, straight black hair pulled back in a single plait that fell from her shoulders to her hips, and her skin was a lustrous brown. She wore an open-necked tunic over a narrowly bound waist and flowing skirts, slit for ease of movement, with trews beneath. The woman looked as ready for a ball as a battle. She stared them all down, eyes so dark they were almost black, as if daring another to try to move. Kissen was suddenly deeply aware that she was wearing weeks-old clothes and covered in dried blood and pigshit, even if her cloak was nice.

'Anyone else?' she said, lowering her bow. The one with the cropped hair stepped demurely back.

Kissen felt a kick on her back, and she lurched forward. A clump of congealed blood from her cheek came forward in her mouth, and she spat it out.

'This one says she's the king's messenger,' he said.

The woman looked down at Kissen, entirely unshaken by the man she had killed. 'Bit underdressed, aren't you?' she said. 'The only messengers we've had are from the other fortresses. What is it this time? Burning? Hanging? Salted earth or torture?' She laughed bitterly. 'Each warning is no better than tinder to the flame.'

The woman's face, Kissen realised, struck a chord of memory in her. Something in its shape, and the set of her frown.

'I said I had a message *for* the king,' Kissen said dryly. 'I'll deliver it to anyone in charge then be on my way.'

'A message from whom?'

This rankled; Kissen swallowed her annoyance at fate making her a god's messenger. 'From the god of the River Aan.'

Everyone fell silent, and Kissen grimaced. She had known that would happen. When the gods were involved, everyone pissed themselves. The woman's eyes narrowed.

'Saying what?' she asked.

'Saying that while you all stare at your navels, the real danger comes from the sea.'

A flash of annoyance brightened the lady's eyes before she turned to the others. 'I'll talk to her,' she said. 'Hostage to gaol, others to the pit. Clear the body.'

'I want my staff,' said Kissen. 'And my arms.'

The woman gave her a slightly amused glance. She was radiant, powerful but contained; Kissen didn't think she had seen anyone more beautiful. Aan liked to tease Kissen with her weakness for good-looking women, but this one had killed a man running, without even a thought. She would kill Kissen too, and Kissen knew it.

'Very well,' she said, and ducked into the tent.

Kissen felt the knot on her wrists tugged, wrestled with, then released. The guard with cropped hair picked her up by the arm, face impassive, then took her staff from the soldier who offered it before dragging her into the tent.

It was warm inside, heated by a small charcoal burner which was almost out, but still hot. There were three heavy chairs set with cushions, and a table in the centre littered with letters. In the corner was a small cot, recently vacated, with a sword leaning against it. The lady stood at the table, appraising Kissen, her face unreadable.

'Hold out your wrists,' the guard said, brandishing a pair of manacles.

'Really?' Kissen said.

'Really,' said the lady before the guard could answer. 'We're no fools, and you look like you can fight.'

'I don't take kindly to being a prisoner.'

'Few do.'

Kissen leaned on her staff and put her hands out in front of her. The irons were cold, closed straight over her wrists and fastened with a pin lock. The lady watched, standing like Elo did, like a knight, her back straight and her mouth firm, her fine fingers resting on the back of one of the chairs while the sunlight through the tent brightened her skin to bronze. In the shelter of the tent, her fierce gaze seemed softer, sadder. Kissen, for once, was silent. She felt as if her tongue had trebled in weight, and found herself blushing.

'Well?' the lady asked. Kissen shook herself and went to one of the chairs then sat in it with a sigh. This drew a raised brow from the woman and her guard. That look again. The familiarity was nagging at her.

'I'm Kissen, a godkiller from Talicia, by way of Blenraden and Lesscia.'

'What is a godkiller doing with a message from the gods?'

Kissen leaned back. She was enjoying the warmth and clean scent of the tent after a night spent rubbing sides with bloodied fighters and suspected it wouldn't last long. She'd be in a cell before the evening was out. She hoped, at least, it would have a bed in it. 'What's a noble doing besieging her king's city?' she asked.

The woman watched her steadily, though tension threaded through her shoulders, and her hand tightened where she still held her bow.

'I'd like to know who I'm talking to before I talk,' explained Kissen after a few long moments of silence. 'Seems polite, no?'

The noble laughed. 'You come marching into my tent, take my seat – stinking to the heavens, might I add – and you want my name? Shouldn't you already know to whom you are giving your message?'

Her accent, too, rang familiar. Her way of phrasing.

'I just came down from the sky on the back of a rude little bastard god in the wrong city,' said Kissen. 'I have no idea what the piss is going on here, why there's a siege in Sakre instead of Lesscia, and I'm scared shitless. So, are you going to give me your name or am I getting an arrow in the back? Because I'd rather know now.'

The noble's mouth quirked in a smile, but it faded quickly. 'My name is Lady Lessa Craier. And this siege is my vengeance, for the gods, my House, and my daughter.'

CHAPTER FORTY-TWO

Elogast

ELO COULD SEE ARREN'S ARMOUR GLEAMING FROM A MILE away. He had scoffed at first glimpse. Such splendour! The Arren he had known had been simple and straightforward, and now he wore a great helm with a crown of antlers and golden rays. Stranger still, he had styled a break in his armour over his chest, more gold shining around it. Arren had clearly anticipated Elo's intention to reveal him and was thwarting him by showing the world what he had done, what he had become. A king one with a god.

And the world loved it. The army was still with him, Knight Commander Peta, Elo's replacement, even Gods Commander Risiah. He had hoped Antoc stripped bare would have made his friend remember, just for a moment, that he was still just a rich boy dressing up.

It should have. But the swift, brutal act of sending his own commander catapulting into the distance had been smarter than Elo anticipated, and crueller. Elo was tempted to send Yether's knights after Antoc to see if he had lived, but that would be a sign of weakness, an admission of fault.

'What is he waiting for?' said Naia nervously. Despite herself, she had not left the wall. Elo wondered if it was her way of making amends.

'I don't know,' said Elo. The army had stopped perhaps three hundred strides away, spilling out into the paths between outer city homes, organised by different commanders and captains, like blue blood through a vein. 'Parley, perhaps.'

But they had sent no requests, and Elo was not about to either. This wasn't like Arren. Elo thought it but didn't say it aloud. Arren was rarely patient, particularly when the advantage was his.

Naia seemed to trace his thoughts. 'Perhaps he is not the man you knew.'

'He isn't,' said Elo, but continued to stare at the figure in gold, seated calmly on his horse, and wondered if Arren could see him, could pick him out amongst all the other figures. He looked around. Faroch had not returned with Yether as they had planned. Something had delayed them.

He turned to Faroch's second, Necrin, who had joined them when the army had been sighted. 'Hold here,' Elo ordered him. 'If they approach the gate, fire warning shots. No bloodshed.'

The second swallowed, looking around. Some of the guards were peering over the wall in a way that was liable to earn them an arrow to the head. 'And if they charge the gates?' he asked.

Elo glanced at the golden king. Sunbringer. 'Hold them,' he said. 'I'll be back.'

He hurried down the ladder, Naia at his heels. 'Where are we going?' she asked.

'To check something,' said Elo. He frowned at her. 'We?'

They moved away from the gate towards the horses kept at bay, saddled, fresh-shod and ready. Naia took the reins of a big one, giving it a pat on the neck. 'Ariam is dead,' she said. 'Canovan . . . gone. You would turn me away?' She looked at him directly. 'I'm the last of the rebellion still standing with you.'

Elo could not help but feel relief, and when he did not protest, Naia passed the reins to him.

'I'll ride with you,' she said.

Elo put his foot in the stirrup and pulled Naia up. She hesitated, then put her arms around him, holding tight to his armour. Her armour.

The chestnut steed was all too happy to be chosen, and Elo barely needed to kick in his heels before they were trotting through crowded streets.

'What are you worried about?' said Naia into his ear as they crossed a bridge over one of the grand canals and into the streets of the new quarter, built as the city expanded with wide avenues and clean water channels that carried refuse down to Daesmouth.

'Perhaps nothing,' said Elo, the sound of the horse's hooves loud in his ears. Should he gallop? No, that might cause a panic.

'You think the "Sunbringer" might cast a longer shadow than you hoped?'

'Something like that,' he said.

They passed through the finely kept gardens, cloaked with the fresh scents of spring flowers. All was calm, and Elo was out of place, sweating beneath his armour and blood still on his skin from the night before. He could smell it under the flowers, like a sewer in a palace.

It wasn't long before they reached the grand gates of the Yether manor and its marble fountain. Two guards stood at the door in yellow, seemingly at ease.

Strange, though: there was a pony, dusty-flanked from the road, drinking from the water trough.

Elo and Naia dismounted and one of the guards greeted him with a wave.

'Commander Elogast,' said one, his eyes alighting on Elo's armour. 'Lion of Lesscia, I'm sure they'll be finished soon. Faroch will be sorry for the delay.'

'Who else is in there?' asked Elo, ignoring the titles. Faroch didn't ride a pony: he had a horse in Yether livery. In fact, Elo could see it by the stables.

'His son came back,' said the guard. 'Begging an audience. Apologising, I suspect. I heard he caused a ruckus.'

Elo frowned and went past him through the door, Naia close on his heels.

'I thought he was banned from the city,' she said. 'All the guards knew . . .'

'We just had an influx of refugees,' said Elo. A moving tide of faces, impossible to track. Ponies, livestock, cloaks and homes. 'He must have come in with them.'

The hallway floor was gleaming in the bright sunlight, and Captain Faroch stood by the door not to the study, but to the library on the other side. His arms were folded, his face a picture of boredom. He glanced up as they came in, his hand going to his sword, but relaxed as he recognised them. 'What's wrong?' he asked.

'The king is waiting,' said Elo, and a flash of anxiety passed over Faroch's face. It was one thing to expect an army or act against a monarch's knights, it was another to be faced with whatever would happen next. 'Your guards are nervous. Where are the Yethers?' He could hear the faint clattering from the kitchen, the hum of a maid stoking a fire. All seemed well.

Faroch tipped his head back towards the door to the library. 'They were arguing in there,' he said.

'Were?' said Naia.

Faroch frowned. 'Went quiet a few—' He trailed off at the look on Elogast's face.

'Open the door,' said Elo.

Faroch's mouth tightened and he straightened up. 'Be careful you don't overstep, commander,' he said.

'Open the damn door, Faroch!'

The captain caught his urgency, but still hesitated. Elo shouldered past him while he havered and shoved his way in.

The room was hot, too hot with a burning fire, and the light within was narrow, stifled by curtains drawn over the window to hide the light.

Elo saw Beloris first. His sat staring into the flames, his neck sweaty, a riding cloak discarded on the long chair he had settled on. He did not look up as they entered, but stayed completely still, his elbows on his knees. His hands were red.

'Oh gods . . .' gasped Naia.

Lord Yether lay in a pool of his own blood, his legs still in spasm, a knife buried in his throat. The blade was in the thick vein, bleeding in throbbing gushes.

In a moment, Elo closed the gap between them, pressing his hand to the wound. But he knew. He already knew it was too late. Red spread across the floor, into the rugs, towards the fire. Yether's eyes rolled back in his head, his mouth working. No noise came out.

'It was better this way,' said Beloris. He looked up, his eyes steady, shining. Burning with zeal.

Arren had done this. Elo would never have thought he could stoop so low, but this new Arren had just sent his own commander to an ignominious death on the back of a horse. He had already burned a House that had disobeyed him. What was a dagger in the dark between a son and a father?

Beloris's mouth twisted in a smile. 'Sunbringer,' he whispered.

'Captain, do something!' Naia cried to Faroch, who had followed him in. His throat bobbed, his hand on his pommel, but his fingers were splayed out as if they would not bend. His lord had been murdered, but it was his heir with the dagger.

'Better than a public execution for a traitor to a king,' Beloris continued, and he reached up to push his hair back, running it through with his father's blood. 'Better at the hand of someone who loved him.'

Elo said nothing, too many moves flicking through his head, as he dismissed one after the other. Beloris had sneaked in with the crowds. How many others had come? How many had Elo let inside the gate with knives and daggers? Who knew where the armouries were?

What could he do? What should he do? Beloris held his gaze as Lord Yether pulled in his last breaths, sips of air that could not survive the waves of blood.

'Captain Faroch,' said Beloris and Faroch flinched. '*Commander* Faroch, if you act wisely now.'

Faroch was frozen, panicked.

'The gaols are open,' said Beloris. 'Middren's knights are freed by writ under my father's seal. My seal.' He held up his bloody left hand, showing a signet with the Yether eagle. 'The gates will open, and what you choose will determine if you die as a traitor, or you save those misled by the false lion of Lesscia. Elogast of Sakre, who has killed my father.'

Elo lowered Yether gently. The man was dead. If his heart was still beating, it was beating his last. He looked at Naia, closest to the door, trying to get her attention. If she ran now, Beloris might forget about her. Chaos was about to break on a city already balanced on delicate threads.

'*You* killed him,' said Naia, oblivious. 'You killed your . . . your own . . .'

'Me?' said Beloris. 'I did not turn my father against the king, nor a god loose on the streets. I did not make my people traitors. I did not kill him.'

Faroch finally looked at Elo, his gaze pitying. Lord Yether was dead, a new Lord Yether had taken command. The Sunbringer played a vicious game. The board had tipped again, and Elo had now lost his most important play.

Elo glanced towards the hearth, its fire blazing on such a warm spring day, and for a moment he thought he saw a face there. The face of Hestra the hearth god. Watching.

'Arrest him, Commander Faroch,' said Beloris. 'Arrest him now. I will grant your guards amnesty, if they do not fight back. You and your family will be well rewarded by our Sunbringer. I swear it to you.'

Faroch closed his eyes.

'Faroch, you can't,' said Naia. 'They have to know. The truth.'

The truth didn't matter. There was only survival. It was no choice at all. Elo or the city. One man who had lost, or a hundred guards who were about to lose more. Elo didn't know whether to fight or flee. He put his hand on his blade. Should he kill Beloris? Would that gain him anything but vengeance?

The captain's fingers closed on his sword. A decision reached as he drew it. 'Commander Elogast,' he said hoarsely. 'You have abandoned your lord.'

Elo drew his own blade, but hesitated. *Commander*, he still called him. *Abandon.*

Faroch charged, and Naia screamed. But he was going for the knee, as Elo had shown Ariam. Elo stepped back, whirling his blade around and under Faroch's, and lifting both into the air. Faroch met his gaze. He was weeping. His eyes were full of grief, pleading with him.

Abandon.

Elo charged into Faroch's chest with his shoulder, shoving him into the wall.

'No!' shouted Beloris as Faroch collapsed with an *oof* of breath.

This was their moment, the only hope Faroch could give him. Elo leapt for the door and grabbed the shocked Naia's hand, pulling her after him.

'Run!'

CHAPTER FORTY-THREE

Inara

THE CANALS WERE BUSIER THAN INARA HAD EVER SEEN them. People were everywhere, clogging up the city from bank to bank. They almost vibrated with excitement, gossip, some applauding the loss of the king's knights, others muttering about retribution.

Inara and the archivists did not make an unusual sight, at least, with their three barges nudging through the water. Especially not with all of them dressed in civilian clothing.

'Watch it, fucking luggers!' snapped one merchant at them as they passed, his own boat barely inches above the water, weighed down with grain. He flicked his oar, and Telle winced as a splash hit the boxes.

Yatho sat with her, and reached across to hold her hand, signing with her other. Ertha, the archivist, was expertly steering the boat, with surprisingly muscular arms, dressed in worn velvet leggings and a purple shawl wrapped around her shoulders and neck. Cal stood at the front of their boat using a staff to prevent the barge being knocked by other craft and Inara sat back with her satchel, her waistcoat, her waxwool cloak, and Skedi. Running again.

This didn't feel right, not to Inara. *I don't want this*, she said to Skedi. He was crouched inside the satchel, whispering his lies that surrounded them with a cloak of obscurity.

They need our help, he replied swiftly, *we should help them.*

They don't need me.

No, he poked his head out of the satchel and looked at her from below. *They need me.*

Inara clasped her hands together, looking down at the green beads hanging from his antlers, next to the button. He blinked at her, his yellow eyes bright in the light from the sky, then they passed under a bridge, and Cal and Ertha had to crouch.

The sudden shade was chill, the reflection from the water trailing patterns on the stone arches above them, and the pillars that held them up. The rippling light revealed a small shrine, set back above the waterline under the nearest arch. It was carved into the stone, and there were one or two cups sitting on it, brimming with a dark wine. The shrine looked as if it had been damaged and rebuilt, damaged and rebuilt.

'What canal are we on?' Inara asked as Yatho glanced over to her, pausing her conversation with Telle. They shone beautifully again, now their emotions were aligned, patterns more lustrous than the gleam on the stone.

'Geniv Canal,' said Yatho. 'Named after one of the builders.'

What had the rose god said? There was a god of the canals still living, still with a shrine.

Inara pressed a thought towards it, trying to distract herself. *What's your name, god of the Geniv?*

Who is it who asks? the god spoke back immediately.

They broke out again into the sunlight between bridges, and Cal and Ertha straightened. They were nearing the river harbour, where the water widened. No one had recognised them amid the crowds, not yet, though Inara had seen more than one grey-robed archivist peering out across the boats.

'I'll miss this city,' Cal said, looking up at the grand buildings rising over them, their colonnades reaching into the water. As if to spite him, another small boat ricocheted off a heavy barge and scraped sides with theirs with a vicious creak. Telle stood up to push them away with her boot, ignoring their angry yelling. Ertha, with a flick of her pole, knocked their oar into the water so they had to scrabble to pick it up.

A cry came from a few streets away and the thunder of hooves on flat cobbles. A horse broke through the crowd, scattering people on the bank, hastening at speed towards the bridge. Its rider was one of Yether's guards, a yellow scarf around his neck and a bow and arrow on his back.

'We have been betrayed!' he yelled to anyone who would hear him. 'Lord Yether is dead. The king is coming!' He continued to run, turning left and over the next bridge ahead of them. 'Lesscia has been betra—'

His yell was cut short. An arrow sped across the water and struck him through the throat before he reached the other side. He fell backwards off the horse and into the canal to a wave of screams. Inara crouched, turning to see who had loosed the arrow. Ertha and Cal kept themselves small, but Solom stood on one of the other boats, his colours startling and livid with fury.

The archer was one of two knights on horseback, in ragged blue-and-gold. The knights Elo had apprehended. They were loose. One blew his horn.

'Be calm!' the other bellowed. The canal fell momentarily silent, and the horse of the guard who had been shot had trundled to a confused halt. Inara met eyes with Telle and Yatho. It had all been going so well.

The guard who had spoken sat up higher. 'The traitors against House Yether will be dealt with, just like him,' he declared, his voice carrying and bouncing between the buildings. Traitors to House Yether? Surely he should have said the king?

Yatho was signing to Telle, who protectively put her hands on one of the boxes.

'The king comes,' the guard added, 'to pay homage to the city. Prepare for him.'

She recognised the knight's voice; she was sure of it. Where had she heard it? Somewhere significant. The only other sound was the knocking of the boats as the ripples from the guard's body falling tipped them in the water. The knight cast another glance around, waiting for someone to challenge him. Hoping for someone to challenge him.

It is better not to act, it is better to be silent, it is better to be quiet. Inara could hear Skedi whispering, but not at her, at Solom, who was bristling with desire to speak.

Skedi, I know his voice, said Inara. *We need to find Elo.*

Skedi didn't answer: his focus was on Solom, on keeping them unseen.

'We shall have peace,' the knight said, 'once more, in this city.'

'Peace?' Solom cried, breaking through Skedi's hold. Telle signalled at him to be silent, but he listened to her no more than he had Skedi, too stalwart in his righteous fury. 'You killed a fleeing man in cold blood!'

The water stirred. The man's blood was seeping into it. In the shrine they had just passed, the god was listening.

The knight bristled. 'We killed a traitor to the king,' he said. 'And if you speak one more word, a traitor you shall be too!'

'Come, Deegan,' the other knight said. 'They're no one, we need to clear the march.'

Deegan.

Deegan's colours were red and bright, the colour of roses that had just bloomed from thorny branches, and they stirred like flames, thick with violence. Inara remembered where she had heard the voice. It felt like a lifetime ago.

'Lucky you're a good shot, Deegan.'

'Didn't stop her yelling, though. Not smart enough to prefer the arrows to the fire.'

Voices in a forest, while they hid, terrified of their own breaths. The smell of smoke in her hair, her clothes, the smell of her orchards burning. The knights who had attacked her home had jested as they rode from the slaughter and blaze. They had laughed, their colours shining.

Lucky you're a good shot, Deegan.

And this was one of them.

'We are archivists here,' said Solom loudly. 'We are a city of knowledge. We say what we see. And I will not look away.'

'Solom, be quiet,' hissed Ertha. Yatho groaned and put her head in her hands.

'There they are!'

Inara whipped her head around. Grey robes on the bank: archivists.

'Arrest them!' one of them shouted, pointing at Solom. 'They're thieves! Archivist thieves and traitors!'

The other knight with Deegan pulled out his own bow, and they both nocked arrows, drawing the strings tight. Solom stared them down, while an archivist from the shore began to leap across the boats, somehow thinking she could apprehend them all on her own as she crossed the canal. Another joined her. Two men in the boat next to Inara's stood up, flexing their fists and taking the measure of their barges.

Inara stood too.

Inara, what are you doing? said Skedi. *Duck, hide, run.*

The canal. The god. Inara stood up. *Help us,* she called.

I don't help anyone for nothing, said the canal god. *I am Daefer. The merchants and the ferries are my folk. They pay for their luck.*

Of course, this was not Skedi, nor Scian. This god was bargaining. An arrow flew from Deegan, skimming just over Solom's shoulder as the boats bobbed with activity. Solom lifted his oar, gripping it with two hands, shaking.

What do you want? Inara threw to Daefer.

Blood and wine.

Inara swallowed, flipping her long braid behind her. She had no wine. Kissen would not want her to give blood to gods. What would her mother do? Inara had no idea. Her mother was dead. This man had helped kill her.

Kissen was not here. Her mother was not here. Elo was in danger, and her last parting with him had been in anger. Whatever he had planned, it was failing, and once again Inara was watching events happen around her. Helpless.

The first archivist reached their boat, Yatho pulled her wife out of harm's way and brought her hammer around with a ferocious crunch into the interloper's leg. The archivist screamed as she fell into the water. One of the men in the boat made a grab for Solom, who turned with his oar and smacked him in the face. Deegan fired again, striking Solom in the arm. The other knight pointed his arrow at Yatho, passing over Inara as no threat.

Inara, please, said Skedi. Telle had seen her standing and was gesturing wildly for her to run.

No, she was not helpless. She had strength. She had power.

I will give you my blood, said Inara, looking around for something, anything, sharp. *Protect us.*

'Your king is a false god!' Solom cried, and Cal leapt off his post and wrapped his arms around the old archivist, kicking at the men who made a grab for them and dragging him down into the bottom of the barge where caged messenger birds were flapping up a feathered panic. Another arrow whistled through where his chest had been and struck a woman in a longboat in front of them, slamming through her cheek. She howled.

I accept, said the canal god.

Inara put her hand to her mouth, staring straight at Deegan the knight. He met eyes with her, not recognising, not comprehending. Her vengeance began now. No more waiting.

'For House Craier!' she snarled, and Deegan's eyes widened. He nocked another arrow, turning directly to her. Skedi flew up out of the satchel despite the risk, eyes wide as he realised what was happening, why she hadn't moved.

'Inara!' he shouted. 'No!'

Inara bit down, hard, into the base of her thumb, channelling all her fury into her own flesh. A crunch, a give, and blood spilled into her mouth.

My blood! she cried, holding her hand over the edge of the boat. Her own colours were with the blood, her fears, her hopes, her anger. *Protect us from harm, take down the knights, get us to port.*

Give it to me, said Daefer. *Give it!*

She squeezed. A drop of red fell to the water, drenched in colour, two, three.

Oh! What wealth in your blood! cried the canal god. *What power!*

The water surged around the boats, then burst outwards, rippling out towards the shore as a wave. The horses reared, their ears going flat as a wall of green water rushed towards them. Deegan fired at Inara and Skedi, but his arrow went high.

The Geniv Canal surged up in a wave of green muck and detritus. It pushed aside the other boats on the river, knocking people from where they clung, their hands trapped in wood, or rope, or their own clothes. A second archivist fell with a shriek, the first that Yatho had struck disappearing under the waves.

Their boats were picked up, and up, pulled to the centre and shoved forward in the current. As they reached a bridge, the god bore them higher. Inara could almost hear him cackling as he did so.

Skedi had landed on Inara's shoulder, his fur blooming about him in panic. Cal was screaming.

'Inara!' Telle shouted. She was holding onto Yatho, who had fallen. *Is this you?* she signed one-handed. Yatho winced, her back paining her as the boat bucked and moved on the waves.

Inara didn't deny it. It was not her power, but it was her command.

Telle paled. *Stop it!* Shouts from the shore, the waves sucked boats in their wake, tipping them, rocking them, dragging unsuspecting folks under the surface. *People are getting hurt.*

Inara shook her head. *I'm saving you*, she said.

Skedi flapped his wings in consternation. *This isn't right*, he told her, digging his claws into her shoulder as they picked up speed, only to hold on.

'None of this is right,' snapped Inara. Telle was staring at her as if she had grown horns and sharp teeth. 'None of this is right till I make it right.' She looked over the side of the boat. 'Daefer, take me to shore!'

As you wish, little one.

Skedi crawled down and dropped to the hull. 'What are you doing?' he said, ears flat, backing towards Telle.

'I'm going to find Elo.'

Skedi shook his head. 'You can't,' he said. 'Elo sent you here. It's too dangerous.'

'I decide what's dangerous,' said Inara. 'I decide what I can do. I'm not going to let that damn king win!'

'You don't want things decided for you,' cried Skedi, 'yet you can decide for both of us?'

Inara steeled herself. 'And you? Have you never decided anything for both of us?'

Skedi flapped his wings. 'That was wrong,' he pleaded. 'What is this but wrong as well?'

Inara stepped back. The water rose beside them, it had shape now. A long-limbed dog, shaggy furred and grimy. Daefer.

'Stay then,' she said in a whisper.

'No . . . Ina, you're my home.'

'You're not mine.'

Skedi flinched, diminishing in size. Inara bit her tongue, wishing she hadn't spoken. Wishing she could take it back. A truth she should never had told.

But it was too late for that. 'You have offerings now. Believers,' she said, and picked up her satchel. Skedi's satchel. 'You don't need me anymore.' Her heart sharpened in her chest, paining her. Skedi had protected her, lied for her, kept close to her, her whole childhood. Her constant companion. Her friend.

But he could not bring back what she had lost. Nothing could.

She turned and stepped onto the wave of Daefer's back. The water felt solid under her foot.

'Inara!' cried Skedi. 'No!'

Inara leapt for the shore and the water caught her, passing her down towards the bank.

'Inara!' cried Skedi, leaping up into the air. 'Come back!'

She landed. The water was loud: she willed it to cover his voice.

Inara, he called directly into her mind. *Please. Don't leave me.*

She pushed him away, closing herself to him, and she ran. Into the alleys, away from the surging water, away from the screams, those she had caused, and she didn't look back.

Ina?

His voice was a shadow, she dusted it off and kept moving.

She had to find Elo. He had ruined his chance, and she had to save him. The connection between her and Skedi was stretching. She moved further and further away from him. Her heart still hurt, but it was a strange hurt, an ache so cold it felt like ice. Their link, it was changing. How much could it take. Half a city? More?

Was it already broken?

But she would not turn back.

CHAPTER FORTY-FOUR

Kissen

ALIVE. SOMEONE HAD TO TELL INARA HER MOTHER WAS alive. And an absolute arsehole.

Kissen told her tale, starting with Inara, and ending with Talicia, with some omissions in between: Inara's connection with Skediceth, her strange powers, these Kissen did not know how to say. But to the story of Blenraden, of Arren, Hseth, Talicia and the war preparations, Lessa listened impassively, her face turning colder and stonier as Kissen spoke. After she finished, the noblewoman sat very still, her eyes resting on her maps. The guard was well trained, they did not speak, though when Kissen had described the burning of the Craier manor she had gripped her swords so tightly their pommels must have left imprints in her palm.

After a long while, Lessa looked up. 'Get the others,' she said.

The guard nodded and left.

'Can I go now?' said Kissen.

'No,' said Lessa. 'My companions are Selainne Vittosk, and Fargast Graiis, regent of the Graiis House until its son comes of age. You will tell them what you told me.'

'What more is there to tell?' said Kissen. 'Your daughter is in a city five days' ride from here, a city that you *know* is under siege from its own king.'

The only indication that Lessa gave that she understood was a slight tremor in her fingers.

'I gave you my message,' said Kissen. 'I belong back home, looking after my *family*.' She had meant that as a barb, but Lessa Craier did not flinch. How did she not understand? How did she not run to Lesscia as fast as her legs would move? Kissen would even take another ride on Faer's back if she could assure herself that the girl was safe.

Lessa was unmoved. 'I have yet to decide whether I believe you,' she said. 'I saw what became of my House, my people. I have been given to false hope before.'

'I am not a liar.'

'Nor I, and abandoning this siege will make me one. I owe more than that to the soldiers who have given their allegiance and their lives to me. Your word pales in the shade of theirs.'

'Then you're a fool.'

'More foolish than a woman who tells me she has been dragged between gods and people for weeks? And has nothing to show for it apart from a good cloak, a tale of doom and a hope that could unravel a war.' Lessa smiled slightly, but there was no warmth in it.

Kissen bit her tongue. She had not met a woman like this before, as hard as iron but softly spoken, able to match her cut for cut.

'The knight you say,' the woman added. 'Elogast. I met him in Blenraden. A smart man, sharp tongued, and a wise strategist. He was almost as dedicated to the king as the king was to him. It would surprise me if he had turned on him.'

'It wouldn't surprise you if you saw the mess the king made of his chest.'

Lessa's dark eyes landed on her. Gods' blood – she wasn't pretty like a doll was pretty; her face was sharp, almost hawkish, when still. But when there was a quirk of movement, a smile, a frown, Kissen found herself watching it like the turn of a weathervane.

The tent door stirred, and through it stepped a broad man with light blond hair streaked with silver, and an old woman with eastern looks and fair skin, who wore leather instead of armour. Etched on her breastplate were two ships sailing, and another sinking. House Vittosk, the lands closest to Talicia. She did not look pleased.

'What's this about Talicia?' said the man, Fargast Graiis, Kissen suspected. 'Lady Craier, we have claimed the Shield. By tomorrow night we will have the Reach, and the Forge. I do not enjoy distractions.'

'I agree,' replied Lady Craier. 'And yet and yet I promised I would share anything that came my way. This person speaks of an alliance between Restish and Talicia. An invasion.'

'Ridiculous,' said Selainne Vittosk. 'It violates our treaty.'

'They are already marching through the Bennites,' said Kissen. 'I have seen them. And their ships are going south as we speak.'

'A mountain campaign would be doomed to fail,' Selainne threw back. 'They have tried it before. The supply lines are too thin.' She sneered at Kissen and looked her up and down. 'We broke Talicia and its ships decades ago,' she added, then directed her words back to Lessa. Vittosk was almost twice the Lady Craier's age, but she looked at her with open admiration. 'They have fat traders only that do not tip at their old god's beating. It is a rotten little land of liars and idolaters.' She smiled without humour. 'Never trust a Talician.'

'Surely a Restish alliance is not out of the question?' said Fargast tentatively. 'That was the same treaty that gave Restish ships untaxed access to Blenraden ports. We broke it first.'

'I'm well aware of Restish's grievances with the east coast,' said Selainne, 'they are closer to my lot than they are to yours.' The Graiis House was in the middle of the north west, far from any relationship with Restish.

'I'm just saying, I would not put their loyalty above their greed.'

Lessa gazed at Kissen, and Kissen wondered what she was thinking. She could not read her face at all.

'And if it is the truth?' said the lady. 'She did not come just with a message; she came with a request. Save the king.'

Lessa's guard had come back in, and she scoffed, folding her arms.

'Save who burned my House, and the people in it,' said Lessa, her hand on her table curled slowly into a fist. 'Who had not the courage to meet me in fair battle.'

Kissen was starting to suspect this would not go her way.

'Save the king who marches on his own cities and fancies himself a god,' Lessa continued, then laughed. 'We should call off our siege, disband our rebellion, lay down our vengeance and our lives at his feet, all on the word of a veiga. No better than a catcher of small gods.'

'A veiga who saved your child,' snapped Kissen.

'Who claims she did. Highly suspicious, I think, to come into the midst of a siege, claim connection to my kin and say I should throw myself at the mercy of a merciless king, because – what? – he's well liked? It seems the enemy has adjusted their tactics.'

The two other nobles laughed a little, relaxing. 'I did not know you had a child still living,' said Fargast.

'Neither did I,' said Lessa, still looking at Kissen as if to gauge her reaction. 'Lesscia will fall,' she said. 'We knew it would be so. Fargast, you have even given your own blood, a Graiis captain in Lesscia, for our cause. Our opportunity is here.'

Kissen realised what Lessa had done: she had used her. To solidify her connections with her allies, to show that she consulted them, but that her lead was still strong.

Well, Kissen never took a tongue-lashing kneeling down. She leaned back in her seat, pushing her thighs apart so she could rest her manacles on her left leg.

'Is this the game you want to play, my lady?' she said, her voice dripping with ire. The guard made an annoyed sound, but Lessa quietened her with a motion of her hand.

'You want some more truths to convince you?' Kissen went on. 'How about that over a moon ago I was summoned to your lands to put an end to a god who had started starving a village under your protection for blood offerings?'

Lessa's brow twitched. A reaction! A cautious one.

'I loitered in a tavern with a very fine lady about to grace my bed. Rosalie, her name. Do you remember your own people in Ennerton? They're in the lowlands near the Bennites, I wonder what will happen to them when the Talicians descend?'

'Are you leaning towards threats now, veiga?' said the guard. 'Now that you do not get your way?'

'I'm just telling a story,' Kissen continued, still looking at Lessa.

'The night your lands burned, your daughter had run from where you were hiding her. Why do *you* think a little girl might come to a godkiller, frightened, with a secret she could not tell her mother?'

The lady stood, her eyes going wide with anger as she began to suspect what Kissen was telling her. 'Be careful,' she said in a low voice.

What would have happened if that night had gone differently? If Kissen had lain with Rosalie and woken to her sweet smile, if Inara had stayed home with her little god? If Elo had continued baking bread and quietly atoning for whatever sins he had committed?

Inara would have burned. Elo would have lost his heart. Kissen would be none the wiser.

'A god,' said Kissen quietly. Lessa visibly paled. 'Didn't you know your own child, Lessa Craier? That she had a god linked to her and would not tell you in case it hurt you?'

Lessa opened her mouth, then closed it, her eyes darted to the others, who were looking at Kissen with renewed interest. 'Hold your tongue,' she snapped.

'Well,' said Kissen, 'I pick up the smart-mouthed little shit – you're welcome by the way – and take her back to her house, only to find it burned, her mother gone. Worse, no one knew who the fuck she was. Sound familiar?'

The guard hissed. Lessa took a step forward and grabbed Kissen by the collar of her cloak, seething with fury as she lifted her from her seat. Kissen was half-throttled, but this was the most she had got from the lady.

'So,' she continued to Lessa's face, 'I take the girl to my family and tried to separate her and her little god, only to later find her still-living mother sitting pretty on a siege while condemning *my* city and *her* child to fall to a bastard king.'

'You will be silent!' said Lessa. Kissen had found a chink in her armour.

'A bastard king *you* want to save,' said the guard, looking likely to draw her sword.

'I never said I liked him,' spat Kissen, sideways, her eyes still on

Lessa. The noblewoman did not just disbelieve Kissen; she was terrified that it was true.

No, there was something more.

'What's this about a god?' said Selainne. 'Your daughter . . .'

Lessa dropped Kissen back into her seat. 'She's just shooting arrows at the sky,' she said quickly, 'hoping one will strike. Every word of it is nonsense.' She looked at Selainne and smiled with a warmth so startlingly real that Kissen immediately saw it as a lie. 'You're right, I should have listened. Never trust a Talician.'

Selainne nodded.

'Are you sure?' said Fargast.

'Look at her,' said Lessa. Her tone, her demeanour, had changed completely. Moments before she had Kissen by the throat, and now she shrugged. 'Stinking, talking about fire gods and invasion. I shouldn't have bothered you with this.' Fargast looked at Kissen, then tipped his head.

'Perhaps you're right,' he said.

Speaking about Inara's connection with a god had been to shake Lessa, to make her understand. But it had only made her deny everything.

That meant she knew something, about Inara.

It also meant she could not let a word Kissen said be the truth.

'I am telling the truth about Talicia,' said Kissen. 'What reason have I to lie?'

'Other than being raving mad?' said Lessa, with a laugh. 'To distract and disrupt us.' She nodded at the others. 'Are you ready for tomorrow?'

Kissen tried to get to her feet.

'Tarin,' said Lessa, barely deigning to glance at her, and her guard's hand shoved Kissen back down.

'Oh, we are ready,' said Fargast, eyes glimmering with anticipation. 'What about her?'

'I'll deal with her,' said Lessa.

Selainne and Fargast left. Kissen, Lessa, and the guard, Tarin, were alone.

'We should kill her,' said Tarin when all was quiet. Lessa pressed her lips together.

'I'm still here,' growled Kissen, though she doubted that would make a difference.

'Inara trusted me,' said Lessa, more to herself than either of them. 'She knew she could trust me. She would never have gone without my permission. She would have told me.'

'She has a velvet waistcoat,' said Kissen. 'Blue, with buttons from your grandmother.'

'Stop it,' said Lessa.

'Her hair and skin are fairer than yours, but she likes to plait it like you do.' A wave of pain passed over Lessa's face. 'She's a good archer too. Better than I am. Almost as good as you. And . . . I care for her. Deeply.'

Lessa closed her eyes for a long moment, then looked at Tarin. 'I want more information. After the Reach falls. But I want no one else near her.'

'Cut out her tongue,' said Tarin, 'she can write her confessions.'

Kissen's stomach went cold.

'Seeing as I can't write,' she said, cautious, 'you'd be waiting a while.' Then she cocked her best smile at Lessa. 'And you'd really be robbing the world of the tricks I could pull with my tongue.'

To her satisfaction, Lessa blushed. Just slightly. Then she straightened her shoulders. 'If even a feather touch of what you speak is true,' she said. 'I would not let this burning king lead us to war.'

She nodded to Tarin, who grabbed Kissen's manacles and pulled her to her feet. Shit.

'Why don't you ask me?' Kissen tried, resisting. 'The god she is hiding. Why don't you ask me its name? He has no shrine other than her, what do you think that means?'

Lessa ignored her, turning her back and staring pointedly at the maps. Tarin dragged Kissen towards the door. 'Keep quiet,' the guard said.

No. Kissen didn't have time to wait for sieges. If Lessa wouldn't save Inara, she would. Her family too. She lifted her arms and wrenched down with her full bodyweight, using the momentum to grab Tarin's belt and tip her over her shoulder. She landed with a grunt of breath and Kissen leapt for the door, but a catch on her leg sent her sprawling; Tarin had grabbed it.

A boot slammed into Kissen's belly, kicking her to the side. Lessa, her blade from her bed in her hand. Kissen rolled with the pain and used the movement to reach down into her boot, grabbing Osidisen's knife. Her last weapon.

Too slow. Lessa dived down, her blade batting away Kissen's as she landed with her knee on her chest. If not for her leather breast-plate, Lessa would have broken her ribs. As it was, she was pinned, breathless, nothing left to give.

The lady dragged her sword to Kissen's throat, pressing it there. The weapon was strange, curved like a seafarer's, like Kissen's cutlass. No sword of a Middrenite noble, but it looked comfortable in her hand.

'Drop the knife,' Lessa said, 'or I slit your throat.' Her hand didn't waver. She was strong for a slight woman, and smelled of musk and lamp oil, with the faintest tang of smoke. Her whole bodyweight was pinning Kissen down.

Kissen put up her hands, released the blade. It was that or die. 'It was a god of white lies,' she said.

The blade on her neck lightened. Lessa caught her breath. 'Skediceth,' she said with surprise.

Tarin was up. Lessa stepped back and her guard dragged Kissen to her feet, forcing a wad of cloth into her mouth. Kissen grunted as her staff was taken and used to lock her elbows behind her back.

Lessa watched, the point of her blade dropping to the ground, her gaze distant.

'You know it?' said Tarin.

Lessa nodded. 'He travelled with Yusef. I did not think . . . he had survived.' She swallowed. 'He has been near us? All this time?'

Yusef. The god of safe haven. Kissen tried to spit out the cloth, to no avail, as Lessa came towards her. She noted her panic, and took a hold of her chin, tipping up her face so they were looking eye to eye.

'If you care for my daughter at all,' she said, 'you will not utter her name to gods or humans again.'

At last, Kissen understood, her suspicion hardening into certainty. Why Lessa Craier had hidden her daughter. Why Ina knew nothing of her father. Why she had fought against the king. It was for Inara's sake.

Her father was a god.

CHAPTER FORTY-FIVE

Skediceth

INARA DIDN'T TURN BACK. SHE DIDN'T EVEN LOOK.

Skedi tried to reach her in his mind, time and time again, but she had locked him out. He could not sense the direction she had taken, leaving him further and further behind as he washed down the canals with the barges, the wave bearing him to the docks. Her connection to his heart was unravelling.

All three barges slowed as they reached the river harbour amid a surge of refuse picked up by the current.

She had gone. Left everything. Kissen's cloak, her sword, her bow. Him.

'Inara,' Skedi whispered, already longing to see her colours.

The others were picking themselves up, looking around and finding themselves safe, away from the mayhem. Telle was checking the boxes. None had been lost. Yatho groaned, easing herself up onto one of the benches as Ertha jumped from their barge to Solom, who was clutching his arm.

Skedi had done nothing wrong. These people knew him. For the first time, they needed him, gave him offerings. Wanted him and his gentle lies. That was his calling, who he was. Inara would deny him that for blood and briddite, war and vengeance.

A wind from the sea rattled his gifts against his antlers. The bracelet, and Inara's button. Both suffused with colours, one of a stranger, the other of a girl he had loved.

Foolish child, he shot at her, angry and hurt. He was a god. A god of white lies, no more, no less. This was where he belonged. She had lived only a fraction of the years that he had.

And protected him for every single one of them he had been with her. Even as a child, she had hidden him. She had done so much to try to take care of him, had tried to forgive him when he manipulated her. What was he doing to protect her? What sacrifices was he making to ensure that she was safe? Safe not just as a child, but as Lady Craier, heir to her own lands, and their avenger?

He shrank down.

He had made a mistake.

A pain.

A sharp tug on his heart, there then gone. If he could weep, he would: the connection between them was still there.

It faded, then he felt it again, more distant. Less pain now, more a hook in him, tethering him to her. His shrine. His home. He had told her that in Blenraden. That he needed only her. Whether she wanted him or not, she needed him too.

He sat up, lifting his wings.

'You're going after her?' said Yatho.

Skedi flinched and turned. Kissen's family were watching him. Telle's face was troubled, and Yatho just looked weary.

'I can't leave her,' said Skedi.

Yatho nodded, and signed to Telle, who swallowed and shook her head.

We should go back for her too, said Telle.

We choose our own fates, my love, said Yatho. *Kissen always did, and it seems she rubbed off on the girl. And they need us here. They need* you.

Telle looked at the others, still shaken, but alive. She reached for Yatho's hand, and they squeezed each other tightly. Their colours seemed to pass between them, shifting in unison, like one life, one soul.

Skedi shifted his position, picking up his wings. How to find her? Through the tug of his heart? He closed his eyes, his ears twitching. Yes, perhaps. There.

'Wait.' Telle's voice.

He paused and looked around. She pulled something out of her pocket; a small, sealed leather tube with a carry-strap. A scroll protector. 'Please, give this to her,' she said, holding it out.

The item was imbued with colour; Telle's emotions: sadness, fear, awe, doubt. For Inara. Skedi bowed his head, and Telle placed it over his neck. He had to grow to carry it, and grow he did, spreading his wings wide to catch the air.

Then he took off. Several people in the harbour caught sight of him, their faces amazed. They pointed and gasped. A bird, hare, deer. A god.

Skedi cast a thought towards the archivists. Telle and Yatho, so brave, so full of love. Solom with his passion, Ertha with her pragmatism, Cal with his pride.

Keep going, Skedi circled them, passing on a small piece of his will. *Keep going: you will succeed. The scripts will be saved.*

A white lie, but one they needed. Ertha helped Solom to his feet. He looked up at Skedi, raising his good arm in a salute.

'We will raise a shrine to you, Skediceth!' he called.

Skedi did not dare hope. He turned back to the city, carried on the river wind, and followed his heart's lead.

The colours below were all eruption, chaos. People were shoving against each other, shouting, moving, praising, frightened. No one was controlling the crowds. There were skirmishes of fists and knives, flashes of yellow swallowed by blue and gold. Most of the activity was down the central streets, from the western gate directly towards the cloche. In the distance, the king's armies were moving forward like a cerulean sea. The gate was open.

Skedi swooped down again. The narrower avenues to the west of the cloche, the winding streets. Inara was here, he was sure of it. He focused between the bodies.

There! Her long braid of hair, her determined stride. Her colours burned brightly, the purples of when she thought of her mother, surrounded with fiery oranges and reds of vengeance, sadness. Heartbreak.

Heartbreak for him.

Ina! he called, but she did not hear him. He dived down, back to Inara. Back to his home.

She shrieked as he flew before her, scroll swinging from his neck, and went straight into her chest with enough energy to send her stumbling backwards. A few people scattered.

'Skedi . . .' Inara gasped.

'I'm here!' said Skedi, fluttering backwards. 'I'm here. I'm with you. But please, talk to me. Don't decide everything on your own. Please trust me again.'

Inara gazed at him, her brown eyes shining, filling with tears. Then she opened her arms. Skedi flew into her neck, and she held him to her.

'I'm sorry,' she said into his fur as he spread his wings over her. 'I thought . . . I'd lost you. I've been losing you. I thought you were gone last night.'

'You can't lose me,' said Skedi, pressing his antlers to her chin. 'You'll always be my home. I'll help you find yours.'

'But . . . I didn't feel it. I couldn't feel you.'

'I know,' he said. 'I know . . . but it's still there. I promise it's still there.'

Inara released him and dashed her hands over her face. It was thick with salt, she had been weeping. Skedi landed on a nearby ledge, drawing a few stares, and she caught sight of the scroll.

'What's this?' she asked.

'From Telle,' said Skedi. 'For you.' He ducked his antlers so she could pull off the leather tube, 'Do you have a plan?'

Another rattle of hooves and two horses ran past in pursuit of a woman on foot. Inara retreated into a doorway, and Skedi shrank. She looked at the scroll case in her hand but made no move to open it.

'Scian was right,' she said at last. 'I know what I am, and it isn't for the archives yet.' She looked down, her eyes straying to the button on Skedi's antler. 'I think I have discovered it. Some of it.' She held her breath, then said only: 'Haven.'

The god of safe haven, whom Skedi had known, her mother had known. She could speak to other gods, not just him, and had called a powerless god of broken sandals from lands away. She had unravelled a wild god's curse, and with just a drop of blood almost flooded a city. Inara wasn't just blessed, her power was her own.

Inherited. If the god of safe haven founded lands for humans, what if Inara was safety for gods?

And what would it mean if humans and gods could make life together?

It meant there were others.

Skedi kept his thoughts close. Too much to unravel, too much to change. But he felt it in his heart. 'Haven,' he whispered. Inara smiled, her eyes brightening.

'I have an idea,' she said.

CHAPTER FORTY- SIX

Elogast

THE QUEEN'S WAY. ELO AND NAIA DIDN'T KNOW WHERE else to go. Home, and her family would be implicated. Perhaps they already were.

'We can't stay here long,' said Naia, standing as far away from Canovan as she could. 'It won't be long before they seal off the gates, the docks.'

'I'm not leaving the city,' said Elo.

Canovan was sitting by the open fireplace, which was thankfully empty and cold. His wounded hand was on the table, linen-wrapped. The cloth had soaked part through, but it looked as if the bleeding had stopped. In front of him was an empty bottle of liquor, another half-drunk, and a tiny filigree bird inset with bright gems, with a key for turning between its wings. Between Canovan's chafed and muscled hands, it looked impossibly delicate.

The inn was empty, though Elo could hear rowdy lovemaking and drunken yelling from the brothels on either side. It seemed some who could not afford a quick exit were instead spending their last coin on a bit of fun. Elo didn't blame them.

'What do you mean, you're not leaving?' said Naia. 'They'll come looking for you. Both of you.' She was a better person than Elo. She looked as if she wanted to throw something at Canovan but she was still trying to save him.

'I'm not leaving either,' the innkeeper muttered, scowling. He hadn't let them in, exactly, he just hadn't stopped them.

'What do you presume to do instead?' said Naia.

'Lick my damn wounds.' Canovan thrust his bandaged hand upwards. 'And watch this gods-damned knight fall the way my wife fell.' He looked back down at the clockwork bird. 'The way Ariam fell for a stupid cause. I have no intention of following them.'

'You *will* follow them, you stubborn old goat!' snapped Naia.

Canovan stroked one of the bird's wings with a tenderness Elo wouldn't have expected. The man was hideously drunk, and miserable with it. 'You want to make doe eyes at the knight, then fine,' he said. 'I will sit on my land and hide it well until they break my illusions and come and take me.'

'So, you will live with your vengeance spent on a few knights and poor discipline,' said Elo. 'And die in spite.'

Canovan smiled at him without humour, then picked up the bottle with his good hand and threw it at Elo with desperate strength. 'I got the fight I wanted, you pompous fuck,' he said as Elo ducked and it smashed on the wall behind him. 'You idiots thought you could win, but this isn't even the battlefield. It's a side piece. A player's gambit.'

'What do you mean?' said Naia.

Canovan cackled, his voice ringing hollow in his throat. 'This little rebellion here is nothing,' he said. 'As soon as the king's army left Sakre, the real fight began. Years in the planning, and they just bloody leapt at the opportunity.' He spat on the floor. 'Told us as a pissing courtesy that they would move on the Reach. To stand down. Stand down!' He lowered his head to the table, resting it against the bird's beak. 'As if they had the right.'

Elo blinked. The Reach? He was trying to make sense of a drunken, grieving man's hateful ramblings. 'Sakre has never fallen,' he said. 'The king is here. The fight is *here*.'

Canovan grinned. 'Lesscia was never more than a distraction.' His smile fell, and he looked at the ceiling. Guilt wracked his face, and he clutched the bird to his chest. 'Ariam died for a distraction, and I am all alone again.'

Elo breathed out. The king had abandoned Sakre with his entire army. He wouldn't have missed that opportunity, had he been there. So, who had taken it? Who had the audacity?

Naia stared at Canovan. 'It was all for nothing?' she said, her voice shaking with rage. 'And you *knew*?'

'What would you have done if I told you?' Canovan grumbled. 'Nothing! You would have cowered.'

'We would have lived!' Naia shouted at him. 'Ariam would have lived. *I* would have lived without blood on my hands! We would have protected the archives, made peaceful work. How . . .' She ran her hands over her braids. 'How can I fix this? Everything is broken.'

The door slammed open. Elo drew his sword and turned, ready to go down fighting.

He almost dropped it.

'Inara,' he gasped.

Her hair was tangled and hanging out of her braid, her satchel at her side. She was back in her blue waistcoat, her waxwool cloak, with Skedi on her shoulder. Behind her, Kissen's horse, Legs.

'I thought you'd gone,' he said.

'I thought you'd been killed,' said Inara, casting her eyes around the room, taking in Canovan, Naia. Her eyes snapped back to Elo. 'We're going to fight back.'

Naia gave a growl of disbelief. Canovan narrowed his eyes at Inara, and it seemed – maybe – that one of his tattoos shifted.

'Arren is going for the archives,' Inara continued. 'Skedi checked. The knights are making an avenue through the city, all the way to the cloche. That's where he's going.'

Of course, a show of dominant splendour.

'The archives,' whispered Naia. She shook herself. 'Who's this little girl?' When Elo didn't answer, she looked to Canovan, who shrugged.

'I'm Inara Craier,' said Inara, and Canovan stood, wincing as he knocked his injured hand on the table. Naia drew her breath, surprised. 'And,' Inara continued, 'like your friend here, I have a way with gods.'

Canovan curled his lips but made no denial.

Inara held Elo's eyes. Gods plural? What had she discovered?

'You,' said Canovan. '*You* broke the curse. You're . . . like me.'

Elo and Inara ignored him.

'I can call them,' said Inara confidently 'the gods that remain in this city. They will help us.'

Elo felt as if he was looking at Kissen in Inara's eyes. Her certainty, her power. He understood neither, but the latter frightened him. How much like Canovan's power was it? How far would she let it go?

'All the gods left here are small, little things,' said Canovan. 'They hide in wells, crevices, shadows. I've seen them. What are they going to do, bite an army's ankles?'

'We just need to slow the march,' said Skedi. 'Give you a chance, Elo . . . A last chance.'

To get close to him. To Arren. King Arren. No, Sunbringer. To face him. Blade to blade. After all this time, all this work, it was a child and a god who still understood him, no matter how many times he had turned them away.

'It won't be enough, Elo,' said Naia, putting a hand to him as if to hold him back. 'Even if you get close you'll be killed as soon as you touch him. He's a king.'

Skedi sat up on Inara's shoulder, lifting his antlers. A glint of light caught in one of the glass beads that hung from them. His voice came into Elo's head, sharp and painful. *If she does not try*, Skedi said. *She will regret it forever.*

'No,' said Elo. Inara swallowed, but he wasn't speaking to her. He spoke to Naia. 'He's not a king. He's a god.' He looked at Inara and saw who she was. Saw that the child he had been trying to protect was no more. 'And we kill gods.'

It was what Kissen had said, when she walked towards Hseth. Walked towards her death. For them, for a future. For this.

CHAPTER FORTY-SEVEN

Inara

LEGS WAS HAPPY TO BE OUT IN THE CITY; HE HAD BEEN cooped up too long. Inara took him to the streets. Her shortsword and Kissen's bow had gone with the boats, but she had found a finished dagger left behind in the smithy. Bea's work, she thought: it had detailed etchings that seemed too fanciful to be Yatho's. She hoped Yatho would find him at the dock as she planned, and that they would make it to Daesmouth.

The streets were no longer heaving, and those who still lingered let Inara pass without comment. The lengthening shadows of the evening found empty cobbles littered with discarded belongings as people either raced to the centre of the city to see what the king would do or fled to whatever home they could find. The light that hit the roofs was pale and gold, gold like the king's armour, bringing glory out of the dusk.

A sharp breeze, scented with smoke and water, stirred the air as she directed Legs as close to the city's centre as she dared. In the distance, she could hear drums and lutes. The sounds of celebration.

Inara tested the knife in her hand. This had to work. Elo was relying on her and . . . if she never saw him again, she had to know she had helped. The way he had looked at her and said those words: she understood. She didn't want to lose anyone, but what if that was all she could do? Help them win, and lose her heart again?

She tugged the reins, guiding Legs to a halt. Then she pulled her long plait over her shoulder, feeling the weight and heft of it in her hand. It did not look like her mother's braid; too messy, too curly. But it was how Lessa wore it, and Inara had liked to pull it when she was young, imagining herself as her mother. Wearing her clothes, walking in her shoes.

Then Kissen. What would she have thought if she knew what Inara planned? What would she say? Inara closed her eyes. Kissen was dead. It did not matter.

She had to let them go. Kissen, Elo, Mother. If she was going to do this, she had to do it right.

A test first. She held the edge of the blade to a curl near her face. Just one god first. One god whose voice she had heard before where it shouldn't be, far from his shrine. She had to be certain.

Inara cast her mind to Kelt, the god of broken sandals. Small. Mouselike. He was bound to Blenraden, as all the gods were to their shrines, but his voice had come to her over mountains and rivers.

Kelt. She closed her eyes and called him again, then sliced through a lock of her hair. This was what she was offering. Herself, her memories of her mother, her childhood hopes. *Come to me.*

Her innocence. Her humanity. Just a little.

A flutter in front of her. Legs whinnied with annoyance, and she opened her eyes again.

The mouse god was there, with his chipped wooden mask. He faded in and out, like a shade in the night.

She had done it. She had called a god.

Kelt, he echoed once more, and looked around. *Where is Kelt now?*
'Lesscia,' said Inara.

Skedi, she called for her god in her mind. *I did it.*

Of course you did, Skedi said back. *This is why I'm safe with you. Because you are haven.*

Haven. Yusef. How had her mother made her? Why? What had Telle sent her in her scrolls?

Lesscia? Kelt spoke the word as if he had never heard it before. He looked up at her. *Girl with button,* he said. *Offering once, now twice.* He cocked his head. *You believe in Kelt?*

'Yes, Kelt,' said Inara. 'I believe in you. And I needed your help to believe in myself.'

She held out the lock of hair, and Kelt took it, his fur rippling with excitement. His mask gleamed, healing somewhat, smoothing. Like Skedi when he took an offering from her. It gave him power.

A gift, he said. *I . . . forget. Sometimes. What Kelt is.* He looked up. *Till you, girl.*

'Inara,' she said. 'Inara Craier.'

Inara Craier, he repeated the name slowly. *This was all you need?*

'Yes . . .' She wanted to ask him for more, but what could she request? She just had to know, for if she could call on a god over such great distances, what could she do in a city she was standing in?

His paws grasped her bit of hair. *I watch for you, Inara*, he said. *Kelt will look out for you.*

Inara found herself fighting back tears. She had wished, and he had come. He should not have been there. By the lore of the gods, they were bound to their shrines, their spaces, their homes. But she could change the lore, and they could come to her if her will was strong, her offering was good. She could ask for their help. She could save them.

Save Middren, if not Elo.

She had to make an offering, enough to give them power. Something that she loved and was desperate not to lose. Her last link to her mother.

Taking a deep breath, Inara put her blade to the base of her hair.

She cast her mind out to the sunset-stained city, thinking of the rose god, the god of the canals, the god of inkers, the gods of the wells, of anything. Scian. Lethen. She called to the old gods, and the new. She thought of Skediceth.

Help me, she sent out through her mind. *Protect this city. Protect your people.*

Her thoughts, her will, passed through the streets she had walked, first with Kissen, then with Elo, and Telle, Yatho and the archivists. The city that had protected her in some of the worst times of her life.

The city she wanted to defend.

'I'm sorry,' she whispered. 'Mother, Elo, Kissen. I'm sorry.'

Help me. Help us.

With a slice of her blade, she hacked through her plait, trying not to weep. Piece by piece, she sawed at it, and her hair flew loose. Her braid came away in her hand, and the ragged ends of her curls tickled her neck, her ears, like the touch of Skedi's wing, or her mother's fingers.

She looked down at the hair she had cut away, weighed it in her palm. So thick. So heavy. Like a knot of rope. But, with a god's eyes, she could also see the colours, all the love, and rage, and hope in it. All her admiration, all her love and loss, shining in amethyst, citrine, and pure white.

It is a good offering, a voice spoke to her. Not Skedi's, but Lethen's.

Inara hadn't finished her summoning. Lethen had come of her own accord.

No. Canovan walked up beside her, his arms running bloody with self-made marks. The scent of moss and dark forest nights grew on the breeze, richer with each palm lower the sun sank through the buildings.

'I didn't think *you* would fight,' said Inara.

'Not for your knight I won't,' said the innkeeper, then looked up at her. 'You have godsblood in your veins.'

Inara hesitated, but then inclined her head: she knew it in her heart to be true.

Canovan nodded. 'Like me,' he said. 'I only ever met one other. Caria, my wife. Grandchild of a smith god, she had such a way with metals.' His voice creaked. 'I fight for her. Everything is for her. For us. Godkind.'

The shadows around them lengthened, grew legs, ink-black. Teeth and wisps that became the lights of their eyes. Legs tipped his head up, his ears going back as he stamped in distress, but Inara held him. Lethen's summonings. Eight of them. And this time, they were on Elo's side. Her side.

'Godkind,' Inara murmured, and cast her will out to the city.

Come to me.

She released her hand. Her offering scattered, picked up into the air and dragged along the buildings, landing on cobbles, in water, in the canals. Inara wondered what Aan would think, the hair of the god still sitting in a vial around her neck. When the river had requested, Inara had given a single hair. Now, she gave it all.

Help us.

The inker god was first to answer. Maira. She manifested on Inara's wrist, slithering down her arm.

Blind their eyes. Test their faiths.

Roses twisted around Legs's hooves. Makioron who had no shape, still was there, Inara's hair tangled in his briars. Water seeped up from the canals at the side of the road, wells overflowing. Daefer, the dog of the canal, rangy and bright-eyed, his fur black and clogged with weeds.

Lethen raised her hands, catching Inara's hair in them like rays of light. Her staff glowed brighter, and the shadows multiplied. Sixteen. Twenty.

More little gods, coming out of hiding, creeping out of their hidden shrines. Gods of the tilers and cracking stone, gods of the weavers and coloured threads.

'Scatter the armies,' said Inara. 'Take the fight to the king. Save Scian's city.'

CHAPTER FORTY-EIGHT

Skediceth

THE PARADE THE KING LED DOWN THE AVENUES TO THE cloche was well guarded on all sides. Knights in gleaming gold and blue shone in the evening light, keeping back the crowds that had seen the city change hands so many times in the previous days that they no longer knew where they were. Their colours beneath their cloth were a cacophony, their emotions all in tangles and knots.

Skedi flitted from roof to roof. Closer, closer.

These waves of emotion, tension, were longing for release. To celebrate, to destroy. Enough for someone's will to slip in and take hold. Sunbringer wanted it to be his will, his glory. He wanted to claim their chaos and tame it. Skedi understood. It was what a god would want.

There. The king was processing down the central avenue, proud and tall on the back of his horse. Golden antlers like Skedi's rising from his closed helmet, beautifully framed by the halo that circled his head. His chest armour was strangely made; torn in the centre, as if a slice had been made through. Skedi paused, ducking down to the roof.

The king was showing it. His heart of a god. He was baring his own betrayal to the world, and still they marched with him.

There, on the breeze . . .

Skedi saw a strand of dark hair, infused with light. And he heard Inara's whisper.

Help us.

She had done it. His heart ached for her. He felt his fur prickle, his feathers stir. There was power in the air. His person's power. His haven.

He leapt up and caught the thread of her hair in his antlers. It was for him too, her offering.

Stop the king. Destroy the sunbringer.

Skedi let the wish infuse him, Inara's emotions running through his god's body. He thrilled with the feel of it, its energy. More than he had ever known, filling his blood with light and warmth, giving it strength, giving him purpose. This feeling, better than anything he had felt. Power. Delicious, intoxicating power.

He knew now why gods could become addicted to such offerings.

He shook himself in mid-air, drawing his mind back to Inara. What she wanted, her will. He knew where she was; heading through the western streets, the gods at her side, towards the cloche to prepare the way. So brave, so determined, so fierce.

He could be brave too.

Skedi took off from the roofs and flitted over the central phalanx, the size of a sparrow.

You are not needed here.

A white lie. He touched the helmets of the guards with it, the soldiers, the knights. Their colours shone like the blues of their cloaks and clothes, the gold that adorned their armour. But there was difference beneath the uniform; the seeds of their personalities, their hopes and dreams.

You are not wanted here.

He pressed the lie to them, so soft they did not feel it coming.

The king doesn't need you. He wants to use you.

Was it a white lie? Was lying all he could do? He wasn't as certain as he once had been. Gods didn't change, did they? But then, gods couldn't survive without their shrine. Gods couldn't be summoned by a little girl.

The world could change, if they wanted it enough.

You should not be here.

Their march slackened, just a little. Swords, before held so high, began to waver. A piper struck a discordant note, a drum skittered off beat.

Skedi turned his attention to the windows, to the people in the street. One or two had pushed their way to the front, throwing rosemary and thyme at the feet of the horses which, when crushed, sent up sweet smells from the march. Others were just watching.

This is not his city, whispered Skedi to them.

Their messy colours rippled as he passed. He spread his strength further, taking power from Inara's hair, Solom's offering. It suffused him with colour, with energy.

You do not want him here. This is not his city. THIS IS NOT HIS CITY.

A child first. An old cabbage. They threw it through an open window, and it landed on the arm of a soldier, who looked up, bright blue flame flickering with confusion.

An old barge pilot standing on the street let out a jeer, low and bellowing, that several picked up.

'Quiet for the king!' a knight belted out, for the king was approaching.

What king? That pompous boy? Skedi pushed his will onto them, telling them what they need to hear. *People starve, trade falters, while his crown weighs heavy with gold.*

Someone jostled a knight, who pushed back. A fight broke out and someone felled a drummer. The rhythm struggled. But still the parade moved, a unit, as one.

Then they stepped into water. Canal where no canal should be. A shout of surprise. Several onlookers splashed in front of the walking knights as not just one canal but all of them broke their banks. In a swift rush, their waters flooded onto the pathways, the roads, sloshing around the boots of the invaders, dirty and thick.

Inara, it's working, said Skedi. *They're fighting back.*

Then, there, as they passed a tilers' workshop, the water turned black, red, ochre, then gleaming pink. It splashed up into their faces, getting into their eyes. A snake-god darted past them, skimming around their feet, spitting colour at the knights, staining their uniforms yellow, magenta, emerald. Anything but blue.

Some of the crowd began to run, others picked up on the spreading anger.

You are not wanted here. You do not belong here. You should not be here.

The people of the city pushed their way through the distracted knights that lined the avenue and waded onto the road, shoving at the paraders. Formation broke, and the march stumbled into a brawl. Skedi stuck out his whiskers, flying in the sunlight. The chaos was spreading, up and down the lines. Disorganised, discordant, irreverent.

Then Skedi saw shadows and lights along the water, he smelled faintly the scent of moss.

Shadow demons were moving down the alley, flanking a tattooed man walking alone, limping slightly, axes in his hands.

Canovan, demigod, son of Lethen of the Ways. She walked with him, a shadow at his back. He was so unlike Elo, bent with abandon and bloody fury. But he used it well.

With a howl, Canovan and his shadows burst into the central avenue, tearing into the king's host like water spilling through a dam. Several soldiers screamed, shrieking back as their nightmares came for them, made real and terrible, and full of teeth.

Not needed here, Skedi crowed into the melee. *Unwanted. Undesirable. Unloved.*

A hiss of air. Skedi tipped out of instinct, and felt his feathers stir as something missed them by a breath.

An arrow.

He swooped and ducked as two more came flying for him from the horses beside the king. The arrowheads were murky grey: briddite.

Briddite could kill him.

The king himself was looking up, his halo and antlers tipped back.

He ceased his playing and dived back towards the rooftops, crashing into tiles and running as two more arrows singed the tips of his hind legs before he barrelled over into the next alley.

Skedi had been seen.

More than that, they knew he was a god, and they were ready for him.

CHAPTER FORTY-NINE

Elogast

THE SCENT OF ROSES FILLED THE PLAZA IN FRONT OF THE cloche. Elo waited, hidden in the deep red blooms from the top of the arch, but there were few enough people to hide from. Two knights in blue were stalking the plaza on horseback, unaware that he had scaled the roofs and crept down to the entrance Inara had mentioned. Elo knelt, his sword drawn, its briddite edge touching the stone far from the roses. He was waiting, steadying his breath.

Kill the Sunbringer. Kill the king before he became the god he desired, with the power to twist people's minds, their thoughts, their loves. Before he demanded the sacrifice of blood for his favour.

Elo put a hand to his chest, reminding himself of the scar beneath Naia's armour.

Drums and pipes were getting closer, though their sound was now discordant, disturbed.

The last golden flush of sunlight was passing over the dome, fading into night, and the scent of roses increased, heady and thick with a hundred summers. Soon, Elo realised why.

Briars were spreading across the walls of the plaza, moving from his arch towards the others that had not yet bloomed. They moved slowly, surely, digging into walls, threading around window ledges, covering over tile. Elo caught the tracing, twice, of fine brown hair tangled in the branches.

Inara: she was doing this.

Elo gripped his sword, passing his thumb over the empty pommel where the lion had been. Kissen would not have liked this at all.

'What—' The knights in the plaza saw what was happening and opened their helms for a closer look. The blooms were descending now as they spread across the wall, budding, ageing, then popping open like blisters of blood. Red petals scattered over the stones. The plaza was almost completely encircled. Below him, the arch he perched on had been blocked off with roses.

'Don't touch it,' said one, panicked when their companion walked their horse closer to the wall. The other gates were closing now, thickening with thorns. 'Go. Warn the king.'

'But—'

'I'll stay here.'

The second knight set off at a run, their horse clattering across the cobbles and through an archway before the briars swallowed it. Elo watched as the plants at his back thickened, sending tendrils back along the street, but did not harm him. He breathed out. Allying with gods during the war had been the smartest move they had made, and the most dangerous. Each one had taken a negotiation and sacrifice; precious cattle, one horse; then several more. The god of war had taken twelve horses, and then when Arren turned on him had almost destroyed them all. This rose-god showed such strength on just a scattering of Inara's hair.

Movement. People in white. Elo looked back. Through another gate, before it closed, walked a trail of people in pale robes, whispering as they looked up at the blooms. Elo shrank back, though he was well hidden. Archivists? Novices? No, not all of them were in robed attire: they wore plain linen, as light as they could afford it, trews and tunics. Scarves.

One of them he recognised. Naia.

She paused as she entered the plaza and looked towards him. She wore perfect white, clean and starched, and had taken out the silver in her hair.

Elo caught his breath. She saw him, her gaze triumphant. What was she doing? Was this her way of absolving what she had done?

There were thirty or forty folks with her, some of them old enough to be grandparents, others closer to Inara's age.

But her expression said more than that. It said, 'This is how *I* fight.'

'Halt!' cried the remaining guard. 'You are not permitted to be here.'

Naia ignored the knight. None of her companions had weapons on them, no shields, no armour. They looked nervous but determined, and she directed them to link hands, spreading out in front of the cloche in a long line. From the dredges of his memory, Elo remembered what the white robes signified; those Scian wore before she was attacked and killed, dirtied, bloodied, darkened with dust as the woman she had been died. The white robes were her innocence, and the darker greys were knowledge.

The guard dismounted, her sword still drawn. 'You need to leave,' she barked, moving towards Naia, who was clearly in charge.

Elo ground his teeth. Naia refused to relent. If he was fighting, she would too, in her way, her peaceful way. He admired her courage, but it could ruin everything. He poised himself on the arch, ready to climb down to her aid.

'This area is under the king's authority,' the knight said, waving her sword threateningly.

'This is our city,' Naia returned, her tone haughty. 'We can stand where we wish.'

'You're not allowed inside the archives.'

'We're not going inside the archives.'

The line of people, fifty, maybe sixty now, reached from one side of the plaza to the other, their arms outstretched in front of the archive doors. They watched the roses, which had filled the square now growing upwards, thickening into a wall. When Elo looked in the other direction, towards the city, all he could see was a sea of blooms, lustrous beneath the darkening sky.

The knight was taken aback. 'Leave now, or I'll make you leave.'

Naia moved back into the others and joined hands with her neighbours. 'All of us?' she said. 'On your own?' She looked pointedly at the roses. 'Through that?'

The harassed knight swallowed. 'The army will come—'

'Then we will wait.'

Elo tightened his hold on his sword, and looked back over the sea of red. He could not yet see Arren's parade, but he could hear it. The drums had faltered.

And there were screams.

CHAPTER FIFTY

Kissen

KISSEN WAS LOCKED IN THE BASEMENT OF A TOWNHOUSE. Craier's presumably, judging by the barrels surrounding her that were all stamped with the three trees and bird sigil. Her manacles had been chained to a crossbeam above her head, so her heels were barely on the floor, and there was no light save for some of the mellow dusk filtering through the windows. This was enough to show that her dagger and her staff were on a barrel not far from her, but much too far to reach. A taunt, perhaps.

Well, at least she still had her tongue. She hoped she would get the chance to tell Telle that not being able to read had finally come in handy.

Kissen was expected to wait for the taking of the Reach. How long would that take? They seemed certain that it would fall. Whatever Lessa had planned, she was assured in a way that terrified Kissen. Nothing was more frightening than a smart woman with a vendetta and a plan.

But to break into the walls of the Reach? Any attempts to scale them had clearly failed. So why *was* she so confident?

Kissen sighed, her breath shifting some of the cobwebs that hung around her. She had tried three times to pull herself down to no avail. Tarin had known what she was doing, which was desperately annoying. She had been abandoned, beaten, dragged through the mountains and through the sky. Her one great victory against Hseth had turned into a charred mess, her country was about to be invaded, and no one believed her warnings.

'Well, if you're watching me now, Osidisen,' she said bitterly, 'I'm pretty sure you and Aan have realised I was a bad choice of messenger.'

Osidisen, of course, didn't answer. If he had any strength at all to see her at this distance, he would need more than the grumble of a godkiller to do anything. Kissen leaned her head back, annoyed with herself. Since when did she ask the gods for help? Why was she wallowing in self-pity? Hoping for rescue? This was not her.

Kissen turned her hands in their restraints. She could move them; the metal was loose at the wrists. That gave her some opportunity. It was possible. But it would hurt.

But then, as a child she'd chewed through a rope that had been hard enough to rip a tooth out. She lived in pain: each day she woke with it, carried it, slept with it. Pain was as steady as her breath. She could use it.

With the strength in her arms, Kissen lifted her knees. Her stomach ached, badly bruised, most likely. She lifted her legs higher, her body beginning to shake, placed her feet against the beam that held her wrists. Then, she shifted her left hand as far down the manacle as it would go, tucking the bone of her thumb into the metal.

She breathed in, twice, quickly, out once. Again. She knew pain. Pain was hers. But she didn't want to do this twice. With a yell she brought her legs and body down on her right side.

The crunch and pop of the bone breaking was enough to turn her stomach before she even felt it. Then: agony.

She came crashing down from the beam and onto her side, hunching immediately into a ball over her left hand as if that could protect her from herself. She first felt cold, then hot; too hot. Her skin prickled as blood rushed through her body, nausea rising in her throat. She clenched her teeth to suppress her scream, half-scared to look. Then she breathed. In. In. Out. Her hand was hottest now. The pain lost its edge, but not its depth. Instead, the flesh of her fingers throbbed.

Kissen took one more breath, then peered at her hand. The skin was bleeding, not too badly, but it was already swollen and going to swell further. The thumb was hanging loose, which might be a good sign. It might have popped the socket instead of snapping.

She sat up, cradling her fist, then took hold of the joint, swallowing as she lifted her thumb. Blood did not bother her, but the dangling flesh was less pleasant. She gently pulled, middle of her thumb. Strangely, it did not hurt as much as she had expected, so she pulled harder, twisting it slightly.

With a sensation of grinding, then a snap, and the bone slid back into place. Blackness shuffled in at her eyes, and she hissed through her teeth while she rode agony's wave. Then, it diminished. Slowly. She could move her thumb, just, though the swelling was already restricting its motion.

The manacle was still stuck to her right hand, but that was nothing a crowbar and hammer wouldn't fix. She dragged herself to her feet and limped over to her staff, picked it up and collected Osidisen's dagger.

'Come on then, old goat. I guess it's time to try my other plan.'

Could those briddite cages ever be lifted from his sea once they had been dropped? Would the god live his dwindling years in pain before he disappeared back into wishes and foam? Kissen couldn't remember the number of times she had wished Osidisen dead, but now she couldn't help but feel pity for him. It was a strange sensation, one she had never thought she would feel for a god, even one her parents and brothers had loved so much. Especially one that had been too weak to save them.

And Inara. Kissen had been ignoring what should have been plain to her eyes. Even gods could not do what Inara could.

For a moment, Kissen wavered. This wasn't her fight. She had always seen to her own problems, done her duty. She should turn her back. What did it really matter to her if the lands tore themselves apart? She could ride out the aftermath with Telle and Yatho. Maybe Inara. Save her from whatever her lunatic mother had done to make her.

But she could not. Kissen had to keep trying, because she was the one who had seen the coming war. If she didn't act, she would always wonder if she could have done more, saved more, tried harder. She had seen what Hseth's followers would do to people, people they knew and loved. Their neighbours, their neighbours' children. What if this new Hseth was even worse? Who knew how many children would burn?

Whatever they were about to do to the Reach, Kissen knew she had to try one more time before civil war spread as fast as Hseth's fires and everyone was either dead or ash.

She slid the dagger into a loop on her girdle for easy access, and shifted her staff under her left arm, wincing as her hand throbbed with pain. She was able to clutch it with her working fingers as she stepped towards the door, pulled at the handle, then cursed. Locked.

Lessa and her dog really weren't stupid.

A thunderous percussion sounded, followed by a tremble in the air so strong that Kissen felt the hairs on her neck rise and her ears pop. Dust fell from the ceiling. The spiderwebs shook.

Another. Closer. The floor shook slightly, and Kissen held onto the door handle with her good hand.

That wasn't thunder Not at all.

A third boom. The ground shook again moments later, and the barrels bounced and rebounded off each other. Kissen crouched against the door as the shaking increased, and the sound. The air roared, and the scent of earth and stone hit Kissen before she yelled and covered her head. The wall of the basement at the far end collapsed inwards in a snap of timber and tumbling rocks. A wave of mud, earth and stone collided with the roof supports and the barrels, splitting the latter open in a howl of noise.

The air stilled, slowly. Kissen found herself caked in dust and mud, and something else that stank sour and acrid. She looked up. Air was filtering in with some of the fading sunlight, spilling through the broken walls of the cellar. She had been saved by standing at the top of the steps: the floor was split, mud and stone filling half the room and shattering the barrels. Kissen had expected them to contain brandy or wine, but instead it was black stuff that had spilled out of them.

Her heart dropped. She recognised the scent of that dust: black-fire powder.

No wonder they had not left a lantern. Kissen herself had used the powder for small briddite bombs. Good for large gods of air or fire. But there was enough here to sink a ship.

Or blow up a building.

And these were the barrels Lessa Craier wasn't using. These were *spare*. What kind of noble could get their hands on a fleet's worth of blackfire powder?

'Lessa Craier,' whispered Kissen, 'what have you done?'

CHAPTER FIFTY-ONE

Arren

THE PARADE HAD SHATTERED INTO CHAOS, BLUE AND GOLD spreading through the streets, fighting locals and gods. Arren forged onward, Risiah and Peta at his sides, leaving their own commanders and generals to do the work. There had been some missiles thrown towards him. Eggs, fruit, stones. None of them hit. His guards had shields and knew how to use them.

Gods. Elo had brought gods into this. Arren shook with anger. How dare he? And how had he done it all on his own?

The streets were filled with water, his knights were being worried on all sides by shadows with teeth, flying ink and cracking tiles. Before even that, the people of Lesscia had become a mob, charging swords with nothing more than clubs and kitchen knives; inkers with stained hands trying to climb over horses to find someone to fight, a madman with two axes had been darting in and out of the fray. Several of Yether's guard had joined in the mayhem, not as quick to break as Arren had expected.

They do not love you as much as you thought, whispered Hestra.

'They will,' hissed Arren. He had hoped for little bloodshed, but he would show Elo consequences.

We'll see.

'Release!' a captain cried, near the front.

They had reformed their ranks where they could, and now the

archers were clearing the way ahead. Two women screamed as arrows found their marks.

'Release!'

This was madness, the madness Arren had been trying to destroy.

And where was Elo, during all of this? Arren had suspected he wouldn't flee when Beloris Yether returned to the fold, desperate to prove his worth. Was he waiting for him up ahead? Arren wished his heart could beat, that it could feel his anticipation of what would come, of seeing Elo's face again.

He needed to make a statement. He needed to make them understand. All gods must die. Only he could bring them safety, security. Gods were weak, susceptible, foolish. Dangerous.

And if the rumours of the nights before were true, then he knew exactly where to begin. In fact, he had already given the order.

The parade was clustering ahead, coming to a halt. Behind him, soldiers were still fighting with the water, yelling as canal weeds and ropes dragged them under.

'Can you smell that?' said Risiah.

Arren shook his head. He could smell nothing; his senses were quiescent.

'Roses,' said Risiah.

A horn sounded: a guard was riding forward, their cloak in blue. 'Your majesty!' They were covered in sweat and mud, with spots of blood across their brow. 'Every entrance to the cloche is blocked.'

'What do you mean "blocked"?' said Peta.

Arren looked ahead. What should have been a street was instead a wall of briars, blood-red, thick, and growing. The thorns were as long as bear claws, the blooms shaking onto the street.

Risiah. This was his duty, and he knew it. Arren turned his helm to face the veiga.

'Take down the gods,' Arren commanded. 'Burn it all down if you must.'

CHAPTER FIFTY-TWO

Inara

INARA SPURRED LEGS TOWARDS THE CLOCHE. THE STREETS of Lesscia were full of water: it was impossible to tell what was bank and what was river in the gloaming evening. Bridges rose from river to nowhere, marked by their balustrades, and boats floated by Legs's belly. Doors were filled with sacks of sand, and windows had been boarded to stop the encroachment of the flood. Desperate families hoisted expensive furniture up steps, their children on their back. An archivist was weeping from their top window, spreading out dripping manuscripts in the very last of the sunlight.

Spray kicked in shining drops from Legs's hooves as he made steady ground. He part-waded, part-ran up the streets. Behind, two shadow beasts followed them, guarding.

Soon, Inara caught the scent of roses, thick and sweet, like the oil the Craier steward had put in lanterns for the summer festivals. The thought might once have been soothing, but now it made her sick with anger.

Then came the sound of swords.

Legs turned into an alley, and ahead Inara could see a street thick with brambles and blooms. Makioron. His power had reached so far. A crowd of knights were attacking the branches, their cloaks printed with a symbol Inara recognised; not the king's usual stag and rays. Two of them held torches to burn away the leaves and briars, their hands and faces bloody. The others used their blades, and at their touch the leaves curled, the bark wrinkled. When the swords cut, the branch would snap back, recoiling like a bitten snake.

Briddite. Inara knew the dull grey of that blade anywhere. These were godkillers.

But Makioron fought back. With each snapped branch more rose-briars grew, richer, thicker than before.

Inara reined in Legs for a moment, unsure what to do. The symbol on their cloaks was the same that had filled Kissen's paper-and-leather ledger. The veiga's sigil, the sign that a god had been destroyed.

The shadow creatures came up beside her. Waiting. Waiting for an order.

A whole section of roses cracked and a hundred petals fell.

'Stop them!' she yelled.

The shadow creatures charged, and their bone-teeth drove deep into the flesh of a veiga. Legs whinnied, rearing back before she could join them. This was not what he was for.

'Come on, Legs!' said Inara. 'Fight!' But Legs would not.

Inara! cried Skedi.

An arrow flew by her, catching Inara's chin with the slightest graze. She winced and looked around. She was surrounded. Behind her had formed a river of bedraggled soldiers and knights on foot, damp in bloodied blue and gold. Further back, there were others on horseback. A man seated in golden armour, a stag's antlers on his head.

The king. Inara thought she met eyes with him, she couldn't be sure. He was sitting so still.

Another arrow skittered across Legs's neck. They were cautious, in case they hit the veiga. Inara cried out, ducking. *Skedi,* she shrieked in her head.

I'm too far away!

A flash of shadow, and a howl, then Canovan came sprinting from a side street. He and four shadow summonings came careering into the front flanks of the march, tearing a bloody hole in the blue.

Inara looked around for a route to escape between roses and

veiga or soldiers. Then she saw one of the godkillers produce a bottle, stoppered with cork, and use his thumb to release it. Inside were seeds. Not just seeds. Seeds full of emotions, of colours, vibrant greens, luscious. Prayers.

A lure. Inara had seen Kissen use them. Prayers that could tempt a god.

'No!' Inara cried. *No, Makioron.*

It was too late. The air stirred as Makioron was drawn in by the offering. Roses bloomed in a stream as a ripple streaked down from the shrine towards the vial.

'Now!' cried the vial-holder.

'Makioron!'

'Release!' came the shout from behind.

Both the march and the veiga released a hail of briddite arrows. One struck through the airy spirit of Makioron, tearing it apart into the dust of burned incense and a spray of sweet mead. To the other side, Canovan screamed as an arrow struck him through the left shoulder, another in his belly.

'No . . .' whispered Inara. Two arrows missed, they flew towards her and Legs, one striking the horse on his haunches, the other embedding itself in his back. A third caught one of the shadow demons, exploding it into nothing. Legs reared, almost throwing Inara off, but she threw her arms around his neck and held on as tight as she could.

Makioron, she called, *come back!* Tears pricked her eyes. This couldn't be right. This wasn't what should happen. *Rose-god, answer me!*

The blooms were turning black. Drying, cracking, gone. Canovan whirled his axes again, diving back towards the knights. 'Run, godsblood!' he cried to Inara. 'Run away!'

Makioron was gone. The rose god was gone, ripped to nothing in a moment. Only desiccated thorns and branches remained, and on these the torches caught, spinning up the skeleton of roses. Smoke erupted, thick and stinking.

Canovan cried out as he took a halberd across his stomach, stumbling almost into another before swiping it away. He was surrounded by illusions, multiplying the number of shadowbeasts, dodging most attacks, but he was losing still.

'Run, little Craier! For us!'

Inara didn't know how to leave, she didn't know how to help. Canovan was bleeding too much, from too many wounds. The shadows congregated around him, the demons protecting their child, then they flew up, darkening, thickening. Inara saw a glimpse of a woman within them, holding Canovan in her arms, then she turned her white eyes on Inara.

Legs screamed. His ears went back, struck by a deep, wild panic. Then he bolted. Inara held onto his back for dear life as he plunged through another alley, turned up a street, but everywhere there were still briars, thick and black.

Makioron was gone. Canovan gone. The roses were burning. Elo awaited the king.

She had summoned them all to die.

CHAPTER FIFTY-THREE

Skediceth

THE SMOKE WAS THICKER NOW. SKEDICETH HAD LOST sight of Inara, but he felt her distress and sped towards it. There were knights at every entrance to the plaza, now scrambling to get through the dead roses. But the first entrance, where Elo was hiding, was going up in flames. The vines were catching, burning, carrying the fire up to the roofs and back down along the avenue. Someone's blue tabard caught light, their voice rising high in panic as they backed through the thorns. The rose-god's revenge.

Lesscia had flooded; now it was burning.

Elo, get down! Skedi called to the knight, he would soon be caught in the fire. *They're through to the cloche. The king! The king is coming.*

He had no energy left. He raced after Legs and Inara. Through clouds of smoke, Skedi saw them. Inara clinging to Legs's neck, hanging on desperately as the terrified horse streaked through the streets. He rounded a corner into another crowd of blue soldiers and panicked, then turned up another street filled with dead briars, towards the cloche.

No, not that way! Skedi called.

I can't control him! cried Inara. Legs had barrelled into a snare of thorns, his animal colours blaring red with fear. He bucked further into the tangle, hopelessly ensnared.

Skedi dived down through the thorns. They tugged at his wings, pulled out his feathers, tore fur from his tail. But his flesh grew back, quick and clean now. He landed on Legs's neck, throwing his will around the beast like a net.

Nothing to fear, there is nothing to fear.

He felt the animal's panic, as immediate and intense as a human's. Confusion too. Yearning for something. A scent, a sense of safety. Kissen.

She's coming back, Legs. She's coming. Skedi conjured up Kissen in his mind, alive and well, and willed it towards Legs. Her scent, her hair, her hands. The sound of her voice. Everything Legs might remember.

Legs's movement slowed till he was no longer damaging himself and Inara with his fear, though the sounds he made turned pitiful.

Ina looked up, her eyes full of tears, catching sight of Skedi. The thorns had scratched through her face and neck, leaving bloody streaks across her hands.

'Makioron,' she whispered. 'Canovan . . .'

'Maira too,' said Skedi, though he couldn't give a whisker about Canovan and his demons. 'The inker god. She went for the king.'

And had died in a flash of colour.

'It's my fault,' said Inara softly. She clutched one arm, which was bleeding badly. She looked up at the dead briars tangled around them. 'All those years, all those prayers, then . . . nothing.'

The smell of smoke was getting stronger. A cloud of it enveloped them. Then, the sound of blades came from further back, and an axe slamming into wood. The bushes shook.

'A god! I see a god!'

Skedi looked back. There were knights hacking through the roses.

Inara gripped Legs, frightened.

'We have to go,' said Skedi.

'There's nowhere *to* go,' whispered Inara. She was right. All around them were briars and walls.

A flash of metal. The blades were coming closer. Skedi tried to push a lie at the invaders: *It's too thick. You can't get through, go another way.*

The knights didn't even hesitate. He had used up too much of his power. A wave of exhaustion consumed him, from so many desperate lies, so many emotions, so much fear.

'You run, Skedi,' said Inara. 'Get out of here. They might not hurt me.'

'I won't leave you.'

'You must! You can fly!'

He could fly. And he could grow. But his power was spent. 'Give me an offering,' he said.

Inara stared at him.

'Something, anything,' said Skedi. 'Please. Trust me.'

Inara held out her hand. It was dripping with blood. 'Is this enough?'

Skedi swallowed. Blood. Though she was already bleeding, her blood was her life, it was her colour. He lifted his wings. He wanted it. Oh, how he wanted that power.

He shouldn't.

She decided for him, reaching across and touching his brow. Her fingers left a stain as she offered her blood to him: red and dangerous, and strong. Power ran through him again. Not to lie; to soar.

He grew. Past a hare's size, past a dog's. A wildcat. Larger. A wolf. He jumped back onto the branches, stretching his wings and shattering those that still stretched around them, feeling them bite him like tiny teeth. Inara held onto his paw as he reared up. Briddite arrows sped past him, nicking his fur with ice-hot burning, but most struck the tangle of forest.

'Hold on,' said Skedi.

'What about Legs?'

'He'll be safer without us.'

Inara leapt for the god, grabbing the top of his wing then pulling herself onto his back. Skedi hauled them upwards, snapping branches with his antlers, his wings, using his powerful hind legs to leap higher. He climbed to the top of the buildings then stretched out his wings, their span spreading wider and wider, then he took off into the night.

Smoke was all around them. Skedi beat his wings hard, higher, trying to escape the reach of lucky arrows, but in every direction there was flame.

There's nowhere to go, said Skedi. He had thought he was pulling Inara to safety, but instead they were exposed. Already he felt the strain of maintaining this size, even with her blood offering. It was not as powerful as her hair, as she had already been cut.

The cloche, said Inara. *To the archives.*

The archives were dark, most lights gone from their windows. The turquoise-and-gold dome still shone, though the light was shadowed by rising smoke.

Skedi was shrinking already. He felt fatigue droop his wings.

There was nothing for it. He dived for the open dome of the cloche, shrinking as he went, Inara holding tight to his fur. Closer, closer. An arrow flew up behind them, missed. Another nicked Skedi's wing and he cried out.

But then they were within the dome's shelter. He flew for the nearest balcony, hit the balustrade and he and Inara tumbled over it, rolling to the floor.

Everything went black.

CHAPTER FIFTY-FOUR

Elogast

THE KING IS COMING!

Elo knew it before he heard Skedi's call. He saw the roses die, and the flicker of flames as the branches caught and the wall of roses began to burn. Sunbringer was unstoppable.

Behind him, Naia's people were still circling the archives, some crying as they watched the fire rise. Before him, he could see Sunbringer's helm as the king guided his horse through embers and ash.

On every side, buildings were starting to spit people onto the street. Not fighting: they were dragging buckets and forming a chain to the floodwater and back to their houses to quench the flames and stop the fire spreading.

'*Makers of ink, marker of tides*

Protector of tomes

Where knowledge resides.'

Naia's people had started singing, the sound barely breaking above the noise of shouting knights, the calls of the citizens as they beat back the fires. Elo winced. The flames near him were getting too hot, too hot to stand. His armour was heating, his chest prickling with the sensation. He was surrounded by dead branches.

Someone yelled. Not far from Elo, from one of the other entrances, a beast erupted from a tangle of branches, its dappled wings spreading into the sky.

Not a beast. Skediceth. He was as large as a lion, his wings spread wide. On his back Elo could see Inara, clinging, bloody, her hair cropped short. A few people pointed as he rose high over the smoke, then dived down towards the cloche.

Behind where they had come from, twenty knights hacked through the last of the branches and ran in, dirty and bloody. A horse clopped through with them, arrows in his flank and back, shaking his head and whinnying. Legs.

'Shit,' hissed Elo. He had hoped Inara would run once her plan was fulfilled. At least she was far away from the flames. Below him, swords were flashing as a second contingent managed to force their way through to the plaza, their backs were stamped with the symbols of veiga.

'The jewel on the river
The star of the south
The bearer of beauty
From wellspring to mouth.'

The godkillers went straight for them, their boots breaking the sound of the singing.

'Move!' the veiga were yelling. 'In the name of the king!'

The godkillers tried grabbing the arms of the singers, but they held fast to each other, refusing to break their grip.

'Scian's home, Scian's womb
Scian's knowing. Scian's tomb.'

Naia's folk held fast, still singing, though it was more shouting than song now.

A wave of smoke filled Elo's eyes, his throat, his lungs. He choked and looked back. The flames were much closer. Too close. Elo covered his mouth, his eyes streaming. This was his leaping point; this was where he had intended to finish Arren from above.

But would he survive the flames?

Would Naia survive the veiga?

'Do it now! For Sunbringer!'

One of the veiga drew their sword. Elo cursed. What did they want? This was more than just a march, they were on some kind of mission, some purpose, and they intended to complete it. Even if it meant killing innocents singing.

The sword came down. The singers screamed, one bleeding from their waist, and they broke for a moment against the shoving of the veiga. Three managed to sprint through, running for the cloche where Inara had fallen before Naia could reform them and push back.

Sunbringer would have to wait. Elo couldn't just let them die.

He grabbed a dead branch, swung himself down and called in his commander's voice, the voice that had bellowed armies into battle, 'Stop! For the love of Middren, stop!'

CHAPTER FIFTY-FIVE

Kissen

OUTSIDE, THERE WAS DEVASTATION. THE EAST WALL OF the Reach had fallen, and from it had opened a deep fissure beneath the palace gardens. Catacombs, of course, and drainage. No one was in the gardens now. That wasn't where the fighting was. All the noise was from the shattered fortress.

So Kissen followed it. She found a metal bar to smash through the other side of her manacles, then went over the crumbled wall that stank of burned blackfire, into the king's palace.

Bodies littered the ground. Most of the defending guard were in tatters, and the first fountain she passed was thick with blood, and there was still a skirmish going on under its arches. Lessa was not among them, nor the heads of the other Houses.

Where? She chased footsteps of mud, higher into the towers, finding only corpses. The force in the Reach was bigger than she had expected, judging by the number of bodies, but still it was no great number. So, why was Lessa here? Claiming the Reach was a bold move, but it would be useless without capturing or killing the king. And no matter how strong Elo was, or how wilful Inara, Kissen had no idea how they would defeat an army.

She rounded a corner with a balcony overlooking several gardens and almost fell into a young squire in blue, his face pimpled, his trews wet with fear, running. He yelped. Kissen flicked her staff, wincing as her left hand twinged with agony, and struck him right in the sternum before he could draw his blade. He doubled over, wheezing, and she grabbed him by the scruff of his shirt, dragging him up and pressing him over the balustrade.

'P-please, don't hurt me!' he cried. 'Please!'

He was just a lad, like the one she had killed. He was terrified just looking at her, and terrifying she must look, her face scarred and thick with blood and dirt, her hands bruised and bloody, her patience at its end.

'Tell me where the intruders might be going,' said Kissen.

He whimpered and she shook him. 'I'd die before I betray the Sunbringer,' he said, his voice squeaking.

'You—' Kissen rolled her eyes. 'Fuck's sake: why?'

He closed his mouth, staring at her.

'Look, I'm a veiga.' She gestured to the white scar of an old god's curse on her face. 'I'm here to help, understand? I'm here to save your skin. Tell me where they're going or your Sunbringer is dust.'

CHAPTER FIFTY-SIX

Inara

INARA OPENED HER EYES, HER WHOLE BODY STINGING. Skedi was beside her, panting, his eyes closed, the size of a mouse. Exhausted. Reduced. His power faded, almost gone. She scooped him up into her hand, cradling him to her.

Skedi, she called him, running her thumb over his fur. *Skedi . . .*

What had she done? Used gods just to exhaust them? Break them? Tears flooded her eyes.

Skedi's ear twitched, the green beads on his antlers glinted, and he opened his yellow eye. *I'm all right,* he said. *Tired.*

I've got you.

Inara tucked him into her shirt and picked herself up, coughing on the smoke that was pouring from the other buildings and peered out below. The people fighting the fire were working hard, minimising the damage and using wet blankets to reduce the sparks, breaking holes in the roofs to draw a line in the burning.

Lethen! she called. *Daefer. Anyone?*

The canal god will not answer you. Lethen answered immediately, as if she had been waiting for Inara's call. *He saw the veiga and ran to his wet little hole. Though now he has other prayers to answer, prayers for water.*

And Canovan?

My child too, cannot go on. He fought bravely. Her voice sounded proud. *I made him, I bore him, but I could not protect him always.*

Inara blinked back tears, clutching Skedi tight. Would her mother have been proud of her? Would Kissen? Or would they have been afraid?

I am glad you saved the knight, said Lethen at last. *This was the most fun I've had in ages.*

Her voice disappeared, and Inara was alone.

She stirred as she heard shouts, yells from below, then footsteps in the forum of the cloche. Inara picked herself up, grimacing with pain, and went to look.

'Be careful, Ina,' Skedi whispered.

She nodded, holding him to her chest, and crept to the edge of the balcony. The sky was dark, and so were the archives below. Smoke drifted between the fig trees, thick and grey.

Movement: knights. No, veiga. Three of them.

Inara ducked. They would have seen Skedi fly in. But there was no shout, no feet on the stairs. It was not them they were looking for.

One instead went to the door she and Cal had sneaked through the night before and tried the handle. It didn't open, still locked from the inside.

'Stand aside,' said one of the others. They shook out their shoulders, adjusted their pauldrons, then stood low like a bull before running into the wood, shoulder first.

The wood cracked, splintered, burst inwards. The stairs below were dark, and they paused.

Moments later, two more veiga ran in to the forum, and the colours of relief bloomed from every one of them. They were carrying some strange equipment, long poles and metal chains, all in shades of briddite.

'Are you ready?'

'Take it down. You two, stay here. We'll get the god.'

Scian. They weren't interested in her and Skedi. They were going to kill Scian.

CHAPTER FIFTY-SEVEN

Elogast

ELO REACHED THE SINGERS. HE GRABBED THE VEIGA WITH the bloody sword and flung him back. The man stumbled and Elo slammed his own weapon through his chest, piercing armour, flesh, bone.

'Elo!' cried Naia. 'What are you doing?'

With a roar he pulled out his blade, turned to another one and charged into her, jabbing his sword up from beneath. His blade connected with her side, then his shoulder with her chest and he shoved her back into another veiga. They both fell.

'Elo, stop!' cried Naia as he stood up again.

One of the knights tried to rise. 'Ser Elogast?' they managed, but Elo was past mercy. Arren had shown no mercy. He brought his sword across their shoulder, their neck, and ended them in a spray of blood.

'Stop!' Naia barked at him. 'Please!'

'You have to leave!' cried Elo, turning. Two singers had knelt beside the one who had fallen, applying bandages with quick hands.

'This is *my* choice, Elo. My fight.' Her mouth tightened. 'My absolution.'

'This isn't a fight! It will be a massacre.'

'We are as ready to be martyrs as you.'

Elo stared at her, at the others. They wept; they were shaking.

But still, they were singing. Scian's song. He recognised one or two of them as the inkers who had fought and killed with Canovan.

'Like our patron god,' Naia whispered. 'We're here to die.'

Elo took hold of both her arms and she flinched as the pommel of his sword bloodied her clothes. 'You mustn't,' he said. He understood. He didn't want it. 'You can be anything, Naia. Do anything! Wash your hands of this, and let the blood be mine. Let it be my guilt. My shame. My death!'

Naia shook her head.

'Elogast!'

Elo turned. There were horses on the plaza. A ragged parade of knights were dragging themselves back into their ranks, ink-spattered, muddy, and exhausted with disrupted splendour. Behind them, the buildings burned. The Lesscians had no time for marches: they were racing to save their homes.

And within the sea of blue was gold. Arren sat on a pure-white steed, unmarked by their battle, his armour glinting in the light from the fires, the lanterns in the windows, the torches of his own knights. And the glowing embers of his chest. Elo hardly recognised him, hidden as he was inside all of his gold and his closed helm. If he had not grown up with the set of those shoulders, the lift of his chin, Elo would not have been sure it was Arren at all.

No. Not Arren. Sunbringer. A god who had to die.

But Elo had lost his last chance to kill him. Peta sat beside him, her nose as hawkish as Elo remembered, her hair grey. And by her, Risiah, who was blinking at Elo. A spray of yellow ink was spattered across his horse.

Elo released Naia and turned. 'These people are innocent,' he said, stepping forward. 'Let them go.'

'There are no innocents who stand against their king,' said Peta, her hands tightening on her reins. Her voice carried over the plaza, quelling the sounds of the people. 'There are no innocents who ally with the gods against the Crown.'

'They are protecting their city!' Elo shouted back, his voice ricocheting around the square. 'From a tyrant who sets it ablaze.' They were twenty paces from him, he had no bow, and he was not as good a shot as he was a swordsman.

Arren tilted his antlers. Gods, he had modelled himself on Mertagh, the god of war who had almost killed him. It sickened Elo to his stomach.

'And what has your king done to deserve your mobs and violence?' he said through his helm. His voice crackled, strange and distant. Flames burst through the gap in his chest. 'I came here in hope, in glory, in reason. It is not I who called the gods upon your streets, filled it with demons.'

A few people had stopped their work; the singers had fallen silent. Listening. 'I have done nothing but give my heart for you,' he said, and put his hand to his chest, to the flaming, artful tear. Elo felt a dull pain in his belly, that spread and prickled over the scars on his chest. 'I gave my family. My blood. My life.'

Elo felt Arren's eyes on him as the king stretched out his hand and lowered his voice, as if speaking directly to him.

'Was my death not enough,' said Sunbringer, 'for your love?'

CHAPTER FIFTY-EIGHT

Kissen

KISSEN HEADED THE WAY THE BOY HAD SHOWN. UP THE tower, over another bridge to a higher one, and ran around an open courtyard with another fountain below, this one unstained. From the balconies, she could see a view of the other forts. The Forge's flagpole was still bare, but the Shield flew with colours that were not the king's. At least one of them was green and silver. Craier.

At last, she heard the chime of blades meeting. She rounded a corner that opened to a corridor with a black-stained ceiling, as if there had once been a great fire that had never been fully cleaned.

There she found Lessa, Tarin, the Vittosk woman, Graiis and guards in the colours of two more Houses that Kissen didn't recognise. They were fighting with a cluster of twelve knights in Regna blue outside a locked double door of brass.

Why here? Why so many guarding a door to a tower, and a courtyard?

The rebels were winning.

'Lady Craier!' cried Kissen. 'Stop!'

Lessa turned to stare at Kissen. 'How . . .'

A knight took advantage of her distraction, bringing her long-sword up and across, but Lessa saw it. She brought her own blade around and stepped aside, sliding the curved sword from point to pommel and through the guard's eye, as cool as rain.

'Now!' Selainne Vittosk had hold of a battering ram the size of a child and was carrying it with two more Vittosk knights.

'Tarin—' Lessa called.

'I have them!' said her guard in the fray. 'Back!' she ordered to the other fighters. 'Push them back! Clear the way.'

Lessa dragged her sword out, sending a spray of blood to the ground as she came towards Kissen, her expression murderous. She looked at Kissen's bloodied hand, her swollen wrist and thumb, her face, her staff, and lack of any real weapon. Kissen could tell she was trying to decide if she was insane or impressive, and Kissen didn't blame her. She was trying to decide the same thing.

'Why did you come here?' Lessa barked. She spoke as if Kissen was her friend rather than someone whose tongue she had threatened to remove. She looked genuinely astounded. 'This is a battleground. You could have left.'

'Please . . .' said Kissen. Her voice caught. She put her bloody hand to her chest and tried for her softest voice. She looked the lady directly in the eyes. No humour. No sting. Just honesty. 'Please, my Lady Craier.' She threw down her staff as the others ran with their battering ram, slamming it into the door and shaking it against its bolts.

Kissen drew her dagger next, Osidisen's dagger, and held it out by the blade, pommel towards Lessa. And then she knelt. Carefully. Painfully. She put her knees to the floor, her breath catching in her throat.

Lessa watched her in disbelief, then levelled her blade at her neck.

The ram hit metal again. A creak. The door was giving.

Kissen had faced death before and had not been afraid to die. Each breath of life she took was time her father had given her, and she never thought she would regret a thing if her next breath was her last. But that was before she had met Lessa Craier, and wondered if she would rather live, if only to see the changing expressions on this woman's face.

'I came for Inara,' said Kissen. 'You have to believe me, or I would be long gone. For your daughter. For her future. If Hseth comes to these lands, she will not have one.'

The battering ram slammed once more against the brass. The door cracked open, and the sweet scent of gently burning woodsmoke rolled through.

A ram again, and the doors flew open. Beyond them was a wide table covered with a detailed map, and a burning hearth. Within it, gently smoking, was a cage, or cocoon of twigs and moss, as big as the fireplace itself. Through the branches, cross-legged in the fire, Kissen saw a young man, handsome, his eyes closed. And his curling brown hair wreathed in a coronet.

CHAPTER FIFTY-NINE

Inara

SKEDI CLIMBED INTO INARA'S POCKET AS SHE RAN DOWN the stairs, trying to recall what she had glimpsed on the archive map. They had landed on the eighth and she sprinted past the seventh, and sixth, to the fifth.

Preservation, instruments and weaponry.

Inara pushed through an open door and raced through the archive rooms. Here were stringed instruments from all over the world, harps and sitars, zithers and violins. Not right.

Skedi was recovering. He rustled in her pocket, and stuck his head wearily out of it, his ears flat and tired, his whispers drooping. 'What are you looking for?' he asked.

'A bow,' whispered Inara.

Next room. Yes. This was it. Swords of strange shapes, circles, discs, spears of stone, of metal, of bronze, arranged on tables beneath frames of wood and glass. These rooms were huge, their scroll-heavy shelves a warren.

'There,' said Skedi, flicking his ears.

Inara turned and saw what she was looking for through rows of shelves filled with parchment: bows. Longbows, crossbows and, at last, hunting bows. They were all strung, seemingly with the correct catgut, and were well cared for. Oiled and ready. Arrows too, though one of each kind, categorised by feathers and heads in tiny, perfect writing.

SUNBRINGER

The doors to the cabinet were bolted, but not locked. She slid one open and grabbed the first bow that looked her size, testing its give.

'What are you going to do?' Skedi asked.

'I don't know,' said Inara. 'Save Scian.'

Skedi batted his ear at her. 'Against five veiga?'

She frowned. The bow she had grasped was too loose. It had been strung for display. Badly. She found another, just a little higher than her chin. The gut sang when she plucked it.

'Just . . .' Inara said, she paused, and looked at him. 'I just want to give her a chance.' She had led two gods and possibly the only other half god to their death already, she couldn't let another die.

Skedi sighed, too tired to lift his ears.

Inara grabbed the arrows next, as many as she could, shoving them into her satchel.

I'm coming Scian! she thought in her mind, throwing it down the stairs, through the stones, past the vaults, to the tomb.

She was not expecting what she heard back.

No, little one.

The papers on the shelves around them rustled. Skedi's whiskers twitched.

I'm going to save you. Inara ran back for the stairs, nocking an arrow to her bow. She could distract the veiga, draw them up. Away from Scian. She could hide Skedi. She could . . . she could . . .

I said no.

A scroll flew off the shelf and flew into Inara, wrapping around her wrist. She shook it off, but another came, for her ankle this time. A third, a fourth. Ledgers smacked into her, long wraps of wood and paper, leather and parchment, flying towards her on the will of their god.

Stop it, said Inara. *Wait for me!*

A scroll tangled around her arms, a codex dragged at her knee. Skedi ducked down into Ina's pocket, frightened.

Your will is not the one that turns the world, little one, said Scian's voice. *Even gods have their time to die.*

341

Inara tried to use her own power to fight back, but she didn't know how to direct her will. At the god? She was too far. At the paper? They wouldn't stop, they were not gods. She pulled the pages from her, their ink smudging with the blood from her hands, the sweat and tears from her face. The bow she had stolen was thickly clogged, its gut unusable.

A shriek from below shook the entire cloche. The bells sounded, dust running from the rafters. The strength of the papers diminished; they fell. Softly, like leaves.

Inara struggled loose, kicking the expensive parchment off her boots and breaking for the stairs again. Down to the fourth, third floor. She glimpsed the guards below, two on the door, their swords drawn, staring up into the cloche.

Inara tore the paper from the bowstring and shook it from her arrow, nocking it again as she ran.

Ina, Skedi whispered. *You can't do it all.*

I can!

Scian had done nothing wrong, she didn't deserve to die. The look on her face when she had felt the people praying for her, the hope, the love. Inara couldn't forget it. Wouldn't.

Next flight. She hit the top step at a stride, losing the last of the paper. At the bottom was another balcony, and she would use that to fire. She kept her bowstring taut. Seven more steps, and she would be there. Four more steps. Two more steps.

And she would shoot someone.

She heard Scian scream. This time her cry set the birds shrieking from the rafters.

One more step.

Ina's bootlace snapped. She felt her breath leave her lips as she fell, putting her arms out to protect Skedi. She struck her shoulder, her head, and sprawled onto the stone steps. Bright light crushed across her vision, then black, and red.

She groaned. Her face was on stone, her head split with pain. She tried to move, winced, her vision swimming, then put a hand to her head. It came away sticky with blood.

I owed you a debt.

That was not the voice she had expected. She looked up,

bile rising in her throat, and saw a mouse two steps above her, its face a carved wooden mask.

He gazed at her, half in shadow, half faded, but his eyes clear.

'Kelt?' said Inara. 'Why . . .'

It is not your time to die, halfling.

CHAPTER SIXTY

Elogast

KNIGHT AGAINST KING. AND THE KING HAD ARROWS. ELO
kept his sword high.

'Elogast,' said Risiah. 'Stand down.'

More and more knights were entering the plaza, their bows
trained on Elo, on the singers. The drummers who were left had
taken up their skins and were rattling out a rhythm. The knights
with them chanted.

'Sunbringer. Sunbringer. Sunbringer.'

Elo stood in front of Naia, unmoving. Instead, he stood very
still. A single shift, and the arrows might loosen, killing him, Naia,
as many as they liked. They had more than enough archers for all
of them. The singers' voices were fading, drowned out by the sheer
force of numbers.

'Lion,' whispered Naia, then shouted. 'Lion of Lesscia!'

The other singers caught her call. 'Lion,' they began. 'Li-on. Li-on.
Li-on of Lesscia.'

Arren's head tipped, his hands tightened on his reins as the
chanters battled for noise. Elo dared not look back. He stared at
the Sunbringer, willing him to fight. Arren sat proud and still,
waiting for something. So they stayed, pinned between fire and
chanting, silence between them.

Elo wished he could see his face. What would it tell him? Would
he see fondness still? Regret? Hatred? Entreaty?

Or would his old friend's expression be as cold as his helm? What if he didn't care that Elo was once again before him, desperate again, betrayed, alone, with no Kissen to save him. Every fibre of Elo, every agonised, limping moment, had been bent toward facing his friend and making him pay for what he had done. Elo's fury burned with a passion as hot as his dedication had once been.

But what if Elo was nothing to him? Just a man he had tried to sacrifice?

Why did Elo fear his indifference more than is hatred?

But he had reached out his hand to him, as if they were lovers in the square.

Someone gasped, then a flurry of cries passed around the Lesscians gathered in the plaza. Elo turned. Out of the tunnel, a veiga emerged. No, two, three. Four. And between them was Scian.

The god of knowledge, who had walked the streets the night before; her neck bound in briddite, the collar attached to chains and poles that held her tight. Her veils were caught and ragged, her face aged and weary. Behind them were two more veiga, carrying armfuls of manuscripts.

'No!' cried Naia, breaking hold for the first time. 'Please, for pity's sake!'

Scian's captors pressed down with the poles, tightening the chains, forcing her lower on the cobbles before the cloche. Risiah and Peta dismounted, the Gods Commander drawing his briddite sword.

In another life, Elo would have been walking there with them. He steeled himself as they marched past, his mind racing. All he needed was a chance.

'This is not the battle you want to fight, Elogast,' said Risiah as he drew close. 'Please. Trust me.'

'Don't speak to the traitor,' snapped Peta, her head held high, her hawkish nose twisted with hatred.

'You know what he is, Risiah,' said Elo. 'That he thinks himself a god.'

The commander paused. He stared at Elo with meaning in his eyes. But Elo didn't understand what he wanted to convey. At last, he nodded.

'Then,' said Elo, 'I have nothing to say to you.'

Peta lifted her arm and shouted. 'Sunbringer!'

The knights echoed her, louder now as more and more followed, drowning out the singers at last. 'Sunbringer! Sunbringer!'

Arren lifted up his arms to a roar of adulation, then he dismounted too. He started walking, not to Scian, but to Elo, his antlered head held high.

One chance.

CHAPTER SIXTY-ONE

Inara

TOO LATE. ALWAYS TOO LATE.

Inara stumbled up the stairs again, blood dripping onto her shoulder. Her head felt like a cracked egg, but she dragged herself to one of the stained-glass windows as Scian was hauled into the plaza. Veiga were piling papers behind her while she knelt in the dust, everything they couldn't save. Elo stood in the face of a hundred arrows, his sword loose in his hand.

They had failed.

A man and woman were walking towards Scian. The first was a veiga, his cloak clearly printed with their symbol. His briddite longsword was drawn, his colours dim, but there. She could not read them. She lifted her bow.

It was a long shot.

Skedi fluttered out of her pocket and crept to the edge, closer to the size of a hare now, his ears lifted.

'I've seen you shoot harder targets,' he said supportively.

Her heart swelled, and she nocked her arrow to her stolen bow. The head was barbed, for tearing flesh. She tried not to think about that. Instead, she breathed in, adjusting for the wind, the sting of the smoke, stretching the gut back, back, further than she thought she could go. She swallowed, her short hair was tickling at her eyes. She had not killed a person before.

The man with the briddite sword reached Scian and looked

347

down at her as the papers behind her were set alight. She flinched but tipped her head and gazed straight back.

The shining king was moving towards Elo, his arms held out as if in greeting. Elo stood still, a pillar of silver flame, the colour of his heartache tipped with blue. His love was diminished by his pain.

Inara turned the bow, shoulder down, feather to mouth. The smoke showed her the way the wind was blowing. Did she shoot the veiga? Or Arren?

'Inara . . .' said Skedi nervously as she pointed the arrow at the king. Did she trust Elo to kill the man who was coming towards him like a friend? 'Inara, if you shoot Arren the archers will fire on Elogast.'

'There is only one true power!' cried the woman commander, her colours a banner of gold-edged blue. She lifted her foot and put it on one of the bars that held Scian's collar. The god bent silently, her forehead going to the floor. 'Only one uniter of the seas. One king. One god. Sunbringer!'

'Sunbringer!' The name came on a wave, and the arrows on Elo stayed steady. The veiga lifted his sword higher, its briddite point tearing the air. The singers in white had mostly knelt, praying.

'Only fools forget their past,' said Scian. Her voice carried. *Only fools forget their past.*

All Elo had wanted was a chance to take his revenge. Could Inara let him fall for her own? Take her vengeance no matter who she hurt?

No. Then she would be no worse than the Sunbringer.

But her shot could save someone else.

Inara turned back and loosed her arrow on the veiga before he dropped the sword. It struck him at the base of his neck and sent him spinning to the ground. His colours flared in shock and pain, and then all of them went out.

A cry of surprise went up from the king's army. Their attention swerved from their king to the god.

And Elo used the moment to close the distance. He flicked his sword up and around in a flash of light, then brought it towards Arren. The king drew his own blade, meeting Elo's strike with a parry, and they slammed together, arms and bodies locking. Too close for the archers to fire for fear of striking the god-king himself.

Inara drew another arrow, a different shape, but then saw the silver-haired woman stepping in where the veiga had fallen, snatching up his sword. Inara cried out, releasing another shaft. Too quick to fly true, it slammed into the commander's arm, but not hard enough for her to cease her swing.

The blade came down.

Scian did not make a sound as she died. She folded like vellum, crumpling, her veils too, her robe. The rebels in white cried out as if their hearts had felt the blow. Across the city, the shrines people had put out on Scian's Day, their prayers, their totems, began to shatter and crumble. The god herself blew away, drifting to the dust the world had made of her life.

Inara stepped back, fumbling her bow. It hadn't worked. She hadn't saved Scian. She had killed a man and the god had still died.

'You tried,' said Skedi softly, reaching up to put his nose on her chin. 'Inara, you tried . . .'

Shock took her by the throat. Another god gone; centuries destroyed. She couldn't believe how little she had achieved. How she had summoned a city of gods and had barely changed a thing. A sob caught her chest, then another, but she was too shocked to weep. She felt as if her heart had stilled.

Something caught her eye. She blinked, straightened up, her eyes drawn east. There: the distant sky was glowing orange, but it was far too early for sunrise.

'Skedi,' she whispered. 'What's that?'

Skedi looked up, his antlers catching in the tangle of her hair. He gave her a worried glance, then followed her gaze. His ears rose. 'That's Daesmouth,' he said. 'Where Yatho and Telle went.'

Inara recognised that glow.

So did Skedi.

'That's fire.'

CHAPTER SIXTY-TWO

Elogast

ARREN HAD COME TOWARDS HIM, OPENING HIS ARMS.

'Come back to me, Elo,' he had said, his voice every bit the same as Elo remembered. Soft-spoken, a twist of humour, as if they shared a secret, not the bellowing god-ruler on a white horse. 'End this madness. Come back to my side, where you belong.'

Elo had tentatively, subtly, pushed Naia behind him.

You are the last thing Arren loves, and he has chosen to lose you.

Unforgivable. Arren had dragged out a peaceful god before her faithful, killed a father with his son's hand, burned histories, families, houses to the ground. He had broken their friendship, their love, over power. No. He would not forgive. Sunbringer, or Arren.

Neither deserved his love.

Then, a hiss of an arrow, a cry behind him. The army and their arrows shifted, wavered, fluttering with panic, fear, distraction. Risiah had fallen, an arrow in his neck, come from above, before he could deliver the killing blow.

Inara.

Arren was but three strides away. Elo picked up his sword and charged.

Swift and sure, Arren drew his blade enough to parry Elo's. A cry of warning went up from the soldiers, and an arrow skittered across where Elo had stood, but it was too late. They were locked, fighting, too close to separate between the smoke and wind and arrows.

Inara had given him his chance.

Elo drove down and stepped in to Arren's parry to strike again. Arren met it, and locked their swords together, strength against strength. He fought like Arren, his footwork perfect, his movements lithe and sure. They broke and locked again, swords clashing.

Elo did not see Scian fall, nor hear the singers howl in sorrow. He and Arren danced across the cobbles as if they were the only ones beneath the fire and shadowed sky.

Arren laughed. 'This, Elo!' he said. 'This is you! The real you, as you should have been. Out for blood, leading armies. My Lion of Blenraden, now Lion of Lesscia!'

Elo brought his sword down towards Arren's head, and the king lifted his blade to take the strike, another, as Elo hammered them down. Arren was stronger than Elo remembered: he did not seem to feel the blows that bit through Elo's elbows even as he threw them.

'I was never yours,' growled Elo. 'I was mine. I chose to serve you. I chose to leave you. *You* chose to betray me.'

'Betray?' Arren moved aside at his next strike, anger in his steps as he tried to make space between them. 'You *left* me.'

Elo wouldn't let Arren put space between him: if he did he would be arrow-bait, and Arren would have him in his power.

Never again.

Fast on his feet, Elo kept their closeness. He aimed his sword for Arren's leg now, and the king was forced to turn and parry or lose it. The edge of his blade ran down Elo's with a terrible shriek and forced both of their weapons down into the cobbles, catching for a moment in the stone.

'Hseth fooled me, Elogast,' said Arren. 'I thought I needed a sacrifice, that it would sever all ties between us and end . . . whatever we are. But all I needed was love. They love me.' His gripped tightened. 'You can again too.'

Arren dragged the end of his blade from the cobbles, sending Elo's flying up, out of stance. Elo pushed his left leg back and leaned as Arren flipped his sword in hand and slid it up towards Elo's side. The blade glanced off his chest armour with a silver spark and skidded down. His breath came quick, but why couldn't he hear Arren's? The king seemed barely to have broken stride.

Elo found his feet and moved in again, ribboning his sword back, then under, around then over, putting Arren on the back foot, defending now. One archer tried a shot, their arrow glancing off Elo's forearm.

'Hold!' yelled Peta, her voice tight with terror. 'Do not harm the king!'

They shifted across the cobbles, and Arren backed away from Elo's onslaught.

'Is this love, for you, then?' said Elo. 'Terror and fire? Blood and gold?'

Arren growled in frustration and caught his next blow, then shoved him back.

'What would you have done?' Sunbringer gestured around them, at the half-burned buildings, the barely contained fires. 'Let the land fall to infighting and civil strife? This? This is as much your doing as it is mine, Elogast.'

His voice had lost its lightness, and instead was thick and bitter. So close, so familiar. Elo clenched his teeth, and Arren shifted his balance, pressing on his back heel and catching Elo's blade at the tip, then slamming it back down to the floor. The pain of the moment shook all the way up Elo's arm, into his still-healing chest.

But Elo released his pommel with his right hand and smashed the back of his fist into Arren's helmet. The king stumbled back, reaching up to resettle it, but quickly rallied. He deflected Elo's next two blows, shoved him to the side with his blade, then found the gap in Elo's armour. He went for the strike, catching his shoulder between the pauldron and the cuirass, where the plates were not built for him. The sharp point sliced in, quick and true.

Elo reeled back, gasping with pain. A trail of blood followed Arren's sword as he yanked it out and Elo dashed it away. They circled each other, moving in closer, then apart. Arren had not tried again to run. He was too angry now.

An opening. Elo ran forward, feinting left then striking right, catching Arren by surprise. He hammered his sword into Arren's blade once, twice, three times, almost breaking his guard. Arren fought back, taking his attack as if he didn't feel it. But Elo had gathered his weakness; Arren had not practised brawling. When he was a lesser prince, Arren had used every trick he knew; now he was Sunbringer, no one tried to kick him down where he stood.

Apart from Elo.

'I did love you,' snarled Elo, advancing. His arm was still bleeding, losing feeling. 'I stood at your side through death and ruin. I put you on a throne above all others, and I will not watch you use it to trample the world.'

Arren ran forward with a yell. He moved with grace and energy, a spinning strike from the left, whirling and turning it into a brutal stab. Elo stepped and caught it. Locked, again, entangled in a dance of swords, each trying to lead.

'Loved me?' the king cried over the screech of their blades. This was more like Arren. Rash. Cross. Passionate. 'You loved me at a distance, Elogast. More and more you stepped away as the world changed from under me.'

Elo was leading him to the centre of the plaza, to open ground. Two pieces on an empty board.

'More and more,' Arren continued, his voice cracking with rage, 'you refused to love me enough to stay. You *never* loved me like I loved you.'

No more playing. Elo had already decided. No more Arren. Elogast moved. He released Arren's sword, and the king brought the blade around to Elo's head, expecting him to block.

But Elo ducked. He fought like Kissen did: he ran forward into his friend's guard and used his shoulder to ram through his chest. Arren stumbled back, and Elo grabbed the antler of his helm and dragged Sunbringer's whole head down onto his knee, crushing the stupid grille into his absent face before throwing him back.

Arren yelled with fury, lifting his sword high to bring it down in a vicious blow.

Elo stepped aside and used his bracer to block. The blow was stronger than he expected – he had hoped it would glance off

– but instead the strike cracked through the metal plate, to his flesh and bone.

Still, Elo was ready, his own blade poised. He pointed it up, a through-strike straight into the gaping hole in the Sunbringer's chest, the cavity where the god's heart must be. Where Arren's heart and their friendship had died. Elo's blade was briddite-edged, it should destroy whatever heart he had.

The blade ran true, out through the king's back, shattering his armour. Arren cried out in pain as the metal went through him. The plaza fell silent, other than the distant cries of the firefighters, still beating back the flames.

Elo stood still, his sword in his hand and through his friend's back, his king's back. He was horrified, terrified, by what he had done. He knew, this time, that if the arrows didn't finish him, his heartbreak would.

'I'm sorry,' said Elo. His voice broke, his throat tightened with emotion. 'I'm so sorry that it came to this.'

Arren lifted his head, his antlers rising.

'I didn't think,' he said in a whisper. 'I honestly didn't think you would do it.' He seemed astounded. 'You truly want me dead?'

Elo held his sword firm, though his hands trembled. 'You died three years ago,' he said. 'The man I knew . . . you are not him.' He closed his eyes. The silence was deafening, no one breathed. 'Now we die, together, three years too late.'

The darkness within his helm looked at him, and then Sunbringer laughed. A hollow, dry, chuckling sound. Like the echo of wind through a furnace.

'No,' said Arren.

He lifted his hand and put it on Elo's.

Something was wrong. His movement was not that of a dying man. Now Elo was close enough to kiss him, he still could hear no breath from Arren's lungs. He could, however, smell woodsmoke. The smoke of a hearth.

'Not today.'

Arren lifted his other hand to the grille that covered his face and swung it open.

He was not flesh. Twigs and branches, sparking with flame. His eyes were embers, his mouth a maw of fire. An effigy of burning tinder. Hestra's creation. Not Arren: his double.

'Today, I'll save you,' it said in Arren's voice. 'Today, it's my turn.'

As Elogast watched, branches grew through Arren's chest, flames licking out, up Elo's sword, over his hands. Twigs and moss grew over him, branches stretched, wrapping them both in a huge cocoon of greenwood and bright, warm yellow light. Arren's power.

Elo.

Skedi's voice broke into Elo's mind, a needle of ice. He looked up. Skedi was huge once again, the size of a lion, blood on his mouth. Inara was clinging onto him as they came swooping down from the sky.

Arren did not look up. Instead, he opened his arms to Elo, and wrapped him in an embrace as Skedi and Inara landed with them.

Then all Elo could feel was burning, ash and smoke.

CHAPTER SIXTY-THREE

Inara

THE WORLD TIPPED SIDEWAYS. INARA REMEMBERED falling, swooping down. They had to know, something was wrong, there was fire in the sky. But Arren had wrapped Elo in a cocoon of kindling, like a huge firestarter of moss and twigs and embers, and she and Skedi had fallen into it.

After that, darkness. A sense of rushing, a flash of light.

She dreamed that Skedi, small again, was clutched in her arms, a bundle of fur and feathers. That she was tangled in her bed at home, hot, too hot. Her throat was burning. The bed was hard. Everything was on fire.

Not on fire. She would be screaming. She was close to flame but not burning. The ground was not a bed, only stone warmed from flame. Around her, twigs cracked and fell to pieces, and acrid air rolled in.

She opened her eyes. Were they dead? Was Skedi? No, the ash in her mouth was thick, the world too real, too clear. Too loud.

She was in a hearth, its walls black with burning, and smoke rose around her through a curved chimney. Scattered across the stones were branches and roots, lint and straw. A few were burning.

From where she lay, she could see one side of a large room dominated by brass trellis-doors, and a wide wooden table bearing a jug of water, a cup, some bread. A large map was spread across it, scattered with ink marks, letters, figurines.

Something stirred in her hand: Skedi, small and silent as a newborn mouse. Others were moving in the fireplace too. Inara saw long limbs, bound in armour, a chestplate resplendent with an Irisian lion.

'Elo,' Inara whispered. He had done it; he had killed the king. His sword had gone through his chest, Inara had seen it. Her knight was bleeding badly from his left shoulder and his bracer, at the sound of his name he groaned. 'Elogast.'

With Elo, holding onto him in a tight embrace, was a young man with curly, brown hair and a circlet around his brow. His eyes slowly blinked open, and he sat up, gaze sharp, bright and gentle blue. He caught sight of Inara, his brow furrowing as he held Elo tighter to his chest.

'Who are you?' he said hazily as if he had just risen from a long, long sleep. 'We did not bring you here, did we?'

Inara's eyes dropped to his chest. There was a hole between his ribs beneath an open shirt, laced with scarring, but not bleeding. Within it burned a ball of twigs and flame.

Inara screamed, leaping back, holding Skedi tight. The king looked different without his armour. Young. Innocent.

Elo's eyes snapped open, and his eyes found Arren. As the king drew a dagger from his belt, Elo grabbed his wrist with his undamaged arm and shoved him back before he could seize Inara. The king wrestled with him; he and Elo struggling for the upper hand as Inara scrabbled out of the hearth and fell to the tiled floor.

Flames burst out of Arren's chest, biting at Elo's flesh, his face. He cried out – injured, exhausted, and confused – and Arren used it to his advantage. He grabbed Elo by his injured shoulder and pulled him back, putting the edge of his blade to his neck. Elo stilled, breathing heavily. His gaze found Inara, then went past her, and his eyes widened.

Arren was also staring, his colours shaking purple. 'How . . .' he said, then his expression hardened. No longer innocent; he looked gaunt, exhausted and afraid. 'What the *fuck* are you doing here, Craier?'

He wasn't speaking to Inara. She followed his gaze behind her, and saw the shattered mess of a doorway, crowded with soldiers sweating and bloody with battle, a battering ram at their feet. They were not in yellow, or blue, but greens, browns, greys. Neutral. Before them stood Lessa Craier.

'Mother,' said Inara, her breath catching in her throat.

Behind her, rather worse for wear, was another dead woman: Kissen.

'Ina?' the godkiller said, her voice hoarse and breaking. She looked terrible. Worse than Inara felt. But Lessa Craier looked wonderful: her blade out and bloody, poised. Her mother's long hair was slicked in a perfect braid, her tabard edged in Craier green and silver, embroidered with birds and leaves, and her leather chestplate was the same one she had kept in her armoury in their manor.

Their burned manor.

It took hearing Kissen call Ina's name for Lessa's mouth to tighten in recognition. No wonder: Inara must look very different to the soft little girl who had never left her home. Her mother's colours fractured out into white, pure panic, then shifted into a fountain of golden foam, love or relief, before disappearing once more. Pulled back inside her frame. Hidden.

Kissen moved. Inara didn't have time to think before the veiga charged past Lessa and pulled Inara away from the fire and into her arms, far from Arren's blade.

'Kissen,' Inara said, tentatively. She was real. She was completely real. No dream could smell so bad. Inara grabbed her back, holding on for safety, for terror and grief.

'You're . . . you're alive.'

She held her, tightly, as tight as she could hold a thing, and Kissen held her back as if she could use her body to shield her from the world. Lessa didn't come to her, Lessa didn't move.

'And kicking,' Kissen said. 'Barely. I'm so sorry, I tried . . . I tried to come back to you.'

'Kissen!' Joy was on Elo's face and in his colours, shining the mellow hues of fresh-baked bread with the reds of Kissen's hair.

'Quiet,' said Arren, holding him tighter, but even the knife to his throat couldn't dim Elo's utter relief.

'Elogast,' said Kissen, her voice gruff with emotion, her eyes going from the knife, to Arren, and back to Elo, calculating. She covered it with a joke: 'Looks like you're in trouble again.'

Elo huffed out a breath of a laugh. 'I should have known . . .' he said, his voice cracking with exhaustion and wonder. He grinned. 'I should have known you were too stubborn to die.'

'What's going on here?' said Arren. 'How did you people get inside the Reach?'

'Enough blackfire to blast a fucking mountain,' said Kissen, and Lessa made a noise of annoyance in her throat.

Arren wrapped his arm possessively around Elo. 'Hestra,' he hissed, 'get us out of here.'

The flame in the king's heart flared, but did nothing.

Inara was beginning to understand, or thought she did: Arren's body had never left Sakre. He had stayed in the capital and, like Blenraden, had sent a twig and flame double made by Hestra in his stead. How much power had that taken? To exist both in him and outside them, then summon them all in flame to Sakre in a moment?

Elo had never stood a chance. None of them had stood a chance in Lesscia against a king of twigs with a heart of fire.

'What are you going to do now, Sunbringer?' said Elo dryly, putting his good hand up to Arren's knife. 'Look around you. You've lost.'

'Says the man with my knife on his neck,' said Arren. He stared back at Lady Craier instead as if he could disappear her with his mind. 'How did you know I was here?' He was playing for time, perhaps till Hestra was strong enough to rescue them again.

Lessa smiled coldly, calm and confident. Inara didn't need to see her colours to taste her satisfaction. 'Perhaps,' she said, 'you should be more careful of playing god around a veiga.'

Arren's hand dropped a little. 'Risiah,' he hissed.

Elo must have felt his arms loosen. He grabbed Arren's hand and wrenched the knife away, twisting it and disarming him. Arren cursed, losing his last advantage.

'Yes, Elo!' cried Inara, sensing victory seeded within their defeat. But then, to her shock, Kissen dived forward with a cry.

'Stop!' Kissen grabbed Elo and wrestled him back before the

blade could land, and Arren broke free from the hearth and around the back of his table, putting it, the map, the jug, between him and everything else. He had no other weapon; he clearly had not expected to need it. He put his hands on the trellis doors. There must be a balcony, an escape.

'Stop!' cried Lessa, starting forward.

Through the gap in the king's chest, Inara could see the flames of the hearth god sustaining him.

Flames. Fire in the sky. The rose god's briars burning, the fire in her orchards, her home. Skedi, so small and weak, his body the only certainty he was alive. Shrineless, desperate, outlawed.

She clutched him to her and reached her other hand towards the king.

No, towards his god.

She threw her will towards them, every ounce of strength and anger, she wrapped it around the god in his chest, binding it, holding it. Tightening her grip.

Be still. Inara spoke to the fire.

It flared in Arren's chest, the flames bursting out with surprise and power enough to send him stumbling back from the door before it dwindled, caught by Inara's will.

Inara held her, the god, binding her with her power. But Hestra fought back. She was small, but she was old, known across Middren, and she had a strong will of her own. The fire flared then sputtered, brightened then diminished as Arren choked. He, however, could move. He grabbed the table, holding himself upright. This made Inara smile: he was not a god yet. Perhaps he never could be.

'Ina,' said Kissen desperately from where she still held Elo, understanding immediately what was happening. Did she know now? What Inara was? What she could do? Did Lessa? They could see her standing, holding Sunbringer at bay. They could all see. 'Don't kill him. Please. We need him.'

Don't kill him? The man who executed a helpless god before her faithful? The man who had driven her from her home?

'He burned my home,' said Inara. 'And Lesscia. The books.' She trembled to think of Scian, how she had not even been close to saving her. 'Now Daesmouth.'

'Daesmouth?' said Kissen.

'Skedi and I saw it, he must have sent ships.' Her throat tightened, her will too, Hestra was bouncing around Arren's ribs like a rat in a cage, half held, half resisting. 'Yatho and Telle went there.'

'Why did you stop me?' said Elo, holding onto Kissen as he dragged himself to his feet. 'Ina's right, he wants to be a god.' He let go of her, and stepped back. 'You're a godkiller.'

'So listen to me this time, baker-knight,' said Kissen wearily, 'when I say this isn't a god we want to kill right now.'

'Inara,' said Lessa in a warning tone, and Inara winced. 'Daughter.' Daughter she called her, in front of them all. 'Get back. Stop this.'

Inara frowned, but did not stop. Everyone in the room, in the corridor, could see what she was doing. They should see. She had a god's power, not Arren. She could win where all of them had failed. If she held the god for long enough, he would die, she was sure of it.

'I sent no ships,' said Arren. His face was paling as Hestra used all her energy and will to struggle against Inara's. Elo stared at him, his colours uncertain. 'Nothing is happening in Daesmouth, girl.'

He was not lying, his colours told her so. They were frightened, angry, but no deception dimmed them. Inara's will wavered for a moment, and Hestra fought back.

Your hearths are cold, your loves are scattered, your home is gone . . . her voice slammed into Inara's head, and her skull split with pain, her heart felt heavy, aching, with the truth of what she said. *Your will is weak, your past is broken, your future lost* . . .

Hestra's focus on Inara did nothing for Arren. His knees buckled, and he went to the ground.

'What are you doing to me?' he said through gasping breaths. His chest was smoking now, thick and dark, not Sunbringer anymore, no light, just charcoal and embers. 'What *are* you?'

Inara gritted her teeth against Hestra's will. 'I am the daughter of the Craier House you burned,' she said. *The house you burned,* she shot her will towards Hestra, a god's echo of a human voice. 'I have fought with gods and against them. I am half haven, protector of the god of white lies.' *Half haven. Protector.* She held Skedi tighter. 'I am everything you tried to be and failed.'

I am everything you tried to be and failed.

Hestra faltered again, diminishing in a shower of sparks and smoke. The king groaned.

'Inara Craier,' said Lessa, still standing by the door, fear in her voice. She and her companions seemed uncertain, unnerved by a dynamic they had not expected, they waited for her command. 'Please. Stand down.'

'Inara,' said Kissen. She came close to her again, her hand on her back, steady, but she didn't grab her, she didn't pull her away. 'You don't want this.'

'I do want it,' said Inara, her head felt light. 'Why shouldn't I want it?' The man who would be king was choking on fire, the man who had taken everything from her, over and over. 'Why shouldn't I tear the god from him?'

'Elo . . .' gasped Arren. 'Help me . . . please.'

Elo swallowed, but stayed where he was, his hand flexing around Arren's dagger. He had already accepted Arren's death, he had already tried to make it happen. It was all but permission for Inara to do it, and Arren knew. Some of the fight went out of his eyes, and Hestra's light all but disappeared. A spark, a tiny flame in his chest, burning on lint. Inara held the god, and the king's lips went blue. This wasn't like Canovan and Lethen, nor her and Skedi. His god's will sustained him, but when Hestra faltered, he was lost. He fell back against the wall and groaned with such pain that Elo flinched.

Kissen tightened her hand on Inara's shoulder. 'I'll show you why, Ina. Why I've been trying to get back to you, all this time. I need you to know before you kill him.' Kissen did look as if she had dragged herself through fire and mud; her cheeks had peeled with frostbite, her hand was clutched to her chest, her leg warped and broken. 'I'm with you. I swear I'm on your side.'

'Don't listen to that woman, Inara,' said Lessa suddenly, strongly. 'She's mad, and dangerous. Come away from danger.'

Inara swallowed. Her mother was alive, her mother had not burned. She trembled. So much of her heart wanted to run into Lessa's arms and tell her everything that had happened. But all that had happened had been without her mother. Inara had been

SUNBRINGER

abandoned and alone, while her mother was alive and well. In command.

Kissen cursed, then, for the first time, she released her colours. Consciously, carefully. Her shades tumbled silver-tipped blue from her, different from Elo's; the shades of a still sea in the morning, tinged with sunrise pink and laced with vivid summer leaf greens. They were steady, hopeful colours, as honest and true as colours could be, but also intense. Desperate.

Then, within them, tangled like Makioron's briars, the red of dried blood, and the white of ice and snow. Guilt and shame. Inara could tell it easily, a persistent tremor, like the shaking of leaves on treetops as the wind descended. Deeper again, yellow flickered, the colour of glowing metal and hot flame, spiking, insistent. Fear was there in her deepest heart.

'Please,' said Kissen. She had a knife in her other hand, but she held it by the blade. It had silver-grey stones that flickered. 'Do you still have Aan's gift?'

Inara blinked, surprised. 'Y-yes.'

No lie, no connivance, no flicker. Kissen releasing her emotions was releasing vulnerability, to gods, to the world, to her.

'Inara Craier,' said Lessa strongly. 'Listen to me, not her.'

Inara ignored her. 'Take it,' she said to Kissen. 'It's around my neck.'

'Inara?' Lessa's tone was both a question and a reprimand, she took another step forward, but Elo moved to guard her and Kissen, lifting his stolen knife. With her as well, her knight, her protector.

'Stay back, Mother,' commanded Inara, and Lessa stopped on the tiles. Inara didn't look back. 'I mourned for you,' she said instead.

Kissen reached for the vial, and wrapped her hand around it. She didn't take it, she crushed it, at the same time closing her fingers on the blade. With the shattering of the glass, the slice of steel, the godkiller's blood flowed, and colour flowed with it. The sea green, the ice, the flame and fear. Colour in her blood. An offering.

'Talician gods of water,' she called, 'show them what you see.'

Kissen had made an offering to a god.

The jug on the table shattered, and the water rushed out,

363

splitting in two. It ran over the map like a flood, some going to the mountains, some going to the sea. Elo turned to watch it as the mountain water turned into an army, a long line of small battalions, flowing over the Bennites, down the land and into Middren.

The other wave washed into the sea, turning into ships that travelled from Talician and Restish shores, washing over Blenraden, and landing at Daesmouth. Where she had seen the flame. There, the ink began to darken, spreading with the water. It washed further north, further west, picking up with it the tiny figurines that had been painstakingly placed along the map.

The water washed them away and toppled them all.

The fire god's followers will overrun Middren, and all the gods in these lands, before the year is out.

Inara knew that voice. Aan's voice. Everyone flinched as it burrowed into their skulls, the river god's warning strong and true. Arren had not lied. He had not burned Daesmouth. They had been so busy fighting each other none of them had noticed.

Save the king, halfling, Inara felt the breath of the god in her ear. *Nothing good will yet be wrought by his death.*

Inara looked at the man she hated, dying on the floor, utterly at her mercy, the god caught in the cage of his chest. But Kissen had never lied to her, or asked her anything without reason. Kissen had stayed with her, to help her, when she had been abandoned and alone.

Not for Aan, not for her mother, but for Kissen, Inara released Hestra, and she brightened in Arren's chest. The king drew breath, coughing and choking as oxygen filled his lungs.

'Restish has betrayed us,' said an older woman by Lessa, at her feet a battering ram. Whatever Aan's will had done, it had run through them all with its power, and a deep terror as fierce as Kissen's. 'If Talicia have already begun to move on Daesmouth . . .' She looked at Lessa. 'They will have struck the east first. My lands. It takes days for a bird to reach us.'

'I was allied with Talicia,' said Arren, wheezing. He stood again, and looked at Elo as if he could advise him. 'Hseth is dead, their god, I bargained with her directly. Talicia has no army.'

'She lied to you,' said Kissen. 'And so did the one who keeps you alive.' She looked disgusted, with herself, with everything, with the world. She looked down at her bleeding hands, then Inara. Her colours, she had hidden again, but the crook of her smile, the flash of her gold tooth, Inara understood. A thank you.

I did not know they would continue with her plan, said Hestra furiously, her flames licking around Arren's skin as his hand went to his chest. At her words, the colour returned to his face. Anger flushed his cheeks, filled him again with life. *Without her, they should have stopped, should have faltered.*

'Like you did,' hissed Arren, his frustration flared about him in shades of ruddy brown and, at their edges, gold and red. 'You rode on her coattails, and now you cling to mine.'

They should have summoned me. Hseth said they would lift me into their hearts.

'Yet she used us both,' said Arren. He looked to Lessa, who was staring at the map, the stained lands in the central lowlands, the Craier lands. It wasn't just Inara she had abandoned, it was her household, her people. Her defences. Then he looked to Elo, whose shades were much like Arren's, torn in red and gold.

Inara recognised those colours, the shades of his deepest terror, the flashes of his nightmares, and the horrors of war.

EPILOGUE

VILLAGES FLAMED ACROSS THE BENNITES, STARTLED BY invaders raging in with the spring, riding the back of the floods and snow.

Blue flags fell from the shattered walls of Blenraden, new ones were raised in place of white and red, adorned with the mark of the bell, and marked by the burning of prisoners. The eastern towers of Daesmouth burned, taken by surprise.

And each flame that rose was an offering. And each offering was a sacrifice, of blood and bone, of cattle, of walls and homes.

And within the flame, a hissing that sounded like laughter. Laughter, that sounded like falling empires, and the crackle of bones on a pyre.

Soldiers watched the flames they had made, at the freshly sown fields of smoke and ruin, offering the skulls of children to the earth.

'Hseth, Hseth, Hseth.'

Then some of the fire twisted, not tossed by the eddies of wind, nor the breath of a mountain. They whirled like the cloak of a soldier, hardening like the armour of war. They flew, brightening the sky like the last light of day.

Within them, an armed woman danced. Her ribs were lightning-white, her feet stamped black scorches into the earth.

And within her chest, a heart already beat. A heart of briddite, blood and flame.

ACKNOWLEDGEMENTS

I DON'T KNOW WHERE TO BEGIN. THREE YEARS AGO, AFTER more than seven years of rejection, I almost decided to stop writing, and here I am typing acknowledgements for my second book.

I first want to thank Eileen and Ben, my parents and my allies, for their support, love and pride. And for teaching me to unlearn the fears that I taught myself. My siblings, Joshua, Felix and Genevieve, for their inspiration, resilience and smarts. I wouldn't be who I am without you.

Thank you to Ali, my person, for your endless, shining passion, intelligence, patience and support. You lift me up, and keep me grounded. I love you.

I want to thank the booksellers and librarians who became my champions – who loved *Godkiller* and put it into the hands of readers. You turned this trilogy from a ripple into a tidal wave. Thank you for inviting me into your spaces, thank you for giving me your time.

Thank you to the Mushens Entertainment Team. Juliet Mushens, leader, powerhouse, legend. Rachel Neely, for keeping the world moving and for your impressive calm. Liza DeBlock, Alba Parnau, Catriona Fida, Kiya Evans – for making *Godkiller* global and being forces of nature.

My heartfelt thanks to Jane Johnson, my very own knight in shining armour. Your passion, skill and energy are both astonishing and boundless, and *Sunbringer* wouldn't have been the book it is without you.

Tom Roberts, I'm so thrilled that I've been able to work with such a talented and skilful artist, and so lucky to be able to call you my friend. You bring these words to life and wrap them in beauty.

To the HarperVoyager teams – in the UK and US. Julia Elliott, Deanna Bailey, Jes Lyons: I couldn't have hoped for a better team to launch my books in North America, you are wonderful, and you have my undying loyalty. Rachel Winterbottom, Natasha Bardon, Susanna Peden, Sian Richefond, El Slater, Chloe Gough and so many others, it's such a tremendous privilege to be able to work with you for another year, thank you for everything you've done and for launching this trilogy into flight.

Finally, to my friends, both new and those who cannot escape me now. My marras from home, my loves from school and university, my pals from Scotland, my folks from far south, my family of families: you are mischief and magic. To name a few of my fellow inkers: Saara El-Arifi, Kate Dylan, C L Clark, Tasha Suri, Samantha Shannon, L R Lam, Elizabeth May, A Y Chao, Kat Dunn, Catriona Silvey, Ian Green, Elvin James Mensah. You inspire me daily.

Finally, thank you to the readers who have become part of this family I've found. I hope you enjoy this book. I hope you are ready for what comes next.

ABOUT THE AUTHOR

Hannah Kaner is the #1 internationally bestselling author of the Fallen Gods trilogy. A Northumbrian writer living in Scotland, she is inspired by world mythologies, angry women, speculative fiction, and the stories we tell ourselves about being human.

DON'T MISS THE FIRST BOOK
IN THE FALLEN GODS SERIES
GODKILLER

"Beautifully imagined and intensely felt . . .
Godkiller is a bone-rattling fantasy thriller
that flies by in a breathtaking rush."
— Joe Hill, #1 *New York Times* bestselling
author of *Locke & Key*

Gods are forbidden in the kingdom of Middren.
Formed by human desires and fed by their
worship, there are countless gods in the
world—but after a great war,
the new king outlawed them and now
pays "godkillers" to destroy any who try
to rise from the shadows.

As a child, Kissen saw her family murdered by a fire god. Now, she makes a
living killing them and enjoys it. But all this changes when Kissen is tasked with
helping a young noble girl with a god problem. The child's soul is bonded to a
tiny god of white lies, and Kissen can't kill it without ending the girl's life too.

Joined by a disillusioned knight on a secret quest, the unlikely group must travel
to the ruined city of Blenraden, where the last of the wild gods reside, to each
beg a favor. Pursued by assassins and demons, and in the midst of burgeoning
civil war, they will all face a reckoning. Something is rotting at the heart of their
world, and they are the only ones who can stop it.